THE DARKEST LORD

Also by Jack Heckel

The Mysterium Series
The Dark Lord
The Darker Lord

The Charming Tales
The Pitchfork of Destiny
A Fairy-tale Ending
Happily Never After
Once Upon a Rhyme

THE DARKEST LORD

The Mysterium Series, Book Three

JACK HECKEL

HARPER

VOYAGER
IMPULSE

An Imprint of HarperCollins Publishers

4/19

This is a work of fiction. Names, characters, places, and incidents are products of the author's imagination or are used fictitiously and are not to be construed as real. Any resemblance to actual events, locales, organizations, or persons, living or dead, is entirely coincidental.

Digital Edition FEBRUARY 2019 ISBN: 978-0-06-269779-0
Print Edition ISBN: 978-0-06-269780-6

Cover design by Amy Halperin
Cover images © VeraPetruk/iStock/Getty images (man); © rendix_alextian/Oleg Krugliak/maxuser/Sergey Peterman/Stephen Coburn/Shutterstock (five images)

FIRST EDITION

19 20 21 22 23   OPM   10 9 8 7 6 5 4 3 2 1

To Carleigh, Heather, Isaac and Taba,
our ultimate natural twenties

"Hush, my dear," he said. "Don't speak so loud, or you will be overheard—and I should be ruined. I'm supposed to be a Great Wizard."

"And aren't you?" she asked.

"Not a bit of it, my dear; I'm just a common man."

—L. FRANK BAUM,
THE WONDERFUL WIZARD OF OZ

THE DARKEST LORD

CHAPTER 1

GOOD MORNING,
TOMB OF TERRORS!

My name is Avery, and I wish I weren't the Dark Lord.

It was a fervent wish. One that I repeated daily, but with no effect, because I was the Dark Lord, and the fact that I was—alongside a number of other regrettable life choices—probably explains why I was lying in a coffin listening to a voice, dry as death, calmly reciting my latest crimes against the multiverse.

"It was meant to be an easy assignment for the Twenty-Second Sealer Division, a Mysterian regiment new to the fighting in Trelari and detailed with guarding the Western Bore, a small supply gateway carved between Mysterium and Trelari, over the past three weeks. The quiet ended in a terrible battle in the Valley Deep at the foot of the Impassable Mountains that saw two regiments of Sealers and allied alchemic golems and undead smashed, then torn apart and completely obliterated."

The voice belonged to Aldric, the semi-lich, my once tormentor who had, of late, turned into a reluctant roommate. I had retreated to his subterranean stronghold about a week ago to recuperate from the last in a long string of battles I'd waged against Moregoth in the never-ending and ever-expanding war between Trelari and Mysterium. It was close to a year now since Valdara had reopened Trelari to the rest of the multiverse and challenged the Mysterium to come and get us. Unfortunately, they had responded with regrettable enthusiasm, and what had begun as a little private struggle with Moregoth had turned into a true Worlds War.

While Valdara's rallying call to the subworlds had not resulted in the mass uprising we might have hoped for, it had been heard and answered by a few. She now led a ragtag group of subworlds against the combined forces of Mysterium and most of the innerworlds. In theory I was under her command, one of her generals, but the truth was she resented needing me, or at least needing to use the means I represented. Not that I blamed her—the Dark Lord was a pretty loathsome guy.

Of course, none of this explains why I was hiding

in the semi-lich's tomb, lying in his coffin, listening to him read me the morning paper. Although, based on the news article, I suspect the first two questions will be answered to your satisfaction before the end of this chapter. As for why the semi-lich had taken it on himself to become my very own twenty-four-hour news network, that is a bit trickier to answer.

This little ritual had begun two days earlier. Every morning, Aldric marched into the crypt I'd been using as a bedchamber to read me articles about the ever-widening war. At least, I assumed it was morning—it was difficult to know time as the semi-lich's tomb had no windows and was buried several hundred feet belowground. He claimed his motivation was purely selfless, that he felt duty bound to keep me informed. You can judge for yourself whether a half vampire, half lich spawn of hell would feel duty bound to do anything, but personally I suspected a more mundane motive. He wanted his coffin back.

The semi-lich cleared his throat and continued his recital. "Over two days, Magus General Moregoth's army was broken by the overwhelming might of the combined forces of Queen Valdara's Paladins of Light and the Army of Shadow, led by the Dark Lord himself. Despite the chaos of the onslaught and the ensuing retreat, the mages of the Twenty-Second "Crimson Claw" Sealer Division made a series of gallant delaying stands before the Western Bore, allowing the remaining forces to escape from the battlefield. The vanguard paid the price though, as only a handful from those brave regiments—fewer than fifty—made it back through the gateway to Mysterium."

There was a pause and a shuffling of paper, which gave me plenty of time to feel truly sick about the growing number of dead on my ledger. Aldric remarked, "There's a section here on casualty numbers and the number of Sealers presumed to have been taken prisoner . . ."

In the dark of the coffin, my heart sank even further. "There were no prisoners," I whispered in a voice low enough to ensure that Aldric could not hear. I wished he would stop, but I was not yet cowardly enough, or maybe I was too masochistic, to make him.

After a few more rustles of paper, a dry cough announced that there was more. "The story of the Twenty-Second's disaster started in the foggy dawn several days ago as the men and golems occupied positions . . . I see there is no mention here of the ranks of the undead," he grumbled. "Typical. They don't really count. They're already dead. Well, they're not! They are undead! That's the entire point! It is literally in our name!"

"If the story is making you angry, you don't have to read it on my account," I said through the velvet-lined lid of the coffin. I sent a prayer to as many deities as I could recall that he would stop. As usual, none of them were listening.

"No, no. It's important for you to know what's being written. Particularly given your *extended* absence from the field."

He stretched out the word *extended* beyond all need and then paused, probably hoping for a response. I gave him none. There was a bit more muttering, and then a sharp crack as the parchment paper was reopened with a great deal more violence than was warranted.

"Now, where was I . . . men and golems . . . positions . . . ahh . . . occupied positions in and around the foothills of the Impassable Mountains at the head of the Valley Deep along a rocky, wooded ridge twelve miles long and a little over a mile wide that fronted the landing zone for the Western Bore. The division was spread pitifully thin along a twenty-mile front." There was pause and then the voice drawled, "Is that a little jab at our favorite field marshal? I think I like this correspondent."

I had been thinking the same thing, and so asked, "What's the byline?"

"It just says, 'By the Mysterium Press, embedded with the Twenty-Second Sealer Division in Trelari.'"

For those of you not familiar with magus media, the Mysterium Press is Mysterium's answer to Earth's AP.

For those of you not from Earth, the AP stands for the Associated Press, which is a news service.

For those of you in realities that are still in a pre-mass media phase of development, first, my congratulations, and second, it's like an official form of the exchanges that newspapers use to fill up their columns when they have nothing original to say.

For those of you in preliterate worlds, how exactly are you reading this?

The point being, the Mysterium Press was as mainstream as it got. Everything that went out over its multiversal wire was checked and rechecked by a dozen editors and censors before it was allowed for release. And using its power over the pen, the Administration had done an excellent job controlling the narrative about the war, even going so far as to plant articles in nonmagical publications in neutral innerworlds like Earth to try to dissuade any wavering diasporic mages from joining Trelari's cause.

If you are from Earth, and don't yet get all your news in 140 or 280 characters, or whatever it is now, you may be saying, "Hey, I don't remember reading anything about a magical war between two alien worlds." You probably have and didn't know it. They are usually cleverly disguised in things no one ever reads: wedding announcements, *Family Circus* cartoons, and your parents' Facebook posts. Still, if you are a magus, the message is unmistakable: oppose us at your peril.

If the Administration's hold on the Mysterium Press was beginning to waver even in the slightest, it might be a sign that an internal resistance to the war was beginning to emerge.

"Interesting," I murmured. There was a sudden,

sharp rap on the side of the coffin. I sat up with a start and banged my head against the lid. "Ow! What?"

"Don't mumble. I can't hear a word you're saying in there."

"Had you ever thought that might be the point?" I asked, rubbing at the lump on the top of my head.

"No," he answered with a sharp hack. Although I couldn't see him, I could picture the semi-lich staring crossly at the closed coffin, the fires of hell literally burning in his eyes. And he wondered why I preferred to keep the lid closed.

"Oh, now this *is* interesting," he said, his voice perking up from dry as death to merely dry as the grave. "There is an article below the fold on the Mysterium's use of skulls, animated cloaks, and chains as a way of conserving necromantic energies. 'For further details, see Necromantic, scroll 5, col. 2.'"

"I really have no interest in knowing this," I said with a groan.

My complaint was drowned out by a lot of muttering and papers being shuffled and discarded. "Where is that fifth scroll? Is this it? Ahh . . . maybe here. Here it is!" he shouted in triumph. He cleared his throat with a vile hacking. "'The Economics of Skulls.' What a great title! 'As everyone who has ever studied magic or economics knows—'"

"That's enough!" I shouted. "It is one thing to have to relive the horrors of the battlefield, but it is quite another to have to sit through an essay on economics *and* necromancy, particularly when you haven't had your morning coffee. I admit the two subjects are inextricably intertwined—I mean, in my own world, Roosevelt effectively accused Hoover of being an economic necromancer during the presidential campaign of 1932. Nevertheless, they are also subjects so mind-numbing and horrible in both theory and application that several innerworlds have labeled their study as a form of indecency—particularly economics."

"Are you quite done?" Aldric asked with a soul-rattling sigh.

"Yes."

"Good. I don't know these liches you're referring to . . . Horror and Roast Evil?"

"Hoover and Roosevelt," I muttered.

"I don't think so," he replied with a polite rasp. "No true lich would ever allow themselves to be called Hoover, much less Roosevelt. It simply isn't dignified. Anyway, whatever their names, I'm sure they never faced the daunting costs of today's necromancy. Inflation is killing the undead," he said with no hint of intended irony. "Now, if you will kindly let me continue."

I carefully said none of the things that I wanted to say and let him read the article, which was every bit as horrible as I thought it would be. I was drifting back to sleep when he finished. There was a long pause, during which he probably hoped I would say something. I very deliberately held my tongue. I was simply not a good enough liar to remark on the article without pointing out that in many worlds his reading that to me would be considered a violation of my fundamental human rights.

When I had said nothing for long enough to consume his patience, there was more irritated shuffling of paper, and Aldric read, "'The attack started shortly after dawn . . .' Surprising. I didn't think the Dark Lord rose before noon," he added in an undertone just loud enough to carry through the mahogany and velvet walls of my coffin bed.

"At this rate your retelling of the battle will take longer than the actual battle," I complained. "Either read it or don't read it."

"Fine." He rustled the paper even more vigorously before beginning again. "'The attack started shortly after dawn with a charge by the Paladins of Light. Led by Queen Valdara, the heavily armored division descended in a sudden and inconceivable rush from the eastern heights of the Impassable Mountains, catching the Mysterium forces not only by surprise but totally unarmed. The paladins' charge swept through the first ranks of alchemic golems and into the heart of Magus General Moregoth's main Sealer force. The ferocity of the initial attack appeared to have broken Moregoth's army, but by early evening they had regrouped and were pushing back, aided by reinforcements from the Fourteenth Elemental Group, which had arrived through the Western Bore during the afternoon. That is when the Trelarian second assault caught the Twenty-Second's right flank, as hordes of blood orcs burst forth from a series of caves concealed in the sheer southern faces of the Impassable Mountains . . ."

There was another pause, and I could visualize the semi-lich tilting his head to one side as he said, "You know, I think these mountains are misnamed. They seem eminently passable."

"The name was Vivian's idea." I felt my pulse race as I said her name. "To discourage Moregoth's armies from exploring them."

"Clever," he replied dryly, and then went back to his paper. "By night the Trelarians had thrown two divisions of blood orcs into the battle and . . ."

I stopped listening. This news was old—almost a week old—and my mind was on Vivian now. Aldric had called her clever, but she was more than that. Drake called her a military savant, while Rook said she had a natural gift for carnage. I think he meant it as a compliment. Whatever you called her, the fact was the Army of Shadow—its discipline, tactics, and strategy—reflected her mind. But sometimes she was loath to commit them to a fight. Unlike me she still felt keenly the loss of every man, orc, demon, or gibberling that died under her command.

How was she doing without me? We had agreed that I needed this break, and for good reason, which

I will come to shortly, but I was feeling more and more guilty about leaving her behind. It wasn't that I was that worried about her safety. Not really. She had Drake and Rook with her, and Valdara was very careful never to let the Army of Shadow roam too far from her own reach, but anything could happen in war.

My mind began spinning out ever-more dreadful and implausible scenarios, and I was well on my way to a full-blown panic attack when I realized Aldric was asking me a question. "What?" I replied.

He hissed his irritation, a noise that I can only describe as the sound a teakettle of the damned would make, if such a thing existed. "I asked how long you think Valdara will be able to convince her paladins to continue to work with your Army of Shadow. All it is going to take is one berserk blood orc at the wrong place and the wrong time and . . ." He snapped his fingers—dry and dreadful.

"It won't matter," I answered wearily. "All of Trelari, the good and bad, are bound together in this fight. My pattern demands it."

Despite my easy dismissal, the question was a good one, and one that Valdara's War Council had argued vigorously for months. It turned out to be a moot point. We had a few disastrous encounters in the early days as we tried to integrate Valdara's army and the Army of Shadow: orcs going on rampages through human villages, humans massacring orc encampments, etc. None of that ultimately mattered. When Moregoth arrived, they banded together as though they had always been allies. In fact, when questioned, most of them couldn't recall ever having been enemies.

That was the most depressing part of the whole exercise, this feeling that everything was predestined. Trelari was under threat and my pattern was trying to stabilize according to its design, by mobilizing all of the world's powers—the dark, me, and the light, Valdara. I suppose I should have been able to predict that reopening Trelari would reactivate my pattern. Perhaps I could have warned Valdara before she cleaved that hole in her world with Justice Cleaver, but at the time I was so relieved that we weren't going to be killed by Moregoth that I didn't give the matter as much thought as I might. Now it was too late. Trelari's position as a central power in the multiverse meant its reality was beyond my, or anyone else's, control.

It struck me that maybe the rise of Trelari was what Vivian had seen all those years ago when we met, when she was looking for a way to break Mysterium's hold over the subworlds. Because of my pattern, Trelari was beyond Mysterium's reach, and the secret that Mysterium had maintained its dominance only by draining and destroying other worlds had been revealed. The multiverse knew now that Mysterium was nothing but a loathsome parasite.

It was my own knowledge of this truth that kept me bound to my hated alter ego. There was only one path forward. The Mysterium had to be stopped and the subworlds liberated at any cost. To do that, I had to be the Dark Lord. At least that was what I kept telling myself, but it sounded painfully hollow when the consequences were printed in black and white in the morning paper and read back to me by an undead sorcerer.

Realizing I would be saying nothing more about how I was planning to keep mortal enemies, like orcs and humans, from each other's throats, Aldric resumed reading. "'Having secured the ridge, the Trelarians massed for an attack on the Western Bore itself. They were stopped temporarily by the Seventy-Second and Fifty-First Necromantic Battalions which fought heroically under Colonel Yorick. They were badly outnumbered, and it was mainly by guts that they . . .' Really? Guts? Surely this reporter must know Mysterium only uses demi-liches. Demi-liches don't even have bodies, much less guts!" he grumbled. "Next, they'll be saying something like 'the skin of their teeth' or 'soulful'!"

"I think the reporter is employing a little innocent, albeit insensitive, poetic license, Aldric," I said patiently.

He snorted his disgust but kept reading. "'It was mainly by *guts* that they held off the Trelarian advance through the night. However, as morning rose, the Dark Lord arrived.' Oh! Here's your part, Avery," he said excitedly.

I tried to sink lower in my coffin, dreading what was to come.

"'Riding atop his dreaded viper dragon, Losh-laith, the Dark Lord descended on the weakening lines. Driven back by the dragon's deadly breath, the necromantic ranks broke and the Twenty-Second's retreat through the Western Bore became a rout. This marks the second gateway Magus General Moregoth has lost to the Dark Lord in less than a month. Despite the recent setbacks, the provost remains confident that the war will be over within the year . . .'"

I stopped listening again. The rest would be propaganda: reports from this general or that about all the advances the Mysterium was making throughout the multiverse, appeals from ministers imploring mages to conserve mystical energy near the sub-world fronts, and of course the never-ending adverts for war bonds.

Not that the Mysterium hadn't been winning battles; they certainly had. But for the provost to predict the end of the war was pure fantasy. If anything, after a year of constant fighting, the conflict was a stalemate boarding on a quagmire. The problem was that there were as many fronts to the war as worlds in the multiverse, and while we had managed to stop the Mysterium's main advance against Trelari, to do so had required us to focus our forces there. A few weaker subworlds that had come into the war on our side had already been taken or destroyed by Moregoth, and there was a real danger that the others might begin to rethink their alliance with us if we could not find some way to end the conflict soon.

"Well, you come out looking quite good in that exchange, Avery. Nothing too dreadful anyway," the semi-lich said in his cheeriest voice, which was about as cheery as a depressed mortician.

Still, he was right. The article was as close to good PR as someone called the Dark Lord was likely ever to get. Except it was a lie. "It wasn't like that," I said soberly.

"As you said, the author has taken certain license with the truth," Aldric replied dryly. "You know how bards and storytellers are. After all, this same publication once claimed that you were dead."

That wasn't it, and I had a sudden need to make him, to make *someone*, understand. I threw the coffin lid open and sat up, staring at him through eyes I only now realized were on the verge of tears. I took a moment to gather myself. "The reporter got almost everything right except about *my* part in the battle. About *me*."

The semi-lich was sprawled across one of his hideously gaudy thrones, the parchment papers he'd been reading draped over his legs and spilling down onto the floor around him. He dropped the rest of the papers and sat up, so his vampiric side was facing me. He fixed me with a smoldering half gaze and asked, "Well, what did happen? What did you do? And does it explain why you've been sleeping in *my* coffin since getting here?"

Now that the question had been asked, I didn't know exactly what to say. There was a lot the article hadn't mentioned. There was nothing about the terrible screams of shock and terror that issued from the ranks of Sealers as first the Paladins of Light and then the blood orcs tore through them, or about how, when the battle was over, the red cloaks of the fallen mages were so thick on the ground that from a distance the ridge looked like a giant ragged scar carved into the side of the hill. It seemed impossible that the reporter could have been there and not remarked on how the crashing and rending of the collapsing alchemic golems had echoed through the valley until it seemed the earth itself was crying out in agony.

And what of the smell? The hideous odor of burst organs, torn tissue, and blood mixed with the stench of the blood orcs and the undead. There were a lot of horrors the reporter had omitted, but none worse than me. Because the truth was we almost lost that battle, and what I had to do to ensure victory may have been far worse than simply accepting defeat.

In the moment, I found none of those words, and eventually Aldric was compelled to remind me he was still waiting for an answer. "Avery? I shouldn't have to tell you, but I am half vampire, and I don't sleep as well in the guest coffin. Also, we need to talk about Harold."

A sudden rush of panic shot through me. "Harold? What about Harold? Is he all right?"

I fumbled through the covers of the coffin and pulled out my multiversal, ether-protected imp monitor, which took the form of a little white orb covered in elaborate mystical tracings. I gave it a shake, but nothing happened. I dropped the orb back into the coffin and craned my neck around to peer across the chamber.

In the shadows at the far end, a ghostly candelabra cast a dim and uncertain light on a pedestal, upon which sat an enormous crystal ball. The ball glowed with an undulating red light, and atop it was a very small imp with a large head and big eyes. For a second there was no movement, but then the imp gave a plaintive squeak followed by a soft snore. He was still asleep. A great rush of relief passed through my body.

"Oh, thank the gods." I glared at Aldric. "You scared the bejesus out of me. He needs to nap for at least another hour, otherwise the afternoon is going to be hell, and you know that."

His only reply was "Bejesus?"

CHAPTER 2

BABY MAKES THREE

I know those of you who have read *The Dark Lord*, and still there could be more of you, may be slightly confused at this point. When I last left you, Harold the imp was old and crusty, and had a habit of smoking cigars and eating dead mice and cursing and being wise and mysterious. Then, well, a lot happened.

Harold died, at least as much as an imp could die, and it turned out that when an imp was resummoned through its mystical connection, they didn't come back exactly the same. Don't get me wrong, Harold still loved butterscotch, and unfortunately cigars, but, well, he was a baby. Same imp, but rather than looking like a hairless bat, an old man, and an overripe banana blended together and then left to bake in the sun for a couple of months, he now looked like a cross between a cute anime baby and one of the more adorable Pokémon (maybe a Mew with wings). He had baby soft skin that was a lovely caramel color, enormously big eyes, and he made the most adorable squeaks and purrs. If I were putting him on a cuteness scale, he would have rated somewhere between baby chick and newborn kitten.

I know. It was that saccharine, especially when he danced, which was often, or at least it was when he was in a good mood, which was unfortunately less often than one would hope. I guessed this last fact was what Aldric wanted to talk to me about.

He confirmed this by repeating, "I need to talk to you about Harold." I raised an eyebrow. His long bloodred nails fidgeted uncomfortably with the satin upholstery of his throne. "It's . . . well . . . I think this may not be the right place for a baby." He gestured at the imp helplessly. "Or whatever he is."

"Oh, is that all?" I chuckled. "I thought it was something serious. It's nice of you to worry about us, but don't concern yourself over me and Harold. The accommodations may not be what we're used to, but he seems to like the new perch, and Vivian and I both agree the tomb is the perfect place for him. We did a lot of research looking for the safest possible location both here and back on Earth. We considered the Castle of Light, the Svalbard Global Seed Vault in

Norway, the secret grove in Silver Wood, NORAD's facility at Cheyenne Mountain. Nothing compares. I'm even beginning to grow accustomed to sleeping in a coffin. It's surprisingly comfortable."

I can't stress this last point enough. A coffin is really the ultimate in sleeping comfort. It is both bed and sensory deprivation chamber all neatly wrapped in plush velvet, polished mahogany, and brass fittings. If you take nothing else from this book, then remember this one piece of advice: don't wait until you're dead to get one. I promise you won't regret it. You will get the best sleep of your life, and as an added bonus, when people ask you what death feels like, you will be able to tell them confidently: snug and cozy. That the dead have been keeping this a secret for so long is downright selfish in my opinion.

Sadly, it was not the merits of coffins that Aldric wanted to talk about.

"Are you crazy?" he shouted and twisted about in his throne to face me, revealing the dividing line between his handsome vampiric and hideously infernal lich sides. I shuddered involuntarily and decided there was simply not enough time in one life to get comfortable with his appearance. He banged his skeletal lich fist down on the arm of his chair. "You do realize this is the Tomb of Terrors? It is filled with the most diabolically dangerous traps in the known world. There are a dozen rooms within a five-minute walk of where we sit that would not only kill your imp, but blow his remains into bits, reduce those bits to ash, and then use that ash to make a memorial plaque commemorating his death!" He was gesturing wildly, sending motes of necromantic power swirling about the room.

"Exactly!" I said, stretching my arms lazily over my head. "That's why your crypt is so perfect. While he's in his immature state, Harold is a major target for abduction or assassination by Mysterium agents. This is the safest place in the world for him. No one can get in here without fighting their way through room after room of death and destruction on a scale almost beyond comprehension."

I clambered out of the coffin and began picking through the clothes scattered around its base, looking for a pair of jeans and a cleanish shirt. A thought struck me, and I asked, "Did the contractor ever fix your water trap room? I need to do some laundry."

"No!" he shouted.

"That's unacceptable, Aldric," I said as I started to pull my clothes on. "It's been more than a year since you discovered the leak. You're going to get a mold in-festation if you don't do something about it soon." An idea struck me. "Hey, you should get Ariella to talk to them. She would get those contractors moving, I can tell you."

"No!" he shouted again.

"Okay, okay, none of my business," I said, waving a sock in mock surrender. "But I'm telling you, she's one tough negotiator, and probably the best rules lawyer on Trelari."

He jumped to his feet, scattering unread parchment to the floor. He seemed very agitated and began striding about the room, swishing his tattered robes and his stylish black cape with its red silk lining back and forth as he went. "I am not talking about the water trap or your elf maiden friend or even the contractors, although they should all be damned to the lowest ring of hell for the overages they charged me. Serpents! Devils!" His eyes flashed with infernal anger, but then he shook his head and the fire flickered and died. "I am talking about you spreading Harold's toys and your dirty clothes across the floor of my crypt, and about all the baby poofing!"

"Baby poofing?"

"You know, the doorknobs that won't turn, and the spell component bottles that won't open, and the little fences you've placed around everything with the latches that won't work, and replacing all of my lovely candles with these nightmare lights." He gestured at the candelabra that I had retrofitted, very inelegantly, with a handful of battery-operated animal-shaped night-lights. "Or, or, making me put my lovely treasure hoard in storage."

I rolled my eyes at him. "Come on, Aldric, even you have to know that the coins were choking hazards. And as for all those weapons? You can't leave rusting knives and swords and morning stars lying about the floor. Harold might cut himself, and he won't have the full protection from his DTaP vaccination until he's at least eighteen months old."

"Exactly!" Aldric said and pointed back at me with such vigor that a bolt of purple energy arced from his finger and hit the wall behind me. "That is exactly the point I'm trying to make. This is no place for a baby. I am a semi-lich, a king of the undead, a fiend of the infernal. I am the thing that the dead fear and the living won't even name! Plus, I have a certain lifestyle to maintain."

Aldric waved his hands helplessly about the chamber. I looked around and had to admit that Harold and I had pretty thoroughly invaded his space. A large playpen had been set up in the center of the room where the treasure hoard and throne had formerly stood. The dark hangings that used to run from high ceiling to floor had been taken down because I'd read that getting tangled in bedding or curtains was one of the chief household hazards for babies. Every step or ledge had been railed in, and every corner padded. The torture rack had been repurposed as a changing table, and the chains on the walls that had once held me and the rest of the Company of the Fellowship as prisoners were covered in brightly colored pictures of animals holding up letters of the alphabet: *A is for ankheg, B is for beholder, C is for catoblepas* (although that one's picture was covered up for obvious reasons). And then there were the inevitable baby things.

Toys and bouncers and strollers and bags were scattered everywhere.

I rubbed a hand across the back of my neck. "We have kind of spread out, haven't we?"

"Kind of?" He began to tick things off on his fingers. "You've clogged my whirlpool trap with bath toys. My hallway of heat has been turned into a drying room for onesies. And I don't even want to go into the smell that is coming from the bottomless pit since you began disposing of Harold's soiled diapers there."

I suddenly felt guilty. We *had* imposed on him without really asking if he wanted us. "Aldric, I'm truly sorry about the mess, and I want you to know how much I appreciate your taking us in. I assure you, it's only temporary. We just need to wait until Harold is little less helpless. As soon as he is old enough to take care of himself, I promise will be out of your hair and your bottomless pit."

His gaze piercing, which was saying a lot when you're talking about a semi-lich, he asked, "How temporary?"

"Let me see . . ." I said, clearing my throat and very deliberately counting on my fingers.

I had no idea what I was calculating, but I guessed that doing so would give me the appearance that the answer I was about to give was going to be based on some objective standard, when in fact, everything about the aging of imps sits squarely in the realm of speculation. I knew this because, after realizing how adorably helpless Harold was and witnessing firsthand how much of a mess a baby imp could make, I had done some research into imp biology and exactly how long he would remain little.

There is no simple conversion like you can apply to dogs or outdoor furniture, but the way Eldrin explained it to me, imps age at an unpredictably accelerated rate based on factors including moon phases, solar flares, and exposure to peanuts and gluten. In other words, I had no idea, but at some point, he'd look like the bat/old man/banana creature I had come to know and love. I didn't have the heart to tell Aldric that it might take anywhere from a couple of days to a couple of months to potentially years to get there. What I ended up saying was "I would guess he'll be out of diapers in a few more months."

"Months?" Aldric gasped, his eyes widening so that the glowing embers of the soul stones at their center were clearly visible.

I nodded. "After that he'll be talking and walking and flying."

His mouth dropped open revealing the portal to the infernal realms in its depths. "F-f-flying?" he stuttered.

"Yes, of course," I said absentmindedly. "You know, thinking about it, you may want to start moving some of the magical artifacts off the lower shelves in your library. If you don't, he's going to start getting into them, and as you learned with your copy of the Necronomicon, he is teething."

"Months! Flying! Teething! Am I to be damned to this hell forever?" he shouted, holding his arms up in a dramatic appeal to the heavens.

I decided it would not be wise to point out that being damned was the very nature of his existence, but I was concerned that all this yelling was going to wake Harold. I put a finger to my lips and tried to shush the semi-lich.

"There is no silencing me, Avery!" he roared. "I will be heard!"

On the other side of the room, Harold gave a squeak of surprise, and his eyes blinked open.

Aldric froze in place, quiet as the undead that he was, but it was too late.

Harold looked at the two of us, gave another squeak, this time a little louder, and then began to emit a low wail that grew steadily louder with each passing second. I nearly tripped over the coffin in my rush to get to him. I scooped him up in my arms, but he was inconsolable. Tears welled from his eyes and rolled down his checks.

Aldric came over, his hands pressed against the side of his head. He said something to me, but I couldn't hear it over the air-raid volume wails Harold was producing. "What?" I shouted.

"I SAID, THE NOISE IS INTOLERABLE! You must make him stop! Place him in the baby containment device." He pointed at the bouncing chair.

"You mean the Mamaroo bouncy chair? That won't work. Not while he's crying. I need the wrap. Have you seen the large diaper bag?"

Hands still clutched to his ears, Aldric began to peer about the room at the mounds of baby supplies. (You may think that Vivian and I had gone a little crazy, but with Valdara, her entire court, Eldrin, Dawn, Drake, Rook, and a surprising portion of the Army of Shadow all buying things off our registry, we had enough stuff for a dozen babies.) While Aldric searched, I tried my best to soothe Harold, singing out my normal mantra whenever he was having a meltdown, "Is someone having a really big feeling?" and handing him in rapid succession a geodesic rattle containing a dozen miniaturized galaxies, a glass bottle filled with warm pureed mouse, and a teether in the shape of the Cthulhu Outer God, Azathoth. All were shoved into his mouth but ultimately rejected.

At last, Aldric thrust a bag into my hands.

"What is this?" I snapped.

"It's the diaper bag, you fool," he shouted over Harold's increasingly earsplitting cries.

"No, that's the Skip Hop day pack, you idiot," I bellowed, shoving it back at him. "We need the Petunia Pickle diaper bag."

Aldric's eyes suddenly blazed with an unholy light. "I am the one, the only, semi-lich," he intoned in his deepest, most sepulchral voice. "Master of the Dark Forces, Keeper of the Infernal Flame. I am not Master of the Stiff Pop or Keeper of the Pestilential Pickle." He held the bag back out to me. "Take it!"

"Make me," I spat.

We stood there glaring at each other, while Harold cried inconsolably in my arms. I could see the purple glow around Aldric's body growing deeper and deeper with each passing second and thought he might simply explode. Then Harold, who had been clutching a wooden block in one tiny taloned claw, gave an enormous shriek and launched it at Aldric. It bounced off the semi-lich's forehead and fell to the ground.

There was a momentary pause during which Aldric slowly, deliberately looked down at the toy, and then a purple flash of pure necromantic rage erupted out of his hands like a star going supernova. The bag he'd been holding disintegrated into ash.

The shock of what he had done, and that he might have done it to me, took both of us by surprise. We looked at each other and began to back away, holding up our hands in mute apology. As we did, Harold's cries suddenly stopped and he began to laugh hysterically and point at the pile of ash.

We both looked at Harold and then back down at the ashes. "Had I known he liked pointless destruction, I would have started blowing things up days ago," Aldric said.

I saw his point, but that had been my favorite day pack. It had this series of cubes that fit inside so you could organize your stuff. There was an insulated cube for bottles and a mesh cube for toys, and—

My diaper bag musings were cut short when Aldric asked, "What is *this*?" He brushed past me and stared into the crystal ball, which was pulsating rapidly with a deep scarlet light.

"Your crystal ball?" I suggested, even though I was pretty sure he knew that already.

"But what have you done to it?" he asked, peering into its depths with disturbing intensity.

"Oh, I retuned it to Harold's imp monitor. I didn't think you would mind. You didn't seem to be using it." As I was speaking, Harold was digging through my jeans pockets, obviously attempting to determine if I had any butterscotch on me. All tears were gone.

"You *what*?" asked Aldric, and the look he gave me almost made me dive for cover behind the coffin.

When he didn't blast me into oblivion, I answered, albeit a little less confidently. "I reset its pattern to link it to Harold's baby monitor. Why? Is it showing you something?"

"Someone!" he said dramatically. "I designed the crystal ball to monitor everything happening in my tomb! Someone is coming. I would have detected him sooner had you not baby poofed it." He gave me an accusing glance before returning to his study of the ball.

Harold had given up on his butterscotch quest and was now standing on Aldric's shoulder peering into the ball, doing an amazingly good impression of the semi-lich.

"This won't be a problem, right?" I asked. "I mean, this is what the tomb and all those traps are for, to keep out the riffraff."

"Normally, yes," Aldric said, stroking his chin, a movement Harold managed to copy after a short study. "But look at this. He's evaded the pits of death, the pendulum of evisceration, the spike trap of doom, the poison gas trap, and he went through the evilly humming white room without any hesitation. I've never seen anything like it."

I shuddered involuntarily, remembering how long my own group had spent debating what diabolical death the humming white room had in store for us, before figuring out that it did nothing more than hum as you walked across it. Curiosity took hold of me and I leaned closer to the crystal ball.

A single figure was gracefully making his way through the tomb. He seemed to be evading traps of the most vicious lethality in an annoyingly nonchalant way. The image quality was not good, but there was something familiar in the way he moved.

"Ah, he turned left. That corridor leads to the spiders of inevitable death! You will want to watch this, Avery! It should be entertainingly gory." Aldric laughed maniacally and rubbed his hands together, another mannerism parroted, disturbingly well, by Harold.

We watched as the robed figure casually disarmed several intricately trapped locks with a gesture and a puff of smoke, only to appear on the other side of the vault door and be swarmed by thousands of foot-long, red-eyed, hairy-legged spiders.

"Those are crimson death spiders," Aldric boasted. "They cost me a fortune but were well worth it. Death from their venom is inevitable. Thus, their name. Ah, well, it was entertaining while it lasted." He gave a contented sigh, and Harold sighed along with him.

At last Aldric seemed to take note of the imp's aping behavior. He did a double take, which Harold copied to perfection. They began studying each other suspiciously, and so missed the next few moments of action as the intruder somehow escaped the room of spiders and passed, apparently unscathed, into the chamber beyond.

"Out of curiosity, what happens if he makes it through the spiders?" I asked.

"That's not really something you should be concerned about," Aldric began and then, glancing in the crystal ball, shouted, "Impossible! In the name of all the demons of hell, he's nearly here! No one has ever made it this far. Not even you."

He slammed his fist down on the crystal ball,

which was followed by Harold slamming his own fist into the ball. Aldric and Harold glared at each other with matching tilted heads. Each pointed a finger at the other.

"Can you make him stop?" Aldric asked, which Harold parroted by babbling adorably.

I looked at Harold and the naughty little grin on his face and decided that this was not a battle I needed or wanted to fight. "I don't think so." I tried to draw Aldric's attention away from Harold's sudden precociousness by asking, "What will you do with the intruder? Do you need some help? I am not without skills when it comes to dealing with the unwanted."

The semi-lich's eyes flared at the suggestion. "The day I need assistance from a mage to protect my own tomb is the day I turn in my soul cage." He rolled up his sleeves and his arms and hands began to glow with a diabolic purple light. "He may have survived my traps, but no one can survive me," the semi-lich proclaimed. "You stay here. I will deal with this trespasser."

Aldric moved toward a door in the east wall of the crypt. He was chanting something incomprehensibly hideous and dark, and his hands were weaving elaborate patterns of purple power in air before him. As the spells took effect, a sheath of lethal damnation surrounded his body and a half dozen shadowy figures appeared in ranks on either side of him.

His preparations were complete just in time. The

door slid open, revealing a hooded figure grotesquely silhouetted in the doorway by the infernal glow of Aldric's spells.

The semi-lich gave a maniacal, demoniac laugh that sent a shiver of horror down my spine. With a bestial growl, he said, "I do not know who you are, but I have made my legend off the foolishness of your kind. Perhaps you have come to steal my treasure, or to test yourself against my traps, or simply to make a name for yourself. Whatever the reason, their fates will be yours—death. For you stand before a true emissary of hell and face all the power of the infernal." He raised his skeletal hand and a ball of swirling, shadowy death formed there.

Now, I have faced many foes in my time. As the Dark Lord, I once had to battle an army of breakaway demons who were trying to overthrow my rule. In the group there were a half dozen minor demons, a couple of demi-demons, a semi-demon (not sure of the difference between the two to this day, except that the demi-demon was a looker and the semi-demon was definitely not), at least three different demon lords (of what realms I was not clear on even at the time), and even a couple of demon princes, and that's not counting all their underlings, which spanned the whole range from type I's to type VI's. (By the way, don't ask me why demons use Roman numerals to label themselves, it seems even more anachronistic than the NFL's use of them.)

The point being that I have been in some bad situations, but I have thankfully never had to stare down Aldric in full semi-lich rage. I will say that, had my place and the intruder's been reversed, I would have run as far and as fast from that tomb as my body and my power would have allowed.

Whoever this cloaked figure was obviously was made of sterner stuff. With no hesitation that I could detect, he stepped out of the doorway and into the main chamber of the crypt.

For a fleeting moment he was illuminated by the virulent purple glow coming from Aldric's body. In the split second before Aldric attacked, I was able to get a good look at the intruder and received the second biggest surprise of my life: it was Eldrin. There could be no mistaking those impossibly handsome elven features, or the way his robe was open halfway down to his navel exposing a great deal of his perfect hairless chest, or the lovely smell that surrounded him.

It was while I was screaming the word *NO* that the semi-lich roared, "Die!" and launched the swirling death orb he had been holding at Eldrin, while the shadows, talons sharp as night, sprang forward. The shadow creatures enveloped and seemed to consume Eldrin even as the horrible ball exploded at his feet. There was a concussion like a thunderclap and gouts of infernal flame erupted in a great circle around him, devouring everything within fifty feet. The violence of the attack was so terrible that the walls shook and the ceiling above Eldrin collapsed, burying him beneath the mountain.

And then, there was silence.

Everything in the crypt was shrouded in a cloud of smoke and debris. I was dumbstruck. My legs collapsed beneath me, and I knelt, breathless and numb, as I tried to comprehend the fact that Eldrin was gone.

Then Harold tugged at my shirt and pointed into the smoky remains. I looked up and watched as Eldrin stepped out of the destruction. He paused in front of Aldric and brushed a bit of dirt off his shoulder with the fingertips of one hand.

"It's not possible!" exclaimed Aldric.

"You mean it isn't probable, but you have to admit it must be possible," he said in that smug voice I swore I would never complain about again.

"But . . . but . . . but . . . all my magic and my traps," Aldric stuttered. "It was foolproof!"

"But I'm not a fool," Eldrin said, and already I was beginning to regret my promise not to get annoyed at him. He gave Aldric a sympathetic pat on the shoulder, and then sidestepped the stupefied semi-lich and made his way over to me. "Hi, Avery! Hi, Harold!"

Harold waved back, and I smiled for the first time in weeks. "It was a neat trick, Eldrin," I said, "but to satisfy my curiosity and restore poor Aldric's sanity, how did you do it?"

"Avery, you know me. Is it that much of a stretch to imagine that with all the free time I have had after being banned from Mysterium that I might have improved my real-time extradimensional communication spell?"

I stared at him for a second before realizing what he meant. Then I laughed, another thing I hadn't done for a while. "You added video!"

"Well, that's a bit of an oversimplification," he said with one of his patented disappointed sighs. "It's a holographic transmission transported through subspace using a heavily modified travel pattern. I need to tweak the multiversal positioning system though. I was off by a good quarter mile, which is the only reason I had to go through all those rooms."

Aldric staggered over. "You're saying that you're not really here?"

Eldrin nodded. "I'm not really here. Your traps and magic are just as lethal as ever and, having observed them close up, may I add, very cool."

The semi-lich, although somewhat mollified by the compliment, was not satisfied until he poked a finger through Eldrin's chest. He fell back into his throne. "That's a relief. I was beginning to wonder how I was going to offload a chamber full of crimson death spiders."

Aldric assumed a classic fainting pose, one arm thrown over his eyes while fanning himself with the other.

I turned back to Eldrin. "If you're not here, then where are you?"

"Dawn and I are still in New York, but we've had to move out of our apartment. It was too well-known, and while technically Earth remains neutral, there are a lot of mages here that are loyal to the Administration. Spies are everywhere." His projection glanced about, and Eldrin lowered his voice. "In fact, the reason I haven't communicated in so long is that I needed to improve the encryption patterns on my communication streams. The old ones were too easy to eavesdrop on. Speaking of which, don't use your old coin. The Administration could be monitoring it and we would never know."

My heart dropped on hearing this. The coin was my only reliable connection to Eldrin and Dawn, who had been stranded on Earth since the start of the war. Now I had no way of talking to them that was safe. "Could you send me an improved coin? Or maybe come to Trelari and join us?" I asked.

Eldrin looked suddenly very uncomfortable, and I knew the answer was no. "Not yet," he said, frowning. "First, I'm not sure how we would get there. Gateways into and out of Earth are monitored constantly, so we would have to take a pretty winding road. But more important, there is a lot of information that passes through Earth. Being neutral, we still have visitations from Mysterium mages, some of which are Avery sympathizers."

I looked at him sharply and he raised his hands. "Their label, not mine. They call themselves Benchers for reasons I'm not entirely clear on."

I grinned. "Because of my bench. Remember, the one I'm sitting on with Harold at the end of *The Dark Lord*? Someone painted 'Avery Lives' on it, and I suppose it became a kind of symbol."

Eldrin suddenly slapped a palm against his forehead. "Idiot!"

"What? What's wrong?" I asked, worried that he'd been discovered.

"Nothing's wrong," he said, waving away my concerns with one hand. "I was just so excited to finally talk to you that I forgot the whole reason I called. Guess what came out today."

He slowly raised a tablet computer into the air between us. On the screen was the title page of a novel. It read, *The Darker Lord* by Jack Heckel.

Harold started clapping.

CHAPTER 3

THE DARKER LORD

I stared at the title—speechless with horror. This couldn't be happening again, and yet, there it was, the words glowing on the screen. The last time this happened, when the multiverse spun *The Dark Lord* out of my experiences on Trelari, I spent months obsessing over every word. Now it seems it had done it again and created a second book about some or all of my life over the last year, but unlike last time, I didn't have the luxury of time to read and reread the book looking for answers to questions I didn't know I should be asking. The worlds were at war. I was supposed to be finding a way to restore balance to the multiverse.

I handed Harold down to Aldric, who was still re-clining on his throne muttering about phantom elves under his breath. I knew the shock of Eldrin's appear-ance and his apparent immunity to Aldric's powers must have been terrible on the semi-lich, because he didn't stir an inch or make any complaint as the imp clambered across his lap and began gnawing content-edly on the gold arm of the throne. I left them there and walked Eldrin's projection to the far side of the room beside the torture rack/changing table, which was still smoldering from Aldric's attack.

Now came the moment of truth. I leaned in close. "Have you read it?"

Eldrin answered with a look that meant the answer should be obvious, and that I was either being incredibly dense or purposefully irritating in asking the question.

I nodded and swallowed hard, trying to work some moisture back into my suddenly dry throat. "How bad is it?" I asked hoarsely.

A smile broke across his face and he said brightly, "Oh, is that what you're worried about? Don't. I gave it a five-star review on Amazon. The dialogue was sharp, the action constant. For a middle book it really moved and had a great ending. The only bummer is that I have to wait another two months to get the paperback."

"That's not what I meant, and you know it," I barked irritably. "And don't start in on that trilogy nonsense again. Despite the tradition of trilogies in Mysterium literature, you know as well as I do that it is just as likely that there will be no more books, or twelve more books, or five more books, but where they base a television show off it and the gap between each subsequent volume increases exponentially."

He waved away my protest. "If you think the universe won't want to record and report the fact that you've taken to sleeping in a crypt with a semi-lich, then you are delusional."

"So," Aldric said in an unenthusiastic monotone, "I will have the dubious honor of appearing as a minor character in Avery's next little history. I cannot wait."

Eldrin and I looked over at him with matching glares, but the semi-lich's eyes were still closed, which was probably a good thing as Harold was now chewing on the hem of his beautiful, if frighteningly foreboding, velvet robe.

"If everyone is quite done," Eldrin said irritably, pausing to see if Aldric or I had the nerve to interrupt again. When neither of us said anything, he asked, "Would you like me to continue?"

I nodded silently.

"Right. Well, thankfully it skips over the months you spent being a couch potato."

"Oh, so maybe his stay here will be the prologue," Aldric muttered just loud enough to be heard.

Eldrin ignored him. "It picks your story up on the first day of class. It follows you all the way from there to the moment Valdara opens the breach between Trelari and the rest of the multiverse. If I had one complaint it was the baseless suggestion it made that my lunch with Dawn was anything more than that." He shook a finger at me. "You, my friend, have a dirty mind. However, I must admit it does serve the story well when you meet up with Vivian in Baum's world—very spicy."

I blushed, suddenly worried about how explicit the book had been in describing my reunion with Vivian. "Can you just tell me how awful I was this time? Please."

Eldrin sighed and shook his head. "You really don't get that you're the hero of *The Dark Lord*, do you?" When I said nothing, he added, "The book tells the truth, Avery."

"Gods," I groaned as I recalled everything that had happened during that short time.

He cut me off with a hiss of impatience. "It tells the story of a mage who does what he always does—the best he can in a series of bad situations. A mage who agonizes every time he thinks he might have done better. More important, it exposes the Mysterium for what it is—pure evil. This is a good thing, Avery. When this new book starts circulating through the subworlds, it will be a rallying cry for the rebellion." He paused and cast his eyes down toward his feet. I would almost say he looked chastened, except I knew that was impossible. "To be honest, if anyone comes out looking like a jerk, it's me. I hope you know how much—"

"Stop!" I said and almost tried to embrace him before I remembered he was a projection of mystical energy and that he was standing worlds away. "You reacted the way any sane person would react. You and I have lived most of our lives under the spell of the Mysterium. Its power is subtle and strong."

"And you were able to see through it like that," he said with an impatient snap.

"Is that what you believe?" I asked and laughed bitterly. "The book may not mention them, but you certainly can't forget those six months before all the excitement started when I was lounging on the couch gazing at my own navel and watching bad TV. What do you think I was doing? I was working through what you had to figure out in a moment. Do you really think I like daytime television? It is awful. Well, except for *Days of Our Lives*. How can you argue with a show that has been running since the mid-sixties? Oh, and reruns of *Gilligan's Island*, of course." I thought about it for a second more. "I also love afternoon anime—*Voltron*, *Pokémon*, *Yu-Gi-Oh!*"

Eldrin stared at me without comprehension.

"'It's time to duel'?" I suggested.

He shook his head in confusion.

"Really, no clue? I mean it is only one of the most popular anime series and trading card games of all time."

"You were trying to make a point?" he reminded me.

"Thank you, Eldrin," Aldric said with a groan of exhaustion.

I shot the semi-lich a glance and, despite his repeated pestering, had to smile as I saw that Harold was gnawing lazily on one of the bony fingers of his lich hand. The appendage must have been totally insensitive, because Aldric gave no reaction.

"Avery?" Eldrin sang, trying to return my attention to our conversation.

"Right. Right," I said, trying to refocus. But I was still flustered by his apparent ignorance of Yugi Mutou and his dueling monsters. "They have sold twenty-five billion trading cards," I pointed out.

"Avery!" he and Aldric both shouted simultaneously.

I acknowledged them with a distracted wave and tried to recollect where I had left off before my mental detour. While I was gathering my thoughts, I could have sworn Eldrin murmured, "Yare yare daze," under his breath. However, when I looked up at him, he had the same stony expression and I convinced myself I must have imagined it.

At last, I remembered what I was trying, in my own roundabout way, to say. I stabbed a finger into the air. "The point is, while you and Dawn were working and living and taking care of me, I was struggling to deny what I already knew. My mind shut parts of itself off from me to keep the truth away. The only difference between you and me is that you were able to arrive at the same conclusion in one tenth the time."

"Only because you showed me the way," he said, and then more gently, "Avery, you can't blame yourself for stumbling and taking a few wrong turns when you are in trackless lands, blazing the trail for the rest of us."

"May I ask a question?" Aldric asked in a croaking voice that only someone already dead could produce. "Who's counseling whom? Avery, are you trying to make Eldrin feel better or is Eldrin trying to make you feel better? And why are the two of you trying to do whatever it is you are trying to do to each other in my crypt while an infant imp gnaws at my very bones?" He lifted his lich hand and Harold came with it, still chewing vigorously on the forefinger.

Eldrin and I looked at each other and laughed. "I have no idea, Aldric," I answered. "But I promise we're done."

Eldrin nodded his agreement.

But my mood was quickly tempered by another disturbing thought. "Is there an epilogue in this one that I should know about?" I asked Eldrin. "You know what I mean, something that may not have happened yet?"

He shook his head. "No, it ends with you in the Castle of Light, having just resummoned Harold."

The tension drained from my body. "That's a relief."

I had one last question but was a little hesitant to ask it. Eldrin noticed my discomfort at once. "Spill it," he ordered.

"You know me too well," I said with a cheeky half grin. Eldrin nodded and gestured for me to continue. I took a deep breath and asked, "Any clues in there about what I should do next?"

"Like leave my tomb?" Aldric interjected.

Eldrin ignored him and raised an eyebrow at me. "Do you need some? I thought something was up when I discovered you had been hiding out in a tomb for nearly a week. And that's before I knew its owner was so ill-tempered." He looked sharply at Aldric and then back at me. "The short answer is no, but one friendly piece of advice—if there is a third book in the series, then abandoning your girlfriend to fight your war for you is not a good look."

"Amen to that!" Aldric said enthusiastically. "And that's coming from one of the damned!"

I felt blood rush to my face in embarrassment. "I didn't abandon her."

There was that eyebrow from Eldrin again— speaking volumes. Even Aldric turned about and fixed me with a look that made my cheeks burn even hotter. I suspected I was nearing lobster red on the shamefaced scale.

"I didn't, it's just . . . it's complicated."

That wasn't true. It was actually very simple. I'd had something close to a nervous breakdown after the Western Bore, and Vivian and I had agreed that, given my mental state or lack thereof, it would be better if Trelari's survival didn't depend on me just now. The problem was I did not know how to explain that. I had come close with Aldric earlier, but I didn't feel right dumping the whole grim and sordid truth on someone I didn't know that well. Eldrin was different. If I couldn't tell him, then I wouldn't be able to tell anyone. Besides, he deserved to know what had happened, and what I'd become.

I leaned back against a wall and stared down at my shoes. "Did you read about the battle at the Western Bore?" I asked.

The question must have surprised him, because there was a slight pause, which Aldric eagerly filled. "If not, there's an article about it I could read you." Then his tone shifted to aggrieved and he added, "If, that is, it hasn't been reduced to shreds by this little beast."

After much effort, he finally managed to detach Harold from his forefinger. Almost at once, the imp started to whine and squeal. Aldric reached into his robe and, disturbingly, produced another finger bone, which he shoved into Harold's mouth. I was about to protest, but the imp seemed happy with the substitution and curled into a little ball, sucking on the bone and cooing happily.

I shrugged and turned back to Eldrin. "The Western Bore?" I asked.

"Of course," he answered, still clearly confused by the question. "Why?"

The true story of the last moments of the battle spilled out of me, soft and low and dreadful. "By dawn of the second day, the blood orcs and Paladins were spent. In the previous twenty-four hours, no one had been allowed to sleep or rest or even eat. The smart thing would have been to pause the advance and allow our troops to regroup, but we were so close to the gateway. Valdara and I were certain the battle was won. We decided to push on."

I grimaced as I remembered our utter confidence as we plotted to tighten the noose around the last pockets of Mysterium resistance. "Valdara and I gathered our combined armies in a tight half circle, pressing what was left of the Sealers and golems back against the sides of the mountains. That is when Moregoth sprang his trap. He had bored three gateways into the valley. The main bore that had been the focus of our attack, and two smaller passages on the heights to either side that he had kept hidden. How he did it was quite brilliant. He knew we would be able see through a normal cloaking spell, so he simply didn't complete the bore. He stopped just short, leaving a thin shell of reality between him and us. Maybe we could have seen through it. I don't know."

"A Deschain Portal Detector would probably have worked," Eldrin said academically and then, realizing the implicit criticism, quickly added, "It would have been hard even then. Maybe impossible depending on the conditions."

"Maybe," I agreed without enthusiasm. I knew he was trying to give me an out, but I had already accepted that my incompetence at not anticipating Moregoth's trick was responsible for everything that came after.

"That morning was spent repositioning our forces into the tight headlands at the end of the valley for our final assault. We were still reassembling them into their ranks when two regiments of Moregoth's Destroyers—the elite guard he built from the remnants of the force that pursued me through the subworld—burst through the gates on either side of us. The fighting was . . . terrible."

Bile rose in my throat at the memory, and I had to pause to swallow it down. "We were blindsided. There was no organization, no lines. One giant scrum is what I saw when I came diving down on Loshlaith." I pointed at the paper Aldric had been reading and snorted. "The news account said I won the battle using the dragon's acid breath, but there was no way. I would have killed as many of my own men as Moregoth's. Still, the crisis was upon us. The Destroyers were pouring from the gateways, more and more with each passing moment. Soon they would have the numbers to sweep over us and break through the valley. What Valdara and I had seen as a relatively minor skirmish over a fairly unimportant gateway was developing into a major new Mysterium offensive."

My heart raced at the remembered fear, and I fell silent. After a few moments, Eldrin, with studied care, said, "If Moregoth had won, he would have been able to merge the gateways. It would have created an enormous tear in the fabric dividing Trelari from Mysterium."

"Irreparable," I confirmed. "There would have been a second permanent crossing between the worlds. Instantly, we would have had been forced into fighting on two fronts."

Aldric had grown more interested in my tale the more it diverged from the printed account. At last he said, "I don't understand. If Moregoth was that close to breaking through, why did the paper portray it as a completely one-sided affair?"

"Because of what I did next," I said with a sigh, and pushing myself off the wall, I began to pace.

Choosing his words carefully, Eldrin asked, "What did you do?"

"Does the new book talk about Griswald's reality key at all? About what it can do? About the cost of using it?" I asked.

He nodded, his body tense and still.

I continued, "I only meant to use it to seal the gates. My intent was clear. My will focused. It should have worked."

"You couldn't close the gates?" he asked.

If only, I thought. Aloud, I said, "No, the gates were woven closed, and had that been the end of it, we would have secured a major victory. Moregoth's two regiments of Destroyers would have been trapped in Trelari. Without support, we would have been able to grind them down. But . . ."

"There was a cost," Eldrin offered.

I started to nod but stopped myself. That was the easy answer, but I wasn't sure anymore. "The magic went out of control," I answered. "It wove the gates closed, but it didn't stop there. It continued to weave, binding pattern to pattern at random. Before I could stop, hands were woven to swords, bodies to armor, feet and legs to ground, enemy to enemy. The battlefield became something out of a diseased nightmare."

I had to stop, because my mind was filled with visions. The melted landscape, alive, like some Lovecraftian abomination. Everything pulsating and moving and screaming and dying. My head swam, and I put a hand out to brace myself against the wall. I looked at Eldrin and Aldric. The elf's normally glittering skin was pale with horror, and even the lich looked slightly ill, something that I wouldn't have thought possible. After all, he was the mastermind behind the Abattoir Hall, which has more spinning, swinging, and slicing blades per square foot than any place in Trelari, and was designed with floors, walls, and ceilings that all allow for the efficient cleanup of any and all blood, bits, and bodily fluids.

"So, tell me," I asked them both. "Did I do 'the best I could with a bad situation'?"

"That's not fair, Avery," Eldrin said, taking up my defense. "The scope of the magic you were attempting was completely appropriate for the situation. You could not possibly have known that would happen."

"Ignorance and good intentions are excuses that wear thin after a time," I retorted, and sinking down to floor, I buried my head in my hands. "The fact is, I knew something *could* happen. For instance, I was willing to take the risk that *somewhere* I was unwinding a reality. Does it matter that the consequences were immediate and visceral?"

None of us had an answer for that, and so we wrapped ourselves uncomfortably in our own thoughts. Only Harold was unfazed. He had clambered off the throne and buried himself under Aldric's discarded newspaper where the sounds of gnawing and sucking could be heard. It was at times like this that I missed the old version of my imp. Old Harold probably would have lit up a cigar and said something insensitive and wise and perfectly timed to shake me out of my latest bout of self-loathing.

Eldrin tried to sit down on an edge of the changing table, but instead he seemed to be floating slightly above it. I pointed at the table. "I think your calibration is off."

He looked down in annoyance and made a couple of elaborate motions with his fingers. His imaged flickered and then reset a couple of inches lower. "You just can't get the same quality of material components on Earth as you can on Mysterium," he complained. "That is one thing I miss. That, and the kebab stand."

"I miss the fogs that roll in every evening," I said. "As fantastical as the place is during the day, at night it felt like you were walking in a dream."

"You know what I miss?" Aldric asked.

"Your coffin," I answered flatly.

"No . . . Well, yes," he conceded. "But what I was going to say is that I miss breathing. It drives you mad not having something to do every few seconds."

Neither Eldrin nor I knew how to respond so we didn't. After an awkward gap in the conversation, which Aldric missed because he was pretending to breathe, Eldrin asked, "So, what's going on? Why *are* you in a tomb?"

"My tomb!" Aldric interjected.

"And don't give me any nonsense about it being for Harold," Eldrin scolded.

"Because the maw of hell is no place for a baby!" Aldric said with clenched fists raised to the sky.

I glared at Aldric. "You know, this was meant to be a *private* conversation."

"You know you are talking to an evil hell-spawn," he said, mimicking my scolding tone.

With an exasperated sigh, I gestured for Eldrin to follow me and walked across to the far corner of the room, ducking into a small alcove that had once held an imp-unfriendly iron maiden. Naturally, I'd had it removed when Harold and I moved in. I looked back at Aldric and whispered, "The truth is, I'm trying to find a place to hide the key and thought I'd see if the tomb was secure enough."

"So, your plan is to abandon the key altogether?" he asked.

"I don't see any other option," I answered with a shrug. "It cannot be used. Even in a reality like Trelari that is strong enough to resist dissolution, the key's powers have grown too unpredictable. And the temptation to wield it is very strong. Even after the horror at the Western Bore, Rook is still making excuses for the bloody thing and trying to convince Valdara to let him try to use it." I glanced back at Aldric again, but he was preoccupied with Harold, who was poking at the semi-lich with the strange finger he had been chewing on earlier. I motioned for Eldrin to step further into the alcove and he did. "Anyway, your little stunt put the nail in the proverbial coffin of this place as a safety deposit box."

"But I only made it through the traps because I'm not really here," he protested.

"I know that. It's more what your appearance revealed about Aldric than it is about the tomb itself. Don't get me wrong, I like him, but he's too clever, knows the tomb too well, and is entirely too evil. No matter where I hid the key, he would find it, probably using that crystal ball of his. And if the key fell into his hands, I'm not confident that Aldric wouldn't use it to try to set up an undead empire."

On cue, the semi-lich called out, "Avery, you had better come and take your imp away before I rend his soul and blast his mortal remains into the realm beyond." He plucked Harold from the top of his head where the imp had been sitting drumming with his newfound finger-bone toy.

"Sorry, Eldrin," I said apologetically. "I guess I better go."

"That's okay, I'm afraid I need to leave also." His projection seemed to look off through the wall to our left and nod. He gave the universal signal for one more minute, which oddly is one or two fingers held up in an alternating and uncertain fashion.

"What's going on?" I asked, but the innocent question elicited an unexpectedly slippery expression from Eldrin.

"Oh, no place in particular," he said evasively.

I put my hands on my hips and began tapping a toe impatiently. "Out with it! I know it has something to do with me, so you might as well confess. What have I done this time?"

"It's nothing really," he said with a dismissive wave of his hands. "It's just the new book let slip a couple of little details about our New York apartment, and

Dawn and I decided we needed to . . . clean a few things up."

"What few things?" I asked.

"Nothing important."

"What!" I pressed.

He let out an elaborate sigh. "If you must know, the book mentions that you and I set up an antigravity field in the stairwell of the apartment building, and now overeager, albeit well-read, joy riders are zooming up and down and breaking all kinds of limbs, not to mention laws of physics. Anyway, Dawn insists that we go over and decommission it before someone gets seriously hurt."

"Another debit in my ledger," I said and rubbed a hand across the back of my neck. "I'm beginning to doubt that I will ever be able to balance the sheets with you."

Eldrin gave a strange, enigmatic smile. "I hope you know that I don't think you owe me a thing, although it would be fun to let you try to 'balance the sheets' with me."

I was trying to sort this comment out when Aldric roared, "Avery! Imp! Now!"

"Looks like you have to go," Eldrin said. "And so do I. Ships and nights, as always."

I nodded in agreement and said, "Yeah, from the way Harold is trying to beat Aldric to death, it's just about nap time over here. Time for the regular ritual—bottle, change, book, bed."

Eldrin raised an eyebrow inquisitively. "So, you are using the Sears method?"

"Actually, a hybrid between Sears, Pantley, and Hogg," I answered as we strolled back across the room. I disconnected Harold from Aldric, much to the semi-lich's relief, and took him over to what remained of the torture rack changing table, where I began pulling on the specially warded robes and gloves I used when dealing with the imp's diapers.

"You're certain that's a wise idea?" he asked.

I took a clothespin and clamped it over my nose before answering. "Yes, but why do you ask?"

He shrugged and watched as I began removing the five-point harness that kept the diaper attached to Harold's bottom. "It's just that you and Vivian are so busy with the war. Those methods require a lot of patience and time. Particularly if you are incorporating Hogg's PUPD technique. I'm just wondering if you've thought about Ferber or Weissbluth."

I paused in the middle of my delicate operation to glare at him. "Vivian and I agree that any technique that includes the word *extinction* has no business being associated with putting a child to sleep."

"Just asking," he said as I took a pair of mystically enhanced tongs and carefully, very carefully, lowered the soiled diaper into a piece of folded reality that I'd modified into a high-temperature industrial incinerator. If you wonder why we needed to take all these precautions to change a simple diaper, then it is clear you have never had to change a baby whose diet consists exclusively of blended mouse carcasses.

The changing operation complete, I took off the robes and gloves and carried Harold and a copy of *Goodnight Moon* over to the coffin.

I started to climb into the coffin beside Harold. Eldrin ran a hand through his perfect hair and shook his head. I could see he was about to opine on the wisdom of my sleeping arrangements. Holding up a finger, I said, "Not a word."

"But—"

"No!"

He sighed. "Have a good nap, Avery."

"Thanks, Eldrin."

We broke the connection and he flickered away. I snuggled in close to Harold and closed the lid.

CHAPTER 4

YOU MAY BE WONDERING
WHY I BROUGHT YOU HERE

I got to *Goodnight clocks* before passing out, which is better than my average by a few bears, chairs, kittens, and mittens! If our pattern held, Harold probably nodded off a few minutes after I did. I can't remember what I dreamed while I was sleeping, but I am confident I was thoroughly enjoying my unconsciousness when I was jolted awake by a blaring alarm.

It was one of the many wards of protection I'd imbued into the coffin. They were warning me that someone had cast a spell either on or near me. Now, before you get too nervous, I want to assure you that there was no danger that this alarm would wake Harold, because it was all in my head. I had long before revised all my warding patterns to silence any aural alarms for fear that they would disrupt the imp's sleep schedule.

Reluctantly awake, I assessed our situation. First, I confirmed that we were still in the coffin. For those of you new to coffin sleeping—and, again, I must stress that you not wait until you are dead to try this highly underrated sleep medium—there are two signs that you should look for: darkness and velvety softness. After confirming both the blackness and softness of my surroundings, I made my second and far more critical check: was Harold still asleep? I quieted my breathing and after a few seconds I confirmed the imp's soft snoring.

Now that the important stuff was out of the way, I could deal with my mystical foe. I focused my will inward on the warding pattern that had first alerted me to the spell. It informed me that someone had summoned the coffin through a travel portal. This was bad, but the good news was that we were still in Trelari. It was having a hard time getting a fix on our exact location but assured me with the greatest confidence that we currently had zero velocity. I silently cursed it and reminded myself to reset the ward's Heisenberg defaults.

The activation of the ward had also automatically activated a cascade of automated defensive protection (ADP) spells. I could feel their drain on my store of mystical energy and notionally prodded them to see how they were holding up. Another piece of good news to add to Harold still being asleep and Aldric having splurged for eight-hundred-thread-count sheets was that all the wards were still intact and not under immediate assault. In theory, this meant it was safe to open the coffin and see what was going on.

But then I have always favored the adage, "In theory, there is no difference between theory and practice, but in practice, there is." Then again, this saying is either attributed to Jan L. A. van de Snepscheut, who infamously bludgeoned his wife before setting himself on fire, or Yogi Berra, who also once said, "I never said most of the things I said."

Still, I had to do something. I looked down at Harold, he was not ready for a full-on fight, if that was what was coming next. I was tempted to transport him straight to Vivian, but I didn't have his portal seat with me, and unrestrained travel at his age had its dangers. Something I would most certainly be bringing up quite forcefully with whatever jackass just yanked us across the world. Also, since I wasn't entirely sure where I was, it was hard for me to be entirely sure how to get him somewhere else.

Instead, being very careful not to disturb him, I drew a series of circles around Harold's sleeping body. As each of them activated, they rotated about, forming a sphere that enclosed him and would theoretically—there's that word again—protect him from all the horrors of my paranoid imagination, up to and including my own death.

Having done as much as I could to keep Harold safe, I filled myself with magic, took a deep breath to steel my nerves, and opening the coffin lid, sprang out.

I was stunned to find that I was in the middle of Valdara's throne room in the Citadel of Light, a vast cathedral of polished stone, gilding, and overly elaborate tapestries all capped by a soaring ceiling supported by an unnecessary, if not obscene, number of pillars. I once compared it to what you might get if a marble factory exploded in an aircraft hangar. It was big, it was gaudy, and it had clearly been designed by someone that knew nothing of Valdara's taste or sensibilities. Of course, none of this mattered when Valdara was seated on her throne, because your eye was drawn to her commanding presence. But what I saw on emerging from the coffin was not the well-ordered, dignified court I had come to expect. Chaos raged all around.

Soldiers and attendants were sprawled on the ground or staggering to their feet. The large war table that usually stood in the very place where the coffin had materialized lay in splinters among the tall colonnades. The queen's banners that lined the walls were in flames, and several of the massive support beams were smoldering ominously. Even the throne had tipped backward and lay on its back atop the high dais that dominated the north end of the room.

I could see Valdara, disheveled in her regal robes, being helped to her feet by Drake, while Sam, outfitted grandly in his new Royal Wizard's robes, sat dazed on the floor as though he had been blasted with a powerful spell. His face was blackened, and his hair stood on end, crackling with the remnants of mystical power.

My first thought was that the castle must be under some kind of assault. I closed the lid of the coffin to make sure Harold wouldn't be disturbed, and dropped into a defensive crouch, which wasn't really a magic thing but something I picked up from repeated watchings of the Karate Kid franchise, particularly the fight between Chozen and Mr. Miyagi in *The Karate Kid Part II*. But after a few seconds I realized no one seemed to be battling anyone. Instead, they seemed to be recovering from some cataclysm.

I deactivated my defensive wards and rushed across the room to Sam. I knelt by his side, my eyes still darting here and there for signs of danger. "Sam, are you all right? What's going on? Are we under attack?"

Without a word, Sam put his hand on my shoulder and levered himself unsteadily to his feet. He swayed for a few seconds, trying unsuccessfully to straighten out his robes, and then slurred grandly, "Great Queen Valdara, Protector of Trelari and Supreme Commander of the Armies of Trelari, may I present, Magus Stewart, Vice General of the Army of Shadow."

Having made this pronouncement, Sam toppled straight onto his backside. It was then that it dawned on me that Sam may have brought me here, and that the destruction around us was simply the aftermath of my admittedly aggressive antisocial wards. I looked back at the coffin, and sure enough, surrounding it on the marble floor were the remains of a mystical circle, still sputtering and sparking with residual power.

This didn't make sense. I knew Sam and he was a very cautious mage. It seemed out of character for him to attempt something so dangerous on his own. Also, he knew about the defenses I used to protect myself. I had personally given him a full list of wards to cast on Harold's crib for when he babysat. Then it struck me that there was only one person who could override Sam's built-in prudence: Valdara.

I looked to the ruined throne where Valdara was just rising to her feet. Anger and confusion warred within me. Anger won out. I stormed up the dais toward her. Already a swarm of guards were setting the throne back upright, and several attendants were trying to untangle Valdara's hair from the gilt filigrees of her crown. Behind her, Drake leaned against his staff and watched the attendants trying to reassemble Valdara's royal person with a frenzy of pins and clips and combs, a grin that perfectly balanced mocking derision and peaceful beneficence fixed on his face.

Valdara brushed the servants aside. I had to admit, even with her hair undone and her crown slightly askew, she still looked imposing. Particularly with Justice Cleaver cradled in her arms. A couple of the royal guards, seeing the look of murder in my eyes, rushed to get between me and their queen.

She dismissed them with a wave. "Let him approach," she commanded and gave her head a little shake as though trying to clear it.

"I'll do more than approach," I mumbled as I pushed past the guards. Valdara, standing with one hip resting against the throne, had her fingers in her ears now and was yawning. "Are your ears ringing, Your Majesty?" I asked, in a sweet, singsong voice. "Is your head a little woozy? Are we maybe a little unsteady on our feet?"

Valdara, still not completely with it, nodded vaguely. "Yes. What the hell happened?"

"What happened was that you tried to pull a magus through the ether by force!" I shouted. "What the hell were you thinking? You could have gotten someone killed!"

The throne room grew instantly quiet. Valdara's eyes sharpened and bore into me like steel javelins.

I suddenly remembered where I was, and who she was.

"I'll tell you what I was thinking, Magus Stewart." Her tone was both low and commanding, and somehow projected to every corner of the vast chamber. "I was thinking that one of my top generals disappeared in the middle of a war without a word. I was thinking that this general had purposefully gone to the one place in Trelari where I couldn't reach him. I was thinking that this same general had ignored two separate summonses to return to the capital for consultation." Then she dropped her voice to a whisper, which only I could hear. "And I was thinking that during our last battle, this general of mine literally melted part of my army and part of my kingdom together using what I can only describe as a doomsday weapon!"

At this, Justice Cleaver jerked to life in her hands, his voice booming and echoing against the stone walls of the throne room. "You are mistaken there, my queen. I am the only doom-bringer. The weapon of weapons. Never challenged. Never defeated. Let me prove my mettle with my metal—see what I did there—against this upstart magician. He shall feel the sting of justice! I will rend—"

Valdara rapped a single finger against the battle-ax and it grew silent. "What is our rule, JC?"

"You talk! I fight!" he answered vigorously. "However, this is an argument, which is a verbal fight. Therefore, I am in the right! Never you fear, my queen. I am as adept with words as I am with my blades. If you will not let me teach his flesh to fear the cut of my edge, then at least let his ears know the righteousness of my rebukes."

Valdara dropped her forehead into her hand and began rubbing her temples. Two of her attendants took this as a sign that she needed assistance and rushed forward with combs and hairpins at the ready. After trying to shoo them away discreetly, Valdara finally roared, "Enough! I want the Royal Throne Room cleared of everyone except for Magus Stewart, the royal wizard, the royal steward, and the high priest! Master of Arms, take this . . ." She took a deep breath. "Take Justice Cleaver to the Royal Armory and keep him there."

A huge man, bristling with armor and weapons and muscles, approached with a large velvet pillow. He was sweating with anxiety. Valdara deposited Justice Cleaver onto the cushion, and the man carefully retreated, eyeing the battle-ax warily. As he exited, Justice Cleaver could be heard saying, "You are right to fear me, unworthy one. Without any great exertion on my part, I could turn you from a Master of Arms into a Master of No-Arms. . . . That was a joke. Did you get it? You may not be aware, but my humor is renowned throughout the known world. Did I ever tell you the one about how many swords it takes to light a candle?"

Valdara and I stood regarding each other in silence as Justice Cleaver's voice faded into the distance and the room was cleared. When the last guard slipped out the side door, Valdara asked, "Can you explain yourself?"

"Only if you will explain yourself," I answered, still angry at being yanked out of the semi-lich's tomb against my will, both because I missed my nap and because it was so easily done.

Her voice hardened to steel. "That is not the way this works, Avery. You agreed when we merged our armies that you would be answerable to me."

"On the battlefield," I retorted. "And I think I've kept my end of the bargain. I take my forces where you command. I confer, but always defer to you on all questions of strategy and tactics. However, I told you before we began that there would be times when I would need to be elsewhere."

"What could the semi-lich have that you need?" she snorted. "Is your Dark Lord look getting stale? Were the two of you comparing evil laughs? Did you catch vampirism when I wasn't looking?"

I started to say it was none of her damned business, but Drake, who had taken up his traditional post to the right of the throne, stopped me just in time. "Valdara, the kid is looking pale. He's got a lot going on with Harold, and I'm guessing he hasn't had much rest."

Trust Drake to know exactly when to turn down the heat. I bowed my head in thanks and said, "Just one of the downsides of sleeping in a coffin."

He smiled his crooked smile in return and was about to say something else when Sam, who had still not managed get to his feet, asked, "Why were you sleeping in a coffin anyway? I thought you'd died, and that I'd summoned you from the grave!"

"When you're living in a tomb with a semi-lich, you don't have a lot of choices on where to sleep," I answered. I glanced back at the coffin and rubbed my chin thoughtfully. "Speaking of which, I don't think Aldric's going to be very happy with having his coffin stolen. He said it really pulled the crypt together."

Sam's eyes grew wide with fear. "I . . . I didn't mean to summon the coffin. I thought it would only pull you through. Do . . . do you think you could tell him it was an accident? I wouldn't want him to be sore with me."

"Semi-lichs don't get sore, Sam," Drake said with exaggerated gravity. "They get evil."

Swallowing hard, Sam asked, "You don't thing he would try to k-kill me, do you?"

"Nothing like that," I reassured him and let him relax for a half beat before adding, "He would probably just enslave your soul for all eternity or turn you into his vampiric thrall."

Sam's face turned a shade of pale that would have done the lich proud.

I felt a sudden pang of guilt. It was wrong to wind him up this much, besides, it was growing increasingly hard to keep a straight face. "I'm sure it will be fine once I explain it to him, and we return his coffin." I shook a finger at him. "However, let this be a warning to you about summoning people without permission. It is a very dangerous practice. Not only do you not know what they might bring with them, but you also don't know what kind of defensive spells they may have cast." I gestured about at the destruction. "Some mages I know use wards that are designed to turn enemy casters into stone or dissolve them into pools of goo."

He swallowed again and said sheepishly, "Sorry, Avery. I've been studying everything I can about portals and transport circles. I read all your notes and even your dissertation. I guess I thought I could do it, and I suppose I wanted to impress you."

"I'm more impressed that you made it through my dissertation without falling into a permanent coma," I said with a tip of an imaginary cap.

"Yes, yes, we are all impressed that Sam managed to blow up my throne room as a result of his study of your work, Avery," Valdara said impatiently. "However, surprisingly, magic instruction is not why I asked to have you brought here." She paused to peer about the room critically. "Where is Seamus? I told him that I wanted him here when Avery arrived."

Sam put his hand into the air, one finger pointing up. Valdara's lips thinned in irritation. "You don't have to raise your hand, Sam. If you know where he is, just tell me."

"No, he's up there." Sam again pointed emphatically toward the ceiling.

"What? In heaven?" Drake barked. "You mean he's dead?"

For a second my heart dropped to my feet, but then Sam began shaking his head vigorously. "No, no. I mean he got blown into the rafters."

We all looked up and sure enough, there was a blackened Seamus standing unsteadily on one of the large oaken beams waving down at us. "Sorry, Your Majesty, I'll be down momentarily."

"How?" Drake asked with a shout.

Seamus started to answer, then scratched his head. "That's not something you should concern yourself with, Your Grace. I'm sure an idea will occur to me on the way down."

Valdara grimaced. "Absolutely not! Sit back down before you fall. We will get someone to retrieve you shortly." She drummed her fingers on the arm of the throne and looked back and forth between Sam and me. "Well, do either one of you have any bright ideas?"

In deference, Sam gestured that I should go first.

"I have seven," I said confidently.

"Great!" she said. "What will it take?"

"Well, depending on the option you choose, the casting will take from an hour to twelve weeks to prepare and may result in some slight but permanent seismic instability in and around the citadel."

Valdara nodded her head wearily. "That's about what I expected. Sam?"

He chewed on his lip for a minute. "I have two ideas. One would require us to somehow get this feather up to him." He pulled a small piece of white goose down from a pouch on his belt.

"A bit impractical, but better than Avery's options," Valdara said. "What would you need for the second plan?"

"A ladder, Your Majesty."

We were all digesting this in silence when Seamus shouted back down, "I've been thinking about it, Your Majesty. It doesn't look that far, I'm pretty sure I could just hop down. Dwarfs are excellent jumpers!"

Valdara closed her eyes, muttered a series of increasingly desperate prayers under her breath, and then shouted, "We'll get you down soon, Seamus. In the meantime, why don't you stay up there and take a rest?"

"It's no problem, Your Majesty," he reassured her. "If you will but move Avery's traveling box a little to the left and open the lid, I'm sure it would be more than sufficient to break my fall."

"No!" we all shouted in unison.

Valdara turned to Sam. "In the royal steward's absence, could I impose on you to get the documents on troop movements from the war room? I want to review them with Avery."

He bowed to Valdara and then whispered to me, "In case I forget before you leave, please remember to explain things to the semi-lich."

Having already forgotten about Drake and my little joke, I asked uncertainly, "Explain?"

"About the coffin . . ."

"Oh, right." I winked and nodded. "Leave it to me, Sam."

He let out a big sigh. "You're the best, Avery."

When he was gone, Valdara fixed me with one of her infamous steely glares. "You shouldn't tease him like that. He is the royal wizard and deserves respect." She turned on Drake and added, "From both of you."

"Respect?" Drake laughed roughly. "He's got more than my respect, Valdara. The kid scares the life out of me. Sometimes I think he has more power than sense."

"Drake has it right. Sam has the ability to do things he has no business doing. I wasn't kidding when I told him not all my wards went off. Had I been off-world when he pulled me through, this entire section of the castle could have been leveled. The only reason they didn't go off is because I thought the only person on Trelari that had the power to perform that kind of magic was Vivian." I shook a scolding finger at Valdara. "If you keep pushing him, he'll do something one day he can't come back from. He needs more time and more training."

"I agree," Valdara said, shaking her own finger back at me. "But must I remind you that one of the things you promised to do was to train him. How are you going to do that hiding in a coffin?"

"That's not fair," I protested. "I have been right beside you every step of the way. It simply cannot be that my taking a few days to deal with some personal matters throws the entire war effort into chaos." Valdara started to respond, but I bravely cut her off. "Let's cut to the chase. What is so important that you decided to ask Sam to perform magic he's never done, risking both him and me, and unknowingly you and your entire court in the process?"

For one of the few times since I'd known her, Valdara was momentarily speechless. She stared at her hands briefly and then locked her eyes on mine. "You're right, Avery. I'm sorry. It was badly done."

I'm not sure who was more surprised, me or Drake, but both of us looked like fish: wide-eyed and openmouthed.

She looked between us and her face darkened. "What? I can admit when I'm wrong."

"Absolutely!" Drake reassured her, followed a half breath later by my "No question about it!"

"One of your finest traits," Drake added.

"Without peer!" Seamus shouted down from above.

"That will do," she said sharply. She stood and began pacing in front of the throne. "Avery, I am concerned about the Army of Shadow."

My mind went to the aftermath of the Battle of the Western Bore. I wanted to avoid talking about the key, if possible, since I had no solution for it yet. Instead, I decided to play dumb—not that hard for me. "Concerned?"

She stopped pacing and looked at me suspiciously. "Yes. It may be impossible for you not to take this the wrong way, but I'm concerned about Vivian."

Behind her, I saw Drake's eyebrows rise up his forehead, which let me know this was as much a surprise to him as it was to me. I'll admit I had a lot of concerns about the Army of Shadow, it being the largest collection of evil ever assembled in the history of Trelari and my having ended our last battle by literally melting a portion of it being the most obvious examples, but Vivian was not one of them. I suspected something else was at play here, and so said diplomatically, "She has the rank of vice general, the same as me. She has been fighting with and commanding the Army of Shadow along with me from the beginning of the war. She is at least as experienced as I am and arguably more competent at logistics, planning, and management."

"A great deal more competent, I'd say," Drake growled a bit too quickly for my ego.

"She does have the advantage of premonition," I said in my own defense.

Valdara sat down on the edge of her throne. "It is not a question of competence. It is a question of trust. Do you both trust her to *loyally* command the army?"

"Absolutely," I answered, but this time Drake said nothing. His silence was deafening. "What is this all about?" I asked. "Has something happened?"

"I don't know. Perhaps," she said, and then, in an abrupt change of subject, asked, "The key of power . . . Does she have it, or do you?"

"Why do you want to know?" I asked, my mind spinning as I tried to figure out what was going on.

Her mouth drew into a tight line. "Out of respect for my position, can you give me an answer without requiring a reason?"

"No," I said with a slow shake of my head. "But out of consideration for all that we have been through, I can tell you that the key has always and will always remain under my control and protection."

Valdara nodded and I thought I saw a little of the tension drain from her face. However, before I could get any further explanation from her, Sam came bustling in with armfuls of scrolls. She rose and, gesturing for the rest of us to follow her, started toward the area of the throne room where her war table had stood before it was obliterated by my entrance. She glanced at the splintered remains and cursed under her breath.

I was about to suggest we spread them over the acres of empty floor when Seamus's voice came floating down from above. "Never fear, Your Majesty, I will fetch a new table at once!"

We all looked up in alarm as the dwarf began lowering himself over the edge of the beam. "Sit down, Master Seamus!" Valdara barked. "That's an order!"

Once Seamus was safely seated again, Drake pointed to the coffin. "We could use that."

Valdara nodded and Sam began laying the papers out on the coffin's lid. They appeared to be troop activity reports that detailed the movement of different units in the Army of Shadow. Each scroll was a map showing a location in Trelari. Black S's, the symbol we'd chosen for units of the Army of Shadow, marched across topographical terrains in a series of annotated arrows.

After studying them for a few moments, I began to see a pattern. The S's on each map were converging toward a single point, but none of the S's combined with the S's on any of the other maps. It seemed Vivian was splitting the Army of Shadow up into a dozen or more smaller forces. Although we hadn't discussed doing this, the strategy, in and of itself, wasn't that unusual. We often split and then recombined different elements of the army to try to conceal the true size of our overall force from the enemy. What was puzzling was that I didn't recognize any of the muster points. Units were being sent to far-flung locations all around Trelari with no apparent strategic value.

Valdara stood beside me. "These redeployments began five days ago." She paused significantly. "The same day you left for the semi-lich's tomb."

It was baffling. It wasn't just that there was no clear strategic objective, there appeared to be no sense to the movements at all. Vivian might as well have taken a handful of darts and thrown them at a map of Trelari. "There has to be an explanation," I said.

"Explanation?" Valdara snorted in disbelief. "The only explanation is insanity."

Drake scratched his chin. "She has a point, Avery." He pointed at one of the maps. "What possible reason could there be for massing thousands of blood orcs on the edge of Silver Wood? Or hundreds of doom trolls in the middle of the Sea of Grass, or an entire division of rage demons at the entrance to the Mines of Maria?" When I said nothing, he asked, "Shall I go on?"

To Drake's surprise, I nodded. It wasn't that I wanted a geography lesson, but something about the locations he was naming was triggering a memory that was desperately trying to bang its way out of my skull.

With a shrug, he continued shuffling through maps reading off names of places. He made it through about a half dozen more before I finally made the connection. It still made no sense and I still had no idea why, but I knew where Vivian was sending the army, and I announced the names of next three muster points as Drake and Sam looked on in amazement. "A mountain pass outside the village of Hamlet, the wasteland where Aldric's tomb stood, the ruins of the Dark Queen's fortress."

"How can you possibly know that?" demanded Drake.

"I need a map," I murmured in reply.

Valdara looked at me, and then at the papers in front of us, and then back at me before exploding. "What do you think these are?" She picked up handfuls of map scrolls and held them in front of my face. "Now explain how you knew where Vivian has been moving the Army of Shadow. Did you know?"

I was too busy trying to divert my mind from the dark paths of thought it was trying to wander down to answer Valdara's more incendiary questions, and instead focused on my very tangible need for a map of the world. I swept the papers we'd been studying off the coffin. "These won't do. I need a map of the whole world. I need to see all of Trelari."

At this request, Valdara turned on her heel and stalked away from me down the length of the throne room. I followed, trying to figure out how I could explain that I hadn't gone mad and may even be on the brink of understanding what Vivian was up to, but she was in no mood to talk. We were somewhere near the center of the Great Hall when she stopped and pointed down. I followed her finger and there, inlaid in the marble floor, was an enormous mosaic map of Trelari.

Without a word, I dropped to my knees and began mapping Vivian's mustering points, marking them on the giant map with random bits of debris from my pockets: a butterscotch candy, my old apartment keys, a desiccated demon eye, the still sealed but pulverized remains of a fortune cookie from my favorite takeout place in the Village. When I was done, I stood and studied the pattern they made. It immediately confirmed my suspicion.

Vivian had moved the Army of Shadow to twelve different encampments, each forming one of the three points or one of the nine intersections of a triquetra that spanned nearly the entire length and breadth of the central continent of Trelari. Coincidentally, each also happened to lie atop an important location in my original stabilizing pattern. I still had no idea what Vivian was planning, but I was filled with admiration at the scale of her accomplishment.

"It looks like it forms a pattern," Sam observed.

I nodded absentmindedly. "It's a triquetra."

"What's it mean?" he asked.

"Depends," I said, still lost in my own thoughts as I spun out the implications. "If you're Japanese, it's the Musubi Mitsugashiwa, if you're German, then it symbolizes Odin, if you're a Christian, then it represents the trinity, if you're a twenty-year-old who's into yoga and cleanses, then it probably has something to do with the Triple Goddess, if you're a Marvel fan, then it's the marking etched onto Thor's hammer, Mjollnir, and if you're a fan of Led Zeppelin, then it stands for legendary bassist John Paul Jones."

"What does it mean to you?" Valdara asked from close beside me. "And is it treason?"

I'm not sure how I would have responded to that question, but it probably would have been a lie. As much as I liked and respected Valdara, I was in love with Vivian, and she deserved a chance to explain herself before I condemned her. Fortunately, I didn't have to say anything, because at that moment a chime went off from inside the coffin. It was the baby monitor. Harold was waking up!

CHAPTER 5

YOU MAY BE WONDERING WHY
I ALSO BROUGHT YOU HERE

The others spun about and stared suspiciously at the closed coffin. "Is . . . is it another of your wards?" Sam asked nervously.

"Oh gods, no!" Seamus croaked from high above.

"Nothing like that," I reassured everyone in a voice loud enough to be heard in the rafters. "It's just Harold's monitor. He's probably waking up from his nap. I'll go check on him."

"Can I come say hello?" Sam asked. "I've got some of those candies he likes." He fished into one of the pockets of his robe and pulled out a handful of gold-wrapped butterscotches.

I looked at them doubtfully. "Okay, but only one!" I warned. "Otherwise, he'll be bouncing off the walls all afternoon and won't want to eat his dinner."

Sam plucked one from his palm and stuffed the others back into his pockets. "I can't wait to see him," he said, rocking forward and back on the balls of his feet in anticipation. "Ariella says that imps Harold's age are nearly as intelligent as a full-grown elf, and twice as intelligent as the average human with an undergraduate degree—whatever that is."

This being exactly the sort of thing I'd expect an elf to say, I let it pass and instead focused on the much more fascinating topic of my baby imp. "Well, Harold's not talking yet, but he is extremely clever," I said, leading Sam back toward the coffin. "Just the other day he was finger painting and drew what I'm certain is an abstract interpretation of the mystical gate that used to stand at Stonehenge—"

"Avery!" Valdara called from behind us, the hardness of her voice more than the word itself cutting off my story midsentence. We both turned. She was fuming, and her green eyes glittered like cold, hard gems. "We have not finished with Vivian. When you are done, I will expect an answer to my question."

Anger flared in me at the not-so-subtle, albeit all-too-accurate, implication that I might try to weasel out of our conversation. I said coldly, "Then an answer you shall have, Your Majesty."

I had never liked this imperious version of Valdara

and liked it even less when she reminded me of duties I was in the process of shirking. My aggravation was so great that I almost jerked the lid to the coffin open. Thankfully, I managed to stop myself in time. Popping in on Harold like a demented jack-in-the-box was a surefire way to ruin everyone's afternoon and possibly for me to lose a few fingers. I took a few calming breaths before gently lifting the lid.

To my surprise, Harold was still asleep. With his eyes closed and his wings folded around him, he radiated an aura of angelic peace, which was weird because he was literally part devil. My anger drained away. What can I say, he had that effect on me.

Sam cooed, "Oh, he's adorable." Then, less coo-ily, "Is that a finger bone he's sucking on?"

"Yes," I admitted uncomfortably. "The semi-lich gave it to him, and now he can't fall asleep without it."

"Gosh!"

"Indeed. It's part of a relic left behind by a sorcerer called Vecna or Varmit or something like that. Aldric was nice enough to let Harold keep it. Actually, he seemed pretty thrilled to get rid of it."

I stared at the finger with new suspicion and made a mental note to research it but had very little faith that I'd remember. Beside me, Sam was buzzing with excitement. "His little horns are so cute! Can I touch them?"

I held a finger to my lips. "There are only three rules to taking care of a baby imp," I whispered.

"First, never feed them after midnight, because if you do they'll produce their own weight in dirty diapers before morning. Second, never get them wet unless you are willing to lose one or more limbs. They really hate baths—turns them into regular little demons. But the most important rule of all is to never, ever wake one up while it's napping."

Sam's eyes went wide. "Why? What happens?"

"They wake up."

While Harold looked okay, I was now worried that the monitor was malfunctioning. I pointed to the coffin. "Sam, could you hold the lid for me while I check on the monitor?"

He grabbed the top with both hands. I leaned into the coffin and, out of habit, checked on Harold's diaper and the wards. Everything was holding up okay. I turned my attention to the monitor. It was only supposed to chime when Harold woke up, needed a change, or was in some other distress. Vivian and I had created the mystical monitor over a period of several weeks. It was one slick piece of magic, if I do say so myself, and we had been using it for months without issue. I decided to check that the spell construct wasn't breaking down.

I carefully reached across Harold to pick up the monitor, but as my fingertips brushed the softly glowing white orb, a shock of magic went through my body, followed by the unmistakable sensation of my brain turning inside out and trying to exit my skull through my ears. We had been trapped by another portal.

Sam, Harold, the coffin, and I appeared in the middle of a dimly lit tent, a circle of glowing summoning runes surrounding us. We were in an Army of Shadow camp. I knew this because the black-and-gray striped cloth of the tent walls was unmistakable, and also because Vivian was sitting cross-legged on a large cushion-covered divan just outside the perimeter of the runic circle.

She was wearing her full Dark Queen outfit: a high-collared, purple-black robe that somehow both fitted her body and flowed like dark water over the edge of the divan to pool on the exotically carpeted floor, and an iron circle of uneven spikes that crowned her blazing red hair and set off her naturally pale face to great effect. Next to her stood her trademark black iron staff. She steepled her hands over the bridge of her nose and studied us, her remarkable gold-ringed eyes glittering mischievously.

My heart both soared and sank to see her. I was, of course, happy, because it was Vivian, and she was in a cheeky mood, and I liked her best when she was feeling slightly naughty. On the other hand, I was not so naïve not to realize that she had somehow booby-trapped the monitor to get me here. Plus, not moments before I had been in a conference with the queen of Trelari debating whether or not Vivian was a traitor. Finally, this marked the second time in less than an hour that I'd effectively been mage-napped, which was not doing wonders for my self-confidence.

"Vivian! What's the meaning of this?"

That's as far as I got before Vivian gave Sam a very un-Dark Queen smile. "Hi, Sam! Nice to see you."

"Nice to see you too, Ms. Vivian," he said and gave her a little wave.

Unfortunately, in doing so he let go of the coffin's lid. I reflexively wedged my arm into the gap as it swung down. It is a testament to either my fortitude or my terror of a grumpy Harold that I didn't cry out as it smashed into my forearm. Biting the inside of my cheek to stifle the litany of curses I wanted to utter, I carefully closed the lid. Once I was certain Harold was safely sealed inside, I spun on Sam, holding my throbbing arm carefully against my body. "What did I tell you about taking care of baby imps?"

He swallowed hard. "Not . . . not to feed them after midnight?"

I nodded and gestured for him to continue.

"Not to get them wet," he added with a bit more confidence.

"Correct, go on," I urged. He fidgeted and stared up at the cloth roof of the tent. "The *most important* rule? About *sleep*?"

Sam smiled. "Not to wake them up!"

"Right! So is slamming the lid to Harold's crib—"

"Coffin," corrected Vivian.

"Coffin," I said with a nod. "Is that a good thing or a bad thing?"

He looked pale and started to stammer an answer, but Vivian took pity on him. "Actually, I have a different question. Why is our imp sleeping in a coffin?"

It was my turn to squirm, and the pain in my arm was momentarily forgotten. "Well . . . that is . . . you see . . ."

"He seems to like it!" Sam said enthusiastically.

I pointed at Sam and snapped my fingers. A new and exquisite rush of pain shot through me. Through grimaced teeth, I said, "Exactly! He likes it. He sleeps like an angel in there. Best napping tool I've found."

"That's a maybe, but it's still a coffin," Vivian said critically.

"Well?"

"Well, don't you think it's a little morbid for a baby?" she asked.

"Once, when Harold was being a picky eater, you said you'd gladly puree Mickey *and* Minnie Mouse if Harold would only agree to eat them." She opened her mouth to respond and then closed it. I smiled because I knew I had her. "He sleeps well in a coffin, so now I travel with one."

She shrugged. "Fair enough."

With the point conceded, it was my turn to question her. "Now, can we talk about why you pulled me out of a fairly important meeting with our boss?"

Vivian smiled sadly. "Yes, we need to talk, but . . ." She glanced at Sam. "Privately."

I nodded my agreement, and we both turned to Sam. "Vivian and I need to talk. Can you watch Harold for a couple of minutes?"

A smile stretched across his face, and he nodded vigorously. "Of course, Avery. Don't worry about a thing. I remember all the rules: no feeding, no bathing, and no waking."

I started to correct him, but Vivian, quite correctly, said, "Thank you, Sam."

"Indeed! Thank you." Forgetting about my arm—again—I clapped him on the back. A thousand knives stabbed into my wrist and ran up to my shoulder. I pressed the injured arm back against my body while inventive and disturbing curses that I am sure would never have been tolerated by my editors fought for escape, but I had promised Vivian I was going to work on moderating my language around Harold, so I clenched my teeth and repeated under my breath, "Damn, damn, damn, damn."

Sam asked, "Do you want me to take a look at it?"

I shook my head. The pain wasn't broken-arm bad, just deep-bruise bad. It hurt plenty, but the last thing I wanted was to have Sam trying to perform some kind of magical field medicine. I hadn't been lying when I told Valdara that he was a remarkably talented mage, but while it is one thing to trust someone to reshape the world around you, it is quite another to trust them to reshape your own innards.

"I'll be fine, Sam," I said and stepped out of the circle, being careful not to touch any of the glowing lines.

I reached out a hand and Vivian took it, standing. She picked up her iron staff, and together we walked to the opening of the tent. We were about to duck through the flap when Sam called out, "What should I do if Harold wakes up?"

"The best you can?" I suggested unhelpfully, and then a thought struck me. "In the meantime, remember how we talked about you needing to learn spells of protection when casting summoning portals?" He nodded. I pointed at the glowing circle surrounding him. "Study that."

He looked at the elaborate runes and patterns and smiled like a kid in a candy store. "Will do!"

I followed Vivian out of the tent before remembering something important I forgot to mention. I ducked my head back through the tent flap. Sam was squatting down near the edge of the circle peering at something inscribed there. "Oh, Sam!" I called. He looked up. "One little detail, that spell is only tuned for Harold and me, so if you touch the circle or try to leave it, you may get a little incinerated."

Sam's eyes grew wide and he slowly drew his hand back from the glowing lines. When I pulled my head back out of the tent, Vivian stared at me crossly. "You shouldn't lie to him like that."

"I didn't lie!" I protested. "That circle is lethal and you know it."

"Of course it is," she said with a dismissive wave. "But it's an exsanguination curse. Do you think I'm so irresponsible as to cast a spell that might potentially expose Harold to open flames?" When I didn't answer instantly, Vivian became even more upset. "You do, don't you? You think I'm a bad parent!" She turned and stormed off.

After a moment's hesitation, during which I wondered at how weird my life had gotten in the past few months, I followed. I caught her soon enough, but she was in no mood to talk. We walked in silence along what had at one time been a well-paved path but was now broken and overgrown. It curved around behind the tent, winding its way through a jagged gallery of head-high rocks and brown and yellow grasses as it climbed drunkenly toward the top of the hill.

After a few minutes we reached a ledge of rock just below the crest of the hill that commanded a breathtaking view of the vast grassy plain at the hill's foot. Below, the land stretched out, placid and rolling, for as far as the eye could see. It was beautiful, and having spent the better part of a week entombed in stone, I breathed in the fresh air gratefully. The only sour note in the scene was the presence of a large force of the Army of Shadow. Its black tents were scattered like a thousand blemishes on the face of the grassy plain.

It was to these tents, and the tiny figures that moved between them, that Vivian's attention was drawn. She gestured me over and pointed down to the camp. "What do you see there, Avery?"

Vivian rarely did anything without a purpose, but I wasn't sure how she wanted me to respond. I also had little patience for riddles. We had a lot to talk about. "I don't have time for games, Vivian. Just tell me what you want me to see."

She turned her gold-rimmed eyes on me and sighed. "Tell me what you see, Avery. *Please?*"

It was the *please* that got me. Over the past year we had grown too used to being at war. Either we were in a battle or preparing for one, and had no time for gentle pleasantries with each other. I looked back down at the camp and was mildly surprised to see how far away it was. The closest tents were at least a quarter of a mile from the base of our hill and were surrounded by a double row of poles or maybe sharpened spears, it was difficult to tell in the glare of the sun. The result was an enormous, irregular circle—a blot, a black scab on the landscape. A shudder of revulsion passed through me.

"Ugliness," I said at last. "That's what I see. Ugliness. The ugliness of evil, of this war, of the means we have chosen to use to fight the war. Is that why you brought me here? To remind me of what we are? If so, you need not have bothered. It torments me every day."

Vivian smiled sadly. "Do you know what I see, Avery? Life." She looked back down, studying the tiny figures. "Do you know what they do every time we set up a new camp? The regiments come together and build a bonfire pit." She indicated a spot in the middle of the black circle. "At night the trolls and the demons, the orcs and the gibberlings all come together to light a fire, and then they dance and chant and sing. There are weddings and funerals and birthdays . . ."

"Birthdays?" I had never considered that orcs might actually celebrate . . . well, anything.

She nodded, her gaze still fixed on the camp. "Yes, birthdays, and all the other tragedies and triumphs that fill the lives of any other Trelarian. And I have begun to think—"

"Weddings?" I did a double take, looking back and forth between her and the camp.

That there are female orcs, and that male orcs find them attractive, is obvious to anyone that has ever observed the explosive growth of orc populations in times when they are not being sent to slaughter in wars. And to those of you that believe they are grown in tanks, I only ask you to consider the problem of scale.

Take Sauron's army at the end of Tolkien's historical trilogy. Estimates put the number of orcs in his army at somewhere between fifty and seventy-five thousand. Presuming it takes an orc somewhere between fifteen and twenty years to grow to adulthood (although since orcs are described as an evil twisting of elves, and elves take substantially longer to reach maturity, I would argue it could be a great deal longer), that would mean Sauron would have needed an orc production line capable of producing thousands of orcs a year at least twenty to thirty years before the war. It's an absurd idea. Although still less absurd than the fact that the Kaminoans based an entire army on a single genetic model. Having said all this, I was still baffled by the idea of orc weddings.

I found myself repeating, "Weddings?"

Vivian's brow knitted in exasperation. "Yes, of course! All the things we are fighting for are happening down there. These *people* have been oppressed, not only by successive evil rulers"—she gestured to me and then to herself—"but also by their current queen. Valdara cares not a whit for their needs or their lives. They get the worst of everything—equipment, training, food— and yet are pressed forward wherever the fighting is the worst. Valdara wants them to die."

"To be fair, they *are* evil, Vivian," I said, stating what I thought was the obvious.

Her eyes narrowed. "And why is that, Avery? Is it because they are inherently evil, or did you inscribe their villainy into your pattern? Ask yourself, you who would otherwise be teaching a class at a university populated with all manner of beings from around the multiverse, including orcs, do you really believe that there are entire peoples predestined to be bad? If you really want to fight the oppression of the Mysterium, what could be more oppressive than having no voice in the arc of one's existence?"

She was right, I supposed, but I was not sure what to do about it. The idea that we also needed to be fighting for the rights of rage demons was too new for me. At my silence, Vivian sighed and went back to her examination of the camp. I, in turn, considered her. She always looked great in her full Dark Queen regalia, but I had never realized how naturally she wore the costume. It fitted her in a way that the Dark Lord persona never had for me. I had always resented the role. More than resented, I *despised* being the Dark Lord. As soon as I left my post with the Army of Shadow, I abandoned my formal evil-wear. Since then I'd worn nothing but my battered sneakers, one of the three pairs of worn jeans that I owned, and something chosen from my extensive collection of ironic T-shirts, like the *Han Shot First* shirt I was currently wearing.

Just thinking about my alter ego made me shudder. I hated everything about the character I'd created. I hated the weight of his cloak on my shoulders and the feel of his make-up on my face and the sound of his voice when I spoke, but most of all I hated the Dark Lord's army. I had always eagerly thrown them into battles they could not win and exposed them to hardships I knew would be impossible to bear. My goal had always been to destroy them. It seemed Vivian's aim was to save them. The questions now were, *how* did she plan on doing it, and should I stop her?

I turned a critical eye on the circle of tents and the surrounding terrain. I could not place exactly where we were on my mental map of Trelari. If it fit into the pattern I'd identified with Valdara, then this encampment was situated on an intersection of the mystical lines that formed my original spell pattern. "Why are we here?" I asked.

"Because you followed me," she answered.

"You know that's not what I'm asking," I said irritably.

"Do I?" she snorted.

I closed my eyes and gritted my teeth. "Right now, Valdara is trying to decide if you are a traitor. I would dearly like to avoid having two people that I love fighting each other for no reason."

Vivian tapped one of her long black nails against her chin. "I was wondering why you were inß the citadel. Valdara must have noticed the troop movements. You always did warn me against underestimating her. Lesson learned." She laughed, but it was bitter and angry.

I swallowed, trying to work some moisture back into my suddenly dry throat. "Is that what this is all about? Some plot against Valdara?"

She gave no reaction to this accusation. More than usual, I found her hard and sharp and impossible to read. "You want to know if I'm betraying Trelari?" she asked.

"I *need* to know, Vivian."

"I suppose in Valdara's eyes what I'm planning might be considered treason."

"What do you consider it? For that matter, what is your plan?"

"What will you do if I tell you, Avery?" she asked, her eyes sweeping back and forth across my face, considering me and weighing the possibilities. "Will you go back to Valdara and tell her everything? Maybe help her stop me? Or would you try to convince me to abandon my course?"

"I don't know," I said, exhausted by the entire conversation. "All I know is that I don't want to hurt either of you."

She said nothing but stared at me with such intensity that I could almost feel her gaze on my body. But in this instance, I had nothing to fear from her powers, because there was nothing to see. I had no idea what I was going to do, or even what I could do. I was one of Schrödinger's cats, floating—both alive and dead—completely untethered to the future.

At last she laughed, this time with real humor. "Why not? As you are playing the hero in this scene and I have been cast as the villain, I will play the villain's role and divulge my entire scheme in a grand monologue."

"You know I don't think of you as a villain."

"But that's the irony, Avery." The bitterness had returned to her voice. "It isn't up to us." Vivian turned away and began walking up the broken path again, saying over her shoulder, "Although I know it is tradition for these villainous confessions to be drawn out, we have to hurry. Harold is probably up by now and we need to get back to him before Sam feeds him his entire pocketful of butterscotches."

I looked at the height of the sun in the sky. She was right. Harold's naptime would be long over by the time we got back to the tent, and Sam would want to keep him happy. Plus, Harold was remarkably good at extracting sweets from the credulous. I had taken several steps when it hit me that neither Sam nor I had said anything about the candies. Either she had guessed, or she had known before we arrived. The aggravating thing was that it was never possible to tell which.

"Where are we going?" I asked, a bit more sharply than I'd intended.

I saw her shoulders flinch at my question, but she didn't answer and I had no choice but to follow. In a few minutes we arrived at the summit, a flat grassy pate ringed by irregular fingers of black stone. The sun was hot, and a welcome breeze blew across the top of the hill. I went to the center of the clearing and spun about, taking in the full scope of the countryside. The distant plain looked golden in the afternoon light as it stretched out to the north, but to the south the land rose up, hill upon hill, to meet a great mountain range that receded into the gloomy skies. As soon as I saw those ragged peaks, I knew where we were. It was the place where I had started my original Dark Lord spell, where the pattern of Trelari, as I had inscribed, was born. My blood froze.

Vivian was standing at the edge of the hilltop near one of the towering black monoliths. Barely containing my anger now, I said, "I will ask you again. Why have you brought me *here*?"

"So, you finally know where you are?" She laughed at me, and it was a perfect Dark Queen laugh, sending chills up and down my spine. "I was a little nervous you would recognize the place from the path, but then you probably never walked up it yourself. Why would you when you could just use the key to pop up and down whenever you needed? Still, the Dark Lord should probably know the spot where his own legend began."

And *that* is exactly where we were. I knew with a certainty that, if you were to scrape away the grass that had grown up in the decades since I was last here, you would find a flat platform of rock, one that extended in an unbroken column from the top of this hill to the very core of Trelari, and onto which I had engraved the initial germ of my pattern.

"Why did you bring your army here, Vivian?" I asked, spinning about, arms half extended. "There is no enemy to fight. There is no land worth conquering. Trust me, I know. I picked this place exactly because there is *nothing* here."

Vivian smiled at me in that sad way she had when she saw something I could not. "There is something here. Something unique and terrible."

"What? Will you stop being mysterious and just tell me?"

"You always sell yourself short, Avery," she said with a sigh. "It's you, of course."

"Me?"

"Well," she said, raising her arms high in the air, "you and the key."

Too late, I realized what was happening. With a violent motion, she struck the iron staff against the ground. There was crackling in the air as magic surged through the hill. I had only enough time to wonder at how easily Vivian had caught me, and then the dormant pattern I'd etched into Trelari's reality so long ago burst to life. Mystical lines of black energy erupted from beneath the thin covering of dirt, burning away the grass to reveal an intricate circle traced with runes and symbols and intertwined lines. I didn't even bother trying to escape. I had designed this trap myself, and it was perfect.

Vivian cleared her throat. "Now, I'll be taking that key of yours, Avery. I promise I'll return it just as soon as I've opened a few new fronts in this little war of ours with the Mysterium."

CHAPTER 6

I AM THE KEYMASTER!

Vivian and I stared at each other across the glowing circle. I decided that she was joking. I had no evidence for this belief and actually quite a lot for her being deadly serious, including the deadly serious way she was staring at me. Nevertheless, I decided to go with it because I had a feeling that if she *was* serious, one of us was not going to make it off the top of this hill.

I plucked up my courage, which was quivering somewhere near the bottom of my feet, and gave her my cheekiest smile. "Where's the laugh?"

"What laugh?" she asked, leaning on her iron staff in a fair imitation of Drake. I suspected not out of flattery for the priest, but because activating the circle had weakened her considerably.

"The evil laugh. You know, like the one you did before. The one that's supposed to follow your villainous reveal."

She said nothing.

I assumed my Dark Lord voice and said, "Now, Avery Stewart, you *will* give me the key." I followed this with a truly hideous cackle.

It was subtle and fleeting, but Vivian smiled. "The Dark Queen does not laugh." She tilted her head to one side, thinking. "At least not like that."

"Like what?" I was exceedingly proud of my laugh. It had taken me several weeks to perfect back when I was preparing to be the Dark Lord.

Vivian shrugged. "Don't try to change the subject. I need the key. I will take it from you if I have to, but I don't want to do that."

Hers was no idle boast. In this circle, I was powerless. In fact, anyone from Mysterium would have been powerless in here. I'd designed it that way. When I started inscribing my stabilizing pattern on Trelari, I had been concerned that my own presence and the Mysterium magic I carried with me would contaminate the experiment. I constructed this pattern to isolate myself from my own spellcasting abilities. Only Trelari magic, or devices with their own reality, like the key to Trelari, would work when the pattern was activated. Of course, this exposed the major flaw in Vivian's plan: she was assuming that I would be unwilling to use Griswald's key, or as Valdara had called it, the Doomsday Key. I decided to raise this point, not because I had any intention of using it, that would be far too dangerous, but on the off chance that the bluff itself might work.

"You *could* take it from me, I suppose, if I let you, or *I* could use the key to break the circle."

I thrust my hand into the pocket of my jeans where I'd sewn a bit of folded reality. My fingers passed over a couple of teething rings I kept for Harold, something squishy that I hoped was my sandwich from the day before, and Eldrin's communication coin before finding the hard, smooth end of the key. Touching it sent a tingling electric shock through my hand, and I felt the metal beginning to shift and morph in response to my will.

Despite my best efforts to look menacing, I could see Vivian wasn't buying it. "Where is *your* evil laugh?" she asked, raising an amused eyebrow. "Nothing? Of course not, because we both know you won't use the key. Not after what happened at the Western Bore."

She was right again. There was no way I was going to use the key, and particularly not here where the flows of magic could be so unpredictable. I was trying to decide what I *could* do or say that might at least extend our conversation when my hand fell on Eldrin's coin. To my surprise, it gave me a little shock.

With it, a spark of hope flared in me. To make his communicator coin work across all worlds, Eldrin had imbued it with its own quantum of reality. The only question was whether it was enough to operate within the circle. It would depend on Eldrin's skill, which meant the odds were pretty good.

"I have no laugh for you," I admitted at last. "But it's only because I don't find anything that's happening the least bit amusing. You tell me I won't use the key, and you're right of course, but you must know that for the same reason I can't give it to you either." I stepped forward, lowering my voice. "You know what it can do. You've taken worlds apart with it. Do you want to be responsible for doing something like that again? Do you truly want to be the Dark Queen?"

"That's where you and I are different," she said in a voice not at all like her own. "You deny what you are, while I do not."

This time she did laugh. It was cruel and cold, and for the first time I considered the real possibility that she might kill me, or worse still that I might have to kill her. I decided, having no other possible recourse, to discard my attempt at gravity and resort again to humor, which after all is the last line of defense for the desperate. Stroking my chin, I said, "I see what you mean about the laugh. Very menacing, but in a Cruella de Vil sort of way."

"Cruella de Vil?" a voice said out of the ether. "I would have thought Maleficent."

It was Eldrin. His ghostly apparition appeared in a flash of green light beside me. Vivian jumped, and I let out a sigh of relief.

Vivian's eyes grew wide. "How did you get here?"

"You mean we," said Dawn, as her equally hazy and shaky image appeared on my other side. "And I think you are both way off. Her laugh has more of a Queen Beryl quality to it."

Eldrin and I stared at Dawn. "What?" she said stiffly. "After last summer, you think I don't know my anime? Avery watched it nearly nonstop for three months. I'm an involuntary expert." When still no one said anything, she muttered, "Screw you guys."

"Can we get back to my question?" Vivian asked. "How are the two of you here?"

"Oh, that's simple," Eldrin said and took a deep breath that meant one of his incomprehensible explanations was coming. "I've modified the subspace communication pattern to temporally compress and transworld-stream apparitional information from the communicating subjects. The codex now captures an image of your auricle emissions and transmits that through an ether-encrypted private quantum tunnel. You have to understand that this is a full AES encryption, not some early gen DES bull—"

Dawn cut him off. "Avery activated his communication coin, and it has video now."

Eldrin crossed his arms and grumbled, "That is a gross oversimplification."

"And yet oddly sufficient," she retorted.

Vivian scowled at both of them. "But neither explains how Avery got the coin to work while completely cut off from magic, which was what I was actually asking about."

I was formulating an explanation of my pattern but was too slow. Eldrin gave the glowing runes a quick glance and said, "Elementary mistake. This circle is designed to keep Mysterium mages from accessing Mysterium magic, not from using items that are themselves magical." His face lit up and he spun about, taking in the surrounding landscape now shimmering under the orange light of the late afternoon. "This must be Avery's genesis pattern. Cool!"

For those of you that haven't had the dubious pleasure of living with an elf, let me explain. Eldrin, like many of his kind, has only two modes of explanation: detailed, by which I mean eye-gouging, fingernail-on-the-chalkboard-of-your-soul over explanation, or no explanation. In this instance, he had defaulted to the latter, assuming that everything was self-evident.

I sighed, but it was contented. It was comforting to know that there were still some things—some people—in the multiverse that you could depend on to behave exactly as they always had. "What he is trying to say, in his own infuriating way"—this comment earned me a glare from Eldrin—"is that I had to use a reality key to form my pattern, but in order to do that I had to make sure that items of that sort would still work from within the activated circle. The coin has a similar, if not as potent, construction."

While Vivian pondered this, Dawn studied the glowing circle. "Which brings us to the *real* question, what is going on here, Vivian?"

"How long have you been listening in?" Vivian asked, still considering, I supposed, how this new information about the circle might alter her plan.

"Long enough," Dawn said impatiently. "Now, would you care to explain why you've caged Avery?"

Vivian frowned but refused to answer.

Selfishly, I decided to speak on her behalf. "Vivian wanted to borrow my Doomsday Key so she could open a dozen or so new fronts against Mysterium and press this war to its inevitable conclusion a trifle more quickly. Naturally that led to a discussion of evil laughs."

"Naturally," Dawn and Eldrin said in unison.

I gestured to the two of them. "You've both heard my Dark Lord laugh. Who do you think I sound like?"

They looked at each other, and I thought I saw Vivian give a warning shake of her head, but they both answered right away. "Skeletor."

"Skeletor? You think I sound like Skeletor?" I said, my voice rising in surprise. "But I was going for a Dr. Claw voice coupled with a classic Mumm-Ra look. I

even used to do a transform like he did, remember?"
I pantomimed tearing bandage wrappings from my
body.

No one had anything to say to this.

"You have to imagine me in my Dark Lord costume,
of course, with the dramatic music playing in the
background . . . da-da-da-da-daaaaaa."

Still nothing. They stood in an awkward silence—
all of them finding much more interesting things
to look at on the ground or up in the sky, anywhere
but in my direction. Chastened, I kicked a rock into
the mystical wall. It bounced off with a crackle and
settled again near my foot. "Well, it never failed to
impress my minions."

"You did pay them to be impressed," Dawn
pointed out with her usual bluntness.

"Besides," Vivian said, finally snapping out of her
introspective silence, "I always assumed you were
going for Master Blaster."

"Master Blaster? As in, 'Master Blaster runs Barter-
town'?" I asked incredulously.

Vivian stuttered, "Um, no?" while Eldrin's specter
tried desperately to shut her up by giving the universal throat cutting gesture.

"What other Master Blaster then?" I asked, straining
to find another relevant cultural reference.

For the first time, Vivian seemed to realize that
she had wandered into dangerous territory. "Does it
really matter, Avery?" she asked.

"Yes," I said, crossing my hands over my chest. "What Master Blaster do you think my Dark Lord sounds like, *Vivian*?"

"You're sure you wouldn't rather be interrogating me about my plans for the key?" she asked.

"Or telling her how she'll never get away with this?" Eldrin asked hopefully.

"Or yelling at her about how she betrayed you?" Dawn asked.

"No."

Vivian sighed, her shoulders slumping. "Fine. If you must know the truth, I thought you sounded kind of like a mean version of Master Blaster from Kidd Video. You know, 'welcome to the Flipside.'"

I could not keep the shock and hurt off my face. "That's just mean."

"Really?" Vivian asked in disbelief. "I've entrapped you in your own magical construct, in an attempt to seize a powerful artifact from you by force, and my characterization of your evil laugh is what is mean?"

"Well," I said in an admittedly forlorn and pathetic sort of voice, "on the one hand you are merely threatening to do something you have no hope of succeeding at, even if I thought you had it in you to carry it off, and on the other you are comparing me to a balding music producer."

Vivian's eyes narrowed. "Oh, I don't 'have it in me'? Interesting. That isn't what you thought after I destroyed Lewis's world."

Trust Vivian to find a way to turn my righteous indignation on its head. "You know that isn't what I meant. I was just trying to say that you aren't capable of—"

"Not capable? Not capable!" she snapped. "I have been carrying you the past few months, and you know it. Without me, the Army of Shadow would be in tatters, and your precious Valdara would be knee deep in dead Trelarians."

"Vivian—" I said, trying to interrupt the tongue-lashing before she could get on a roll. It did not work.

"Not to mention that without me you would never have made it back to Trelari in the first place." She leaned in close to the edge of the circle pointing a sharpened black thumbnail at her own chest. "It was *my* spell that found Sam and Ariella, and *my* spell that kept us alive despite Moregoth's best efforts to kill us."

"Vivian!" I shouted.

Eldrin and Dawn, who had been standing to one side of us, their heads going back and forth like tennis spectators, both jumped back in surprise.

"What?" Vivian asked, her eyes still flashing with indignation.

"I only meant to say that I didn't think you were capable of killing me for the key," I said in a fatigued monotone, staring down at the burnt grass along the edge of the circle. "Which is what you are going to have to do to get it from me. If you think for a moment that I have anything but respect for your abilities as a mage, then I am sorry. I had always thought our mutual admiration was a given."

"Oh," she said softly.

Our eyes met. "Why are you really doing this, Vivian?" I asked. "You're probably right about the creatures"—she glared—"people . . . people of the Army of Shadow. While I think they would probably cut our throats given half an opportunity, they have never been given a chance to be anything more than what they are. But I can't believe you would betray me solely on their behalf. At least not this way."

I looked out over the sweeping plain. The sun was dipping behind a range of distant hills, painting the rolling grasslands a burnished copper.

"You know as well as I do that our one advantage in this conflict, if we have one, is our ability to control where the fighting happens," I continued. "It is why we attack so hard every time Moregoth opens a new gateway. If you succeed, you will be opening Trelari up to assault on a dozen fronts at once. Even if Valdara were aware of your plan, and all our forces arrayed to defend the new openings, we would have less than an even chance of succeeding. Without any preparation, the Mysterium will roll over us. It's madness."

Vivian didn't say anything. All she did was stare at the setting sun. Maybe it was a trick of the evening light, but I thought I saw the gold rings around her eyes glowing. I wondered if she was looking ahead, and what future she saw. I tried to imagine the inevitable battle that would come if Vivian managed to open a portal here. A shudder of horror passed through me.

"You would turn Trelari into a tomb," I whispered.

Vivian blinked and gave a sigh of disappointment. "That is Valdara talking, not you. She has convinced you that the only way to win against the Mysterium is by a war of attrition. To fight and fight for years—generations—if necessary. To let Moregoth and his mage army batter themselves against the wall between the worlds, and to fight them only when they break through and we have the advantage of Trelari's reality under our feet."

She was right that Valdara's plan basically amounted to wearing the Mysterium down. Trelari's reality being as strong as Mysterium's—if not a bit stronger—meant Moregoth and his Sealers were at a disadvantage against us here on our world. Valdara and I both believed that, given enough time, the Administration would be bound to lose the means and the will to keep the war effort going.

"I happen to agree with her," I said wearily.

"And so did you," Dawn pointed out to Vivian.

Vivian nodded thoughtfully. "I suppose I did . . . at one time."

"So, what changed?" I asked.

She hesitated. I could see that she was struggling over what or how much to tell us. Unfortunately, she never got a chance to decide, because at that moment a dozen flashes of light erupted about our position on the hilltop.

Reality bent as gateways rippled open and a scarlet wave of Sealers poured in around us, their Wands of Certain Death already charged for firing. Behind their ranks, I saw the dark silhouette of Moregoth emerge. He was in full spiked-hair glory, his Death Armor radiating an aura of despair and bleakness that made it difficult to look at him for more than a few seconds without losing all hope that life was anything but a pointless charade in which death was a happy outcome to be embraced as a welcome lover.

Reflexively, I pulled my hand from my pocket. Eldrin and Dawn winked out as the connection was broken. I began to weave a spell of protection, and . . . nothing. There was no magic. I had forgotten that I was utterly powerless within the circle.

Vivian cast a quick spell of warding about herself as the first deadly black bolts struck. She rapped her staff on the ground and the hillside rang like a bell. The sound, deep and urgent, washed over the plain and rebounded off the mountain and echoed over and over. *To me! To me! Rally to your queen!* It seemed to say. A muted roar of fury erupted from the camp, and tiny figures rushed out and toward the hill like angry ants from a trodden nest. The Army of Shadow was coming, but would they make it in time?

Already there were fifty or more Sealers on the

hilltop, firing an unending barrage of spells at us. The bolts that hit the black wall of the circle surrounding me simply evaporated, snuffed out like candles by the powerful enchantment, but those that hit the thin blue shell of protection around Vivian flared and sparked. Her ward was holding, but the attacks were having an effect and eventually it would fail. I gave it another minute or so, hardly time enough for Vivian's hordes to reach the base of the hill, much less make the ascent. It was hopeless. By the time they arrived, we would be dead. There was only one thing to do: Vivian had to leave. As for me . . .

Moregoth's voice rang out. "Cease!"

The ring of Sealers opened like a scarlet curtain and he emerged, a smirk of satisfaction traced across his black-painted lips. "Dark Lord and Dark Queen." He gave us both mocking bows. "So agonizingly pleasant to find you here. Dark Lord." He nodded to me. "As always, I find you hiding behind your betters. You really are the most delectably miserable creature I've ever met." Turning his back on me with a derisive chuckle, he faced Vivian. "As for you, Your Majesty—" he ran a black finger along the edge of her ward, sending sparks of deep violet energy crackling "—I look forward to breaking you free from this futile prison of despair and emotion and renewing my, admittedly excruciating, examination of your soul."

Despite the situation, I felt a flicker of hope. Moregoth was talking, and a talking Moregoth was someone I could deal with. It was just a matter of keeping him gloating over our situation long enough to figure a way out of this.

"Moregoth!" I shouted. "Aren't you tired of losing to us? It's been, what, a year? And what do you have to show for all those dead mages? A new piercing or two to hang from your overly burdened earlobes?"

"I will soon have your corpse to hang from the top of the Provost's Tower, Dark Lord," he said coldly.

"Well, I'm standing here," I said, spreading my arms wide in invitation. "Take your best shot. Surely you and all these big, burly mages of yours can take down little old me."

He raised an elaborately groomed eyebrow. "I think not, Dark Lord. I have observed that this ward you've cocooned yourself in is different." He gestured at it but did not venture to touch it as he had Vivian's. "I perceive though that it is somehow linked to the lady. So, we will simply encourage her to remove it."

"No chance," Vivian said. "I can hold this all day, and"—she cocked an ear at the still-distant but on-coming roar of her army—"I don't think you have much time left. Best if you tuck your overly groomed tail between the legs of your skinny jeans and leave before they arrive."

While Vivian was talking, my mind raced through our options. They were few and universally bad, and the only one with even a puncher's chance of working was the one I had sworn I would never use again. Of course, as any follower of cinematic superheroes will tell you, moral codes are only valid up to the point that someone you care about is in danger. At that point, all bets are off. Think Superman reversing the rotation of the earth to save Lois Lane, or Captain America going all rogue to help the Winter Soldier, an admitted mass murderer.

In keeping with that grand, and thoroughly irresponsible, tradition, I moved my hand toward the pocket of my jeans where I knew the key was eagerly awaiting my further descent into corruption.

"Ah, ah, Dark Lord!" Moregoth said in a sepulchral singsong. "Keep your hands out of those pockets, or I'm afraid Vivian will have to *suffer* for your sins."

Saying the word *suffer* made Moregoth way too happy. After carefully lowering my hands to my sides, I decided to explore the topic in hopes that I could keep him talking. "Why did you go goth, Moregoth?" I asked.

"What do you mean?" he asked, somewhat taken aback by this sudden turn in the conversation.

"I mean why all the somber clothing and corpse-like make-up and turns of phrase that sound like lyrics from a Bauhaus album?"

"Bauhaus?" Moregoth asked with a shrug.

"Oh, come on," Vivian snapped and flung out her hand to indicate his clothes. "You can't dress like that and not know who Bauhaus is."

"I have no idea what either of you are talking about," he said grimly.

I turned to Vivian and shook my head in mock sadness. "Mall goth."

"Total poseur," she replied with an equally theatrical nod.

"Mall goth? Poseur?" He glanced back and forth between Vivian and me, and then his eyes widened slightly and a knowing smile split his blackened lips. The game was up. "I know what's happening here. You two think you can keep me talking long enough that someone will come to your rescue. Who will it be this time? Griswald? No, he's dead. Harold? Also dead. More vicious apes? Terrible lizards? A lightning storm? A kraken?"

He laughed, a deep throaty chuckle that rose at the end to something terrible and unhinged. "Oh, that was a good one. Or, perhaps something new like . . . like giant birds." He laughed again, and seemed right on the verge of true hysterics, but then slowly stilled his body. Running a somewhat shaky hand through his spiked hair, he said, "With all the possibilities of rescue, it is probably better if I kill you right away!" He leaned in close to Vivian and said with a lecherous smile, "It is a pity, my dear, I do *love* your new look. So elegantly dreadful."

Before either of us could react, he marched back to the edge of the circle, turned, and raised a hand. Ever so calmly, he said, "Kill her. Then him."

The calculation was an easy one. With all the firepower of the Sealers directed solely at Vivian's ward, it was sure to break.

I shouted, "Drop the circle, Vivian! Get out of here!"

She gave me a small, sad smile and shook her head. My heart sank as I realized that Vivian had made her own calculation. She knew the only thing keeping me alive was the circle, but the only thing keeping the circle empowered was her. If she didn't maintain the magic, it would fail before I had time to do anything. A sinking dread filled me. Moregoth had won. There was no way out for either of us. We were going to die. The only question was who would die first, and that was Vivian's call to make. It turns out she was brave enough to die for me, but not brave enough to watch me go first. In her place, I would have done the same.

I turned back to Moregoth and clenched my hands in supplication. "Don't do this. Please, I'll give myself up. I'll do anything."

He gave me a wink and dropped his hand. A wave of black energy erupted from the scarlet wall and rushed toward Vivian. I may have screamed something. I may not have. There was barely time to think. The only certainty was that there was nothing in this creation I could do to save her. I yanked the Doomsday Key from my pocket. My mind was bent on death and destruction, and the key eagerly complied. I felt it twisting and morphing into something dreadful, and as it did, I could feel the reality of Trelari shifting with it.

I had one final glimpse of Vivian, still smiling, before the spells smashed into her ward and their black energy blotted her out. There was a brief flash of brilliant white light from within the protective shell, and then it shattered with an explosive concussion. The protective circle surrounding me flared and a black curtain rose upward in a roar of magical energy, briefly obscuring everything outside. Then, like a dying fire, it sputtered and went out. Where Vivian had been standing was nothing but a blasted area of withered grass, churned earth, and splintered rock.

Moregoth's hand went up again but never came down. The key had found its form and through it, I felt a well of magic as deep and as vast as the multiverse. In my rage, I called upon it. All of it.

Power rushed through me, an uncontrollable torrent that shot up into the air—a purple-black geyser—and then rushed outward. Wave upon wave of pulsating destruction burst forth. It rolled over the Sealers, dashing them from existence like sandcastles in a hurricane and toppling the circle of rough rocks that ringed the hill's perimeter.

Moregoth alone survived the initial blast, but even he could not escape. While he was strongly warded, he was powerless against the overwhelming force of the magic I'd unleashed. I watched, merciless and emotionless, as the cold glow of his protective spell flickered and failed. As it died, the power caught and tore at his body. Still he struggled. His hands moved, trying to weave spells even as his fingertips dissolved. His mouth uttered soundless words of magic above the roar of the power.

Little more than a ghost remained, his reality all but extinguished, when I lost him. A brilliant white lightning line of power appeared and connected with the swirling motes of what had once been Moregoth. It was gone as quickly as it came, and along with it so was he. Only the vapor of his black armor shell and flowing cloak remained, to be wiped away in the next instant by the ferocity of the key.

CHAPTER 7

YOU CAN'T MAKE AN OMELET . . .

I roared wordlessly as Moregoth slipped from my grasp, and the key surged with my anger. The ground began to roll and twist beneath my feet like something was straining against it from below, trying to burst free. Even within my body, there was a vibration that I could feel growing more violent with every passing moment. I was not sure what was happening, but had enough sense to know it was not good.

I turned my mind to the problem of how to stop what I'd started, but it was a bit like standing at the bottom of Niagara Falls with a sponge and a bucket. The power of the key was overwhelming and relentless, and it was growing stronger with every passing moment. I could feel Trelari's reality straining to contain it. If nothing was done—and soon—the fabric of the world would tear itself apart.

That's when I got the seemingly brilliant idea to channel the output of the key into the pattern.

The initial blast from the key had exposed the stone tracings of my original pattern. I staggered to its center and fell to my knees, driving the point of the key into its heart. I had no expectation that this would stop the flow of magic, but hoped that it might redirect it.

That part worked just great. The magic of a thousand worlds poured into the pattern. The energy raced along the tracings, making them glow with an otherworldly bright light. The vortex of energy that had been churning about me began to waver and fade, then the ground shuddered with a single terrible jolt that knocked me off my feet, a hideous crack came from somewhere deep underground, and the hilltop broke in two. A ragged line of fractured stone opened beneath me, slicing the circle that had been the keystone of my original pattern in half.

Never having been in a world-ending cataclysm—at least of this sort—it is hard for me to describe what happened next. For purposes of simplicity, let's say that the world seemed to stutter or blink, as though it were on the verge of winking out of existence entirely. The power, which had been momentarily constrained by the circle of my pattern, rushed out again. But this time it didn't have my anger to direct it, or the Sealers as a target. The power was pure and formless, and everything it touched started to warp as reality itself began to unravel. The toppled rock pillars melted, flowing like candle wax across the ground. The hillside started to buckle and twist under the strain. And somewhere below the hill's summit, I could hear muted screams as the wave of chaos met the lead elements of the Army of Shadow.

Horrified, I tried to redirect the flow of energy, but this time I sent it into myself. Either my will would be strong enough to master the key, or I would die. For a fraction of a moment, the world was in my hand and the thoughts of every being on Trelari flooded my mind. Then it all came crashing down. The images and voices became a pounding cacophony, and the power a torment. My nerves burned and my blood boiled. I was being stabbed with a thousand knives. Someone was screaming, and I thought it was probably me.

I was on the verge of letting go when I felt a familiar weight on my shoulder. It was Harold.

He said nothing but laid a tiny taloned paw on my head. The pain lifted and a sudden calm washed over me. The power was still there, still burning through my being, but somehow the imp had taken away the symptoms of my ongoing destruction. I turned my head to look at him. His eyes were closed tight, his body rigid, and his face was set in a pained grimace. I suddenly worried what the effort might be costing him.

"Harold? Are you okay?"

There was no outward sign he'd heard me, but his strained voice echoed in my head. *The key! Solve the key.*

"Solve the key? What does that mean?" I asked.

Edges and midges, his voice croaked. *Hurry!*

At first, the words made no sense. Certainly, I recognized them, because they were mine. It was the solution I'd suggested to Rook when we were running from Moregoth and needed to fix his traveling box—the hypocube. He had pointed out what looked like a scrambled puzzle cube as the trouble, and I'd told him that to solve it we needed to first solve the edges and the midges. But the key was not a puzzle cube . . . or was it?

In a sudden flash of insight, I knew what Harold was trying to get me to see. The solution to shutting off the flow of power was not to contest the power itself, which was beyond my abilities, but to solve the key. When it had first tapped into the magical source that was now flowing through it, the key had assumed a very specific configuration of teeth. I needed to detune it.

I focused all my will, not on trying to shunt the power somewhere else or shut off its flow, but to force the key, tooth by tooth, to fold in on itself. At first even that seemed an impossible task, but after an enormous exertion, I felt it move, just a little. And then it moved a little more. And then I had it. As more of the key's structure disappeared, the construct lost its hold on the source of its power. The stream of mystical energy flickered and died.

Everything went utterly quiet.

I exhaled with exhausted relief and stared about at the melted landscape in disgust. I had stopped the world from destruction, but only just, and at what cost? My pattern was gone—shattered. I could feel its hold on Trelari leaking away in a cosmic sigh. As it did, the key pulsed in my hand with what I can only describe as deep satisfaction. With a curse, I hurled it away.

Then my eyes fell on the circle of scorched earth where Vivian had last stood. I staggered to it and fell to my knees. "Vivian!" I choked.

Left on my own, I honestly am not sure what I would have done. If I had been able to focus enough to cast a spell, it is likely that I would have chosen to simply vanish from the rest of my own story, but magic was impossible. I was totally wrung out, exhausted, physically and mystically.

In my despair, I felt Harold's paw on my head and raised my hand to hold it. "She's . . . she's gone." I stopped, unable to say anything more.

Harold hopped off my shoulder to stand, tottering, before me. At first, I thought it was my imagination, but no, he had grown. In the last few minutes he had aged years. "What happened, Harold?" I asked.

He tilted his head, not seeming to understand. "Vivian?" he said, the first word he'd spoken aloud since returning to me.

Tears welled in my eyes. How could I explain? "Vivian . . . Vivian is gone."

The little imp shook his head and pointed to his chest. "Vivian."

"Gone," I moaned.

The imp sighed in response and, grabbing my hand, placed it against his chest, somewhere near his heart. "Vivian!"

It was pointless. The one thing that might have brought me comfort would have been Harold's counsel, but the old Harold was gone, and now my stupidity had cost this new Harold years of his life. My frustration rose at the rising cost of my incompetence. So much to regret.

I took a breath and pressed my hand against his. That was when I felt it: two tiny strands of power. The familiar/mage line that had connected me to Harold since he transferred his loyalty from Griswald, and a new one that stretched from the imp to some distant place far across the multiverse. I felt him grasp this new line with his will and give it a pull.

There was a slight delay and then a responding tug.

In that instant, my mind was filled with the smell of Vivian's hair and the sound of her laughter. I don't know how I knew, but there was no doubt in my mind that she was alive. Where was she? How could I find her? How might she be brought back? Would she want to come back? I knew none of the answers to any of these questions, but it didn't matter.

With a whoop of joy, I plucked Harold from the ground and spun him around. "She's alive! She's alive."

He was still giggling when my mind finally comprehended what I was seeing whirling about us. The tortured landscape, as far as the eye could see, spoke of a terrible cataclysm. I slowed to a stop as a cold weight settled into my chest. The hill was unrecognizable—a melted mass of stone and plant and dirt and bone. But the true scope of my destructive rage was almost beyond imagining. The tops of the wild hills that had once marched toward the distant mountains were sheared off in a clean line, as though a giant scythe had been run over them. Even the mountains themselves, leagues away, were marked by a dark monochromatic line, like the ring in a bathtub, where the wave of power had finally come to a stop. In the other direction, the golden rolling fields of grass were gone, replaced by a wasteland of gray ash. And where the encampment had been, was nothing. All that was left was a black void where the first link in my old pattern had been burned from existence. I wondered briefly if any of Vivian's orcs had survived, and a bit longer about what had happened to the other encampments of the Army of Shadow and whether the entire face of Trelari was cratered with these pocks—more evidence of my wrath.

"What have I done?" I whispered.

My initial rush of joy drained away and I found myself sitting once more on the ground. Harold clambered up my side and hugged me tightly around the neck. With his face buried in my chest, I heard him murmur his one word. "Vivian."

He had a point. I wrapped my arm around his tiny body and hugged him back. After a few seconds he wiggled loose and scampered across the hill toward the key. "Leave it," I called out. "That's the last thing either of us need."

Harold pointed at the key, which had returned to its natural form: a featureless gray rod with a loop at one the end. "Vivian."

"Yes, she wanted it, and I wouldn't give it to her, and now look where we are." I picked up a rock from the broken ground and threw it in frustration. It clattered over the side of the hill. I could hear it bound and rebound off the path below. In answer came the sound of dozens of harsh voices and rushing feet.

Harold and I stared at each other with wide eyes. "Vivian?" he asked.

"What's left of her army anyway." I stared down at my clothes. There was no way I would be able to convince them I was the Dark Lord wearing a T-shirt and a pair of worn jeans. "We have to get out of here. Now!"

At my pantomimed urging, he retrieved the key from the ground while I gathered my will to form a quick transport circle. But nothing happened. There was residual magic in the air, but my will had been fragmented by the maelstrom of the key. I found it impossible to even grasp the magic, much less form it into anything. It was like trying to sculpt with dry sand or motes of dust. I wondered idly if I would ever be able to use magic again.

I was still waving my hands, when the first of the orcs came over the top of the hill. Vivian's army was upon us. My rage had taken a terrible toll. Of the hundreds that had started up the hill only a couple dozen remained. What had happened to their companions I could only guess, but vengeance was in their eyes.

I thrust Harold behind me and tried to strike an intimidating pose. Raising a fist into the air in the best mimic of myself, I shouted, "Forces of darkness, spawns of hell. I, your Dark Lord, command you to halt!"

To my credit, they paused. To their credit, they quickly recovered. There was a roar of laughter, followed by much drawing and brandishing of metal pointy things. They surged forward. That was when I started to panic. Okay, to be accurate, I continued to panic. I made a last desperate attempt to seize the magic I could feel floating around us, but I might as well have been weaving with moonbeams and unicorn farts. (Although a unicorn fart would have at least been useful. They are quite magically potent and smell like warm brownies.)

The sword arms drew back, the spears were flung forward. I gave a last impotent shout of command. And then a most welcome orange light surrounded us, and power grabbed hold of the back of my brain and tried to yank it through my skull. We dissolved just in time for me not to get impaled.

When the magic reassembled us, we were standing in the middle of the tattered remains of Vivian's tent. The center pole was bent almost in two, and the cloth and furniture had melted into grotesque shapes. Sam was standing across from us next to the apparently untouched coffin in a litter of butterscotch wrappers holding a feather, his eyes wide with fear. "Avery—"

There was so much I needed to tell Sam: Vivian's betrayal and escape, the destruction of my pattern, the cataclysm of the key. But first, I pointed an accusing finger at the wrappers. "Did you give Harold all these candies?"

He nodded, still wide-eyed. "But, Avery—"

"I can't believe you would be so irresponsible!" I lectured. "Do you know what that amount of sugar can do to an imp his age? This is totally inexcusable!"

First, Sam shook his head, then he nodded. "But, Avery, why do I need a feather to fly?" he asked in a voice so bewildered and lost that it transformed my outrage instantly to concern.

"What?" I asked about a half second before a large blue circle appeared around all three of us.

We were yanked out of the tent, to reappear with a flutter of candy wrappers in the Citadel of Light—again—this time in front of Ariella and a very stern-looking Valdara. "What the hell have you done to my kingdom?" she asked while Ariella gave us a cheerful wave.

While Sam and Harold waved back, I prepared what seemed destined to be the most awkward explanation in history. How exactly do you apologize for breaking someone's reality? I was still formulating my answer when a smaller black-purple circle enveloped me. I think I said something like, "Gods! Not again!" and then, once more, my mind was scrambled as Harold and I disintegrated only to reintegrate back in Aldric's crypt.

He was standing across from us in full lich-mode, tapping his foot irritably. "Why did you steal my coffin? I am getting very tired and very grumpy."

By this point I was out of breath. I also had a couple of questions of my own that could not wait. I held up a finger to forestall Aldric's interrogation and pulled out Eldrin's communicator coin. His ghost appeared looking very unhappy.

"Avery, what are you doing?" he asked. "I warned you that Moregoth might be listening in."

"Don't worry about that," I said, bending over and taking a few deep breaths to try to clear my head. "I think he's dead. Well, mostly dead."

"How mostly?" he asked. "Like Loki in *Thor* one, two, or three?"

I thought about it for a second and answered, "Like something between one and three."

He visibly relaxed. "Oh, in that case we're probably safe. At least for a while anyway. What's up?"

I stood up and crossed my arms over my chest. "Maybe you should be asking me something like, Avery, the last time I saw you, your girlfriend had imprisoned you and Moregoth was about to kill you. Are you okay?"

He shrugged, his starry eyes glittering. "Why would I do that? You're obviously fine. You just told me Moregoth is dead-ish. And as for what you and Vivian get up to in your spare time? I may not be into that sort of thing, but you are both consenting adults."

"Typical bloody elf answer," I muttered, and it really was.

I was still running through my mental list of reasons to hate elves, which is quite extensive, when I heard Dawn in the background say something like, "Your turn."

He glanced in what must have been her direction and shrugged. Then he turned back to me. "Not that I don't want to talk to you, Avery, but Dawn and I are sort of in the middle of something. What do you need?"

"Yes. Why did you call him?" Aldric asked sharply.

I looked back and forth between them and sighed. I had been hoping to work my way up to the tough questions, but I supposed it was only fair to cut to the chase. "Well, if we must be all business, I have two serious questions to ask you."

"Okay," Eldrin replied suspiciously, probably because we rarely were serious about anything.

I hesitated. Now that the moment was here, I was nervous to ask my question, because I was terrified of how Eldrin might answer. I rubbed my hands together in agitation. "Let's say—hypothetically—that I broke my Trelari pattern. What might that do to the world?"

He cocked his head to one side and tapped his chin. "Well, I can think of two possible outcomes— the cataclysmic and the merely catastrophic."

I wasn't really sure what the difference between a catastrophe and a cataclysm was, but neither sounded good. "Give me the best case first," I said in a voice far squeakier than I would have liked.

Eldrin's image started pacing across the crypt. "Well, in one scenario, destroying your pattern would simply erase the rules and routines that have governed the behavior of Trelarians for the past dozen or so generations, plunging the world into chaos and internal strife."

"Or?"

He spun and stared at me sternly. "Or, your pattern was the anchor binding Trelari to Mysterium. In that case, destroying it would destabilize the world, sending it drifting farther and farther into subspace until its reality weakens to the point that it begins to unwind around you."

"So, that's the difference between a cataclysm and a catastrophe," I murmured. Harold tugged at my pant leg and I absentmindedly lifted him up to rest in the crook of my arm while I thought through the implications.

"This is just a hypothetical, right, Avery?" Eldrin asked.

"Of course," I said unconvincingly. "But it would put my mind at ease if someone with access to a subworld observatory could let me know if Trelari is drifting."

"Gods, Avery! What have you done?" he asked.

I shrugged and asked sheepishly, "Have you ever had one of those ideas that you think better of in hindsight?"

"Like what?" he asked in reply.

After a brief pause while I tried to think of an appropriate example, I said, "Like putting a malevolent ring on while you're being attacked by beings called *Ring*wraiths, or pissing off the only fairy in all of fairy-tale history whose name literally means 'to do evil.'"

"Oh," he said, rubbing his chin. "Like tearing a hole through reality that ends up creating the thing that will ultimately try to destroy you."

"Exactly!" I said excitedly. "Think Ged or Garion."

"Beidomon," he offered.

"Kidd Video," Dawn said, stepping into view.

He tilted his head to one side at this last example. "Kidd Video? Really?" he asked.

"Of course," she answered. "Only their sweet, sweet tunes could have drawn Master Blaster from the Flipside."

While Eldrin stared at her with a delicious look of disbelief, I said, "Getting back to the point I was trying to make, this was one of those ideas. I cracked my pattern in two. It's gone."

He was still digesting this when Aldric asked, "Avery, how long will this inquisition of shadow Eldrin last? Now that my coffin is returned, I need to rest. I think I am beginning to hallucinate. Of late I have found myself questioning odd things, like why holy symbols, even of faiths I have no knowledge of, are so frightening to me, and why it is that my gaze only scares people if they are within ten feet of me. Why not eleven or even twelve feet?"

Eldrin and I blinked at the semi-lich.

"You really did it didn't you?" Eldrin asked me.

I nodded and murmured, "How messy do you think this will get?"

In answer, he simply gestured at Aldric, who was still talking, mostly to himself. "It can't be that my appearance frightens them or it would work at any distance, as long as they could see me." The semi-lich paused to consider. "What if my eyes emit a power that only travels a certain distance, but that causes fear in people when it strikes them?" He paused again to think about this new idea. "But then if I were to look at my own reflection in a mirror, would the power not be reflected back at me? Would I not be frightened of myself every time I checked my hair?" He chuckled nervously at the idea.

"I see your point. I think I'd better go, Eldrin." I began to break the connection but paused. He was one of the only mages in the multiverse that had the ability to confirm whether what I had done was cataclysmic or merely catastrophic. I needed him to go back to the observatory on Mysterium and see if, in fact, Trelari was shifting back into the subworld. I had asked him earlier, but I had been pretty oblique about it. I had to make him understand that this was not optional. It was essential. The only problem was that I couldn't ask the way I needed to, because what I was asking was insanely dangerous, and if Dawn heard about it, she would insist on going. That was something Eldrin wouldn't forgive. Instead, I locked my eyes on his and raised an eyebrow. It was a questioning look. One I knew he would not mistake given what we had just been talking about.

He rolled his eyes. "Of course I will. You know you didn't have to ask. I was going to do it anyway."

I mouthed a thank-you, and that might have been the end of it if Dawn hadn't been standing there. "What were you going to do anyway?" she asked suspiciously.

If I'd been under the scrutiny of those monochromatic eyes of hers, I would have blown it, but Eldrin must have built up a limited immunity, because he was as smooth as ever. "Answer his second serious question?" he asked.

"It can wait," I said, suddenly embarrassed I'd thought to ask it in the first place.

"I really don't think it can, Avery," he pressed. "That first one was a doozy."

I let out a long sigh. "Well, it's about my Dark Lord voice. Do you think Vivian had a point? Does it really sound like Master Blaster?"

"Gods! Not this again!" Dawn groaned. "Come back to the game, Eldrin. It's your turn. I did a Synchro Summon."

His head snapped around at this. "You can't do that. You didn't have a Tuner in your field."

"Wait a minute!" I shouted. "You told me you didn't know anything about Yu-Gi-Oh!"

Dawn slapped a hand over her mouth and shuffled

out of sight. Alone under my scrutiny, Eldrin shifted about nervously. After a pause long enough to seal his guilt in any court of law in any world at any time, he said slowly, "I don't?"

Of course, it was at this critical moment—a moment where at last I had Eldrin right where I wanted him—that yet another circle opened at our feet and I was yanked once more through reality.

CHAPTER 8

SO . . . ABOUT THAT PATTERN . . .

We appeared for the third time that day in the Great Hall of the Citadel of Light, on a familiar carpet of discarded butterscotch wrappers. This time a committee was waiting for us. Sam, Ariella, and Valdara had been joined by Rook, Seamus, and Drake. None of them looked particularly happy. Of course, neither did I. As I have tried to document for my readers, going through portals isn't the best feeling in the world, and although I did it with a great deal of regularity, my body was distinctly aware that I had spent most of the day bouncing from place to place. I felt drained and more than a little nauseated. Plus, I had been yanked away right before I could prove definitively that Eldrin had been playing Yu-Gi-Oh!—something he had categorically denied.

I turned, fists clenched, ready to unloose my anger, but Valdara beat me to it. "Avery!" she shouted.

My name crashed through the hall, echoing over and over. Harold, who had been mercifully quiescent, likely from a combination of mystical exhaustion and sugar crash, gave a sudden start and burst into tears and wailing. His cries rang out, drawing the attention of every court hanger-on and servant in sight.

I glared at Valdara and plucked the little imp from my shoulder to cradle him in my arms.

"Give him a butterscotch!" Sam hissed.

Gesturing to the litter of wrappers, I said in as calm a manner as I could muster, "If you will recall, someone gave him all of them."

Sam had the decency to look appropriately abashed.

There are few things in the world more terrible than the sound of a crying infant—perhaps a banshee's wail, or The Shaggs's 1969 album, *Philosophy of the World*, or "My Humps" by The Black Eyed Peas, or—shudder—"Sussudio," the sound of which is literally like fingernails on the chalkboard of my soul. Even worse, Eldrin really likes anything by Phil Collins and had a weekly habit of playing his entire discography from start to finish in our dorm room. The point being, a lot of bad sounds have been produced over the years, but nothing like a Harold meltdown. Our collective anger was forgotten as the little imp's screaming unnerved us far more than any amount of death, destruction, or weird-ness ever had.

"Avery, you've got to do something," Valdara said, while Rook, putting his hands to his ears, just kept grunting, "Make it stop. Make it stop. Make it stop!"

"Everybody," I said in a singsong voice that I hoped would relax Harold. "We need to stay calm. Sam, check my pockets for a butterscotch." I rocked back and forth and swayed as I spoke. Harold responded with a shrill piercing cry. It made my teeth ache. I wanted to scream myself, but when I looked down, large impish eyes were pleading and giant tears streamed down his cheeks.

Sam ran around me, desperately searching my pockets. "Could you stop moving?"

"No," I sang. "The motion helps."

"Not bloody enough," Rook groaned, his hands still clasped against the sides of his head.

Meanwhile, Sam was pulling all sorts of things from my jeans: pacifiers, a piece of fazechalk, a baggie full of carrots—he waved these at me and I shook my head (even I could admit carrots were not equivalent to candy)—a pattern-tuning crystal, a hell-spawn dagger, a bottle of sunscreen. I stopped him as his hand reached for my right front pocket—the one that held the key. After a moment's hesitation, he moved on and found baby wipes, a sippy cup half-filled with shadow venom, Harold's favorite finger bone. As Sam yanked this last item out, I snatched it from his hand like a rat pouncing on a cat. (I do live in New York.)

"Is that a real finger?" Valdara asked in an unnaturally high-pitched voice.

"Yes, of course," I answered, not really registering her revulsion.

I popped it into the imp's mouth with a blessing to whatever powers protected baby imps and mages who nearly destroyed the multiverse. As I had come to expect from him, Harold demonstrated remarkable recuperative powers. The tears stopped in an instant, replaced by peals of giggling laughter as he sucked on the finger. I looked around at the others with a smile of relief only to be met with nearly identical looks of disgust, at least from everyone but Sam, who had seen it before, and Rook.

The dwarf dropped his hands from his ears. "What's wrong with all of you? Haven't you ever seen an imp chewin' on a bit o' corpse?"

"Actually, no," Drake answered as the rest nodded in agreement.

"Oh, well, they do that sort o' thin'. Perfectly natural," Rook said with a broad smile. "Just thank yar stars he has no' developed a taste for eyeballs." He rocked back on his heels and gave a low whistle. "What a mess."

Apparently, that was either enough small talk, or enough talk of eyeballs, for Valdara. She strode forward and positioned herself directly in front of me.

Somewhere between the last time I was here and now she had donned full battle dress, and even Justice Cleaver was present, strapped ominously to her back. A shaft of sunlight streaming down through one of the upper windows shone on her armor, making it gleam. Whether she planned it or not, it was a great effect. If she'd had wings, she might have passed for an angel sent to deliver divine retribution. As it was, she was looking excessively regal. She uttered one word. "Vivian."

"Yes, it was Vivian," said Sam before I could respond. "She was planning to launch her own assault against the Mysterium using Avery's key. She thinks it's wrong to wage a war of attrition. She thinks we need to bring 'it' to the enemy." He dropped his voice conspiratorially. "She never did reveal what 'it' was that she was going to bring them."

"Sam . . ." I said, a warning note in my voice.

He ignored me and continued. "Of course, Avery wouldn't give her the key. They fought and there was a huge explosion. If I hadn't been in the circle, I might have been turned inside out like the bed in the tent did."

"How could you possibly know what Vivian and I talked about?" I asked, finally silencing him.

"Oh, I was listening in," he answered happily.

"You were eavesdropping!"

"I didn't drop any eaves," he said defensively. "I just used a little magic to listen in on the two of you." He

flushed under my continued stare and started studying his feet and shuffling. "Well, I was worried about
you. Anyway, I don't exactly understand it, but right
after the earth shook and the tent melted, I started
questioning things I'd never questioned before. Like,
why when I invoke my spells I need to use things
like pearls and gloves and talc and balls of bat guano."
He began pulling random bits of this and that out of
a pouch at his side.

Ariella put up a hand. "I was just talking to Drake
about the same thing. Why is it that every time I want
to understand an item of magic, I have to drink a glass
of wine infused with an owl feather and a miniature
carp?"

"Which you have to swallow whole!" Sam said in
disbelief and horror. She nodded.

"Or," Seamus piped up, "why is it when Valdara
carries eighty pounds she can move thirty feet in
six seconds, but if she is carrying eighty-one pounds
she can only go twenty feet, whereas carrying extra
weight doesn't seem to affect me at all?"

"It's ninety-one pounds," Valdara interjected. "And
no matter how much I try to build up my strength, I
can never seem to carry ninety-five pounds. That has
always bugged me."

Drake stroked his beard and growled, "Yeah,
something has been bothering me too. Why in my
years as a priest have I been called everything from a

curate to a lama? I mean, those titles aren't even from the same religious traditions."

"Point of fact, Drake, a llama isn't even human," Rook said significantly.

"No, I meant a one-*L* lama," Drake explained.

"Oh! That makes more sense," Rook said with a sage nod. "That second *L* makes all the difference."

Valdara glared at the two of them until they shut up, and then turned her attention to me. "I think you owe all of us an explanation, Avery."

I looked around and tried to decide how I could explain the consequences of what had happened when I didn't know myself. "Where to begin?"

Valdara folded her arms and tapped her foot. "Why don't you start by telling us what happened between you and Vivian?"

I shrugged at the question. "Sam gave you the important details. We had a fight over the key, but it is over now."

"And the near-melting of Sam?" she pressed.

"That happened later," I explained, my voice hollow at the memory. "During my . . . argument with Vivian, Moregoth showed up. I . . . I had to use the key."

"Does the 'argument' with Vivian also explain the wave of confusion that has been washing over everyone in my court?"

It sounded like a simple question, but the answer

was devilishly complicated. I briefly considered going into the details, because I knew they might help to obscure my guilt. Instead, I decided to take my dad's advice, and, as he would say, *eschew obfuscation*. (Since you've never met him, I'll tell you he's a little strange and prone to irony.) Valdara deserved a direct answer, and so that is what I gave her.

"Not exactly," I said. "I think what you are experiencing is the result of my using the key, but Vivian had nothing to do with it. After she left and after Moregoth was defeated, I tried to shut off the flow of power to the key using my pattern. It broke under the strain. Whatever has been done to Trelari is my fault alone."

She looked down on me in judgment. "You told me you were the only one who could handle the key, and now my people have been plunged into chaos because you could not. I trusted you, Avery."

The disappointment in her voice cut me far more than even Justice Cleaver could have. Had I been there by myself, it's not clear how things might have ended. I was feeling too guilty to defend my actions, and besides I agreed on the whole with Valdara's summation of the case against me. However, I was not alone. In addition to Harold, who had climbed onto my shoulder and nestled into my neck and was purring quite contentedly now that he had his finger bone pacifier to chew on, Sam was also with me.

He took that moment to clear his throat and

bravely stepped forward. "I don't think it's right to blame Avery for everything, Your Majesty," he said and then wavered a little under her gaze. "Well, not exactly anyway."

"If I'm not *exactly* right, then how *exactly* should I feel?" Valdara asked sharply.

Anyone else probably would have given up their defense of me at this point, but Sam raised his chin. "I think it's more complicated."

"It usually is," Drake grumbled.

Sam scratched at his already mussed hair, causing half of it to stick straight up on one side. "Well, as I understand it, Avery destroyed his own pattern, not Trelari's."

"Is this a case of tomatoes or tomahtoes?" Valdara asked.

"No!" boomed Justice Cleaver. "This is a case of high treason. These tomatoes and tomahtoes have no relevance except to show the keen edge of my blades." I couldn't help but snicker at the infomercial quality of this statement. "Do you doubt the fine cutting edge of my steel? Bring me a dozen tomatoes or tomahtoes and I shall slice them all!"

"I'm sorry," I said as I tried to bring my fit of giggles under control. "It's just back in my world there was a company called Ginsu that sold knives. One of the selling points was that they were able to cut through nails or tin cans and then finely slice tomatoes—"

"Ha! Child's play!" declared Justice Cleaver. "No

knife can stand before my might. Bring me this Ginsu and I will defeat it in an epic nail-and-tomatoes duel that shall be known throughout the worlds."

"I think, JC, that we have gotten off topic," Valdara said sternly enough to quiet the blade. "Sam was explaining how it was not so bad that Avery destroyed the pattern of Trelari?"

"No, Your Majesty," Ariella said and she moved to stand beside Sam. "He was saying that Avery didn't do anything to Trelari's pattern except perhaps to restore it."

"Restore it to what?" Valdara asked.

"To what it was before I came here," I answered, stepping between the two mages so that I was once more the focus of Valdara's wrath. "I burned out *my* pattern. The pattern I overlaid atop Trelari's pattern to stabilize it. The reality you are experiencing now is the 'true' Trelari." I spread my hands out, gesturing to each of them in turn.

"So, that's a good thing?" Valdara said uncertainly.

"Well . . ." I began, but before I could say anything more, Rook pushed his way through everyone to stand before us, his thumbs firmly tucked in his belt in what I knew all too well was lecture-mode.

"Of course not! What they're sayin' is that the rules of existence that you and generations of Trelarians have come to rely on are gone." He snapped his fingers. "Like that."

"Is this true?" Drake asked.

I nodded. "Probably. It would explain why all of you are beginning to question things you've held as fundamental truths for all your lives."

Valdara's eyes grew wide. "But if this is happening all across the kingdom—"

"Chaos!" Rook boomed. Harold looked around with a start and all of us hissed at the dwarf to keep his voice down. He continued in a whispered scream. "Chaos! All the accommodations and contracts and understandings that kept your world from conflict are gone. Wizards will question why sorcerers don't need spell books, sorcerers will question why wizards can cast more spells, and both will wonder what the hell a warlock is. Priests, like Drake, will want to know why they can't learn to use swords. Goblins and orcs will be baffled by the fact that they've treated each other as different species all these years even though they are the bloody same thing!" He glowered at me and shook a finger. "That was just sloppy scholarship, by the way, Avery. You have to read the source material. Tolkien, only the father of the term 'orc,' clearly refers to Azog as both the 'goblin' that killed Thorin's father and as a 'great orc.'"

Rook was one hundred percent right about the orc/goblin thing, and I only had myself and my tendency to revise up until the last second of any deadline for the many inconsistencies that cropped up in parts of my dissertation. But before I could even concede the point, he was off again on another rant. "And everyone, everywhere, will wonder how everybody knows how to speak the same language, no matter how isolated they are from the rest of society."

"And why is it called 'Common'?" Ariella asked from behind us.

Rook spun about, pointing. "Exactly!"

"This is going to be a disaster," Valdara groaned. "Oh, Avery, why?"

The answer, of course, is that when Vivian and I are together we have a tendency to sow disaster, but I didn't want to go down that conversational path. The others already didn't trust Vivian, and if they ever found out the full story of what she had been planning, there was no telling what they might do.

Unfortunately, Sam would not let it go. "It's not his fault," he protested. "Vivian had him—"

That's as far as I let him get before I literally stepped on top of him, or at least on top of his right foot. "I lost control," I said.

With a grunt Sam pulled his boot out from under my sneaker and moved to one side so he could be seen again. "But only because—"

"The key went berserk," I interjected, and to forestall Sam from making any more admissions on my behalf, I added, "The fact is, I tried to use the key again and lost control just like at the Western Bore. When I saw what the dark energy was doing to Trelari, I realized there was only one other place I could direct it. This is my fault."

They were all staring at me with such horrified looks I wasn't sure how to continue, but I did know that it was time to tell them everything. That Rook's prediction of chaos was probably a best-case scenario. That there was a chance I had doomed Trelari. Oh, and also that there were better than even odds that I had burned myself out as a mage—I still couldn't grasp even the tiniest tendril of magic, which explained why everyone and their brother had been able to pull my string since the pattern fell. I decided to keep that last part to myself, though at this point my magical impotence might have been considered good news by some, if not all of them.

Harold had begun to squirm again. I handed him to Sam and moved back into the middle of the circle of waiting, anxious faces. "Rook is right, but there is also a chance that there may be worse to come."

"What could be worse than my kingdom in total chaos?" Valdara asked.

I took a deep breath and let it out before continuing. "I don't know for sure, but it is possible that the loss of my pattern will destabilize Trelari's reality. That the world will begin to drift from Mysterium back into the subworld, and that Trelari will gradually grow weaker as it does."

Valdara said nothing but paced slowly back to her throne. We all followed as she sat, shaken but unbowed. "And this was all done with this key?" she asked. I nodded, and she directed her next question to

Rook. "You have said that this key is also capable of great wonders. Could it restore Avery's pattern?"

"No!" I said firmly.

The dwarf's bushy eyebrows came together as he glared at me. "Yes, a' course, but only in the hands of a master pattern builder."

Valdara nodded. "Avery, do you have the key with you?"

The moment I had been dreading had come. What would I do if Valdara commanded me to use the key? Would I obey? Did I have the right anymore to say no? I decided I would have to put my case before them and hope they made the right choice.

"I have it. But Valdara, we've got to destroy it. It can't be used. It's too dangerous. The key has no real power to create. All it can do is consume and destroy."

"Tha's not true, laddie," Rook said, sweeping a finger in a wide arc at the group. "We've all seen it create magical portals, shields, and spells of great power."

"But it creates nothing of its own," I argued. "To work, it must draw energy from other places. I've seen it pull worlds apart and drain their realities until nothing remains. I want to win this war just as much as you all do, but there are some sacrifices that are too great. The key is an abomination, an utter horror, and everything it creates is, in turn, accursed."

Rook rubbed his beard and licked his lips. "So you say, and yet you and Vivian have used it over and over. Convenient now that it may pass to someone else that you should want it destroyed."

"Yes, I know, but you must trust me. It is the only way."

"Trust?" he asked with an odd chuckle. "Fine, let us say that yar right and the key must be destroyed. What is yar plan? How would you propose to destroy it, lad?"

"Good question," said Valdara, folding her arms.

"Well?" asked Rook, folding his arms as well and tapping his foot impatiently.

I'd actually been thinking about this for some time and for once had an answer. "The only thing that I think might be able to destroy it is—" I steeled myself for what was to come "—Justice Cleaver."

"Aha!" shouted the battle-ax from its sheath on Valdara's back. "All becomes clear. Forged from the energies of the Mysterium and the pattern of Trelari, I am the greatest weapon for good the multiverse has ever known. Let this vile key taste the bite of my blade, then it shall know the repast of justice!"

"No," Valdara proclaimed.

"But, Valdara!" I protested. "The key is beyond control. It *will* destroy more worlds if we don't destroy it first. Worlds like Trelari."

"You canna know that, lad," Rook protested.

Drake's brows drew together in a troubled expression. "And yet, if there is even a chance that Avery is right, then there seems no choice."

"Well, I believe him," Sam said with determination and looked to Ariella. But she was clearly not as sold.

"He has been wrong on a number of occasions," she pointed out quite accurately.

Valdara drew Justice Cleaver and laid the great battle-ax across her lap. It glowed with power. I could see the edge of the blade forged in the mystical fires of Mysterium. It had to be able to destroy the key. It just had to. She spoke, perhaps as much to the others as to me. "As I understand it, the pattern of our world has been damaged, and it may mean that we will be overcome by the Mysterium. This key might have the ability to repair it."

"No. It cannot," I objected. She looked at me sharply, and I held up my hands. "I am not arguing that it can't create, although I maintain that it can't create without destroying, I'm only saying that you cannot repair my original pattern. It is gone—obliterated from existence. You could, perhaps, create something new that might function like it, but it would not re-create what was."

"What does that mean for us?" she asked Rook.

He shrugged and, to my surprise, Ariella spoke up. "It means that everything and everyone might be changed. Trelari, as we know it, would be gone."

"And it might be completely destroyed in the process," I added.

"Nonsense!" Rook grunted.

"You didn't *see* it. You didn't *feel* it," I urged, remembering with an unwanted thrill the way it snatched and grabbed at the power. "I want . . ."

"What do you want?" Sam asked.

The question brought me back to the moment. That was when I noticed my hand firmly lodged in the pocket where the key was hidden. I pulled it out again like I had been burned and looked around—confused. "What?" I asked.

"You were saying that you wanted something?" he prompted.

I had but could not recall what. I shook my head, trying to clear the buzzing that had started there, and answered, "Nothing. I meant to say that I don't trust it. In my estimation, it's much more likely to destroy Trelari than it is to save it."

"Still, you admit that it could work," Valdara countered.

"And it may be our greatest weapon against the Mysterium," Rook said as he eyed my pocket suspiciously.

"Impossible!" Justice Cleaver boomed.

"Enough, Justice Cleaver!" Valdara commanded. Impressively, the battle-ax said nothing more.

Still a little disoriented, I put a hand to my forehead and mumbled, "I forfeited my right to make decisions about Trelari long ago. The choice is yours, Valdara."

She bent her head in thought. After a time, she hefted Justice Cleaver and stood. "You are wrong, Avery. This decision is not for one person to make. The fate of Trelari hangs in the balance. I am calling for a gathering of the Company of the Fellowship. And as chance would have it, I think we are all here and assembled. We shall have a council and we will *all* decide. Together. Are we agreed?"

The last question was undeniably rhetorical, as no one in their right mind would have considered objecting to Valdara at that moment. Particularly not with her in full military gear holding Justice Cleaver as she was. While the others recorded their votes by silent nod, I made a mental note to myself that if I ever needed to make a hard rock album, I would have Valdara and Justice Cleaver as the cover art.

"We will meet in the inner council chamber where we can have more privacy." She looked suspiciously about at all the courtiers who had been hovering as close as they dared to hear what they could, and then spun on her heel, sheathing Justice Cleaver as she went.

The rest of us began to shuffle after her, but Drake said, "We are missing someone."

Valdara paused and half turned. "You are right. Luke isn't here. Sam, Ariella, find him. Drake, with me. Rook, Seamus, look after Avery until Luke can be brought here." She smiled, but there was little humor in it. "I wouldn't want him to be snatched away again."

As Drake hurried to follow her out, Rook and I stared at each other. After our recent rather heated arguments, neither of us knew exactly what to say.

"Well, this is a little awkward," Seamus said with a nervous laugh and a tug on his beard.

An evil grin stretched across Rook's face. "Nothin' a friendly game of chess can no' fix." He slapped a chessboard down on top of Aldric's coffin and shouted, "White or black?"

CHAPTER 9

LOSING, LOSER, LOST

I tried to find some excuse, any excuse, not to play chess with Rook, but it was not to be. The good news was that the game was quick. The bad news was that it was brutal. By this I mean that chess, at least as practiced by Rook, was a frightening combination of graduate-level examination and ultimate fighting. Not that we actually fought, but that with each move, whether good or bad, there was much thumping of shoulders with his fists and hugging the breath out of me with his treelike arms. If nothing else, the game, or rather Rook's enthusiastic game-play, made me forget about the bruise on my arm from where the falling coffin lid had hit me. By the midpoint of the match, I was bruised all over! Mercifully, I managed to maneuver myself into checkmate before I came to any real harm.

"Excellent game, Avery!" Rook said with a great deal of un-dwarf-like gusto and further thumping and squeezing.

"Yessss," I gasped after an extra firm hug.

Rook let me go and tucked his thumbs into his belt. "We should do it again sometime."

I nodded and felt at my ribs to make sure they were still intact. He and Seamus started dissecting the game in the most colorful terms: *destroying, crushing,* and *thrashing* being the most common descriptors. Harold, who had been growing restless watching the game, padded across the room to where Ariella and Sam were engaged in a heated argument over how to find Luke. I took the opportunity to apologize to the dwarfs and followed after my wayward imp.

Ariella and Sam were standing over the giant mosaic map of Trelari embedded in the floor of the Great Hall. They had magically animated it with all sorts of glowing lines and arrows, tiny figures, and mystical symbols. It was incomprehensible to me and was made more so when Harold began growling at and pouncing on the little moving figures like a cat. Still, I suppose it must have meant something to Ariella and Sam, because each was very passionately explaining why the other was wrong.

"I still say our best bet is to go back to where we left him," Sam said.

"Total waste of time," Ariella countered. "That area has been searched a half dozen times already." She pointed at a section of the map where several red arrows converged.

Sam ran a hand through his hair with a frustrated sigh so that it was standing on end. "The problem is everywhere has been gone over a half dozen times."

I peered over their shoulders. If the red lines and arrows were any indication of where they'd already looked, he was right. They crisscrossed the map and overlaid each other, in some cases many times.

"How long have the two of you been looking for Luke?" I asked, amazed at the level of detail in the map, and at the amount of time that must have gone into making it.

Ariella and Sam looked at each other and then back at me. "Us personally? About fifteen minutes," Ariella said. "But acolytes of Luke have been obsessed with finding him since we returned from our quest against the Dark Queen. As he was the only red shirt to survive, people thought he had some secret power. A force that kept him safe."

"A force? What sort of force?" I asked.

Sam shrugged. "Hard to say. I don't know if his acolytes ever agreed on what it was exactly. Some people said it was a power that could surround you and bind you together. Others thought it was something in the blood. In the end it didn't seem to matter in the slightest as long as you had something they called 'the High Ground.'"

Nodding her agreement, Ariella said, "They pestered him so much about how to reach this High Ground that he ended up running away to live out the rest of his life as a hermit. Since then people have been searching Trelari for him and building this map."

"Well, given how complete they've been, it looks like we should be able to find him by process of elimination. Like what about there?" I pointed to a small section that Harold was hopping up and down on. It looked to be the only part of the map that hadn't been animated, a strange void in the otherwise dizzying cartographical light show. "It looks like no one has bothered to check it out."

Their faces fell. "That part of the map is missing," Ariella said. "We could not possibly know what's there."

I studied the small hole. "Based on the scale, it couldn't cover more than a few hundred square miles," I observed. "With the right scrying spell, you two could examine it in detail in less than an hour."

"Didn't you hear her, Avery? It's hopeless," Sam said with a depressive sigh. "Unless we can get that missing piece of the map, we might as well not even try." He sat down on the floor and buried his head in his hands.

It was at this point, trapped between the burgeoning insanity of Trelari's two greatest wizards and the pure and unadulterated violence of dwarf chess, that I was saved by a young man in the queen's livery. He marched into the center of the chamber, snapped to attention, and announced, "Queen Valdara, Protector of Trelari, summons all of you to an audience in the Council Chamber."

With a sweep of his hand, he gestured to one of the side doors. I scooped up Harold, and while Rook began meticulously collecting his chess pieces, the rest of us trooped after him. The chamber we were led to was long and had a high ceiling gilded in a reddish gold. An ornately carved fireplace, laid but unlit, was set in the wall at one end of the room, and a bookcase overflowing with leather-bound volumes and cases of parchment scrolls stood along the opposite. A large table littered with maps filled the center of the room. Valdara sat at the midpoint of the table opposite us, with Drake standing at her side. Behind them, a line of tall windows looked out onto a beautiful courtyard where a fountain sparkled and danced. I blinked against the afternoon sunlight.

Valdara's eyes fixed on Sam and Ariella. "Did you find Luke?"

Sam swallowed. "Um . . . no. Ariella thinks it could take months, or maybe years."

"Oh, I was definitely thinking years," Ariella chimed in cheerfully. "But only a few."

Having been burned once on this topic, I wisely kept my mouth shut. Any suggestion I made as to a potential magical solution might, in turn, lead to a request that I actually *do* the magic. I was fairly confident that was beyond me at this point, and I was still reluctant to make this fact public.

Valdara sighed. "The armies of the enemy keep attacking Trelari and our allies. If the breaking of Avery's pattern does mean that our reality is weakening, then every moment we delay, Moregoth and Mysterium become stronger, and in turn we grow weaker. It will not be long before the Mysterium will be able to wipe us out with a snap of their fingers." To emphasize the point, she snapped her fingers.

As the echo of her snap faded, Drake said, "We must decide on our course now, without Luke."

Valdara looked around the table, and we all gave our silent assent. She nodded sharply. "As we are in agreement, I call to order this first gathering of the Company of the—"

"Wait!" Ariella cried out. "Before we start, I need to do something." We all looked at her and waited. "Well . . . you see . . . the thing is . . ." Under the weight of our collective gaze, she seemed to melt, slumping down in her seat, her speech grinding to a halt.

"Must I remind you of the urgency of this meeting?" Valdara asked. "As I just explained, there appears to be every chance that we are facing the destruction of everything we hold dear."

Ariella squirmed a little more before pulling a wrinkled piece of parchment from her pouch and placing it carefully on the table. "Valdara, my parents want you to sign this slip before they will let me participate."

Seamus picked it up and gave it a quick read. "Is this a permission slip?"

Blushing as I had never seen her blush before, Ariella gave a sheepish nod. "After the incident on Mysterium, they said that I couldn't be a part of the Fellowship anymore unless Valdara gave her word that I would be safe."

"That seems reasonable," Valdara said as she read over the form.

"It is not!" Ariella shouted. "I only have ten more years until I'm an adult and they are treating me like I'm a child."

"But doesn't that mean you are still a child?" Sam asked.

If looks could kill, Sam would have been instantly incinerated by Ariella's answering glare.

Actually, now that I think about it, the entire expression *if looks could kill* is nonsensical. There are a remarkable number of circumstances in which looks will kill you. Off the top of my head, I can think of basilisks, gorgons, Demogorgons, cockatrices, beholders, certain dragons, and whatever those things were that flew out of the ark in the first Indiana Jones movie.

Anyway, Sam may well have been turned into a pool or a pile of something had it not been for a bright young man in a sharp uniform. He opened the door with a snappy salute and announced grandly, "High Archon Solon, Guardian of the Gleaming Wood, Defender of the Fey, and Keeper of the Unicorns, and High Queen Allaria, the Infinite Mystic, Eternal Light of Life, and Oracle of Fate."

"Oh, I forgot to mention my parents are here," Ariella announced with another blush. "They have a few questions."

We all went silent as through the door glided an elven lord and lady who radiated nobility. The high archon had a level of poise and grace that put Eldrin to shame. Simply the way he held himself made him seem several inches taller than me, despite the fact that I was looking him in the eye. But if Ariella's father was impressive, her mother was the moon in a sky full of stars, or the just-risen sun on a clear, crisp autumn morning. Radiant, beautiful, enchanting, breathtaking . . . Forget it. I can't even hope to describe her. She was a goddess.

"Wow!" Sam exclaimed. That about sums it up.

"Mom, Dad," said Ariella, "may I introduce you to the Company of the Fellowship?"

The high archon bowed respectfully to Valdara and Drake, and then his eyes locked on me and seemed to flare to life. "Avery Stewart! The Dark Lord!" I took a step back as he pointed an accusing finger at me. "I was there, on the Plains of Drek, in the last great battle between good and evil. I was witness to the failure of your courage as you were slain and finally driven from this world."

I was not sure how to respond to this. Frankly, from the look he was giving me, I thought there was a good chance that he might strike me down on the spot. I shifted Harold to my shoulder so my hands would be free. Not that there would be much I could do against him except beg for mercy.

Fortunately, Drake had my back. "Valdara and I were there also, High Archon. In the actual room with him when he fell, and since then he has proven himself, time and again, as a friend of Trelari."

The elf lord's glare stayed in place until Ariella's mother murmured, "Solon, don't tease him so."

In answer, his eyes, which seemed to have irises that shifted color with every mood, sparkled, and he burst out laughing, in a magical elven way that even I had to admit was not entirely insufferable. "Please, you must forgive me my little joke. I cancelled your Order of Execution over a year ago." He slapped me on the back while I took in the sobering fact that, in the recent past, an elven executioner had been hunting me. "Besides my daughter Ariella has very much been an advocate for you. It is because of her that we are here. I have a request of the Company."

Valdara stepped forward and bowed. "Name your request, High Archon, and if it is in our power it will be done."

He nodded gravely and reached into his robe. I am not sure what I was expecting. Part of me still had not gotten over the whole Order of Execution and was half braced for some further dreadful revelation. I can tell you that the last thing on my mind was my novel, but there it was in his hand. A copy of *The Dark Lord* by Jack Heckel. He held a quill in his other hand.

"Could I get you, all of you, to sign my copy of *The Dark Lord*?"

Ariella hid her face in her hands while the rest of us exchanged puzzled looks. At last, Valdara answered, a bit uncertainly. "Of course, High Archon, it would be our . . . honor?"

A wide smile stretched across his face, and he rubbed his hands together with unelven glee. "Excellent! I am trying to get autographs from the entire Company of the Fellowship. Can you imagine how jealous the dwarf lords will be? To say nothing of any mortal men I might come across."

While the others lined up to put their signatures in the book, Allaria, who I must mention had a voice that sounds as if it comes from Seventh Heaven (a delightful subworld, for the record), leaned over to me and whispered, "I do apologize. He can be quite obsessive with his collecting. He has kept the shattered pieces of your old staff for years, because he claims they are bound to be valuable one day."

"It's true," said Solon, who was suddenly standing next to me with the book. "One day I will reforge your staff. It will be a collector's item. This I swear." He put the quill in my hands. "By the way, why write the book under a nom de plume?"

"A what kind of plum?" asked Sam quizzically.

"It just means that it was written under a different name, even though it's my story," I said as I signed. "Although technically it isn't a nom de plume because I didn't write either of the books."

"Books?" said Solon, perking up his pointed ears.

"*The Dark Lord* and *The Darker Lord*." I handed him the book and quill back. "A sequel recently came out."

"There's a sequel? I must have it!" he exclaimed.

"It isn't available just yet. In Trelari, I mean," I said, trying to figure out how to explain an e-reader to an elven lord.

"Wait," said Drake, "does that mean we are in the third book at this very moment?"

I shrugged and sighed. "I don't know what it means. In my world, most series are trilogies. After the third book, everything is over. If that holds for us, this should be the end. Eldrin is convinced it is."

Sam swallowed. "So, are we all going to die?"

"No," said Ariella, who seemed to have perked up now that the book signing was over. "I researched Mysterium literature a great deal in preparation for school. It just means that this arc will come to a conclusion. We might all live. One of us might even get a spin-off series."

Solon was examining the autographs in his book and something struck me. "Hey, you didn't get Ariella's signature yet."

"Mine was the first he got," she said, and it was clear from her tone that she was none too happy about it.

"How else do you think she convinced me to let her come back?" Solon intoned. "She is still a child after all."

"I am not a child!" Ariella said with a petulant stamp of her foot. "I am nearly four hundred now."

"Yes, yes, dear," her mother said soothingly. "You are a tri-centurial. We know that is very different from being a child."

Solon chuckled. "Our Ariella always was an emotional one. But if you think she's difficult now, you should have seen her in the decades leading up to her three-hundredth birthday." He whistled meaningfully.

Allaria leaned in again and whispered, softly but not softly enough, "Those tween years always are difficult ones. So many hormones."

The glare Ariella was giving her parents made me think of another half dozen things that could kill you at a glance, including the catoblepas (which I kid you not is a species of killer water buffalo), pretty much anything from the Cthulhu cosmogony, and the Ravenous Bugblatter Beast of Traal. I know what you're thinking, but if you look at it, it will kill you.

Valdara cut the silent tension before it could grow too thick. "Well, now that you're satisfied, High Archon, we do need to get on with our gathering."

He held up a finger. "Almost, Your Majesty. If I could just get Master Rook to sign?"

Valdara looked around. "Where is Rook?"

"He was just with us," said Sam, turning his head from side to side and looking under the table, as if Rook might be hiding there.

"I don't remember him leaving. Did he follow us in here when we were summoned?" Ariella asked.

"No," I said. "Last I saw him he was gathering his chess pieces after our game." I wondered if he was avoiding the room because of Ariella's parents. Mysterian or not, Rook was a dwarf and many dwarfs (or is it dwarves?) feel understandably uncomfortable around elves.

"I certainly didn't see him come in," Drake confirmed.

"The lazy bugger. He must still be out there," Seamus grumped and marched out the door to the Great Hall.

Despite Seamus's confidence, I was unsettled. I had the distinct feeling I had missed something or was missing something. Something more than just Rook. That's when Seamus came storming back in.

He threw his hands in the air and grumbled, "He's gone. Bastard always did hate meetings."

My hand, shaking, went straight to my pocket. I knew it would be gone before I checked, but when I felt the empty place where it had always resided the significance of the key's absence came crashing down. "He's gone," I said, and then more quietly, "It's gone."

Seamus tugged irritably on his beard. "That's what I'm trying to say, the guy's scampered." He swept an apologetic bow at Ariella's parents. "Sorry, Your Majesties, he always has had trouble with authority. He also may have a bit of a problem with elves."

"No!" I shouted. "The key! I don't know how, but Rook has stolen the key!"

No one moved or said anything, except Solon, who leaned in close and whispered excitedly, "This sounds like an important plot point. Do you think it means I will be in the third book?"

CHAPTER 10

GET ROOK!!!

Everything became a blur. I recall my heart pounding in my chest. I recall Ariella's parents, in an event that may be unprecedented in elven history, high-fiving over the fact that they would be in the next book. I recall wanting to vomit, at least partially over the insufferability of the scene of two impossibly beautiful elves attempting a five-step handshake. But mostly I remember the panic and fear and anger that churned through me. I needed the key. Griswald had entrusted it to me. It was mine. And I had allowed it to be stolen.

When I finally collected my wits and felt like I could breathe again, I discovered that everyone was shouting at each other, but mostly at Seamus. Harold was giggling and screaming, apparently in joy at the chaos. Seamus held up his hands for silence and roared, "And why do you all assume that I would know anything about Rook? Is it just because I'm a dwarf?" He shook his head and muttered something about profiling. Then he put his hands firmly on his hips and began to lecture. "Well, let me tell you something, I'm not surprised Rook made a run for it, not because he told me he was going to do it, but because he owes me money." He shook a finger at all of us. "None of you will believe me, but he's terrible about paying off on his bets."

"I thought he disputed owing you money at all," I pointed out.

"You're right, he did," Seamus said with an irritated tug on his beard. "But last time there was some question of whether or not the bet had been accepted. This time was different. We shook on it and everything."

"What was the bet over?" Drake asked with a throaty growl.

"A game of chess," the dwarf answered. "We played in the Great Hall not ten minutes ago. Right after he thrashed Avery."

"Well, I wouldn't say thrashed . . ." I began, and then the real oddity of Seamus's story struck me. "Wait. You two played and finished a game of chess in under ten minutes? That was fast."

Seamus puffed out his chest proudly. "Yup. I caught him in a classic Scholar's Mate. It was a thing of beauty. I was actually thinking of taking the nickname Bishop in honor of the victory."

This story seemed less and less likely the more details I learned. "Isn't the Scholar's Mate something that beginners typically fall for?" I asked. Seamus nodded. "Rook may be a lot of things, but I would not call him a beginner at almost anything. Particularly where chess is concerned." He started to protest and I held up a hand to silence him. "Could it be possible that he let you win so quickly to give himself time to escape?"

"Absurd!" Seamus snorted, then he thought about it for a second more and asked less certainly, "Why would he do that anyway?"

I started pacing. Behind me, Harold played my shadow, marching at my heel, stroking his chin in mimic. "He must have taken it from me during the chess game. All that hugging and thumping." I threw out my hands in frustration, and Harold mirrored me perfectly. "He was playing me the whole time."

"Isn't that the point of chess?" Seamus asked.

I shot a look at him and so did Harold. "He's wanted the key since he first saw it. Our meeting to discuss destroying it must have driven him to action. I think he's taken it to prove that it can be used as a weapon. Maybe he's even gone to attack the Administration directly!"

"Is that such a bad thing?" Seamus asked.

"Yes!" I barked in exasperation. "The whole point of this meeting was to decide how to destroy the bloody thing."

"No, Avery," Valdara said authoritatively. "This gathering was to decide *whether* the bloody thing was to be destroyed."

"Haven't you been listening to Avery?" Sam asked. "The key drains reality. You saw it with your own eyes while you were traveling with him. You didn't understand what you were seeing then, but you must now."

"Maybe so," Valdara said noncommittally.

"Then again, maybe Rook is right," Seamus said and stared about the room with a challenging gaze. "Maybe it is safer with him than in the hands of a former Dark Lord who is too busy parenting an imp to help us in the war. A war you started, I might add." The dwarf wagged a finger at me.

"Right or wrong, the choice was not Rook's to make." Valdara gripped my shoulder tightly. "Avery, can you find either Rook or the key?"

I was about to say no, but Sam answered for me. "Yes. Yes, he can. He knows a scrying spell that can find him. Remember, Avery, the one you were telling me and Ariella about?"

"Do it. Take up your magic! Find the dwarf!" Valdara ordered and released my shoulder. I felt the blood start returning.

Leave it to Sam to drop me in the soup with the best of intentions. It isn't that he wasn't right. In theory, what he suggested was eminently doable. I had held the key. I had used it—more often than I should have actually. If Rook had it somewhere, it should have been a simple matter for me to sense it, especially if he was still in Trelari. There was just the little problem of my recent inability to actually do magic. Still, I had to try.

I concentrated and stretched out my senses, trying to see if I could perform the simple task of finding a source of magic. It was impossible, like trying to hold on to emptiness. The part of me that channeled magic was broken. I could feel now that there was a tear in my own pattern.

Someone—probably Valdara—cleared their throat, and I looked up. Everyone was staring at me expectantly. I dropped my hand from where it had been gripping my hair, and Harold dropped his also. I opened my mouth to tell them the truth, that there was no way I could track Rook, but instead found myself saying, "I'm going to need to make a proper tracking circle. I will need space and . . . some assistance. Sam and Ariella?"

Ariella nodded, while Sam said, "Neato."

The table was moved to the side and then I quickly ushered everyone but Sam and Ariella out of the room. Once the door was safely closed *and* locked against intrusion, I pulled a piece of fazechalk from my pocket and began to draw the complex pattern I would need to have them activate so I could track Rook without using any magic of my own. As an afterthought, I put in a few extra lines and symbols so the circle would act as a homing portal—just in case. Once it was finished, I stepped into the middle. Harold, who had been pretending to draw his own circle on the tabletop, sprang forward and clambered up my leg to nestle in his favorite place on my shoulder.

I nodded to Sam and Ariella. "I will need the two of you to imbue it with magic."

Sam, who had been studying the circle quite carefully, asked, "Why?"

Ariella rolled her eyes. "Isn't it obvious? He can't channel magic. He probably hurt himself when he cracked the pattern. If he was willing to be an invalid for a few weeks, I'm sure my mother would be able to heal him. She has always been good at mystical ailments."

"How did you figure it out?" I asked.

Ariella positioned herself at the edge of the circle. Sam joined her on the opposite side. When they were in position, she said, "Because I know you, Avery Stewart. When Sam transported you here the first time, you nearly blew the roof off the Great Hall, and yet you allowed yourself to be bounced around Trelari two—no! Three more times without any resistance. You may make yourself out to be a ridiculous, second-rate mage in your books, but the fact is you are as meticulous and creative in crafting your spells and protections as anyone I have ever studied."

I thought this was a little harsh, and at the same time too generous, but she didn't give me a chance to say so. "For example," she continued. "I notice this circle is not just a scrying circle, but also a—"

"It's a portal!" Sam cried, pointing to the extra symbols I'd added to the pattern. "You were going to leave us—again!"

They both crossed their arms across their chests and glared at me. I stood in the middle of the circle—powerless—and sighed deeply. "It's nothing personal, Sam. It's just I thought I could handle this Rook problem on my own."

"With no magic?" Sam asked.

He had a point, but not one I would concede yet. "Look, between driving Vivian away and probably blowing up most of the Army of Shadow, I've caused enough trouble for Valdara and Trelari. If I take her two best mages away—"

Sam cut me off. "But we aren't Trelari's best mages. You are."

"A mage without magic is not a mage, Sam," I pointed out. "All that is left is a physically unfit fellow with no discernable talents dressed in a voluminous robe and a funny hat and waving around a little stick not even substantial enough to beat someone with."

"Good point," Sam said with a little more enthusiasm than I might have wished. "And you don't even have a robe . . . or a hat . . . or a wand for that matter."

"Enough, Sam," Ariella scolded. "The point is, Avery, either you take us with you, or no one goes."

I tried to think of some way around this impasse, but there wasn't one. I needed their magic to activate my circle. I hissed my frustration. "Fine. But, if your parents get mad at me—"

"Don't!" she ordered, and that malevolent glare of hers brushed past me.

Cyclops from the X-Men, his look could kill. In fact, I think it did several times. That guy really needs to find a better way of securing those glasses to his head. They always seem to fall off at the most inopportune of moments. I shuddered. "Sorry."

"You should be," she muttered. "Now, can we get on with this?"

I gave them both a little bow and gestured for them to join me. They stepped over the boundary line and soon the circle was glowing with magic.

In an instant, mystical lines swirled around me and I saw Rook's path. He was using the key to travel, and it was leaving a trail like a comet through the multiverse. I quickly did some multidimensional calculations, diagonalized the Zelazny matrix, and determined the transdimensional vector that he had taken. It didn't tell me where he was, at least not exactly, but it did tell me the path he was traveling to get there. As I suspected, the trail seemed to be leading in the general direction of Mysterium, although along a surprisingly curvy path. That fact didn't tell me anything about what he was planning, but I suspected it wasn't going to be healthy for anyone.

I looked across the swirling pattern at Sam and Ariella and said, "Rook's left Trelari. I don't know where he's going exactly, but it's in the direction of Mysterium. If he tries to get in, he will probably be caught. Worse, even if he does make it without getting caught, he's using the key, which means he is destroying subworlds as he goes."

There was silence for a heartbeat, and then Ariella asked, "What do we do?"

"We go after him," I answered.

"We need to tell Valdara first," Sam said and began to leave the circle.

I shook my head. "You know if we tell her, she will demand to come with us. I'm not sure what Rook is trying to do, but whatever it is, I don't think Trelari should risk her queen and greatest warrior going after him. We can handle this, but we have to go now. Every moment we waste gives him that much larger a head start."

What I didn't say was that there was a rising sense of panic growing in me. I had to find Rook. I had to get that key back!

Sam was not convinced. "I'm not sure," he said and glanced back at the door to the Great Hall, behind which the others were waiting.

"It's okay, I can handle this," I said and then thought about it and added, "with your help."

"Either step out now or stay, Sam. We are going," Ariella declared.

His face was troubled, but he gave a definite nod of agreement and stepped back into the center of the pattern. A second later, a pulsing glow of magic passed over us. Suddenly, I remembered I'd forgotten to tell them something.

"Just a heads-up," I warned as the chamber blurred. "I haven't worked all the kinks out of this spell, and it has a tendency to make some people a little queasy." Before either one of them could say anything, we were swept through the dimensional currents like a leaf caught in a maelstrom.

My caution was not idle. What we were using to travel was a spell I called a slip portal. It was a mode of transport of my own devising and was a bit of a hybrid between Rook's absurd hypocube and the prescient gateway Vivian made when we were trying to escape Moregoth on our way to find Sam and Ariella. At the time, I had been impressed that their portals were able to transport us to a location even without the caster knowing where it was or how to get there. What had been annoying to me was how slow going it was. At every intermediate point, you had to stop for an indeterminate period of time: a few minutes, a couple of hours, a day, a week.

Wanting to speed up the process, I modified those constructs so that the traveler would pause in each world only long enough for the spell to determine if the location contained the target. If it didn't, the spell would slip the traveler to the next location. The result was fast, but somewhat disorienting. When I tested it with Vivian, she had likened the experience to watching a laser light show in a Tilt-A-Whirl after having eaten a dozen raw eggs and two quarts of sour milk while someone was punching you in the gut. Then she puked on my shoes. In hindsight, I should probably have given Sam and Ariella more than a heads-up.

We dissolved out of Trelari and appeared in a landscape of tangerine trees and marmalade skies. We paused only long enough for me to take note that the trees had been juiced before we passed on. A shredded and torn world of paper children and depressed magic dragons came next. We slipped past it with a sudden stomach-churning lurch. In the next few minutes we traveled through innumerable worlds but only long enough to catch horrifying glimpses of shattered lands—a place where superhumans on motorcycles had once battled ancient gods, now silent; a land where once-delicate ice crystals had grown upward to an infinite sky, now melted and deformed;

a brutal desert marked with the skeletons of ancient monsters, but where now the sand was coarse and rough and irritating; a dungeon filled with living stuffed animals having tea. Actually, I wasn't sure if anything had been altered in that last one except that the stuffed animals didn't appear to be enjoying their tea. I suspected they had been served something horrible like Lemon Zinger or pumpkin spice.

We accelerated faster and faster until the worlds were little more than whorls of color and shape. Then, with a final, abrupt shudder, we came to a stop.

We were in a massive cavern. The walls soared up to meet a vaulted stone ceiling that was lost in the shadows above us. Colossal metal statues of what might have once been dwarven warriors, but whose faces had been erased of all features, stood guard over a huge forge. The smell of coal dust and the tang of iron filled the air, memories of former days when dwarfs might have worked here, but now the fires were cold.

Sam fell to his knees retching, followed almost instantly by Harold. Despite having been prepared, my head was spinning so badly that I had to put my hands on my knees to keep from falling over. Only Ariella seemed unaffected. She stood, poised as always, and watched us being sick with a detached curiosity. "Interesting," she said.

"Elves!" Sam groaned between convulsions. I silently agreed and added immunity to motion sickness as another of my grievances against her race.

It was Harold who seemed most affected. He kept puking long after Sam and I recovered. I will say this only once, after which you'll understand why I'll never say it again: you have never experienced anything that matches the horror of a baby imp projectile vomiting pureed mouse. The sights, sounds, and odors produced are so terrible that there are pits of hell that would seem a paradise in comparison. In the *Inferno*, Dante might well have been prophesying our initial moments in that ancient dwarven forge when he wrote of the Eight Circle: "All the diseases in one moat were gathered, such was it here, and such a stench came from it as from putrescent limbs is wont to issue."

When at last the sickness had passed, Harold started wailing inconsolably. Despite the smell, I picked him up—a sure sign of either insanity or parenthood.

Sam put his hands to the sides of his head. "What was that?" he said, still gagging and retching, although at this point he might have been reacting to Harold's aftermath rather than the motion of the spell itself.

It was while I was trying to explain the principle of a slip portal to them and simultaneously clean the imp up—wet wipes are an amazing invention—that Rook came storming out of a side passage, a troop of angry dwarfs at his heels. Or, at least I thought they were dwarfs. Something was odd about them.

I didn't have much time to study them though as Rook, hand held over his mouth to protect against the worst of the smell, demanded, "What in the name of my grandfather's beard are ya doin', Avery?"

"And why are you doing it all over our floor?" asked another, who was wearing an impressive horned metal cap and a shirt of shining silver rings.

I pointed a soiled wet wipe at Rook. "I could ask you the same question."

"But he hasn't done anything to the floor," the dwarf with the pointy helmet said.

"Except erase all our carvings," said another.

"He explained that. It wasn't his fault. It was the key!" exclaimed another dwarf.

"That's what extinguished our forge also!" bellowed another.

"Lads . . ." said Rook with a warning growl.

"It's true," the horn-helmed dwarf agreed. "First it erased the seven forge runes, each a work of art that we'd spent the last hundred generations carving into the walls. Then went the faces of our forefathers." He gestured with a silver hammer at the four statues. "Then there was the gallery of master weapons—"

Rook cleared his throat. "That's probably enough, fellows—"

"Axes, shields, swords, maces, each the most wondrous of its kind," a dwarf extolled.

"The Regalia of Mightiness!" one shouted.

"The Rod of Mightiness!" another yelled.

"The Helm of Mightiness!" yet another bellowed.

"I think they get the picture!" Rook barked.

"Even my beard vanished!" one dwarf groused.

"So did mine!" said another.

"And mine!"

"And mine!"

I looked around, and realized what I had found so strange about them. All of them were clean-shaven.

Ariella gasped and Sam shook his head. "That's not right. Not right at all," he said.

We all turned back to Rook. I took a step toward him and held out my hand. "Give me the key before you do any more damage."

The dwarf shook his head. "I canna do that, Avery. Not yet. I need you to see somethin' first."

My anger boiled up at the request. Here we were, standing at the end of a line of irrevocably damaged worlds, and he was still trying to convince me to let him keep the key. I gestured at the extinguished forge and the featureless statues. "If this place is an example of your control of over the key, then I don't want or need to see anything you have to show me."

"You *need* to see this," he said firmly. "I'm afraid I'm no' gonna give you a choice, lad."

"How dare you!" I shouted. "Look at this place! Look at them!" I gestured at the beardless dwarfs, who smiled back at me uncertainly. I realized that I had never seen a dwarf smile before, not really, because their beards always covered most of their faces.

It was pretty creepy. I pointed a finger, shaking with emotion, at Rook. "Admit that the key is beyond your control. That it drove you to steal it from me. That it is an agent of pure destruction. That it has to be destroyed."

"Granted, but I'm still no' gonna give it back," he said and raised the key between us. He looked past me to the troop of dwarfs. "Sorry, gents, but it's all for a higher cause."

I felt a ripple in the fabric of the subworld and sensed rather than saw the gathered dwarfs vanish as a glowing circle appeared around us. "Rook, don't!" I yelled, but it was too late.

A desperate, sinking feeling settled in the pit of my stomach as the world, diminished as it was, faded around us. We appeared in a frozen and barren land that perfectly matched my mood. It was cold, desolate, and quickly sapping my will to live, or at least my ability to live. It was bloody freezing!

CHAPTER 11

A DWARVEN WASTELAND

We were standing on a rough circle of black rock in an empty landscape of ice and snow. A full moon shone down on us with a cold blue light. A fierce wind was blowing across the broken plain, driving sheets of freezing rain against us. We had been here only a few moments, but already the cold was growing unbearable. Harold buried himself in my shirt, his teeth already chattering.

"N-n-need . . . w-w-warmth spell," said Sam with a shudder.

He was already casting. A soft glow, like the light of a campfire, surrounded him and he let out a sigh of relief. I started to go through the motions of the spell and realized I was literally doing just that, because I was still without magic. I edged closer to him, trying to leech some of his heat, and turned hopefully to Ariella. Unfortunately, I had not counted on her irritating elvishness. She was standing, cloak and hair streaming out behind her in the wind, a satisfied smile on her face. She must have seen the mix of disgust and envy on my face. "Is something wrong, Avery?"

I gestured at her with shaking hands. "Y-y-yes! Y-y-you! How can you n-n-not be . . . be c-c-cold?"

Ariella shrugged. "I suppose it is a little chilly. Do you want to borrow my cloak?"

She pulled her cloak from around her shoulders and held it out to me. I debated the shame of taking a young woman's coat from her in the middle of a freezing rain versus the growing numbness in my fingers for all of about a half second before grabbing it. I wrapped it around myself. It was like being plunged bodily into a fine spring day. Warmth and the smell of a flowering meadow surrounded me.

"So, what they say about elven cloaks is true. I always thought it was hype, but they are awesome," I murmured contentedly while Harold rooted deep within the cloak's lining. Now that I wasn't in danger of freezing to death, I could be angry. I rounded on Rook. "That's it! I am done being transported all over the multiverse! Give me the key now!"

He shook his head. "No' until you see what you must."

"And what is that?"

He pointed across the icy plain. I followed his finger but couldn't make out anything more than a patch of vague darkness on the far horizon. "What? What is that? A sea? A mountain?"

"It looks a bit like a junkyard or backstage at a playhouse," Ariella answered. "There are lots of bits of lots of things. Does it always move like that?"

For the first time the dwarf looked shaken. "How can you possibly see that, lassie?" he asked. "It's more than two leagues from here."

"Elves can see farther than the rest of us," I answered as though this were the most obvious question in the world.

Rook yanked at his beard and sputtered, "This has nothin' to do with visual acuity, you ninny. Even the human eye, which is inferior to most, can see a burnin' candle at ten leagues, and if you look into the night sky, you can see stars that are millions of light-years distant. But the plain we're standin' on has a curvature similar to yar Earth, which means she'd have to be dozens of feet tall to see what she says she's seein'."

We both looked at Ariella for an explanation. She shrugged and smiled. "What makes you think elves see in a straight line?"

"Common sense!" Rook barked.

"Physics?" I suggested.

"Neither of which bothers elves particularly much," Ariella answered with unnerving tranquility.

I thought about it and she was right. Physics, or more broadly science, would insist that elves shouldn't be able to do a lot of the things they manage to do with regularity. Like run on top of snow, even when much smaller and lighter beings sink. Or go without sleep their entire lives. Or live forever for that matter. Oh, or defy gravity by running up falling stones. Or never run out of arrows. Or control a troll by driving daggers into its brain. Or surf on shields while firing arrows with perfect precision. Or have their bloody eyes change color every other bloody scene. Meanwhile, common sense would tell you that immortal beings able to do all the things listed above would rule the world, not hole themselves up in forests and wait for ridiculous creatures like me to save them. Yet here we were again.

All I ended up saying was "She's got a point."

After a brief pause to consider, Rook grunted his agreement and started marching in the direction of the dark stain on the horizon. We fell in behind him, trudging through the snow, or in Ariella's case, lightly dancing along its surface.

We marched on for about half an hour before the shadowy patch of land at the edge of the ice began to resolve itself into an indistinct, ever-shifting black mass. At first, I thought it might be a sea or a lake, but it didn't seem to be moving right. It was swirling around and around like a whirlpool lay somewhere at its center. Sam and I pestered Rook with questions about it, but all he would say, when he would say anything, was *wait*, or with greater frequency, *shut up*.

As Sam's and my curiosity grew, Ariella's seemed to wane. Whereas before she had raced ahead of us, she fell back as we neared our destination. At last, as we reached the top of a slight rise where the ground sloped down toward the strange sea, she stopped entirely. I thought it might be fatigue, which would have been amazing and given me no end of pleasure, but she wasn't breathing hard. Instead, she was just staring out at the swirling black sea, her eyes wide with shock.

"What's wrong?" I asked.

"The sea isn't a sea at all," said Ariella. "It's . . . it's . . ."

Sam huffed up beside us. "I really need to start running more. Either that or convince everyone else to run less." He squinted down the slope toward the whirling vortex. "What is it? What are you all staring at?"

"Don't you see, Sam?" said Ariella, pointing her shaking hand. "It's all getting broken to bits."

"Who? What?" he asked.

Before Sam could get around to asking how, when, or why, Rook answered, "Everythin', laddie. This is where realities come to die. You can watch 'em gettin' ground up into nothin'."

It sounded mad, but now that he said it, everything I was seeing made sense. Those strange shapes floating on the surface of the shifting black, swirling and changing, were bits of places. I could see chunks of buildings and trees, pieces of hills and creatures. The seething body stretched out into the shadows, one incomprehensible mass of debris and ash—the dead remains of worlds. A strange, cold sensation ran through me, and it had nothing to do with the temperature. This place was dreadfully wrong.

"Where have you brought us?" I whispered.

Rook let out a sad sigh before answering. "To most it is known as the Well of Worlds, but I call it the Waste. We are standing at its border." He pointed into the maw of the chaos. "That down there is another reality entirely, or rather, the remains of many realities."

"I'll grant you it's grotesque," I said with a grimace, "but I still don't understand why we are here. What does this have to do with us and the key?"

He ignored me and began wandering down the slope toward the edge of the whirling mass. In unspoken agreement, Sam and Ariella and I followed. It wasn't clear what other options we had. With him holding the key, I was pretty sure we would lose if we tried to overpower him.

Soon we were standing right at the edge of the pool. This close, the air was filled with the sound of grinding matter and the smell of pure fazedust. It was also possible to make out details of the destroyed worlds. In among the rubble, I even thought I saw one of the statues from the world of the dwarfs, ground to nothing but an indistinct torso.

A horrible thought struck me. "Were these realities destroyed by the key? Is that what this is all about? Did the key do all this?"

Rook gave me a one-eyed stare until I grew silent. "There are lots of ways to destroy subworlds, laddie. These days, mages do it without a thought, they cast a spell, and—" He picked up a rock and threw it into the swirling mass. It skipped across the surface before flaring with power and disintegrating. "But if yar thoughtful about it, you can also mine reality. And if yar very, very careful, you can take the material of those realities, you can smelt 'em down, you can cast 'em, and you can form 'em into things." He reached into his belt and pulled the key out. I felt my throat catch as I saw it. "This key is one of dozens that were made. Forged from the ashes of dead worlds."

"So, who made them?" asked Sam. "Dwarfs?"

"No, of course not!" Rook snapped, pointing the key at Sam furiously. It swiveled and twisted, and its edges began to glow.

"Okay! Okay! It wasn't the dwarfs!" Sam said, holding his hands up in surrender.

Despite Sam's attempt to calm him, Rook continued to direct the key at him with a hand shaking with emotion. I needed to draw his attention away before something happened that we would all regret, particularly Sam. "If it wasn't the dwarfs, who did forge the key?" I asked in as calm a tone as I could muster.

Rook spun on me, the lethal key now pointed at my chest. "The Mysterians, of course!" he answered with a grunt of disgust. "You know, for a professor, you can be awfully dense at times, laddie."

"Rook, I knew it was the Mysterians," I admitted.

"Then why did you ask?" he asked, his breathing coming in ragged gasps.

"I wanted to keep you talking," I answered and gestured at the key, which was still pointing disturbingly close to where my heart was located. "You seemed to be on the verge of dissolving Sam with that thing." Beside me, Sam nodded his vigorous agreement. "At least now it's me you would be turning to goo. An improvement from Sam's perspective, less so from mine."

"Dissolve you? Why the hell would I dissolve you, you great gobshite?" he shouted. "I brought you here to make a point."

"About the key?" I asked. Seeing as how he still had not put it away or even lowered it, I was having trouble thinking of anything else. All I knew was that I needed him to give it to me. Then I needed to make sure it was destroyed.

"Yes, about the key, which you are obsessed with by the way, laddie," he said, waving it at me.

"That could be because you are still threatening him with it," Ariella pointed out with a calm that only an elf can assume.

He looked down at the key in confusion. "Once and for all, I'm not trying to kill Avery or anyone else." When none of us relaxed at his assurance, he grabbed hold of the end of his beard and tried to yank it off. "Fine. If it will help the three of you focus, I will put it away." He jammed the key into his belt where it began turning featureless again. "Happy?" he asked. We nodded. "Good. Now, getting back to what I was saying, the point of this little journey is to prove to you once and for all that the key is just a tool. One of many that the Mysterians made long ago. It isn't inherently evil. It isn't inherently anything."

"You've got to be kidding me!" I shouted, unable to restrain myself. "You just ripped through a dozen worlds and dismantled a dwarven civilization that for all I know was a reflection of your own mind with that 'tool,' and now you say it isn't evil. Well, whether it is good or evil or indifferent, my mind hasn't changed. The key must be destroyed."

His face twisted into an angry smile, more of a snarl really. "To what purpose, lad? To salve your conscience? And to what end? So that this little fragment of the Mysterium is destroyed? Why no' use it?" He began pacing back and forth, tugging at his hair and gesturing with the key, which I doubt he was even aware was in his hand again. "What we need to do is go to Mysterium. We need to unravel its pattern. To extinguish, once and for all, the forge that feeds this madness." He turned on us, a manic light in his eyes, as the key pointed first at Ariella and then at me and then at Sam and back again along the line. "This was our fault, and it's only right that one of us should fix it."

Ariella took a step forward, hands outstretched. "Rook, haven't you been listening? We can't use the key. There's no telling what might happen."

"She's right," Sam said, moving up beside her. "I was there when Avery turned it on Trelari's pattern. I felt the magic. It was . . ." He shuddered, unable to describe it.

"It was uncontrollable," I pleaded.

"And yet you controlled it!" he barked and stabbed the key in my direction.

Its tip was beginning to glow again, and we all backed up a few steps. I had to make him understand that, whatever the key had once been, now it was a danger to anyone holding it and even more of a danger to the people at the other end of it. There was only one way to do that. It was time to confess the truth about what shutting it down on Trelari had cost me.

"Look at me, Rook," I ordered. "I mean really *look* at me. You will see how well I was able to control that thing."

Something, perhaps the hollowness in my voice, finally made him listen. He made a ring of his thumb and forefinger, a simple trick experienced mages sometimes use to make a quick scrying circle, and stared at me through it. I could see the washed-out gray of his eye studying me. When his brows climbed up his forehead in surprise, I knew he'd seen the hole in my pattern.

He let out a sigh. "Sorry it happened to ya lad, but do no' despair. It's no' permanent."

"It just as easily could have been though, and you know it," I countered. "A fraction more power or a little less skill and—" I shrugged.

He hunched over, considering the key. "I do no' care what happens to me, lad. The mages have been drainin' the life from subworlds to power their magic for too long. Their lives, their lifestyle, their status as lords of the multiverse, all of it comes from this." He looked back toward the Waste, gripping the key even tighter. "Their greed created this horror, and yet you want to destroy the only thin' that might be able to put an end to it."

"Because I know that we would just be replacing one horror with another," I said, and now I began pacing, sickened to death that we were still having this argument. "You want to destroy the Administration for what they are doing by doing exactly the same thing. It will achieve NOTHING but more destruction!"

His face flushed red with anger. "What is the sacrifice of one, two, a dozen, or even a hundred worlds, if it stops this defilement once and for all? Are you really no' willin' to pay that price? You of all people?"

And there it was. He believed that once he destroyed the Administration, he would be able to stop. It was the belief of every tyrant, that they would be benevolent where others were not. I knew the truth, because I had been trying to be the good guy for years now, and every time I failed. There was always another reason to wield the power: for Vivian, for Harold, for Trelari, for myself. Since learning the true nature of Mysterium, I'd spent every day desperately trying not to use my powers, but always finding an excuse to do so.

"Well, Avery?" he pressed. "What would you sacrifice to right the wrongs done in yar name?"

From the hard set of his face, I knew he would not move on until I'd given him an answer. The only problem was I didn't have one, so I said the one thing I knew to be true. "I don't know, but I do know that you if you use the key, you will regret it. Stopping Mysterium by doing evil won't buy the redemption you seek."

I thought it was a pretty good line, coming, as it was, off the cuff and unrehearsed, but Rook gave a derisive snort.

"When did you start talkin' in clichés, Avery?

Next thing you are goin' to tell me that two wrongs do no' make a right, or that an eye for an eye will make the whole world blind, or some other claptrap. Do you really think you can convince me to change course by a simplistic appeal to some sort of Tolkienian dualism or Eddings dialectic?" He laughed bitterly. "I knew those guys when they were still in school, an' I'll let you in on a secret. It's easy to be good when you define what's evil. First divide the world—Mordor versus Gondor, the West versus the East, communism versus democracy. It does no' matter what you call them as long as there is an 'us' and a 'them.' Then name your villain and make it ominous soundin'. Voldemort, Sauron, Torak. Or if those are too subtle, just give the bad guy a name that defines their villainy off the bat. The Wicked Witch, Thulsa Doom, the Beast—"

"The Dark Lord," suggested Ariella.

Rook swiveled in her direction and stabbed out with the key. "Exactly!" he said excitedly. "Avery's whole theory about how to stabilize Trelari rested on the idea of creatin' an evil so great that the world would have to rise up defend itself. That's all I'm trying to do."

I silently cursed Ariella, because she'd given Rook a pretty powerful argument in favor of his strategy. I was trying to figure out what her angle was when I saw her eyes flicker once to me and then to Sam, before returning to focus on Rook. I did the same and saw that Sam had very quietly managed to creep quite close to Rook. I also saw that one of his hands was buried in that spell pouch of his. Rook was too busy holding court to notice anything. He turned back toward the Waste, and Sam took the opportunity to advance even closer.

The dwarf threw his arms out to embrace the destruction before him. "We need to do the same thin' to the multiverse! We need to make ourselves the greatest destructive force ever created. Shake reality to its core—"

"Lord Farquaad," Sam said out of nowhere, and his face scrunched up in distaste.

All of us turned to stare at him. He had managed to position himself right next to Rook on the edge of the Waste. When Rook turned to face him, it brought the key tantalizingly close to Sam's reach.

Sam did not appear to notice. Instead, he looked back and forth between us in confusion. "What? Vivian was telling me the story of that poor, poor ogre. Imagine having to share your house with a donkey! Also, Farquaad is another hideous name. It reminds me of the sound a toad makes when you step on it."

Rook shook his head and muttered, "Has anyone ever told you that you've got problems, lad?"

Sam nodded enthusiastically. "Yes, but I really believe I will master long division . . . eventually."

Rook's eyes rolled in disbelief, and the arm with the key dropped to his side—momentarily forgotten. "Gods preserve us."

Sam shrugged, and then in a lightning motion his hand came whipping out of his pouch already glowing. A string of power lashed out from the end of his finger and looped around the key. Then he opened his palm and the line retracted, much like a yo-yo, tearing the key from Rook's grasp. The dwarf looked in disbelief at the key, now clutched firmly in Sam's grip, and then launched himself at the young mage. While Ariella and I rushed to Sam's aide, he struggled with Rook.

"Don't be a fool," Sam grunted. "I've got the high ground!"

"Is that some kind of short joke?" Rook growled as he tried to pry the key from Sam's grip. "I've always known you had something against dwarfs."

"No! Rook! The Waste!" Sam cried.

They had been wrestling on a hill that sloped down into the Waste. As Rook had stepped back to get more leverage, his foot slipped and sank into the swirling mass. The dwarf gave a terrible scream. Sam dropped the key and grabbed Rook's arms as the whirlpool began to drag the dwarf under. Ariella also rushed to Rook's side and took hold of whatever part of the dwarf she could get a grip on. Even Harold emerged from his hiding place in my cloak to wrap his arms around Rook's neck, his wings fluttering with all their might.

While they fought for Rook's life, my attention was entirely on the key. It seemed to drop in slow motion.

As it landed, I could hear it echo in my mind, though it made no sound in the soft snow at the Waste's edge. I had actually turned and taken a step toward the key, when something pulled sharply at that part of my being deep within the center of my chest. I followed the sensation with my mind to Harold. He was glaring at me. I watched him clench his teeth and there was another sharp tug. The force of it actually made me gasp, and the coursing pain snapped me out of the strange stupor I'd fallen into. I realized everyone was shouting.

Ariella was yelling, "We're losing him!"

"Avery! Help us!" Sam screamed.

Still in a half daze, I stumbled to Rook's side and started to pull with them. The force of the Waste was terrible and relentless, and had it been one of us alone, Rook would have been lost, but together we slowly dragged the dwarf to solid ground. As soon as he was safe, Sam and I collapsed, panting from the effort, while Ariella hovered over the dwarf, who was groaning softly.

"I really do need to exercise more," Sam puffed. "I thought being a mage wouldn't require so much . . . so much . . . constitution."

I nodded my head and gasped. "Con . . . constitution is a highly underrated characteristic, Sam. It helps you survive being poisoned or getting sick—"

"Or running," he groused. "Always there's the running."

"Avery? Sam?" Ariella called. "I need some help with Rook."

My initial thought was that he was going for the key again. I jumped to my feet in a panic, but it was still lying right where Sam had dropped it. I clambered over to it and picked it up. It felt cold and oddly heavy, and I gave a sigh of relief as I felt its thrumming power in my hands. I carefully tucked it back in my pocket and then joined Sam and Ariella, who were bent over the dwarf.

Their faces were pale, but Rook himself seemed quite at peace. He was breathing easier and I couldn't see any blood on his clothes. But as my eyes traced down his body, I saw what was wrong. The leg that had been caught in the vortex was simply gone below the knee. There was no wound, no blood, simply an absence. It had been erased.

"Gods, Rook!" I gasped as a wave of nausea swept over me.

Harold flew past me and wrapped his arms and wings around Rook's head and started cooing. Rook opened his eyes at this and smiled, and the smile wasn't bitter or angry. It was just Rook. He patted the little imp on the head and sat up with a shake of his head. "You know what else constitution is good for? Losin' parts of your body. Course, dwarfs are well-known for their stoutness, otherwise this development might be distressin'. Odd thin' is, it doesn't hurt at all.

In fact, now that it's gone, I can no' remember ever havin' a leg."

I dropped to my knee beside him. "I'm sorry, Rook. I never meant for this to happen."

"Yar apologizin' to me?" he asked with a grim chuckle as Harold burrowed into his neck. "You have a nasty habit of stealin' all the blame for yerself. Look, lad, I'm the one that brought us here. I'm sorry . . ." He looked about at our faces. "All of you. I did no' understand. I really thought it was meant to be mine. There was a kind of, well, a—"

"Madness," I suggested.

He nodded and started to gently disentangle Harold from his beard. "While I held it, I really thought I could unmake Mysterium and fix everythin'." He shook his head in disbelief. "Insanity."

"This isn't any one person's burden. It belongs to all of us," I lied. In truth, I had known for quite some time that the key was meant for me. It was why Griswald had passed it on to me specifically, and why it seemed to respond so naturally to my command. Still there was no reason to worry anyone with all that right now. "Besides," I continued, "I'm the one whose dissertation started all of this by swinging Trelari's orbit out of alignment, mixing my pattern with the Mysterium's and Trelari's, and so on."

"Lad, you still do no' understand, do you?" Rook said with a grunt as he levered himself to his foot using Ariella and Sam as braces. "We set you up. Griswald an' I had been watchin' you for years. Why do you think I was in Trelari?"

I had suspected this was true for some time, but having it confirmed did send a little pang of sadness through me. I had always trusted Griswald. To think that he had been plotting with Rook about me, even if it was for the good, left me feeling empty where I had once been full. "I think I've known for a while now," I said, and then lied for the second time in so many minutes. "In the end, it doesn't matter. I trusted him, and I trust you. Now, let's get you to a kick-ass healer so we can grow your leg back. Being a dwarf is one thing. Being a lopsided dwarf—"

"Watch it, lad!" said Rook sharply, and then softening his tone, he added, "Besides, there is nothin' to be done about my leg."

"Don't be so dramatic," I said confidently. "A real Mysterium healer—"

"Would no' be able to do anythin' either," he said firmly and pointed a finger at the Waste. "I told you that's a different reality. That's true and not true. It's actually an area of the multiverse that deconstructs reality. Once somethin' goes in, there's no gettin' it back. I was no' bein' dramatic when I said I don't remember what it was like havin' a left leg. I do no' because it's been permanently removed from my pattern." He stroked his chin. "Which I suppose is a blessin' because I understand phantom pains are a real nightmare."

I'm not sure when I started crying, but my eyes were suddenly wet and the landscape blurred when Rook grumbled. "Stop the waterworks, lad. And please do no' slobber on me, Harold. I'm gonna be fine. Havin' a limb missin' is a mark of distinction among dwarfs. I just do no' know what got inna me." He sighed.

I knew. Though I couldn't see it, I could feel the key in my pouch, pulsing with power just ready to be used. If I focused on it, all sorts of idea about what I might do would begin to flood my mind: taking on the Administration single-handedly, toppling the Provost's Tower, bringing the war to an end.

"Avery? Are you okay?" Sam asked.

I found the key in my hand. Its tines were beginning to twist and turn. I grabbed at my head and focused on what I knew was real: Sam's voice, the smell of the forest that seemed to imbue Ariella's cloak, the connection between Harold and me. Slowly the key began to fade from my mind, and my thoughts were once more my own. I took a deep breath, held it, and let it go. No wonder Rook was rolled so easily. The key was either growing more powerful, or this place and its proximity to such a concentration of magic was feeding it. Either way, I needed to get the key back to Trelari and, hopefully, deliver it to Justice Cleaver's blade as soon as possible.

And then something Rook had said struck me. I stared at the key and then at the grinding horror of the Waste. Could it be that simple?

"Rook, if the Waste is a reality dismantler, would it erase anything we threw into it?" I asked.

The dwarf, who had been trying to pry Harold from around his neck, looked up at me sharply. "You thinkin' of throwin' the key in?" he asked.

I didn't know how to answer. Now that a real solution seemed to be at hand, I wasn't sure what I wanted to do. Still, I wanted to know, so I nodded. (For those of you keeping track, that was the third lie I'd told since we pulled Rook from the Waste. I was on a roll.)

"It might work," he answered. His eyes, weighing and judging, never left my face. "Then again, it might not. Those keys were forged before my time, when the First Mysterians were masterin' their arts. They are made from pure reality dust and are meant to survive anythin'. Including a trip through the Waste."

"Couldn't we just try?" asked Sam.

"You could," Rook answered, and still his gaze was fixed on me. "But if the key does survive, then there's no guarantee we could get it back. It would probably travel through the vortex and pop back into existence somewhere else in the multiverse."

"So it would be lost?" Ariella asked.

"Possibly," Rook answered. "It might appear here right next to us, or it might appear in Moregoth's hand. There would be no tellin'. Depends on whether you think the key's travel would be driven by random chance or no."

I had found myself relaxing more and more as Rook explained each complication. At last, I tucked the key back into my pocket with a sigh of something very close to relief. "No," I answered, and that's when Rook looked away. "The key has shown itself to be unpredictable and we can't take the chance that we might be handing it right to the enemy. We will take it back to Trelari and deal with it there."

"All right then, let's start walkin'," Rook ordered as he handed Harold back to me. "It's a long way to the portal point, and trust me, you don't want to try to do any travelin' this close to the Waste. It has a tendency to suck things into it and not let 'em go again." He laughed as we all looked down at his missing leg.

Our humor was to fade quickly though. There was no way Rook could walk on his own, and even with us taking turns supporting him, our progress through the snow and over the rough rocks was agonizingly slow. Nor could we think of any clever magical solution. If we had a proper circle and the right materials, we could have ensorcelled him an artificial limb, but the desolation provided nothing but rock and ice, and none of us could figure out how to fashion that into anything useful. At points, we were forced to carry him over ravines or up rises that had given us no trouble on the way out. Our slow pace did have one benefit; it gave us plenty of opportunity to discuss Rook's actions while he was under the key's spell.

"If your goal was to attack Mysterium, why didn't you?" I asked. "And why did you visit the dwarfs?"

He scratched at his head. "I do no' know. I seem to recall feelin' that . . . that the Mysterium was far away, and the way difficult and windin'."

"But it is actually fairly close these days," Sam pointed out.

"True," Rook agreed. "Then again, I thought it was important to sneak up on them and . . . and . . . I don't know. There was always the promise that the key would help me destroy Mysterium, but there was always one more thin' it needed me to do firs'."

Ariella chimed in. "Do you really believe what you said about sacrificing dozens of subworlds?"

Rook thought quite a bit on this question before answering, chewing on his beard and muttering, "I did, and, yes, part of me still does." Ariella looked sharply at him and he smiled and waved a hand, as though putting the thought behind him. "Do no' worry, lass, I'm okay now. But I do feel like I'm partly responsible for all of this desolation. The multiverse has suffered for centuries because my people, the

Mysterians, were so arrogant that they could no' imagine anyone bein' able to steal their power. And I do think there is a greater good to be had by destroyin' the mages once and for all—whatever it takes. Vivian told me once—" His voice trailed off.

"Vivian? What about Vivian?" I asked.

"I do no' know, laddie. She told me lots of thin's. Some she'd seen in her visions. Some were her own ideas. Some were just hopes and dreams." He studied his boots. "She thought it was important that you not know. Can you trust that she might be right and leave it for now?"

I nodded. In my heart, I knew that she probably was right, but it still hurt that she wouldn't confide in me. Our relationship, as strange as it had been at times, had been punctuated (bookended, one might say, depending on whether there was another chapter in the works) by her secrets and schemes. I was pretty sure she loved me, and if I didn't love her, I didn't know what else to call how I did feel about her, but I sometimes wished she couldn't see the future. Her visions always tempted her to maneuver events to help me, whether I wanted the help or not, and whatever it cost her in the process.

I put a hand under my cloak and stroked Harold's back, probing as I did that tenuous line that ran from him to Vivian. That it was still there meant she was still alive, and I thought about asking him to give it a pull, but I wasn't sure what I would do or say if she took it as an invitation to come back. I felt alone, and the feeling brought to mind a vague remembrance of a Walt Whitman poem, but I could not recall it.

We walked the rest of the way in silence, lost in our own thoughts and in the physical struggle to help Rook. When we at last reached the portal rock, the light was beginning to gray. I wasn't sure if that was because night was coming or even if there was a night, as the clouds were so thick they would have obscured any sun that might have been in the sky. Regardless, I was cold and tired, and thinking of Vivian had not helped my mood. I was ready to be gone from this forsaken place.

"Sam, would you do the honors?" I asked.

"Fine by me," he answered and began to draw the circle.

"What will you tell Valdara?" Rook asked me, a little nervously.

"The truth," I said, and he gave a slight grimace. "That we all want the same thing—to destroy the Mysterium once and for all. Every trace of it." He nodded. "Including the key." There was a pause, and then he also nodded his agreement to this. "Sam, if that portal's ready, let's go home."

"As the Treants would say," chimed Ariella in an attempt to cheer us up, "let's . . . leaf this place."

Rook and I groaned at the joke, but then as we stepped into the circle, Sam asked, "Do you really think the Treants would say that?"

We looked at each other and a wicked smile stretched across Rook's face. "I do no' know, Sam. You've got me . . . stumped."

I rolled my eyes and whispered a prayer of protection against dwarven humor, and then as Sam activated the portal, he said, "I don't think they would. I've always heard they're too . . . wooden."

Our groans of dismay, stretched and distorted, were carried with us as the portal pulled us across the multiverse toward Trelari.

CHAPTER 12

AXING FOR IT!

I was back in the Citadel of Light for the second . . . No, third . . . Wait. Let me think about this. First, Sam pulled me from the crypt, and then Ariella transported Sam and me back from Vivian's tent, and then both Sam and Ariella yanked me back from the crypt again. Fourth! I was back in the Citadel of Light for the fourth time that day. We reappeared in the Council Chamber. Someone was knocking at the door.

"Avery? Are you finished with your spell?" Drake was asking in his familiar throaty growl. "I don't like to interrupt you while you're doing your magic doodles, but it's been fifteen minutes and Valdara is getting antsy." There was the meaty sound of someone being hit followed by a muffled oath from Drake. "Not antsy! She is not antsy, more . . . eager. No! No! Anxious." He let out an audible sigh of relief. "Yes, she is anxious that we get started."

"Just another minute!" I called out as we lowered Rook into one of the chairs. I gathered the others around him and said in a low voice, "This is a bit of a break. It's obvious that time moves considerably faster where we were."

Rook rocked his hand back and forth. "Yes and no. Let's just say that time is extremely indefinite near the Waste. Pockets of fast or slow time can swirl out from it in strange ways." He pointed to Harold. "I think your imp got caught in one, because it looks like he's grown a solid two inches since we met up in Dwarrows." He sighed when all of us looked confused. "The dwarf world you were on is called Dwarrows. It literally means dwarfs."

"It does?" Sam asked.

"Are you doubting me?" Rook asked, a slight red tinge creeping up his face.

"No. You are the expert on all things dwarfish," Sam answered. Rook nodded in satisfaction. "Just one more question though? About dwarfs."

"Ask me anything," Rook said, puffing out his chest.

Sam smiled and asked brightly, "If Dwarrows literally means dwarfs, then why did you tell us that the plural of dwarf is dwarfs? Why isn't it dwarrows?"

The question clearly caught Rook off guard because he tried to cross his existing leg over his nonexistent one, only to rediscover its absence. But this only flustered him for a second, because after firmly planting his one good leg back on the ground, he said, "First, Sam, you must understand the ancient origins of the word *dwarf*." He then launched into a highly complex explanation of protolanguages and cognates and things of that nature.

Not wanting to get in the middle of a subject as touchy as the pluralization of *dwarf*, I began a careful inspection of Harold to see if Rook was right about his having grown again. This was made difficult by his extreme squirminess. After much giggling, a few attempts to bite my fingers when I extended one of his wings, and a couple of butterscotch bribes, I concluded that he was, indeed, considerably larger and much more physically active than before. It was almost as though he had been transformed in an instant from a toddler to a young child. I prayed that meant potty training was also over.

"Harold?" I asked. The imp cocked his head to one side, listening. "Can you understand me?" A cheeky smile spread across his face as he shook his head no.

Unfortunately, I couldn't explore the question any further as there was another knock at the door. Rook had just reached the climax of his explanation. ". . . which originated from the word *dhwergwhos*, which means 'something tiny,' and so from the old dweorgas, to the middle dwarrows, to the modern dwarfs. Understand?"

Sam shook his head. "Can you repeat that last bit?"

"Which last bit?" Rook demanded.

"Umm." Sam scratched his head. "The stuff right after 'first.'"

The knocking came again. "Avery?" Drake asked in a harried voice.

"There's no time, Sam," I said. Rook, who had begun to sweat with the effort of his explanation, visibly relaxed. I put a hand on the dwarf's shoulder. "Are you ready for Valdara?" I asked. Rook shifted uncomfortably in his chair but nodded.

"Don't you worry, Rook," Ariella said, draping an arm around him. "We won't let her be mean to you. She has to understand that you weren't yourself. That the key overpowered you. You were like a helpless lamb, or something even cuter, like a bunny."

Rook had been growing more and more uncomfortable with Ariella's attempt to comfort him. This last suggestion was a bridge too far. "Not that! I refuse to be compared to a bunny! I just won't have it!" he barked.

At his shout, the door came crashing open. Valdara, Drake, and Seamus were standing at the entrance to the room. Valdara had Justice Cleaver drawn with its head resting on the ground. Drake was holding his staff and giving his sternest, most disapproving look.

Seamus was holding his money pouch with a bright and greedy look in his eyes.

"Rook, explain yourself!" demanded Valdara.

The dwarf opened his mouth, but it was Sam that stepped in front of him, hands on hips. "Nothing to explain. He just doesn't like being compared to bunnies. I happen to agree with him. Bunnies are no laughing matter. They have huge sharp teeth, and they can leap at you—" Sam looked around at the grim faces of Valdara and Drake and even Rook. "That wasn't what you meant, was it?"

Rook shook his head. "No, lad, but thank you anyway. You are a true friend, but this is somethin' I must face myself." The dwarf met Valdara's gaze. "I lost my mind. I thought that if I had the key, I could find a way to win the war. I thought it was both my birthright and my responsibility." He bowed his head, putting his beard on his chest. "You have every right to call me a traitor and have me locked up. But before you do, let me say"—he paused to mutter something that sounded like encouragement under his breath— "I'm sorry. I should no' have taken the key."

"A confession!" Justice Cleaver crowed. "Now it is time to show this miscreant the true force of our righteous ire. I will rend his bones to the very marrow."

"JC!" Valdara barked, and then whispered, "Remember what we talked about? If you are unable to control yourself, I will be forced to carry a—"

"Don't say it," the battle-ax pleaded with what appeared to be a metallic shudder.

"Sword!" Valdara concluded. The ax let out a wounded gasp and then grew quiet. She turned back to Rook. "As for you—" Her eyes grew suddenly wide. "What happened to your leg?"

"It's been cleaved off!" Justice Cleaver said excitedly, adding the professional observation, "A clean cut. Very well struck!"

Valdara held the ax out to Seamus. "Take him away." Only after the battle-ax had been removed from the room did she turn back to the four of us. "Tell me what happened."

"What about my betrayal and the key?" Rook asked.

She waved off the question. "Yes, yes, we will all decide your fate in due time. Right now, I want to know why you came back missing part of your body, and what my mages intend to do to make it right."

Sam, Ariella, and Rook all began speaking at once, but I was distracted. Now that we were so close to the moment of the key's destruction, I was having trouble thinking about anything else. Even now I could feel the weight of it. I reached into my pocket and sighed. Touching the cold metal seemed to have a soothing effect on me, which was worrying in and of itself.

"Gods! It must be destroyed," Valdara thundered. "I cannot believe that a place of such horror exists in the world. If this is what the key does, destroys worlds and drains their essence, then my vote is clear."

This pronouncement shook me from my troubled thoughts. I looked about and realized that I had completely missed the retelling of our story at the Waste.

"I agree," said Ariella, her voice quavering a little. "It is the most terrible of places. If I have a vote, then it is that we ensure that the key can never be used again—ever."

"I also agree," Drake said grimly. "I may no longer be a holy man, but if we use the key, then we are no better than the Mysterium, and I won't sink that low."

Valdara looked to Sam, who simply nodded his silent agreement. Then she turned her attention to me. Normally, I would have said something, but I found myself lost in a swirl of thoughts. We needed to destroy the key, but I found myself reluctant to say so. The feeling was reminiscent of when I was a child waiting at the doctor's office to get a shot. I didn't want to go in, but the sitting and waiting to go in was far, far worse. I wanted everything over and done. Still, I couldn't help but wonder if we were making a terrible mistake. What if Rook was right? What if the key was our only hope?

Valdara cleared her throat. She was still looking at me. "Avery, it is you that requested we destroy the key. What have you to say?"

The key was suddenly very heavy indeed. I stumbled to the table and sagged down into a chair across from Rook. I was so tired, and I couldn't marshal the energy to sound anything but dispirited as I answered.

"It drains worlds, Valdara. It could drain energy from this world, maybe even my home world, Earth. And while in a place like this or Earth, where the reality potential is very high, it is unlikely to consume everything, on a subworld, it can. I've seen it . . ."

I shrugged helplessly before deciding that there was no way to explain all the potential horrors. The best I could do was to describe the things I'd seen myself. "Imagine the color being drawn out of a painting, except it's not just the color, it's the spirit of the image. When you look at that painting after, you will still see the figure, but you will no longer feel what you used to feel about it. Its meaning is gone. That is what the key does to worlds—drains them until there's nothing left."

"Except ashes," muttered Rook.

"Yes, ashes," I said, nodding to him. "Whatever it consumes is gone forever. However, that's not the worst of it."

"What?" said Drake in astonishment. "How in the Seven Hells can that not be the worst of it?"

Valdara nudged him. "You used to not curse so much."

"That was before I was enlightened," he said with a bitter chuckle. "When I still had faith. Before I found out that all the divinity I had believed in was just some student mage's vision of the divine." He tipped an invisible cap to me, but there was real pain in his voice. Whatever he was now, there had been a time when Drake had been a true believer. Count that as another thing I'd taken from Trelari. "But all that is ancient history," he grunted. "The important question right now is how consuming entire worlds can't be the worst of it."

I looked about and saw confusion in their faces. How could I explain things to them when I was having trouble focusing my thoughts on anything but the key? I decided the only way was again to relate my own experiences. "The worst of it is what the key does to the wielder," I said at last. "How it can change your perceptions and control your emotions. How it can make the answer to any question and the solution to any problem be itself. It happened to me on the pattern." I swallowed as I recalled how I had felt when that first rush of power had pulsed through me. "And I think Rook can attest to the same thing."

"Aye, laddie." He nodded and gestured to his leg. "It's easy to lose yerself, even bits of yerself, when you are holdin' it. Look, I know I shouldn't get a vote, but if I had one, it would be to destroy it. I know now that I can't trust myself to wield it, and I'm too suspicious a dwarf to trust anyone else."

Valdara stared sadly at Rook's missing leg and seemed to come to some decision. "Avery, if the key is to be destroyed, I understand you mean to do it with Justice Cleaver. How exactly?"

I heard Valdara's question, but it was as though I

were at the bottom of a well, and the key was a great weight on my chest, pushing me under the water. It was getting hard to breathe, much less speak, and the thrumming it was making was so loud in my ears. Then I felt a tiny paw on my head. I opened my eyes to see that I had laid my head down on the top of the table.

Harold was standing in front of me, stroking my brow. "Butterscotch?" he asked.

I smiled and, with a great effort, fished in my pockets until I found one. He tore the wrapper off, but then rather than shoving it in his mouth he held it back out for me. I tried to push it away, but he was insistent. To humor him, I took it and popped it in my mouth. I had never tried one before, and now wondered at what I'd been missing. They were amazing, and after sucking on it for a few seconds, I felt a rush of energy. I don't know what was in them, but it was probably illegal.

"Avery?" Valdara said again.

I turned to answer, but that tiny paw grabbed hold of my sleeve in a remarkably powerful grip. I looked down at Harold and he gave me the sweetest smile. "Thank you," I said, and gave him a pat. Still he didn't let go of my sleeve. "What?" I asked.

"Butterscotch!" he said firmly.

My eyes narrowed, but I handed over a candy, and Harold happily began gnawing at it.

"Avery!" Valdara shouted.

Both Harold and I jumped, and I blurted out, "Yes! Justice Cleaver!" Valdara's eyes narrowed impatiently. She was obviously waiting for a more detailed explanation. "I believe that if you strike the key with a single strong blow from Justice Cleaver that the battle-ax should be able to cleave the key in two, severing its pattern and destroying it."

"Will that really be enough?" she asked. "From everything I've heard, this key is truly otherworldly."

As usual, Valdara had put her finger directly on the weakest part of my plan: my lack of any real evidence that it would work. I believed it could work, but the fact was I was guessing. After hesitating long enough to ensure that everyone would doubt whatever answer I came up with, I said, "Justice Cleaver is an artifact of immense power, formed from Mysterium-matter, fueled by both the patterns of Mysterium and Trelari. There is every chance he can destroy it."

A shout came from down the hall. "Aha!"

Valdara gave me a sidelong glance. "If you're wrong . . ." I shrugged, and she put a hand to her head and began massaging her temples. "Bring in Justice Cleaver, Seamus!" she shouted.

The dwarf came trotting in, holding the battle-ax before him like a flag. Justice Cleaver was in full monologue mode.

"There can be no doubt that I am the greatest battle-ax in history, and I am far and away superior to any magical swords, even if they have better heralds and more bardic songs written about them. A pitiful, bladeless, weakling key can never stand before me. I shall cleave it from this multiverse and prove to all that doubt me that I am not just the ultimate weapon, but also the penultimate, the antepenultimate, the preantepenultimate, the propreantepenultimate, and even the forepropreantepenultimate—"

Seamus handed the battle-ax, which was still engaged in forging new and ever more ridiculous links in the monstrous chain of prefixes he had invented, to Valdara. The dwarf bowed to her. "Your Majesty, with all due respect, I must disagree with this."

"What!" Justice Cleaver boomed. "You dare to doubt my greatness, dwarf! I shall chop you down to . . . well, down further in size!"

"Quiet!" Valdara roared. When Justice Cleaver was finally mostly still, though still muttering to himself about how difficult it is to chop up dwarfs given that you so often swing over their heads, she turned to Seamus. "I take it you have a different view about what should be done with the key?"

Seamus nodded and started to say something but stopped himself after glancing at the battle-ax. He made a sweeping bow to it. "Besides Justice Cleaver, the key is the most powerful weapon we've got. At the end of the day, it's just a tool. And if the responsibility of using it is too much for Avery or Rook, then let's give it to someone with more willpower, like you, Your Majesty. Or maybe Drake. We need help fighting the Mysterium. I don't know where they keep getting all these Sealers from, but I have had enough of them. If I never see another red-robed mage, it'll be too soon!"

Valdara shook her head. "Justice Cleaver is enough for me to handle. I don't want another magic intelligence sharing space in my brain."

"I could do it," said Drake. "I've got the willpower." Valdara raised a questioning eyebrow. "It's the truth. According to legend, while we were questing for the Dark Lord, I went without food for two weeks so the rest of you would have enough to eat. In those pious days, when I was called—wait a moment." He reached into a fold in his cloak. To my surprise, he pulled out a copy of *The Dark Lord* and flipped to a page near the beginning. "Here it is," he said. "On page nine, 'the gibberlings and I liked to call him St. Dork the Insufferable.'"

I felt my ears begin to redden. "Yeah, um . . ." I hesitated, silently cursing Jack Heckel for including that line. "Sorry about that. I did a lot of growing up in that book."

Valdara stepped in. "We can debate the merits and demerits of the book and what Avery put in and left out later. Trust me, Avery and I need to have a long discussion one day about his admiration for the 'curves of my body' and my 'taut bare stomach.'"

The blush that had started on my ears spread across my face. "A lot of growing up," I repeated.

She waved at me to be quiet. "Drake, are you saying you would be willing to wield the key?"

"No, I'm saying that I could," he growled and, leaning heavily on his staff, pointed a finger at me. "That monstrosity Avery keeps in his pocket must be destroyed. I won't touch it. It is my belief that we will find a way to defeat the Mysterium, but we are going to do it the right way—"

"Don't say it!" Rook grunted. "Just don't!"

Drake stared at the dwarf and gave him a half smile. "That's what makes the difference between being good guys and bad guys."

The dwarf slapped a hand across his face and muttered something about saccharine drivel.

Valdara ignored the dwarf and smiled brightly at Drake. "I can't argue with you when you have that righteous fervor in your tone. We will find another way." Seamus opened his mouth to argue but was silenced at a glance from Valdara. "The matter is decided," she said firmly. He dropped his head in defeat but was too devoted to Valdara and the crown to make any further protest. Satisfied that question really had been settled, Valdara rose to her feet. "Everyone come. We will do it at once."

"No' to be antisocial, but I think I'll stay here," said Rook with a good-natured slap at his missing leg. He looked at me and raised an eyebrow. "If I were you, laddie, I'd do the same thing. Give the key to someone else." That's when I noticed the tight set of his face, and how his other hand was gripping the arm of his chair so tightly that his knuckles were white.

I shook my head. "No, I have to see this through."

Valdara stepped over to one of the tall, windowed doors that led onto the courtyard, and we followed her. A pool lay at the center of the courtyard, surrounded by a ring of willowy, white-barked trees. Here and there, a bust of a former ruler of Trelari stood atop a low pedestal of solid marble. It was to one of these that Valdara went. She lifted off a statue of a dignified-looking man with bright eyes and a very prominent nose and placed it on the ground.

"Avery," she said, pointing to the empty pedestal. "The key."

I felt my heart catch. We had decided the fate of the key. It was time to destroy it. I was sure that this was the right thing to do, and yet, I yearned for a reason not to. Harold seemed to sense my hesitation. He wrapped his arms around my neck, and a tension I had not known I was carrying fell from my body. With an enormous effort, I pulled the key from my pocket. The cold, smooth metal felt so solid in my hand. There was something immensely satisfying in the feel of its weight. I carried it over to the stone pedestal, but did not set it down. I took a last look at the key, watching how it reflected the light, reveling in its simple beauty.

"Avery?" Valdara said softly and glanced from my hand to the pedestal.

I nodded but still made no move to put it down. Instead, I twisted the key around in my hands. I could feel the power in it. What if Vivian was right? What great feats might I be capable of if I kept it? Could I fix everything? For a second, I had a vision of standing on the edge of a precipice above the Waste, but instead of destroying realties, the storm was birthing them. World upon world, wonder upon wonder was flowing from the vortex of the Waste. I knew in my heart that it was a delusion, but I was also dangerously close to giving in to it.

It was Harold that brought me back from the brink. He reached into one of the pockets of the cloak Ariella had given me and pulled out a handful of gray dust. It might have been dust from anywhere but for its smell. It reeked of barely contained power. I had only known its like once before, at the edge of the Waste. All the memories of that horrible place came rushing back. The whispers of dead worlds that blew on the wind. All that ash that had once held the dreams and lives of all those lost people. I dropped the key on the stone as though it burned, and stepped back almost to the courtyard's edge.

Everyone fell silent, expect for Harold, who was

whimpering for yet another butterscotch. I passed one to him to keep him quiet. He clutched it in his claws, cooed, and popped it in his mouth. I tried to focus on him and not the key, and I'd like to tell you I succeeded, but since this is for posterity, know that I failed miserably.

Valdara held Justice Cleaver with both hands and measured out the stroke. She glanced at us. "I'm not sure if there will be a backlash when I do this, but in case there is, you may want to have protective spells cast, or at least, stand back."

Sam nodded and made a casual gesture. A mostly transparent blue wall of mystic power formed between us and Valdara. "Nicely done," commented Ariella. I had to agree. Sam had improved his abilities significantly in the last few months. He also seemed to have begun to kick his reliance on spell components. I wondered how much of his progress as a mage had been my mentorship, how much had been necessity given the strife with Mysterium, and how much might even be credited to my pattern's destruction. Regardless, there was a part of me that wished he was not the royal wizard, but simply a second-year student at Mysterium U. Not that I thought he would be a better mage in this alternate reality, but it would mean that the world was a better and more peaceful place.

"Prepare yourselves!" Valdara warned.

Her words snapped me out of my mental wanderings just in time. She took one last practice stroke, then hefted the mighty battle-ax high over her head and brought it down swiftly and solidly upon the key.

I had braced myself for a massive explosion of mystical energy. I even considered the possibility that the power released by the destruction of the key might blast us all to pieces, or tear a hole through reality, or that it might even generate a permanent rent through multiple worlds. It didn't seem likely that any of those things would occur, although the blowing-us-up option was running about 60:40 in my estimation. What I didn't expect, what I hadn't even considered was what happened. Which was nothing.

Okay, that's not exactly right. There was a clanging sound, followed by a crack. The pedestal split in two. And although he would deny it later, I quite distinctly heard Justice Cleaver say, "Ouch!" The key itself appeared unaffected.

Valdara stared at the key lying, quite serene (if a key can be serene), in the fragments of the pedestal and blinked a few times. I don't ever recall her looking that surprised before.

"Did . . . did you miss it?" asked Sam.

"No, kid," said Drake. "She hit it dead-on. It just didn't break."

"How is that possible? Is that battle-ax not as impressive as it always claims to be?" asked Seamus.

"Nothing's as impressive as Justice Cleaver *claims* to be," said Drake, which may be the most accurate statement ever made in the history of everything.

"Avery? What happened?" Valdara asked.

I wasn't sure how to answer. I really didn't understand. "Sam," I said, "can you kill the shield spell?"

"Sure." He gestured several times and tapped the mystic barrier. It vanished in a puff of blue smoke.

Valdara was quite at a loss. "I hit it. My blow was swift, my aim was true." She pointed to me and then to the battle-ax. "Both of you assured me that nothing could withstand him!"

A small voice came from Justice Cleaver. "Actually, can we tone down the rhetoric? My blades are still ringing."

There were so many unprecedented admissions in that short statement that I was gobsmacked, and I'm pretty sure no one outside of Britain has been gobsmacked since women were called dollies, men clydes, and daddy-o was considered a compliment. Justice Cleaver had allowed two questions to his greatness to go unremarked. He sounded humble. And he had actually asked that we tone things down! It was beyond comprehension.

I moved past Valdara and knelt over the key. My fingers hovered above its surface, tracing its outline. It was completely unharmed. Not only that, but if I had to use one word to describe the feeling radiating from it, that word would be *smug*. My blood turned to ice. I was no longer sure there was a way to destroy the key.

Valdara grabbed the front of my robe and turned me around. Her eyes blazed accusingly. "What is going on? Why was Justice Cleaver unable to damage this thing?"

Sweat broke out on my forehead, and I felt my face flush. "I have no idea. It should have worked."

She continued to glare at me, but I was too dumbfounded to flinch. Drake put his hands on both of our shoulders and separated us, prying Valdara's fist from my shirt as he did. "We are all friends here. It didn't work. We need a new solution." He picked up the key and shoved it into my chest. "What's next?"

I wasn't sure what to say, because I had no ideas. Thankfully, Rook chose this moment to poke his head out through the glass door. He had fashioned a crutch from what looked like one of the chair arms. "Did no' work, did it?" he asked. "Never thought it would. Always dangerous to put your faith in somethin' made by a grad student."

Thank you, Rook.

CHAPTER 14

A VENTI REUNION*

The key, and its heaviness, and its soft thrum were back. I felt a sense of relief mixed with a sickening dread. I had no idea what we should do next. And

---

* Astute readers will note that Chapter 13 has been skipped. While normally not a superstitious person, you must remember that in the preceding chapters I had a rather rotten string of bad things happen: Moregoth's attack, breaking the pattern, burning myself out, losing the key, Rook losing a leg, failing to break the key, and so on. Given all this, I decided not to risk compounding my bad choices with bad luck. After all, despite being a devout rationalist, I also put a lot of stock in Jean Cocteau's views on the subject: "We must believe in luck. For how else can we explain the success of those we dislike?"

despite the gleam of *I told you so* in Rook's eyes, I didn't think he had any idea either. However, it occurred to me who might know. "I need to talk to Eldrin."

Valdara looked at me with what I can only call deep disappointment. "Whatever. Do what you think you must," she said in a dull monotone.

Ignoring the grim mood and bleak looks of the other members of the Company, I pulled out my communicator coin. Unfortunately, this was when the sugar rush from the last couple butterscotches hit Harold. He clambered out along my arm, grabbed hold of the coin, and fluttered off with a shriek of impish delight. I made a grab for him, but it was too late. He made it to one of the trees and clambered up to a high branch before I could get my hands on him.

I stood under the tree and shook a finger at him. "Bad imp! If you don't come down right now, you're heading for a time-out, mister."

Harold made a rude face at me, showing his small fangs and hissing.

"That's it! You are officially in a time-out. No candy for a week!" I stated firmly.

I'm not sure if it was my tone or the threat, but whatever it was, it made an impact. His face crumpled, and he flew over to Ariella, burying himself in her arms and sobbing.

"Avery, don't be so hard on him. He's little!" Ariella scolded.

Of course, while she was chewing me out, Harold took the opportunity to climb into the pouch where she kept her elven butterscotches. "Hey, what are you doing?" she asked. A soft wail issued from within and he poked a tearstained face out from under the pouch's flap. "Fine," she said, handing the imp a sweet.

"You're spoiling him," I muttered, plucking Harold from her pouch. I retrieved my communicator coin and stuffed him into one of the voluminous pockets of the cloak she'd given me and which I had every intention of never giving back. Seriously, it was warm when you needed warmth, cool when you needed to be cool, it felt like silk without being overly slick, and was strong enough to survive an imp ripping at it with his needle-sharp claws. Was I somewhat bitter that even elven cloth was superior in every way to every other cloth? Yes, I was. Would that stop me from keeping the cloak and wearing it on every occasion I could? Nope.

"You need a babysitter," Drake observed with a growl.

"More like an exorcist," Rook muttered, but loudly enough to ensure I heard him.

"Yes, I know!" I barked. "That's why I was staying with the semi-lich!"

The revelation that I had been using the undead to watch Harold elicited a rain of criticism that ranged from accusations that I was criminally negligent to declarations that I was a straight-up monster.

I'd had enough advice from a bunch of permanently single curmudgeons. "I am open to suggestions!" I roared. Of course, this was followed by dead silence from the peanut gallery. "I thought so," I muttered.

"And I thought you were going talk to your friend Eldrin about what we should do next," Valdara said. Her arms were folded across her chest and she was tapping her foot impatiently.

"Right. Sorry." I studied the coin for a moment. I could feel its magic, but it was just beyond my grasp—out of reach. I grunted in frustration and ever so subtly shifted the coin under cover of the cloak. Harold was tucked in his pocket, sucking on a candy. I gently prodded him with the coin. In response, he spat the half-eaten butterscotch out of his mouth and held up three little claws. I shook my head and countered with one. He popped the candy back in his mouth and three little claws appeared again. Once more I shook my head, but this time silently proposed two candies. He rolled his eyes and disappeared into the pocket. Only when he was safely inside did a little paw with three fingers come shooting into view. I ducked my head under the cloak.

What followed was a whispered, one-way argument that I was losing spectacularly when Valdara cleared her throat again and asked, "Problem, Avery?"

I emerged from the cloak with a quick shake of my head. "No. No problem. Just establishing a connection. I'm getting some interference." I looked into the sky. "Probably all these trees."

I shot a quick glance at Sam and Ariella, and while they both looked uncomfortable, neither took the opportunity to reveal my condition. I put up three fingers and thrust the coin back under the cloak. A quick shock of power rushed through my palm and the transdimensional connection sparked to life. I hoped against hope that the Mysterium wouldn't detect the link, and that Eldrin would realize the urgency. A moment later, he appeared.

As Eldrin's image flickered to life, Sam pointed at it and shouted, "A ghost elf!"

Eldrin burst out into broken laughter. It seemed the coins were having trouble keeping in sync, because his image kept jumping around. "No . . . no . . . no, I'm a transdimensional-l-l holographic pro . . . pro . . . projection, an illusory simulacrum that can interact with my actual self, and sync t-t-time and space in the process." His imaged blurred for a second before resolving itself again. "Where are . . . are you? This connection isn't very good. I'm getting so . . . som . . . some kind of interference."

"It's the trees!" Sam said enthusiastically.

"Trees? That doesn't make any sense—"

"Never mind all that, we need help," I said, cutting him off so he would not reveal how ridiculous the thought of trees obscuring a mystical transdimensional connection really was.

"What's the . . . the . . . the trouble this time?" his image asked as it stuttered like a latter-day Max Headroom. His face grew cross. "Th-th-th-this is r-r-r-r-ridiculous. Let me b-b-boost the gain." His image vanished altogether and then reappeared, only without all the choppiness and much brighter.

A troubled expression passed across Eldrin's face. "The communicators have never behaved like that. Very strange." He stared at the coin in his hand for a few seconds, turning it over and over between his fingers.

Having seen him stay in such an attitude for hours at a time, and knowing Valdara would probably run out of patience with me in the next five minutes, I cleared my throat meaningfully.

Eldrin looked up as though surprised I was still there. "Anyway, what was your question? Something about your evil laugh?"

My eyes went wide with alarm and I made a slashing gestures with my hand across my throat to try and get him to shut up. Reverting in my panic to the only secret language I knew, pig latin, I hissed, "Otnay ere-hay! Aldara-vay is-yay istening-lay!"

What I forgot to take into account was Eldrin's literal mind and utter lack of discretion. "I think your audio stream is getting scrambled, Avery. Your words are coming out middle first. That won't do, particularly if Valdara is there listening. Let me see if I can make a few adjustments." His hands disappeared into what looked like a hole in space and there was a momentary high-pitched squeal that made my teeth ache.

The headache had arrived. I massaged my temples and muttered, "Never mind. It should be fine now."

"Don't worry, Avery," Eldrin said with a smile. "I think I've fixed it." He rubbed his hands together. "Now, let's get down to business. What's the problem? Do you need some advice on tactics? I've set up my old Trelari game and have been running dozens of scenarios—block formations, Quavashildamian skirmish and retreat strategies—"

I heard Dawn in the background. "Eldrin, give Avery a chance to talk. He called you, remember? Although if consulting with Valdara will convince you to pick up all the games you have scattered about the place, definitely do that."

Valdara's patience had officially run out. She strode between the two of us, planted her feet, and pointed at Eldrin. "We are not here to talk about battle tactics . . . at least not right now. We want to know about the key."

Eldrin arched an eyebrow. "The key? The one you and Vivian—"

"Yes! That key!" I said, cutting him off. I really didn't want to revisit my disastrous destruction of the pattern again. I stepped around Valdara and tried to seize back the initiative of the conversation. "We need to destroy the key but don't know how. We tried to use Justice Cleaver, but it didn't work."

"Well, yeah," he said, as though any other result would have been absurd. "The only question I have is whether that battle-ax is still in one piece."

"Of course I am!" Justice Cleaver roared, but then immediately let loose a groan of agony, as though the act of shouting itself was painful. "Although, it did hurt a lot," he admitted.

"Why?" I asked.

"Well, because it was really hard," the battle-ax answered.

"I was talking to Eldrin!" I shouted. The battle-ax moaned piteously at the noise, but otherwise made no further comments. I turned back to Eldrin. "Why is it so obvious to you that using Justice Cleaver to destroy the key could not work?"

"Because of the pattern that was used to imbue him with magic, of course," Eldrin said with a roll of his eyes—the ultimate sign that he thought I was missing something obvious.

I'd thought of that, and the fact that I couldn't figure out what I was missing was driving me mad. I started pacing and running my hands through my hair. "But Justice Cleaver was forged in the patterns of both Mysterium *and* Trelari. He should have been doubly empowered."

Eldrin tried hard not to show his disappointment, but I could tell from the way he wouldn't look right at me that I had made a fairly fundamental error in my magical reasoning. He let out a low whistle and winked. "It's a good thing you're so handsome, Avery."

"Enough with the wisecracks. Tell me what I'm missing."

"It's all about the patterns," he said and grabbed hold of the lapels of the flower-patterned silk shirt he was wearing, a classic sign that he was entering Socratic-mode, a particularly annoying subgenre of lecture mode where he asked a lot of exceedingly difficult questions some of which had no apparent answer. "On Trelari you used the world's core pattern to power the ax, but what about on Mysterium? What pattern did you use?"

"The Mysterium pattern, of course," I said impatiently.

"Are you sure?" he asked, in a tone that told me if I was I shouldn't be.

"Of course, I'm—" I came to a dead stop, my eyes wide. "The student pattern. I used the student pattern. That's the only one I had access to." He nodded and gestured for me to continue. "But it is only a copy of the core Mysterium pattern."

"On the other hand, the key would have been forged in?" Eldrin prompted.

"The main pattern," I answered and started pacing and thinking. "But that would mean—"

"That the only way to destroy the key would be to bring it to the main pattern of Mysterium," Eldrin said, finishing the thought.

"What does that mean?" Valdara asked both of us. "And be exact!"

I felt my stomach twist into a knot at the answer I knew Eldrin was about to give. He did not disappoint. "It means the key would have to brought back to Mysterium, sneaked into the main pattern chamber, which is in a heavily secured area of the Provost's Tower, and then exposed to the pattern's full power by a mage capable of directing that power into the key in the most destructive way possible."

"So, you're basically saying a suicide mission?" she asked.

"Well—" Eldrin began, and I knew that we were about to get a detailed explanation and statistical analysis of the odds of such a scenario succeeding. I zoned out.

Valdara was right that what Eldrin was proposing—to journey to the main pattern of Mysterium—was inviting death. However, putting that aside, which I suspected I would soon have to do, it really was a good idea. To imbue the key with sufficient power to manipulate realities across the multiverse, it would have been necessary to empower it on the main pattern. This also meant that the only way to generate sufficient power to overload and destroy the key would be to take it back onto the pattern and channel the pattern's full strength into the key.

". . . basically, to short it out," Eldrin concluded in remarkable synchronicity with my own thoughts.

Unfortunately, it turned out this was only the conclusion to the preface of Eldrin's remarks. Fortunately, we were saved from any further lecturing by a blare of horns, the shouts of sentinels, and a terrible roar that shook the castle.

"That's the celestial dragon," Drake announced.

"Impossible!" Seamus snorted. "She was bespelled to only awake if the forces of Mysterium were at the gates of the citadel itself."

"It's an attack!" declared Valdara and ran from the Council Chamber, waving a gleeful Justice Cleaver, with a cry of, "Follow me! To arms! Defend the citadel!"

"For the Light!" Drake shouted as he followed on her heels.

"Aye!" yelled Seamus, awkwardly trying to brandish a hammer and grab a shield while rushing to the door. "For honor and the forge!"

The others were right behind them, weapons drawn and spells at the ready. I started to follow but stopped at the threshold of the chamber. In the hall beyond, I could hear the frantic sounds of battle: running, shouts of challenge and screams of pain, the clash of arms. I closed the door, silencing them. But for the holographic Eldrin, I was alone.

He stared at me. "Um . . . Avery? Aren't you going to help them?"

Shame welled up in my empty breast. "They'll be fine. They have each other and a celestial dragon.

Besides, I'm not going to be a lot of help. I've kind of burned myself out." His eyes widened at this, and I waved away the inevitable questions. "That's not important right now. What is important is this." I reached into my pocket and pulled out the key. "I need to destroy this, Eldrin. I can't bear to watch another world destroyed or another of my friends corrupted by it."

"But what about your friends?" Dawn asked. "You can't abandon them."

"If I wait, they will either not let me go, or they will insist on coming with me," I said with a sigh of regret. "I don't want to risk either. This could be my last chance to slip away and do what must be done."

"You do know this attack is probably your fault," Eldrin pressed in the most self-righteous tone I've ever heard. "You pinged me with the unsecured coin—again! The Sealers obviously detected it. That was probably the interference we experienced."

I sighed again as explosions echoed through the citadel. He was right, of course. This was almost certainly my fault. I added it to my very long mental list of things for which I needed to atone. "Yes, I know," I conceded. "But destroying the key must take precedence right now."

Before Eldrin could explain why I was wrong or describe how depraved I had become, someone behind me cleared their throat. To be clear, I do not mean that this someone was behind me in a different world that had been reflected through a transdimensional connection, but right behind me in the room. I spun about and there was Rook, sitting at the table, his makeshift crutch resting across his lap. I felt the blood drain from my face.

"Sometimes bein' the slow one works out. You know, tortoise and hare, and all that crap," he said with a knowing wink.

"Rook," I gasped. "I was just . . . It isn't what . . . You see—"

"Don't panic, lad," he said with a chuckle. "I'm no' gonna turn you in. You are doin' exactly what I would have done." He stroked his beard. "What I did do for that matter—until you caught me anyway. I'd even go with you, but I need some time to get a new leg." He patted at where his limb should have been.

I let out a sigh of relief. "Thanks, Rook."

"Oh, I do no' think I'm doin' you a favor, lad. In fact, this is probably one of the most selfish things I've ever done, but I'm still gonna do it. Now, if I were you, I'd get outta here before someone notices you're gone." He pointed his stick at the door meaningfully.

I crossed the room and put my ear to the door to listen. The sounds of fighting were already starting to fade, which might mean that the battle was coming to an end. Rook was right, I needed to hurry. I turned back to Eldrin. "I need to get to Mysterium and not from Trelari. Can you bring me and Harold through to Earth?"

Eldrin scratched his head. "I could, but—" Dawn said something to him that I couldn't hear, and he shrugged helplessly. "What am I supposed to do? You know he'll find a way, just one that's way more dangerous. The question is where to bring him." He started pacing again. From the short back and forth, I thought he was probably still somewhere in New York where space was at such a premium that you couldn't even pace properly.

"Why not bring me to where you are?" I asked.

Eldrin shook his head as he marched back and forth. "It's too dangerous to bring you directly to us. The Administration could track you right to our location." He stopped and looked at my clothes. "If you take off that surprisingly stylish cloak, I could bring you to a different location in the city though. Just keep the imp out of sight."

I could hear the sound of approaching boots outside in the hall. Was it the enemy? Worse, was it Valdara? "Anywhere! Can you just do it? Now?" Then I thought of something else. "Oh, and make sure to weave a protection against summoning into it if you would. I have been popped back and forth between dimensions so many times today I think I'm getting whiplash."

"Do you want the protection to be lethal or just the 'hey, back off' kind?" Eldrin asked.

"Nonlethal, you demented elf!" I shouted. "They are my friends."

"Okay! Okay! Don't get so excited. Jeez!" I watched as he began to sketch out a fascinating little pattern on the ground between us. When he was done, he dusted the fazedust off his hands and said, "Okay, that should do it."

"Thanks, Eldrin," I said and stepped into the circle as the thudding footsteps stopped outside the door.

"No worries," he said with one of his classic crooked smiles. His image began to fade but then stabilized for a second. "Oh, one last thing, when you get here, order me a macchiato and Dawn a"—Eldrin turned and addressed someone out of sight—"a black tea. We will be along shortly."

The request sent a tingling rush of panic through my body. "Wait! Where are you sending me?" I asked as the portal illuminated at my feet. Unbidden, a green-and-white logo appeared in my mind. "Not there!" I protested. "I don't want to go there."

It was too late. Rook smiled and winked as I faded out. "Give my regards to the barista."

My mind folded inward, was shoved through a crack in the universe, and then unfolded again. I was in the back corner of the coffee shop near where the entrance to the Mysterian secret base had been. Now, some of you may remember that this coffee shop was destroyed in *The Darker Lord*, and you may be asking yourself how it was that I was standing in a perfectly rebuilt version of it. I'd like to tell you that it's an example of corporate efficiency and the sheer demand for overpriced coffee drinks. But the real truth is that it's standard practice for the Administration.

Anytime the Scalers trash something in the inner-worlds, which happens more often than you might suspect, the Administration sends out a cleaning crew to cover their tracks. They use lots of different excuses: water main break, sinkhole, natural gas explosion, red tide, and depending on the world, a dragon or a sand-worm or the like. Once the immediate danger of exposure is passed, they go into rapid rebuild mode, using magic to reconstruct the place. They then put a blanket order barring mages from visiting the location for somewhere between six months and a year and a day, to make sure there aren't too many magical "accidents" in a row.

The benefit of all of this to me is that despite its notorious past, Eldrin had probably brought me to the one place in New York where I wouldn't en-counter anyone from Mysterium. Besides, key or no key, I wanted a latte. You won't believe what passes for coffee in Trelari. There is no steam, no foam, no blending, no caramel, and no macchiato.

While I whipped off my elven cloak, being care-ful to keep Harold wrapped inside, I did a brief scan of the room. It told me what I should have known without looking, that everyone was too engrossed in their laptops, their smartphones, or in some exceedingly rare cases, each other, to pay any attention to me. If anyone had noticed my sudden appearance, they didn't show it. I got in line.

"What would you like?" asked the barista.

I ordered my usual. "A grande coffee, quad shot, nonfat, one pump mocha, no whip, extra hot. Please." A little claw poked surreptitiously out of the cloak bundle and jabbed me. "And a blueberry muffin," I added. I decided against ordering for Dawn and Eldrin, because after having been gone for so long I was perilously low on Earth dollars and was positive gold coins would not go over well.

I got my order, stuffed the muffin into the folded cloak and went to sit down at a table. I had just settled myself when my wrist blazed with pain. I only barely managed not to spill my coffee in my lap. With a muffled curse, I set my cup down on the table and pulled back my sleeve. Eight tally marks were tattooed there.

I was puzzling on this when a book was thrust under my nose. It was *The Darker Lord*, and it was attached to an attractive wrist. I followed the arm up to the face and found myself looking at Stheno, the Gorgon woman who had hypnotized me for close to a year at the bidding of the Administration. Her hair was wrapped under a scarf, but I could see slight movement there. Suddenly the tattoo made sense. It was my old spell of warning.

Naturally, I reacted with cool grace, by which I

mean I shot up out of my seat and spilled my coffee all over her.

"Ughhh! Relax," she said as she wiped the coffee from the front of her shirt. "I don't work for the Mysterium anymore. They fired me. Thanks to you . . . and this damnable book." She tossed it down on the table.

I wasn't sure how to react, or what to say, or whether I really *could* relax, or if she was actually here to kill me. The thing to do would have been to see if she was smiling or literally baring her fangs, but I refused to look at her face for obvious snake-related reasons. Instead, I shot my eyes frantically around the room. Nothing had changed, except for my heart, which was beating rapidly, and my lifespan, which had been shortened by at least a couple years. Why was she here? At this place, at this exact moment in time? Was my life that messed up? Okay, I already knew the answer to that one.

"Relax," she repeated and twisted around and down so she could look me in the eye. I quickly looked away again "I'm not here on some sinister plot," she sighed. "I got a message about you." She proceeded to lift a rather large purse onto the table. It made a loud thunk as she set it down, and I heard a distinctive "ouch!" from within. "Look inside please," she said.

I sat back down and hesitantly, ever so carefully, opened the bag. A yellowed skull stared back at me with small balefire pinpricks for eyes. "Hi, Professor.

It's me, Gray, but then you probably knew that from the stench. What did you call it? 'A mixture of rotten eggs and teriyaki sauce'?"

I closed the purse again. These kinds of coincidences should not have been happening. But then that was something I was saying to myself a lot these days. Muffled protests came from inside the purse. Stheno bent over and opened it. "Shhh!"

"Easy for you to say, sister," Gray hissed angrily. "You didn't just travel between worlds in a handbag full of feminine odds and ends only to have someone close you up in said bag like a used tissue."

I leaned forward and whispered, "Can we cut to the chase? What are the two of you doing here?"

"Talk about gratitude!" Gray said with a demonic cry. The coffee shop went dead silent, and everyone stared at us. Stheno riffled through her purse and pulled out a cell phone. "Sorry," she said to the general world and pretended to silence it. She peered back into the bag. "If you don't keep it down, I'm going to close the bag for good. Understand?"

Gray nodded, but the glare in his eyes told me he had a lot more to say on a number of subjects. Although, to be fair, his eyes were glowing portals to the infernal realms, so I'm not sure how much I should have been reading into them. Nevertheless, Stheno's threat seemed to have the desired effect. Gray lowered his voice. "All I'm saying is that this is the life of a skull. No respect. No dignity. Is it my fault that Avery decided to commit the crime of the century on my watch at Student Records? No! And yet after he got me fired, what do I get when I put myself at bodily risk? A thank-you? A well-done?"

Some perverse compulsion made me say, "Can you really put yourself at *bodily* risk, Gray? You have no body."

"Oh, ha, ha!" he said sarcastically. "Look who's the comedian now?"

"You're right. That was a cheap shot," I said. "I'm sorry. I didn't know that your helping me would put a target on your back—"

"My back! My *back*! You can't help yourself," he spluttered, which is never pleasant when you're talking about the undead. "Is it my fault that necromancy cut its animation budget so that I only came back with a head?"

"I'm sure he didn't mean it that way, Gray," Stheno said sweetly over the skull's muttered grievances. "Now, wasn't there something *else* you wanted to say to Avery?"

"Yeah," he said, and the fire dimmed in his eyes a little. "Thanks for giving me some free publicity in *The Darker Lord*. It's really helped boost my profile. I'm a bit of a folk hero among the bodiless undead. Of course, you also incriminated me as an agent of the Resistance, so I can't show my face—" I opened my mouth to say skulls don't have faces, but he silenced me down with an infernal glance. "—my face!—

anywhere near Mysterium anymore. So, a bit of a mixed blessing really. I mean I can't even go to open mic night, because I'm a wanted criminal."

Stheno cleared her throat and Gray fell to muttering again. I decided to ignore the skull. "Stheno, can we go somewhere else to talk? I'm a little nervous being in this particular place with two other refugees from Mysterium."

She shrugged. "We can take a walk, but look around us." I did, and even after Gray's outburst, everyone was staring at their smartphones again. "People here are strange," she said. "How can they not notice that my hair keeps squirming? Or that your wadded-up cloak is making very distinctive munching noises?" I swear I heard a hiss or three of agreement from beneath her headscarf.

I nodded along with them. "That's Earth for you. The inexplicable is commonplace here. Pabst Blue Ribbon selling for $44 a bottle in China, David Hasselhoff's almost cultlike popularity in Germany, or the fact that *Garfield: A Tail of Two Kitties* is the highest grossing animated film in Asia. None of it makes sense. I mean, Hasselhoff? Is it just the name? Is it his inimitable smolder?" Stheno and Gray were staring at me with identical looks of utter confusion. I realized neither had any idea what I was talking about. "The point is, who sent you? The Triflers?"

"No," replied Stheno. "They've gone underground."

"So, they're in hiding?" I asked.

"Sort of," said Gray. "They literally went into the Underground. You know, that maze under Mysterium, the one that the Architecture Department's been building for the past few centuries? The Dungeon of Deficit, we undead types like to call it. I mean really, they can afford that boondoggle but not a body for me?"

I sighed and nodded my head. The Underground is a notoriously endless Mysterium construction project. The initial goal had been to create the largest and most complex dungeon possible. To make sure they got it, the university funded several teams to compete against each other. This was a fine enough, if insane, plan, but there was a minor snafu on the paperwork. Instead of requesting an "8-year grant," someone had accidentally flipped that number sideways. Of course, no one, not the requestor or the grantor, would ever confess to the screw-up, so the money just continued to pour in. When the teams discovered that they had guaranteed employment for life, things went off the rails. It was in everybody's best interest to keep the competition going as long as possible. Each team dug deeper, made their traps more mind-bogglingly complex, and stocked them with strange and dangerous creatures from throughout the subworlds until they became veritable menageries of mythic beasts. After a time, the separate diggings began to intersect, so it became impossible to distinguish one dungeon from another. Students and professors have consumed reams of graph paper trying to map it over the years, but they are rendered obsolete almost at once.

I bit the end of my finger in consternation. "If they've gone to the Underground, they could hide forever. Assuming, that is, that they don't get zapped by any traps or eaten by wandering monsters or something similarly gruesome."

"What do they eat?" Stheno asked.

"Who?" Gray and I asked at the same time.

"The monsters."

"Oh, that," Gray said breezily. "Most of the Underground is overlaid with redundant vitality spells. As a result, they don't have to eat or drink or even sleep, and thank the gods for that."

I nodded in agreement. "Can you imagine the smell of the place if those creatures functioned naturally?"

"Maybe a mixture of rotten eggs and teriyaki sauce," remarked Gray a little bitterly.

"Leave it," Stheno warned.

"Oh, I do!" Gray retorted. "Apparently, everywhere I go! And another thing, do you have to drink coffee in front of me? Do you know how much I long for a digestive tract? Or even a taste bud? It's hell I tell you."

We ignored Gray, which elicited another round of mutterings. There was a burp from under the cloak in my lap, which I took, along with his silence and good behavior, as a sign that Harold was enjoying his muffin. In the relative peace of the moment, I asked, "If the Triflers didn't send you, who did?"

"We don't actually know," Stheno admitted. "I received a note that told me what to do. It had instructions on every detail, how to find Gray, how to find you—"

"Wait a minute!" Gray said, his fiery eyes narrowing. "I also received a note. It said that I should go with the snake, and that you would be here and would need our help. I figured it was from you, Avery."

"Me, too," said Stheno.

"I didn't send it," I said. "I didn't even know I would be coming here. In fact, Eldrin picked this location right as I was leaving, so no one could have known."

We all came to the same conclusion at the same time. Gray was just the first one to say, "It's a trap!"

Stheno shut the bag and stood up. "We need to get out of here."

In a flash, we were out on the crowded sidewalks of New York. It felt so strange being back in New York. For a second, I almost forgot about the key and what I was supposed to be doing with it. Then, after a couple of blocks and turns, Stheno pulled me into a shop doorway. "Do you know where we should go next?" she asked.

I wanted to say something like, "I don't even know why you are here," but I realized that we were remarkably close to my old apartment. "I was supposed to meet up with Eldrin. We could try our old place?"

"That sounds as good as any other plan and better than being on the street," she said and then leaned in close. "We're being followed."

I started to turn around, but she pulled me back. "Don't look, or they'll know that we know they're following us."

This is the sort of thing that people say when they are being followed, and I'll admit that it seemed perfectly logical at the time, but in retrospect I just don't get it. Why wouldn't you want your follower to know that you know you're being followed? It might discourage them from doing it. In fact, the only reason I can think to keep them from knowing is if you are planning an ambush.

"Are we planning an ambush?" I asked excitedly.

She nodded, and we pushed our way through the crowds toward the apartment building. When we got there, we figuratively flew up the stairs, which disappointingly means that we had to run up them. It made me sad to think that the reverse gravity field Eldrin and I had installed, with no small effort I might add, had been permanently dismantled, although not being able to channel magic, I wouldn't have been able to use it anyway. Eventually we made it to the fifth floor. I was surprised but pleased to find that my key still worked.

We slipped inside, and I closed and locked the door behind us. The air was stale, which meant Eldrin and

Dawn had not been here in some time. I was a little disappointed, but it was probably for the best. This place was too well-known. I'd put it down as my home address and Eldrin as my emergency contact for Human Resources, so the Administration definitely knew about it. Still, it was depressing to find it empty.

But there was not time to get sentimental. I turned on Stheno and asked, "Quickly! Who is following us? What did they look like?"

She shrugged. "I don't know what they looked like, only that they were following us."

"That doesn't make any sense," I said. "Either you saw them, or you didn't see them."

"Humans!" she said and meant it as an oath. "You are all alike. It is impossible for you to imagine the experiences of creatures unlike yourselves. Yes, I have sight that works like yours." She pointed to her own luminous green eyes. "But I also have them." She patted the scarf on her head, which gave a subtle shift in response. "One of my snakes saw a figure following us. All she can tell me is that he looked normal and boring. Actually, I think she called him plain as dirt."

"Irrelevant!" barked Gray from the purse. "The question is, what's the plan?"

I couldn't think of much that I could do without my magic. As always, my hand was in my pocket before I noticed. As I ran my fingers along the key's cool surface, I wondered if I could still use it even if I personally was burned out. I decided not to try. Several of Eldrin's favorite games were piled around the corners of the room. He would never forgive me if I erased his collection from reality.

I was still trying to come up with a plan when we heard footsteps outside in the hall. As we watched, a magical glow illuminated the doorknob. Whoever it was didn't have a key, and they were using magic, which meant only one thing: they were from Mysterium. In a rush, I hissed, "I'll jump him and hold him down while you hypnotize him."

"Right," Stheno said and reached up and pulled off her head scarf.

The sight of all those writhing serpents sent chills up and down my spine. I studiously avoided their gaze and moved to one side of the door while Stheno positioned herself opposite. I had just gotten in place when it burst open. A hooded figure that I thought was probably a man stepped into the room. I let him move past me two paces and then grabbed him from behind with a shout. It was a good thing he wasn't that big, because my headlock was not very lock-like.

As you might anticipate from everything else you've read about me, I'd learned all my wrestling moves from the WWE. At least, I thought I'd learned moves. It turned out to be harder than it looked. Thank goodness I started with a simple headlock.

Had I tried something more advanced like the DDT, the Million Dollar Dream, the Tombstone Piledriver, or the Stone Cold Stunner, there was no telling what might have happened. At a minimum, I probably would have ended up in traction.

While I continued to grapple with the intruder, Harold leapt out from the bundled cloak, which I had set down near the door, and began gnawing on the man's ankle. The struggle lasted only a few seconds. Stheno knelt in front of him, the snakes swayed back and forth, and a moment later he was snoring. I laid him down and removed his hood.

It was Sam.

"Oh, come on!" I protested. "Can my life get any more messed up?"

"Sure, you could be a disembodied skull," Gray suggested. "Well, a bodiless skull anyway."

Stheno and I both glared at him. "Do you know this guy?" she asked.

"Yes! It's Sam," I said with a muttered curse. "He must have followed me from Trelari."

"Sam, of Sam and Ariella? The ones who were on the ship with ED and EDIE in *The Darker Lord?*" she asked.

I nodded. "How long will he be out?" I asked.

Stheno shrugged and started wrapping up her hair, which hissed in protest. "I didn't hit him really hard—only three snakes. Probably no more than ten or fifteen minutes."

"Not good," I said, and it really wasn't. It had been a mistake to come back here. If Sam could track us from Trelari to Earth, then the Administration could also. I ran a shaking hand through my hair. "We need to get out of here. Now!"

"What's going on?" muttered Gray. "We got the guy."

"Yes, but I'm worried about the guys that may have followed the guy," I said and went over to pick up Harold, who was jumping up and down on Sam's chest with little squeals and grunts. I stared down at Sam's prone body. "How are we gonna move him?" I asked.

Gray cleared his . . . well . . . not his throat since he didn't have one of those, but he made a sound like someone who had a throat and was clearing it. "If you are unwilling to use your mage-like powers, Mr. Mage, then you might remember that I am a floating skull. Among my powers is the ability to float things." He stared at Sam, there was a brief flash of diabolical light and the odor of rotten eggs and teriyaki sauce, and Sam's body rose off the ground.

We were at the door before Stheno asked, "How are we going to walk around this magic-less world, unnoticed, with a body floating along behind us?"

I looked at Sam, back at her, and then back at Sam before shrugging. "Trust me, it'll be okay. If anyone notices, and in New York that isn't a given, they're bound to think we are performance artists." What I didn't say was that even if we caused a riot, it would be better than staying here and waiting for the Sealers to arrive.

Had I been paying more attention or thinking more clearly, what happened next might have been avoided, but I wasn't doing either. Instead, I reached out and grabbed the doorknob. At my touch, a sickly gray-green beam of energy struck us. My whole body started tingling and we all fell over. We were awake and aware, we just couldn't move. I hate paralysis spells.

There was another flash of light from somewhere on the other side of the room, this time of brilliant white, and I heard footsteps approaching. I cursed myself a dozen times over for my stupidity but didn't even have the pleasure of saying them aloud. What made it worse was knowing that I had delivered not just myself but also Stheno and Gray right into Moregoth's hands.

I was still composing new and inventive ways of calling myself an idiot when the shadow of a figure loomed above me. Would it be Moregoth himself or just some random and incredibly lucky Sealer who had been left on Earth in case someone like me did something stupid? My eyes, which seemed to be the only part of my body I could still move, darted up, and there was Eldrin in all his sparkly-eyed, flowing-haired, unbuttoned-linen-shirt-ed glory. "It's Avery!" he shouted.

"I told you it would be," Dawn answered from another room. "Tell him he's an idiot."

He leaned in close—gods, I forgot how good elves smell. A smile broke across his face. "It's good to have you back, but you really are an idiot you know."

CHAPTER 15

DARK TIMES AT THE DARK TOWER

Eldrin and Dawn and someone else that I couldn't quite lay my eyes on, dragged us away from the door and laid us side by side across the floor of the tiny living room. Harold had been placed on my chest and was snoring quite comfortably there. If you are worried about the effects of a paralysis spell on a young imp, don't be. I wasn't fully convinced that he *wasn't* just napping (imps being immune to all sorts of spells). Anyway, there was a great deal of coming and going and moving of this piece of furniture or that, and arguing about this spell or that, but it was hard to follow, because from my vantage point, all I could see was the underside of the couch. I couldn't even begin to count the number of dies, miniature figures, assorted bags of chips, soda cans, and unidentifiable bits and scraps that were strewn beneath it. I was relieved when the activity died down enough for me to follow along with what was being said.

"How long would you say we have?" Dawn was asking.

"Five, ten minutes tops," Eldrin replied.

"So, Avery really does live!" said a woman whose voice seemed vaguely familiar.

"Yes," replied Eldrin. "Although I'm afraid he's going to have a nasty headache when he comes out of this."

"How long will it take for them to recover?" she asked.

"Too long," Eldrin answered with an irritated huff.

"Can't we do anything for them?" she asked.

I heard something heavy being dragged across the floor and he grunted, "No, we can't."

"But surely paralysis spells are reversible," the woman argued. "I think I can even remember the spell framework from my basic Rowling course. Wasn't it *petrificus notal*—"

"Susan, stop!" Eldrin shouted.

Susan? The only Susan I knew was the green-skinned Susan from the Resistance who had helped me break into Student Records. If it was her, how had she gotten here? Would everyone I'd ever known show up in New York? Why was I so bad at sneaking away? In other stories people manage to sneak away quite successfully all the time. Okay, Frodo couldn't, nor could Harry. Come to think of it, maybe sneaking away isn't that easy after all.

When I came out of my latest thought detour, Eldrin was apologizing to Susan. "Sorry about that, but had you finished your incantation, we would all have been paralyzed in the backlash. I designed this trap myself, and it's pretty good. The paralysis is temporarily permanent. Basically, you can't dispel it for about fifteen to twenty minutes. Enough time for me to pop in and check on who is mucking about in the place. That's why it's activated when you try to leave, not when you try to enter. Once you are paralyzed, any attempt to deparalyze you will backfire on the person making the attempt. Also, and this is particularly clever, the paralysis is chained to a proximal immovability field, which means the paralyzed person can't be removed from the apartment until the paralysis wears off. I call it the Sealer Motel trap." He laughed at his own joke, and, yes, it was as insufferable as it sounds. "Get it? Sealer Motel? The Sealers check in, but they don't check out?" He laughed again. If I weren't paralyzed, I would have ground my teeth in frustration.

Susan almost managed to suppress her groaning sigh as she asked, "Okay, that explains the shouting, but why did you have us stack all those game boxes in front of the door?"

Before he could answer, a disembodied and slightly mechanical female voice announced, "Sealers approaching, dear. You have thirty seconds." By the sound of it, Eldrin had modeled it off the computer from the original *Star Trek* series—after it had been reprogrammed on Cygnet XIV.

"Well, here we go," he said, and if anything, his tone sounded a little too excited for my taste.

"What do we do?" Susan asked.

"Not a lot," Dawn replied without much enthusiasm. "Eldrin has devised a rather unique defensive screen he's been longing to try."

Eldrin could contain himself no longer. "I invoked all the protective spells I put on my games!"

"Games?" Susan asked. "How will that help?"

The sigh he let out told me exactly how disappointed he was that she didn't get it, but that didn't mean he wasn't willing to explain himself. "I designed the wards to create a multiplexed, faze-aligned, interlaced network so that when a multiplicity of them are activated and their proximity fields overlap—"

"The wards combine, and the more of them that he turns on, the more powerful the overall protection," Dawn said sharply, interrupting what was beginning to look like a classic Eldrin lecture.

"How many are there?" Susan asked.

Thousands, I answered in my head right before Dawn said, "You do understand that he didn't just put wards on each game, but on each piece of each game.

Each map. Each rulebook. Each die. Each miniature. Everything!" Dawn laughed. "Sorry, Susan, but your expression is too precious. It perfectly encapsulated the wonder and dismay I feel every time I think about how much effort my boyfriend has spent casting individual protection spells on a bunch of tiny plastic playing pieces."

"But you're not dismayed now, are you?" Eldrin asked.

"Well—" Dawn started to say, but then the lights in the apartment dimmed and flickered, and the temperature fell dramatically.

"They're here . . ." Eldrin said in a fair *Poltergeist* imitation.

A moment later his sultry ward announced, "The Sealers have arrived, handsome."

Dawn growled, "Eldrin!" as a terrible explosion shook the building. It was strong enough that bits of plaster from the ceiling fell onto my face.

"Now what?" Susan asked.

"I turn off the computer voice," Eldrin said regretfully.

"Not about that! About the Sealers!" Susan shouted.

"Oh, we wait," Eldrin said with supreme confidence.

"Dearest, your shield is down to eighty-five percent," the ward's computerized voice announced.

"Now, Eldrin!" Dawn said sharply.

"Fine! Majel, shut down!" he ordered.

"Oh, poo," Majel sulked before going quiet.

There was a brief silence. "Happy?" Eldrin asked.

"Eminently," Dawn replied.

Eldrin muttered something, and I heard drawers and cabinets in the kitchen opening and closing. This was followed by a rattling noise, which in other circumstances I would have pegged as dice rolling, but even Eldrin wasn't that mad. Or so I thought, because a moment later Dawn asked, "Why are you rolling dice?"

"Without Majel, I need them to monitor the strength of the defenses," he grumped. "They show how the aggregate of the shields is holding up." Then his voice dropped lower in concern. "It looks like she was right, the first assault knocked them down to eighty-five percent. That's a bit more loss than I expected." He rolled again.

What I wanted to tell him, but couldn't, is that the reason the attack was knocking down his wards so fast was that Moregoth was leading it. I can't tell you how I knew this, but every cell in my body was screaming that this was so.

Another blast and another rocked the apartment. I could feel the tremors running through the floor as mystical energy continued to strike the shields. The dice also continued to rattle on the tabletop. I wondered how we were doing. It was infuriating not knowing, and also knowing that even if I did know, I couldn't do anything because I'd burned myself out messing around with the key, and finally knowing that even if I knew and even if I could do something that none of this would have been necessary had I simply not been the idiot Eldrin correctly called me. Let's just say, I was at a low ebb in the self-esteem department.

Someone stepped over me. I think it was Eldrin. "They should be coming out of it soon," he said. "Let's get a portal ready so we can get out of here as soon as they are deparalyzed."

Another even larger jolt shook the apartment, rocking it back and forth. "Whoa," said Eldrin. "That was a big one. Dawn, can you roll the dice for me?"

There was a rattle and she announced, "Forty-seven percent."

"It could be worse," he said, and then quieter, "but, not much worse."

"Not much worse!" shouted Gray, who must have just come out of paralysis. "Only an elf would say something that daft."

"First one's back up," announced Eldrin. "I'll start sketching a portal."

"Start! What were you doing this whole time?" Gray asked derisively. "Instead of sitting over there chatting until they attacked, you could have been preparing our exit. It would be just my luck to be captured and made some Sealer goth's candleholder because you couldn't be bothered to do your homework. Students!" He said this last word like it was a curse.

The floor of the apartment jumped under us, and Harold tumbled off my chest with a little squeak. He fluttered back onto my chest and sat there yawning.

Dawn came over and scooped him up. "Good morning, Harold! My, how you've grown." The imp giggled. "I think you might be ready for some solid food. Do you want a mouse?" She took him toward the kitchen where I lost sight of them.

"Shield check!" Eldrin called out from somewhere near the closet we used to use for portals.

There was a rattle in response and Susan said, "Twenty-four."

Eldrin came back into view. He picked up my hand, dropped it again, and then flicked his finger at my nose. He seemed to be checking me for responsiveness, but the nose flicking I'm certain was purely for his amusement. "Susan, can you fill up three pots of water? We need to speed up this process."

If I could have widened my eyes I would have, but of course, I couldn't even do that. I just had to wait while the pots clanged together, and the tap ran and ran, and then Eldrin was standing there with a soup pot full of water. "Sorry," he said, but with a smile on his face that was not at all sorry.

With glee in his eyes, he tipped the whole thing onto my head. I shot up off the ground with a shriek that was echoed by Sam as Dawn dumped a pot of water over his head, and Stheno and her snakes, who issued an entire chorus of shrieks, as Susan poured a saucepan onto her.

"I told you they were close," Eldrin said with a satisfied smile. "All they needed was a little shock to the system."

"Dammit, Eldrin!" I literally spluttered. "Did you have to pick the largest pot in the apartment? I'm soaked."

He looked at the pot and then back at me. "No, probably not."

"So, you just did it out of malice?"

Eldrin put his head to one side in thought. "Not entirely, although I am pretty pissed that you led Moregoth to our apartment. All you had to do was wait in the coffee shop like everybody else."

"What do you mean, everybody else?" I asked.

Dawn yelled from across the room, "Can you two do this later? We're kind of in a hurry right now!"

On cue, there was an explosion, and several boxes of obliterated games came flying into the living room.

"To the portal?" I asked.

He nodded, and we jumped to our feet. Stheno was already up, leaning against a wall, but Sam was more disoriented. He was sitting on the ground, shaking his head, and repeating over and over, "Where am I? What?"

Eldrin and I each grabbed an arm and pulled him to his feet. "Time to go, Sam," I said.

"Where am I? What?" he asked.

As we made our way across the room to the closet where Dawn and Susan were working together to activate the portal, there was another explosion. A shower of melted miniatures and flaming dice pelted us as the shield gave a little more. A large crack had formed in the wall of boxes. Through it, we could see Moregoth standing on the other side. At least, I thought it was Moregoth, but he looked different. His body was wispy and flowing, like it was made of smoke or living shadow. Only his face and clothes seemed somewhat substantial.

His voice, however, was unchanged, and a deep maniacal laughter I knew all too well filled the apartment. "Avery Stewart! What a dark delight to see you again. I was hoping you would be foolish enough to visit this place again. We have much to talk about. I want to thank you for allowing me to experience the morbid squalor of the afterlife, albeit briefly. Oh, and also to wreak my vengeance upon you!" This proclamation was followed by a wheezing rasp.

As we dragged Sam toward the closet, Eldrin said, "He's right, you know, you do have a lot to answer for." He glanced toward the front door. "I'd say about forty-five mint-condition games thus far."

By the time we got to the portal, Stheno and Susan were already gone, and Dawn was stepping through with Harold in her arms. She disappeared, and we waited with Sam for the faze to stabilize.

He looked lazily between us and then focused on Eldrin. "You're so pretty." .

In silent agreement, Eldrin and I pushed him into the closet. With a flash of light, he was gone, leaving only me, Eldrin, and—I realized as a demonic cough sounded behind us—Gray. He was lying motionless on the table. "Hey! Will one of you kindly pick up the bodiless skull!" he screeched. "Seriously! Am I invisible?"

"I thought you could float! You made a big deal about being a floating skull ten minutes ago," I said, my voice right on the edge of panic.

"Couldn't have been more than eight actually," Eldrin corrected.

"Eight, ten, does it matter?" the skull groused. "Do you know how hard it is to create a levitation field when you're still half-paralyzed?" Eldrin and I looked at each other and then shook our heads. "Well, it isn't easy!"

Another explosion shook the room. Eldrin and I took a quick look around. The shield and most of his game collection were gone. Moregoth began to literally flow between the cracks in the shield like water through a shattered glass.

"I'll get Gray!" I shouted to Eldrin. "You get through the gate!"

Eldrin almost argued, but then took another horrified glance at Moregoth and dove through the portal. I really couldn't blame him. Somehow, in almost killing him I had made my archnemesis even more powerful, not to mention creepier. I really did have a lot to answer for. But now was not the time. While Moregoth reassembled his bits, I raced across the room and snagged Gray from the table.

"Ouch! My eyes! You've put your fingers in my eyes!" shouted Gray.

"Here, let me get them out for you," I growled, and doing my best impression of The Bowler from *Mystery Men*, I hurtled him across the room and through the portal as he screamed, "Noooo respect!"

I started to follow, but it was too late. Moregoth was standing, fully formed, or as fully formed as he got these days, beside the shattered remains of the door. Mounds of plastic pieces and cardboard maps smoldered around him. I edged my way around the far side of the couch, trying to put as much distance between us as I could, which I must stress was not a lot. Hell, even if we had been on opposite sides of the apartment it wouldn't have been enough. As it was, only about twenty feet separated us. I glanced at the portal, trying to gauge whether I could make it through before getting killed.

Moregoth coughed and raised an ethereal hand, which began to glow lethally. "I wouldn't try it, Avery Stewart, unless that is, you wish to feel the ghoulish embrace of sweet death."

Normally, my strategy would have been to keep him talking while I came up with a clever plan or someone saved me, but I saw no point. I was trapped. Moregoth had the drop on me, I had no magic to defend myself, and through the front door of the apartment, I could see a wall of crimson-cloaked Sealers. I would like to say that my first thought was relief that everyone else escaped, but that would be a lie. My actual first thought was, *Damn!*

I sighed and started to raise my hands in surrender, when I had my second thought, which was way more useful than my first had been. In the frenzy to buttress the door with piles of games, several got scattered across the apartment. One of them was sitting on the couch in front of me. If I could grab it, maybe it could provide enough of a shield to at least get me to the still-glowing portal. Now I had a reason to bullshit.

I raised my hands, palms out, in front of my chest in the least threatening manner possible. "I'm done running, Moregoth. I surrender."

"Very sensible, although tragically disappointing," he said with a frown. "But then again, you've always been a disappointment."

He sighed and his outstretched arm dissolved back into his body. I didn't spare a thought for how disturbing this was, but reaching down, I grabbed the game box and, holding it behind me Captain America style, ran for the closet door. I had taken no more than two lunging steps when I felt something deathly cold and extremely lethal strike me in the back. The force of the spell was so great that it threw me the rest of the way across the room.

I had no time to figure out whether I was dead or alive. There was a flash of brilliant white light, the portal spell flared to life as I entered, and then it automatically closed behind me.

CHAPTER 16

AN UNDISCLOSED LOCATION
OF MY OWN

The portal twisted me like I was performing a reverse quadruple somersault in the pike position. Of course, I nailed it. When my head stopped spinning, I saw that I was lying on my back in a big, empty, featureless cube of a room. Eldrin and the others were standing in a semicircle around me. He offered me a hand up and I took it.

"We were beginning to worry a little that you weren't going to make it," he said, and the relief in his voice told me that he had been more than a little worried.

"I almost didn't," I said, remembering the spell that hit me. I put my hands to my back to feel for a wound. There was nothing. I breathed a sigh of relief. "Moregoth had me, but thanks to your mad penchant for protecting your games and your general untidiness, I was able to make it out."

I pointed back down behind me where a large box sat, a smoldering hole blown through its center. I'm not sure what I was expecting from Eldrin—maybe a "job well done" or an expression of relief at my escape—but instead, he fell to his knees with a cry and clutched the ruined game box to his chest. "Not my 1978 original printing of *The Campaign for North Africa*."

None of us knew quite what to say. Okay, I knew what I wanted to say, but held my tongue because I had managed to destroy a collection that had taken him a lifetime to build in the space of fifteen minutes. Dawn, on the other hand, knew what he needed to hear. She put a hand on his shoulder and murmured, "I'm sorry, Eldrin. I know how special that game was to you."

He was holding the box on his lap staring at it. "It had 1600 pieces. A ten-foot-long map. Two different rulebooks. Four different books of charts. A log where you could keep track of fuel and food consumption for your units, and if you were commanding the Italian army, whether you had enough water to boil pasta." He choked up a little. "It . . . it was perfect."

"I know. I know," Dawn said soothingly, stroking his back.

Despite the absurdity of the moment, I couldn't help but feel guilty. "I'm sorry, Eldrin. I didn't know."

At first, he said nothing, although I did see the knuckles of his hands go white as they gripped the box tighter. Dawn nudged him in the back. At her prompting, he muttered, "It's . . . okay, Avery. I'm just . . . glad you're alive."

Dawn rolled her eyes, but sat down next to him, and waved for me to go away. With a shake of my head at the madness of elves, and particularly elves named Eldrin who collect games and had been my roommate for years, I left them in their "grief" and joined the others who were examining the room.

It was about twenty feet cubed and was about as plain as a room could get. The walls were smooth and gray and stone and, like most walls in Mysterium, radiated a light bright enough to see by but not so bright that there was a noticeable glow. The only obvious feature was a door set into one of the walls of the cube. Sam and Stheno were standing to the right of this door studying something on the wall. I walked closer and saw that there was a small brass plaque with some writing on it. Squinting at the small script I read, RESERVED FOR PROFESSOR AVERY STEWART. My eyes widened.

"Very puzzling," Stheno said, and her hair agreed with a series of puzzled hisses.

"Does it mean you know where we are?" Sam asked me. "Could this be another house you don't know about?"

I almost answered no, but then the significance of the sign and the odd emptiness of the room struck me. With a whoop of joy, I said, "Yes! I do! This is my private portal room."

I spun around, taking it all in. Having a private portal room may not be the highest honor a Mysterium mage can receive, but it is certainly the most coveted. I couldn't believe I was actually here and that the Administration hadn't seized it back when I turned traitor. Then again, nearly fifty percent of the contract I'd signed when I became a professor related to the issue of portal rooms and under what circumstances they could be moved, transferred, or revoked. After many centuries of negotiations and renegotiations and revisions, it basically took a unanimous act of the gods to take one away.

"But I thought you didn't know where your portal room was," Stheno said.

She was right, I didn't, but then I hadn't brought us here. Eldrin had. The question was how did he know where it was when I never had. I turned and stared at him. He and Dawn were standing over the remains of the game box, giving it what I can only describe as last rites. I moved so I was standing next to them. Their heads were bowed in respectful silence. When

I judged that we had mourned a bunch of cardboard chits long enough, I asked, "How?"

Dawn gave me a little shake of her head to indicate that it was too soon, but Eldrin muttered, "Do you mean how did I know where your private portal was, or how am I going to get over the destruction of one of the greatest accomplishments in war-gaming history?"

"Both?" I said uncertainly.

"Well, I will never get over the loss of the game," he said bitterly. "It was my retirement plan."

Now I did feel guilty. I put a hand around his shoulder. "I hope you know I never would have put it at risk had I known it was that valuable. If I can, I promise I will repay you for it. Maybe when this war is over, if we win and I'm not imprisoned or killed by the Administration, I can sell my house and—"

"What are you talking about?" he asked sharply. "How is selling your house going to help?"

"I . . . I just meant I could give you the proceeds."

He let out a sigh that was so deep that I knew at once I had entirely missed the point. "Gods, I forget how human you are sometimes," he said. "I don't mean the game was so valuable that I was going to fund my retirement off of it. I meant the game takes so long to play that I was planning on spending the better part of my retirement completing it." From the expression on my face, he must have seen that he had lost all my sympathy. He turned to Dawn for support but saw the same thing in the way her monochromatic eyes were turning darker and darker by the second. "You two just don't get it," he muttered bitterly.

"No, we don't. Because to *get it* we would have to be insane people!" Dawn said with an aggravated groan. "Now, tell Avery how you knew where this place was."

Eldrin's shoulders drooped at our lack of compassion. "Vivian wrote to me and told me where to find it."

He whipped out a piece of paper and handed it to me. There was her distinctive script, telling him that when I asked to be transported to Earth from Trelari that he should send me to the coffee shop and then it gave the coordinates to this place. But the note wasn't signed, and I was pretty sure Eldrin had never seen Vivian's writing before.

"How did you know it was from her?" I asked.

Eldrin ignored me and began grumbling to himself under his breath about ignorant Philistines, so Dawn answered for him. "He showed it to me. There's no way I could mistake her writing. I did room with her for two years after all."

Sam came over at the mention of a letter. He leaned over my shoulder to read it and immediately shouted, "Hey! That's the same handwriting from the note I got that told me you were going to try to make a run for it and where to find you on Earth."

The others crowded around. Each in turn recognized the writing and pulled their own notes out. It had been Vivian. I'm not sure why I hadn't seen her hand in all my impossibly coincidental encounters earlier. Only someone with her divination abilities could have managed such a reunion. Although, knowing she was involved didn't explain *why*. If she could see where I was going and what I was planning, why in the multiverse would she want to help *me*? The last thing she wanted was for me to destroy the key. It made no sense.

Whatever her intentions, I was both impressed and terrified by how much influence Vivian was able to bring to bear. We were chess pieces in some grand strategy only she could see. And yet, despite all her machinations, I still had the key. At the thought of it, my hand went automatically to my pocket. The feel of the key's cold, smooth surface both calmed and excited me. It whispered ideas. Filling my mind with images of what might be if I turned its power loose on Mysterium. It wouldn't take much. Just enough anger.

Dawn shook my shoulder. "Avery, come back to us."

I shook my head. "Sorry. I was thinking."

"Before you do too much more of that," she said, glancing at my hand, "Eldrin has something he wants to give you."

Eldrin himself seemed completely uninterested

giving me anything, but Dawn shoved him forward with a hissed, "Get over it! This is important!"

He shuffled forward and drew a handful of coins out of his pocket. "I've made copies of my new communicator device. Everyone should take one," he said unenthusiastically and handed them around.

Sam stared at his. "What makes this coin different from the old one you and Avery used to use?" he asked.

"'This one is a *bimodal* information transmitter that uses a blockchain-based network that is Sybil resistant and invokes thermodynamic security," he said significantly, a little bit of his normal enthusiasm returning at the subject. Naturally, we ruined his mood by not understanding a word he was saying. He gave a frustrated grunt and said, "It means we should be able to communicate securely with each other."

Speaking for all of us, Sam said, "Gosh! Thanks, Eldrin. I'm just thrilled to have my own communicator coin!"

"It's not a communicator coin," he said between clenched teeth. "It's a bimodal information transmitter."

"Right!" Sam said with a nod. "A bi . . . mood all . . . transit . . . Can I just call it a BIT coin?"

Eldrin's face went red with frustration, and Dawn led him away before he could say what he really thought.

"I see I don't get one," Gray said from where he was sitting on the floor. "But don't worry about me. I won't take it personally or anything."

"How would you carry it?" I asked. "You don't have hands."

With a puff of blue smoke that made my throat burn, he rose off the floor to hover before me. His eyes blazed with indignation. "You really don't know how to stop yourself, do you? For someone who supposedly spent a year studying necromancy, you could use some undead sensitivity training, Professor Stewart."

I wasn't sure how to respond, and thankfully I didn't have to, because at that moment the door to the chamber was thrown open and in strode Dean Yewed. He had discarded the tie-dyed robes he had been wearing the last time I'd seen him and was clad now completely in white. He held aloft his staff as Nabilac, his massive stone golem assistant, rumbled in behind him.

"Smoke rises from the Provost's Tower, the hour grows late, and Avery, the Dark Lord, comes to Mysterium seeking my counsel. For that is why you have come, is it not?" He looked at the obvious confusion on my face and added, "At least, that's what the letter said." He waved another of Vivian's notes in front of me.

Maybe it was the growing smell of Gray, or the sheer number of people and complications I was running into, but I suddenly had a splitting headache. I rubbed at my temples and said, "Please tell me she also told you what advice I was supposed to seek from you."

He tapped the piece of paper against his chin thoughtfully. "She didn't, but the most pressing issue I can think of is your publication record." I groaned as he launched into a lecture about Jack Heckel's novels. "You must understand, Professor Stewart, that while the department does support and even expect publication from our faculty, there are certain standards that need to be met. Point of fact, we are rather concerned about the nature of your last two works. I am speaking now, of course, of *The Darker Lord*." He whipped out a copy of the novel.

I grabbed it out of his hand and flipped through it. "Wow! It's out in paperback already?"

Yewed cleared his throat. "Yes, but I think you are missing the point, Professor Stewart. We expect our faculty to publish their research in peer-reviewed journals and to stick to areas in which they have subject matter expertise. Imagine if our most illustrious faculty went around writing crime fiction or novels about local parish council elections? It just wouldn't do. Take this new . . . novel of yours," he said, the word *novel* sticking in his throat. "Putting aside the over-the-top narration, why in the world did you think it was a good idea to publish an account of *everything* that transpired? It is only by my considerable powers"—the golem cleared his throat stonily— "and Nabilac's fleetness of foot and trunk space, that I'm not in the clutches of the Sealers right now. Oh, I also marked my copy with a few discrepancies regarding my description. I expect you to make corrections before the next printing."

I flipped open the book to find it bleeding with the red ink of his annotations and remarks. "Yes, sir," I said reflexively, but my mind was on larger questions: who was this bloody Jack Heckel and why were we all here? Since I knew there was no way for me to answer the first, I focused on the second. It was clear now that Vivian was behind this meet up, but why? The more people she added to the mix, the less I understood what she was trying to do.

The dean was not going to give me time to ponder it out though. "My question for you, Professor Stewart, is what you are doing here, and where is Rook? The Triflers have been looking for him for some time."

Since I wasn't sure how to answer the first question, I decided to answer the second. "Rook? He . . . he couldn't come," I said vaguely.

I had, of course, forgotten about Sam, who said quite cheerfully, "He lost a leg! He's probably trying to get Ariella to put it back on for him right now."

"He lost what?" the dean asked sharply.

"It's a long story," I said, because it was. "Do we have time to sit and talk it over? How secure is this place?"

"Theoretically, it is undisclosed," the dean said confidently.

"What's that mean?" Sam asked.

This being one of his favorite topics, Eldrin answered before the dean even had a chance to take a breath. "In order to transport somewhere, you usually have to know where the place is or, in the case of desire-driven portals like Avery's Tilt-A-Whirl-esque slip portal, at least *that* it exists. But there are ways to shield locations so that not only is it impossible to know where they are but even that they are. Places like that are called undisclosed locations. It should make it theoretically impossible to travel here unless you already know *that* it exists and *where* it is."

"Well explained," Dean Yewed said, though it was clear Eldrin had lost him at the Tilt-A-Whirl reference. "The problem is if the Administration has the coordinates."

"But according to the collective bargaining agreement the faculty signed last century they aren't supposed to collect data on personal transport rooms," I protested.

"They also aren't supposed to employ sociopaths to hunt down innocent students . . ." he said, glancing at Sam as his voice trailed to silence.

An excellent point. I found myself looking about at the corners of the barren room while he continued. "Whether or not it was at one time undisclosed, with all this traffic, Moregoth is bound to keep tabs on it from now on. I'm sorry, Professor Leightner," he said, turning to Eldrin. "I'm afraid that you won't be able to use this route to sneak into Mysterium any longer."

"Sneaking! Sneaking!" Dawn roared. She advanced on Eldrin like a storm. "You've been sneaking into Mysterium?"

Eldrin's eyes went wide with fear. "Uh . . . it's not what you think?"

"So, you haven't been risking your life to sneak back into Mysterium behind my back?" she asked, her eyes twin spots of black anger.

"Oh, I guess it is what you think," he admitted. "But it was for a very good cause. Avery needed—" He clapped a hand to his mouth, but it was too late.

Her black eyes were now fixed on me. "Avery?"

In an act of incredible bravery, I admitted, "He's telling the truth. I asked him to come back and use the Mysterium observatory to monitor Trelari in case my destruction of the pattern caused it to destabilize." I sighed, because it highlighted two more clear examples of my selfishness.

"Well, is it?" she asked me.

"I haven't heard yet," I answered. "I assumed he would tell me when he found a way to get back here."

"Well, is it?" she asked Eldrin.

He shrugged. "I don't really have enough data yet—"

Dawn was having none of it. "How much data do you have?"

"Only a dozen data points," he said with disgust. "I would need at least a couple hundred to be able to apply a Satterthwaite approximate confidence limit, much less a one-way ANOVA or a combined R&R standard deviation."

"You thought you were going to come back here hundreds of times?" Dawn and I asked in unison.

"Well, if you want it done right," he replied as though that were the only possible answer.

Dean Yewed nodded his agreement. "You should be taking notes, Professor Stewart. This is the voice of good scholarship."

Dawn rubbed her forehead. "Could you give us your preliminary analysis?"

Eldrin clearly struggled with this request, but under Dawn's unrelenting glare he finally caved. "There's been no shift. Yet! But there is a great deal of work to be done still. I really need to run some spectral analyses and get on the big scope in the main hall, and then—"

"Enough!" said Dawn. "You do realize our ultimate plan is to bring Mysterium University down, right? All of this, the spectral analyzer and the big scope and maybe even the main hall, everything"— she waved her hands around—"will be gone or at least transformed beyond our imagining."

It was the truth, but none of us had ever actually said it aloud. We stood in silent contemplation until Susan said, "But it's a good thing, right? The current system is corrupt. It needs to be brought down. That's what Avery showed us."

"True," agreed Stheno.

"I suppose," said Eldrin sadly.

"It would be nice to die again," Gray admitted.

This statement left us all preoccupied by our own morbid thoughts. It was the dean that reminded us why we were here, or at least that we were here. "Not to bring the mood down—further—but if Moregoth is tracking you all, he might be here at any moment," he said. "Which brings me back to the question you are avoiding, Professor Stewart. Why did we all receive urgent missives about you needing help? What exactly are you planning?"

Everyone was staring at me and waiting for an answer. I suppose I should have given them a story, but since my sneaking away had failed so spectacularly, I decided on the truth. "Right now, I'm not trying to win the war or bring the university down, at least not today. But I do have something that needs to be destroyed, and the only way to do that is to get it to Mysterium's true pattern."

"What is this 'something'?" the dean asked.

For some reason I was hesitant to speak openly of it, so I left my answer vague. "It is something that is too powerful and too dangerous to risk using. If it fell into Moregoth's hands or even if it stayed in my hands, there's no telling what kind of damage might be done."

The dean's look told me that he was not terribly satisfied with this answer, but to his credit he didn't push me. Instead, he focused on the BIG question.

"How in the name of the gods do you plan on getting to the main Mysterium pattern? It's only in one of the most heavily secured sections of the most heavily secured building on Mysterium."

I shrugged. "I was hoping for some help in that area."

A profound silence greeted this request. Whatever the reason for everyone being here, it was clear that they had no idea how to help me get to the pattern. But then Eldrin cleared his throat and pulled a second folded letter from his pocket. "Don't worry, I've got a plan!"

"What is this 'plan'?" Dawn asked.

"Distraction," said Eldrin.

"What?" asked Dawn.

"Well, the main Mysterium pattern is under the Provost's Tower, right?" We indicated agreement with this statement with various and sundry nods. "And the Provost's Tower, during a time of war like this, is guarded by the Provost Guard and probably the main part of Moregoth's division."

"Yes, to keep the provost safe," the dean announced authoritatively.

"So, we just need to create a distraction large enough and disruptive enough to pull the provost out of his tower. The guard and most of the Sealers will follow, and Bob's your uncle, Avery is in."

"'Bob's your uncle'? Did you let him watch *Mary Poppins* again?" I asked Dawn.

"Yes, and if he sings "Supercalifragilisticexpi-alidocious" one more time, I'll scream," she said through clenched teeth.

I couldn't help myself. I gave her a crooked smile and said, "It is something quite atrocious."

"But!" Gray shrieked. "If you say it loud enough, you will always sound precocious."

"We will have no more of that!" Dawn shouted and then let out a shuddering breath. "I want some more details of Eldrin's 'plan.' Exactly what kind of distraction did you have in mind?"

This seemed to stump him. "Something . . . big?" he suggested unhelpfully.

"Okay, so, to be clear, you never really had a plan," Dawn said.

"I did."

"One word is not a plan!" she shouted.

I decided Eldrin needed saving and said, "I think this distraction plan may work. All we need to figure out is what kind of distraction would pull the provost out of his tower."

We stood in silence for a few minutes and then Sam suggested, "What if we sneaked the Army of Shadow into Mysterium through your private portal room? We could catch the university totally by surprise. That would surely get their attention."

I don't know which of us went paler at the idea, but considering how much blood had drained from my face, I think you could have punched me in the nose and I wouldn't have bled. But apart from me not really wanting to lead an army through the heart of campus in the middle of the school term with so many innocent students running around, there was another problem with the plan. "That would be quite a distraction, Sam," I said slowly, trying to find the right words. "But presuming we could sneak enough of a force into the university undetected, an army showing up would only make the provost increase the guard on his tower. He is not exactly a 'lead from the front' kind of ruler like Valdara is."

"If an army is out, then what?" he asked.

"If you want to attack the Administration, then attack the bureaucracy," Dean Yewed suggested.

"Hey, that's not a bad idea," Eldrin said with a snap. "If we were to raise an issue within the university that required a full board meeting, then the provost would have to leave his tower to attend. They always meet in the Grandiosium."

For those of you that haven't had a chance to visit Mysterium University, the Grandiosium is a private club on campus that only full-tenured faculty, upper-echelon administration, and other dignitaries can join. I've heard Tolkien may have been a member, then again that might have been a lie. I think it likely he would have been considered too radical for membership. The point is, it is exclusive in a way that exclusive clubs on Earth only aspire to be. I've never

THE DARKEST LORD 297

been there. No one I know has ever been there. You have a greater chance of winning the lottery than of ever being invited to join. It is everything rotten and awful and elitist about the university rolled into one breathtaking piece of faux-Grecian architecture, although I'm told the clam chowder they serve on Friday is to die for.

"What could we do that would guarantee a crisis sufficient for a full board meeting?" Dawn asked.

"Well, we could file a Petition on a University Question and demand a full board hearing with oral argument," the dean proposed.

"File for a PUQ hearing?" Dawn asked. "But on what question?"

"It would have to be something they considered a threat to the university itself," the dean admitted.

There was a great deal of head-scratching at the question, except for Gray, who was idly burning rude graffiti into the walls with his death gaze, and Harold, who was too busy trying to knock the floating skull out of the air. At last, Susan's hand shot up.

"We aren't in class, you can just say it," I prompted.

"How about we raise the issue of subworld equal rights?" she asked.

I shook my head. "I don't think it would work. Maybe before the Trelarian war broke out, but not now. They are more likely to declare whoever filed the petition an enemy of the state and lock them up."

"How about something financial? That always gets their attention," suggested Stheno. "Just spit-balling, but how about adjunct professor pay? It's ridiculous how many classes they can be required to teach compared to tenured professors."

This one hit awfully close to home. Thankfully, Eldrin shot it down. "I've got a better idea," he said. "What if we file a petition on behalf of all current and past graduate students seeking overtime pay? Can you imagine the potential ruinous financial conse-quences to the university if they had to reimburse all those graduate students from the beginning of time? With interest?"

"My god, man," said Dean Yewed, whose face now matched the color of his snow-white beard. "Must we resort to such dire tactics?" He shook his head gravely.

On the other hand, Nabilac rumbled, "Overtime pay!" with as happy an expression as I had ever seen on the golem.

"It's brilliant!" Gray shrieked like a thousand out-of-tune violins being played at once. "I was a graduate student here five centuries ago. Assuming they owed me even just twenty Mysterium dollars, with com-pounding interest at a seven percent rate, that would be . . ." He shrieked with joy. "It would make me the richest man in the multiverse."

"What is compounding interest?" asked Sam. "Is it a kind of magic?"

I took hold of his shoulder, looked him straight in the eye, and said, "Yes, Sam. Yes, it is. Maybe the most powerful magic in the world."

"Cool!"

Dean Yewed cleared his throat. "Yes, well, I'm certain that will send the entire Administration scrambling, and certainly precipitate a full board meeting."

"Which will clear the way for Avery to head to the Mysterium pattern with little interference," Dawn said. "However, who is going to file the petition? All of us are kind of personae non gratae up above."

"Am not!" Sam said indignantly. "I have all my hair."

There was a confused silence at this. "It just means we aren't welcome at the university," I explained.

"Oh, that's true. They tried to kill me last time I was here," he said happily.

"Which still leaves us missing a person to file the papers," Dawn pointed out.

"If Susan can use her knowledge of Student Records to get the graduate record files, I will be glad to file the paperwork," offered Stheno. "As you all know, I can be very persuasive." Her snakes hissed their support. "Plus, unlike the rest of you, I'm not an outlaw. According to *The Darker Lord*, I'm still a loyal member of the Administration who was over-powered by Avery's magical prowess."

She ended the comment by shooting a half dozen

glares at me. Have I told you how unpleasant it is to have your private thoughts reprinted for everyone to read? No? I can't believe that. Remind me to go into it in some detail later.

Dean Yewed cleared his throat. "Yes, well, thanks to that same book, I *am* an outlaw, so I can't be the help I might have been. However, I know the Underground and can show you all secret ways into most of the buildings."

"Since it was my idea, I'll go with Susan to Student Records," Eldrin said. "Besides, the undead there swoon over elves."

"Depressingly true," Gray muttered from a cloud of blue smoke near the ceiling.

"I'm going with Eldrin," stated Dawn.

"I'm staying with Avery," said Sam.

I started to protest, but Sam interrupted me. "You know you need backup right now. Besides I can help with Harold." He pointed at the imp, who was now chewing on one of the paving stones of the floor.

"Right! Now that you all know where you want to go, I will tell you how to get there," the dean said. He pointed through the door to the hallway beyond. "Everyone going with Stheno and Eldrin to Student Records, proceed through here and to the right. Nabilac will go with you to show you the way. Everyone going with Avery to the Provost's Tower, go to the left. Gray, if you will do the honors?"

"Gray?" I asked.

"What? Don't you believe an undead skull can be useful?" the demi-lich asked.

The dean tsked disapprovingly and, putting an arm around my shoulder, led me a short distance away. He lowered his voice. "You have to be more guarded in your language, Professor Stewart. Times have changed since you were a student of necromancy. These days we are more sensitive to their needs and feelings. When we get out of this, I will have Undead Resources send you a copy of their pamphlet, *The Undead and You: Living and Unliving Together.*"

I gave a throaty growl of irritation but said nothing. There was no point in trying to explain that I'd quit necromancy, not because I hated or feared the undead but because I loathed my fellow necromancers. And, no, the monster mash Eldrin teased me about in *The Darker Lord* was not a reference to the adorably quirky 1962 Bobby Pickett song, but to a repulsive annual tradition in which the Necromancy Department would extinguish undead thralls by crushing them when they were nearing the end of their enchantment lifespans. I hope it goes without saying that I was not amused.

Of course, just as I had never told Eldrin the dark secrets of the Necromancy Department, I explained none of this. Instead, I said, "All I meant was *how* does Gray know the way?"

"He's a demi-lich of Mysterium," the dean said with a shrug.

"And?"

"And for centuries I've been taking messages from here to there and back again. The Mysterium's little messenger boy," Gray spat with disgust. "Trust me, if you want get to somewhere in the university, then I know the way."

"I have no escape plan," I admitted. "We probably won't make it out."

He gave a shrill laugh. "Are you trying to scare an undead by telling them they might die? Trust me, the second time around doesn't hold quite the same dread."

I suppose I should have said something deep and meaningful, but what do you say to someone who has decided to go on a suicide mission with you? How do you find the words? I clearly didn't know, because all I managed was "Thank you."

Gray smiled and started humming "Monster Mash" to himself. While he bounced along to the tune, the dean pulled me away again. "I don't mean to be the one to break up this little party, but I am getting worried about how much time we've spent here. This room may be foolproof, but Moregoth is no fool, and from what I'm hearing from the others, he had plenty of time to observe your open portal. If I were you, I would say my goodbyes and encourage the others to be off."

"I'll see to it," I assured him. "But before I do, I have one question about Professor Griswald's book on Trelari."

His brows came together in puzzlement. "Yes?"

"Did you really burn it?" I asked.

A sly smile passed over his face. "No. I could never bring myself to burn something so beautiful as Griswald's treatise on Trelari. It was an old copy of Lorem Ipsum I had rebound to look like his text. But I did have you going. Didn't I?"

"You sure did," I said with a laugh.

I can't tell you how much lighter my step was, as I made my way over to the others, knowing that Griswald's old writings still lived on a shelf somewhere. Particularly as they were now incredibly relevant, given that my pattern was gone and Trelari was in the process of reverting to its original form.

Stheno had gathered her group in the doorway. Sam had joined them, and he and Dawn were playing a tickle game with Harold. I went over and retrieved the imp, transferring him from her shoulder and perching him on mine. "The dean thinks we should be moving soon," I said. "But before we split up, I wanted to thank you, all of you, for doing this." I embraced each of them in turn, even Nabilac, although hugging him was like hugging a building only if the building hugged back. When I caught my breath again, I shook a finger at each of them. "Just promise me you won't take too many unnecessary risks, and if it looks like the Administration is catching on to our ploy, then leave. Whatever you do, don't wait for me!"

Eldrin laughed and said to the others, "Ignore him. He's just trying to get out of having to replace all the war games Moregoth destroyed."

"How droll," I replied in a deadpan voice. Then I put my arms around Dawn and Eldrin and said to Stheno and Nabilac, "Can I borrow these two for a minute? I just need to confirm one thing with them." Stheno nodded and I led them a little further down the passage, which, like my portal room, was painfully featureless. When I judged that we were far enough away not to be overheard, I whispered, "Why did you both think I was trying to mimic Skeletor as the Dark Lord?"

"Is that seriously what you wanted to know?" Dawn asked in something approaching a bellow. "Right now? In the middle of all this?"

"Of course," I said, because, of course.

She looked at me and then at Eldrin, who was taking my question with all the seriousness it deserved, which was a lot. She rolled her eyes and muttered, "The two of you." And then louder, "Fine. If you must know, it's because of the language you used."

"What do you mean?" I asked.

"You used to call Cravock a wimp-lash behind his back," she offered.

I dismissed the observation with a wave. "Anyone would have called him that. Cravock was literally a wimpy half lizard, half man."

Eldrin defended Dawn's point with one of his own. "Even if you accept that *anyone* would have called Cravock a wimp-lash, you also once insulted Morgarr as, and I quote, 'a furry, flea-bitten fool,' and threatened to 'cover your throne with his hide.' Which, I believe you stole almost verbatim from an episode of *He-Man and the Masters of the Universe*."

He was right of course. "Season one, episode twenty-eight," I sighed in resignation.

Dawn shook her head. "Wrong! It was episode twenty-nine, 'Prince Adam No More.'" Both of us turned to her, mouths open. "What? I thought you both knew your He-Man." When we still said nothing, she shrugged. "Too old school? I suppose you preferred *The New Adventures of He-Man*."

I saw Eldrin flush bright red with indignation, but before either he or I could launch into a defense of ourselves or how the 1983 version of He-Man—along with Danger Mouse—was the gold standard for afternoon cartoon programming, the dean shouted, "The Sealers are coming."

We ran to the doorway and saw the wall opposite give way. A black vapor with Moregoth's face and his hideous laugh poured through the opening into the room.

"Fly, you fool!" the dean cried. "Fly!"

At his command, Gray came rocketing out of the door on his blue cloud. The dean's hands blurred with action. A shield ward snapped into place between him and us, and the door slammed shut.

We stood in the hallway, staring at the closed door. Nabilac put a hand against it and bowed his head.

"Aren't we going to help him?" Susan asked.

"I agree with Susan, we can't just leave him," Sam protested. No one said anything, and his face went red with anger. "Well, if you all won't help him, Susan and I will."

He pulled out his wand and reached for the door, but Nabilac intercepted him. Reaching out a stony hand, he crushed the handle into inoperability with an effortless squeeze. Sam looked at him in disbelief, and the golem said, "We must go on! For the dean!"

"He's right," I said with all the certainty of someone who had no clue what he was doing or if it was actually right. "If we go back in there to help, our mission ends before it can begin. Dean Yewed thought it was important enough to risk his life. Let's not second-guess him now that he can't argue with us."

I won't say Sam and Susan were convinced by what Rook would call my saccharine clichés, but with the others in solid agreement, eventually they gave in. We all embraced and wished each other luck, and then we were going our separate ways. The hall was straight, but not completely straight, and as it bent, I looked back. Eldrin did the same. He gave a little smile and a wave, and then he turned and disappeared from sight.

"Well, looks like it's you and me, Sam," I said, slapping him on the back.

That's when Gray cleared his throat, a sound like kittens being tortured. I turned around and saw him hovering just behind and above us. "Sorry, and you, Gray, of course."

"He did say fly, and I assumed he meant me," Gray said with a heavily aggrieved huff. "But no, I'll just go back and die . . . again!"

"Gray, I'm sorry."

"You're sorry? It's the dean who should be sorry. After ragging on you for your insensitivity, he dares to call me a fool! Another thing, what was that crack Dawn made about needing a 'person' to file the paperwork? I used to work in Student Records. I can do paperwork. This is what I'm talking about, the world is person-centric. If you don't have a body, you're nothing . . ."

And on it went.

And on.

And on.

And on . . .

CHAPTER 17

GOING AROUND
THE UNDERGROUND

The nondescript hallway continued to bend in a slow and steady arc to the right. Now and then we passed a door just as plain and gray and unlabeled as the door to my portal room. I wondered if these led to other portal rooms for other faculty. If they were, then there was no getting into them. A private portal room was designed to open only from the inside and only to the owner, which begged the question of how Dean Yewed had managed it. It also begged the question as to why this hallway existed. Portal rooms are meant to be transit points, not destinations. No one would transport themselves into a portal room and then try to walk from wherever it was to wherever they wanted to be. They would simply create another portal.

"Gray, where are we, and by that I mean what is this place?" I asked.

"Maintenance corridor," he answered briskly. "It provides access to the portal rooms in case of eventualities."

"Eventualities?" asked Sam.

Gray nodded from atop his cloud. "You know, a mage dying during transport, or blowing themselves up during transport, or turning themselves the wrong way around during transport, or creating some human-fly hybrid abomination during transport. Stuff like that."

"So, the Administration has keys to all the portal rooms?" I asked. The skull nodded again, and I felt a righteous indignation rise up in my breast. "But according to our Employment Agreement, the portal rooms are supposed to be sacrosanct!"

"Oh, grow up!" Gray said with a derisive snort that made a little flame spurt out of his nose hole. "The Administration is also supposed to give me one night off every fifteen years. Do they? I ask you, do they?" I didn't know what the right answer was, so I guessed and shook my head. "Of course they don't. Miraculously every fifteen years on exactly my break night, some ghoul or ghast comes down with some ailment, usually minor like decorporation or disintegration, and who has to fill in? Me!"

We walked along in silence for a time, or semi-silence as Gray spent it grumbling about someone named Gary who always managed to get himself turned whenever the demi-lich had a date lined up. There were so many things I didn't want to know about Gary and about Gray's social life so I decided to try to distract Gray from his own thoughts.

"Will this hall take us to the Provost's Tower?" I asked.

". . . and that's why you never give a banshee the keys to your apartment, no matter how cute she is," he muttered before registering that I'd asked a question. "What?" he asked sharply.

"Can we take this passage straight to the Provost's Tower?"

He laughed at the idea. "Of course not. These tunnels are designed not to connect to anything. I mean, what would be the point of having an undisclosed location if anyone could stumble on it and make it disclosed?"

This left both Sam and me confused, but Sam asked the logical follow-up question first. "If these tunnels don't connect to *anything*, Mr. Gray, then how will we get anywhere?"

"I never said they didn't connect to anything. I said they weren't *designed* to connect to anything," he corrected. "But the designers of this portal cluster never planned on two things—the interminable additions to the Student Records Building and the never-ending nature of the Underground Competition. Over the years as both have expanded, their complexes of tunnels and chambers and sub-basements have encroached on any number of other underground parts of the university. Shortly, we shall take a detour through a janitorial closet and be in the actual Underground, and that will take us where we need to go."

Sure enough, after about five minutes more walking, Gray led us through one of the nondescript doors, and we found ourselves in a tiny room filled with brooms and mops and a shelf loaded with cleansers and rags and other tools of the cleaning trade. I had never noticed before, but cleaning supplies look pretty much the same no matter how exotic the world or how magical the residents. Gray instructed us to pull the shelf away from the wall. We did and found a grate about four-feet high behind it. This pivoted on a hidden hinge, revealing a low passage.

Stooping low, we followed this and soon stood in a narrow hall that did not have the advantage of a magical light source of its own. Illuminated only by the glow of Gray's eyes, it seemed to stretch greenly and demonically into the distance. This hall was different. It was rough-hewn and seemed to meander along, curving one way and then another, but consistently upward.

We were fortunate to have Gray with us, as he seemed to have a downright infernal sense of direction. After some prodding he also admitted to having worked on part of these tunnels at one point during an externship ("Back when externships meant real work," he said). Of course, having him in the lead was what started the trouble. As I described in *The Darker Lord*, demi-liches propel themselves on a cloud of noxious nether gas that, at the time, I described as being what you'd get if you mixed rotten eggs and teriyaki sauce. I also said that after a while you go nose blind to it. That was a flat-out lie. After about twenty or thirty minutes walking in his wake, my eyes were watering and my throat was beginning to clench like a vise. Sam was wheezing beside me, although that might have simply been a symptom of his general lack of fitness.

"We need to stop," I gasped.

"Why? I know this place like I once knew the back of my long-lost and still-rotting hand," Gray shrieked, which I must reemphasize was his normal speaking tone.

"Yes, but . . ." I looked behind me and Sam was bent over, hands on knees, I think trying not to retch. I lowered my voice. "It's Sam. You're so competent and sure. I think he feels like an unnecessary appendage . . . I mean a third wheel," I hastily corrected, not wanting another lecture on my insensitivity. "I was thinking if you were to allow him to carry you, he could feel like he was playing more of a role. Even though you and I would know you were guiding the way."

He turned about and swept his sickly gaze over Sam. "You have a point. He seems particularly pathetic, even as mages go. All right, I'll do it." Before I could thank him, he added, "But you'll owe me one."

Gray cleared his throat, which I won't even try to describe as this is meant to be a PG book. "Creating my levitating cloud is tiring me," he announced in a suspiciously slow cadence. Then he turned to me and one of the fiery embers momentarily vanished. I think it was meant to be a wink; at least, when I winked back, he seemed satisfied. "I need to be carried from here on."

I looked down at Harold, who I'd taken into my arms from where he'd been resting comfortably behind my neck in the hood of Ariella's cloak. I looked down at the still-struggling imp and shrugged. "I have to hold Harold. Could you take him, Sam?"

"Of course," he said with a happy smile. "I've always wanted to carry around a skull like one of those sorcerers in the picture books."

To my nose's great relief, Gray turned off his cloud and dropped into Sam's hand. "Keep moving," he ordered. "Don't worry, it won't be much longer now."

Despite his reassurances, we continued on and on—always upward, slightly upward, or even only ever slightly upward, but still irritatingly upward—

for what seemed, even to me, to be a great deal of time. Harold had time for food, a nap, a change, a period of heartrending activity during which he kept trying to grab anything that he could get his paws on. Even I started to feel an aching in my feet and knees, and from the pain in my toes, I knew I had at least two blisters forming. That's when I remembered that the concept of time to a being like Gray that's been dead for centuries was not to be trusted. I was about to ask what he meant by "not much longer" when we turned a corner and there was a door. It was a real honest metal door, marked with an elaborate rune, and set into a well-carved archway in one of the passage's walls.

Both Sam and I shuffled to a stop. Gray asked, "What are you doing? Straight on."

Sam pointed at the door. He had been suffering even more than I had. His cheeks were pink and he was puffing. "Door?" was all he said.

"No! We go on!" Gray barked, which demi-liches should never be allowed to do.

So, we did. As we went on, the texture of the dungeon walls began to change. More and more the wall to our left had a smooth, finished look to it, and we kept passing doors: a triangular door with eyes carved on its face, a ponderous wooden door with ever-burning torches mounted on either side, an eerie circular door framed by a stone carving of a snake. Gray did not even pause but continued on his course, following the path of this endless, upward, cavernous hall.

At last, we came upon a double door of polished alabaster set in an alcove. A reflecting pool fed by a trickling fountain lay in front of the door and a gracefully arching bridge seemed to invite us across. When Sam and I hesitated, Gray fixed his sickly gaze on us and ordered, "Move on!"

"Why?" I asked, crossing my arms over my chest and decidedly not moving. "Where are we going?" I pointed at the door. "We are obviously trying to get to the Provost's Tower but we've walked far enough to have circumnavigated the university two or three times!"

"Ten, actually," Gray said with irritating smugness.

"Ten?" Sam moaned and sat heavily on the foot of the bridge, the demi-lich cradled on his lap.

"Ten!" I shouted and regretted it as the hallway echoed with my shout for far longer than it should have.

Gray rocked back and forth in Sam's hands in what I assumed was a nod. "Of course, how else do you expect to get to the Provost's Tower?"

If I could have strangled him, by which I mean if he'd had a neck, I would have. Instead, I pulled my hair and shouted, "Not by going in circles around the university! The Provost's Tower is in the dead center, so we need to go toward the center! Not go around and around and bloody around the outside!"

"Avery's plan does seem better," Sam said, having finally caught his breath.

Gray grinned. "Look how smart you mages are! Stupid skull running you in circles? Shortest distance and all that, right?"

"Right!" Sam and I agreed.

Gray's smile vanished, and I realized I needed to be more specific. "I meant right about the straight line, not about the stupid thing. I know you're not stupid. I just don't understand the plan. We need to get to the Provost's Tower as soon as we can."

The demi-lich shook himself. "No! We need to get to the Provost's Tower alive."

"Granted," I said.

"I wouldn't take that for granted, Professor Stewart," he said with chilling menace, the embers in his eyes settling into a truly demonic glow. "The Provost's Tower is the most heavily guarded structure in a world of paranoid mages. Trying to enter it from below is hideously difficult. Do you know why the Underground Competition was started in the first place?"

Sam and I shook our heads.

"To stop people from doing exactly what we are trying to do. The idea was to prevent people from tunneling into the tower by building a web of dungeons around and below it so densely intertwined, so bafflingly complicated, and so absurdly lethal that anyone stupid enough to try to dig their way in would be caught up in it and killed. These doors we've been passing mark the twisted boundary of the Underground. Any one of those doors leads you straight into that mess."

"So, what's the passage we've been walking along and walking along and walking along?" Sam asked.

Gray turned around in Sam's hand to address him directly. Sam's expression told me he wished Gray hadn't. The mage put the demi-lich on the ground and stood at attention. "This is a maintenance tunnel to the Underground. As the competition went on, it became harder and harder for teams to access their own digs without going through someone else's. An agreement was reached that there would be one tunnel carved that no team could alter. Each team was allowed to put a single door from the tunnel to their dungeon complex. A 'backdoor,' so to speak. This is that tunnel."

I was confused. "If the Underground was designed to be a bulwark against tunneling into the Provost's Tower, then presumably the Underground itself never actually touches any of the subterranean parts of the tower."

"Correct."

"And this tunnel skirts the outer circumference of the Underground?"

"Correct again."

His smile told me he was genuinely happy I was following along, but I was more confused than ever. "Then how can we ever get to the Provost's Tower from here? Won't there always be parts of the Underground between us and it?"

Gray simply laughed. Another thing demi-liches should never do. After the ringing in my ears stopped, I heard him say, ". . . and that's why living mages are so limited. They've simply never had the experience of worms burrowing through their brains."

"Excuse me?" I asked, while Sam stumbled back in horror and almost fell into the reflecting pool.

The demi-lich let out a rattling sigh. "I said, that would be true if the diggers had been working from any sort of plan. In that case, you would design the Underground to grow ever larger the closer to the surface you were, creating a sphere or cone of protection around the Provost's Tower. But because the Administration wanted to make it random, and gave no one any plan, that didn't happen. There are areas where the Underground is thinner than others."

"So, we are going to use the Underground to get into the Provost's Tower?" Sam asked.

"Not exactly," Gray replied. "We are going to use the Underground to get into the basement of one of the buildings not far from the Provost's Tower. Can you guess which one, Avery?"

I thought about the many quads that led off from the Provost's Tower. There were six or seven, depending on the season. And on one was . . . "Student Records!" I said with a happy clap, that unfortunately woke Harold from his latest nap.

"Why is that important?" Sam asked with a groan as he carefully lowered himself to sit on the bridge.

While I mixed up a new bottle, Gray explained, "The Student Records building has its own underground, that may be as complex as the Underground itself."

"It's certainly more bureaucratic," I said, while Harold snatched the bottle from me and then, to my great surprise, ripped the top off and started guzzling, leaving rivulets of pureed mouse dripping down his chin.

"You may need to move on to sippy cups or even solid food, my friend," Gray said with a hiss. I had to agree.

Sam sat up and said, "Wait!"

"Why?" I asked. "He clearly is ready to get off the bottle. Dawn actually fed him a solid mouse and he seems fine." Gray nodded his agreement.

"Not about Harold!" Sam said and ran his hands so vigorously through his hair that he left it standing on end. "About Student Records. Weren't the others also going to Student Records? Couldn't we have all gone together?"

Gray and I both couldn't help but laugh at the suggestion. I held up a hand to forestall Sam's further protestations. "We are not trying to be mean, but it is easy to forget you don't know anything about Mysterium. Saying that Eldrin's group is also going to Student Records is equivalent to saying that we both want to visit Trelari. The building is vast, and the section that we are going to could be miles away from the section they need to reach."

"It's actually about seven and a half leagues," Gray specified.

"Well, what's so special about this part of the building we are going to?" Sam asked.

"Good question," Gray conceded. "You are right that the extensive nature of the underground part of the Student Records building means that there are actually many places where dungeon complexes of the Underground and portions of Student Records touch. But there is one point in all of this vast underground jumble where a dungeon of the Underground hits a sub-basement of Student Records that itself also nearly touches one of the underground levels of the Provost's Tower." The demi-lich's eyes lit up with excitement. "That is our destination."

"Don't the Sealers know about this place?" asked Sam.

"Possibly they know about the connection between Student Records and the Provost's Tower," Gray admitted. "It is fairly well traveled by messengers between the two. But almost no one knows how to get to it from where we are. Also, there are confusion, misorientation, and misdirection spells all around us to keep people from using this tunnel as we are. They're designed to send the unauthorized directly through the first door they see. Have you noticed how you and Avery have been tempted to enter every one we pass by?"

We both nodded and Sam asked, "Why aren't you affected, Gray?"

I was beginning to suspect Sam's curiosity was less a function of him wanting to know about the Underground and more about giving him time to rest his feet. I noticed his boots were off and he'd been dipping his toes ever so discreetly into the pool. Unfortunately for him, Gray finally caught on.

His eyes blazed. "Because you can't confuse an unliving skull with underground trickery. This is literally my element. Now, enough questions, it's time for us to move on. And if you don't want your feet to turn to stone, I'd advise you to remove them from that pool."

"Stone!" Sam shouted, jumping to his feet and frantically toweling them off with his socks at the same time.

"Or so I assume," the skull added with an evil grin.

Sam either didn't hear this proviso or didn't care. He danced from foot to foot, wiping one and then the other, all the while bouncing from heel to toe to see if any stiffness was setting in. Harold joined in the wild dance, screaming and shouting and trying to steal Sam's socks. Suffice it to say, it is a good thing Sealers weren't near us, because they would have caught us with our . . . well, with our socks down anyway.

I coaxed Harold into submission with two candies, but it took a good five minutes for Sam to be convinced that his feet were going to be fine. Even then, he was so preoccupied with them, bouncing up and down on his toes or suddenly taking his boots off to feel for hardening, that I had to carry Gray.

There is not much to say about the rest of our journey. The hall continued twisting and turning and climbing, Gray kept up a constant chatter of bad jokes, Sam continued fretting over his feet, while I kept myself distracted from them and the increasingly uncomfortable pinch between my first two toes by trying to come up with a plan for what we were going to do once we actually reached the Provost's Tower.

I was in the midst of a highly improbable solution involving the construction of a large wooden rabbit when Gray announced, "We are here!"

I nearly dropped the demi-lich in shock. Meanwhile, Sam was on such autopilot that he kept going for about twenty more feet before the words sunk in. He rocked to a stop and spun about, mouth open. "What?" he asked, but it sounded more like, "Whaaaaaaat?"

"Right through that door," said Gray casually.

Sam and I turned together and looked at the door. It was nothing special. Okay, that's not true. The door wasn't so much a door as an elaborate metal gate formed into the shape of a spiderweb with a handle set in the middle that resembled a gothically evil spider with glowing ruby eyes. A breath of air issued through the gate that spoke of death and decay within. It was cool in an evil, *you're going to die if you come in here* sort of way. What I meant by nothing special was that we'd passed so many different bizarre or ominous or threatening doors along the way, and one that I swear was identical to Boo's in *Monsters, Inc.*, that I could see no reason why this one should be it.

"So, through there?" I asked, pointing at the gate and shuffling closer. Another sudden gust of air came out. I coughed.

Gray shifted in my hand, nodding. "We just need to walk through that gate, take a right, another thirty feet, find the secret door, turn left, go through the filing cabinet, and we should be inside the Provost's Tower."

"Filing cabinet?" I asked.

"It will make sense once we get inside," he said authoritatively, an attitude that was ruined when Harold poked a claw through his ear hole. He tried to shake the imp off, but Harold only thought it was a game.

Sam was inspecting the gate carefully. "What do you think, Sam?" I asked.

"I don't like the smell of it, but I'll take it over more of this walking," he answered pitifully.

With Gray held in front of me to light the way with his eyes, I pushed the gate open. Did it squeak? Do people carve pumpkins on Halloween and eat too much candy and wear sexy whatever-it-is costumes? Yes! The gate squeaked ominously, hideously, and oddly it continued to squeak even after it had stopped moving. That's when I saw that the spider handle had skittered to the side and was shrieking.

I tried to shoo it away, but it kept dodging me and making that awful high-pitched noise. It ran here and there across the gate and only shut up when we were all inside and I had finally slammed the gate closed behind us.

"Bloody thing!" I roared.

Of course, that's when I realized how dark and quiet and creepy and smelly the dungeon was. I slapped a hand over my mouth, but the echoes continued for a good minute. When everything was quiet again, Sam illuminated the end of his wand, but even with that and Gray's eyes fully lit, it was impossible to see my hand in front of my face. From what I could feel of the walls, they were rough, like the passage, but the air was filled with the tattered hangings of what I assumed were decayed webs. It smelled like a cesspit filled with body parts and the despair of lost children that had been blended together and left to marinate in the sun.

We stood in silence. There was no obvious direction to move in. There was a feeling of space in front of us and instinctively I stepped back, thinking to put the gate at my back. But when I did I felt nothing but stone. The gate was gone!

"The door has disappeared," I hissed.

"Of course it has," Gray said calmly. "The entire point is to trap people and kill them. Unless you have the pass key, the only way out is through the other end!"

"That makes sense," I whispered, trying not to panic. "So, we need to go through this dungeon?"

"Are you kidding?" he said with a howl of hushed laughter. "We'd be dead in ten minutes. If we were lucky."

"Is it that dangerous?" Sam asked.

Gray shrugged. How can a skull shrug? All I can say is that when you see an animated skull shrug, you'll know. Anyway, he shrugged. "Well, there is a giant spider somewhere in here that is pretty much immune to magic and a drop of whose poison could kill an elephant. And I mean Tubul, Jerakeen, Berilia, or Great T'Phon, not just any elephant." This reference went right over Sam's head, but I knew what he was saying, and it wasn't helping my nerves. "But none of that would matter if Avery could still cast spells." His little demonic embers flickered up to my eyes and away again.

"That's why I'm here," Sam said with way too much enthusiasm. "Avery brought me along because, well, he is magically challenged right now."

Gray looked at Sam as if he'd sprouted . . . actually, never mind. Sprouting heads and arms is way too commonplace in Mysterium. Let's say, like he was crazy. "You knew he was magically impotent and came on this mission anyway? Either that's true friendship, or you have some hellacious life insurance you want someone to be able to collect on."

Sam laughed. "You're funny, Gray. Now, which way do we go?" He started walking forward.

"If you want to die and cash in on that policy now, take about six more steps forward," Gray answered. Sam stopped in midstride, his foot wavering in the air. "Otherwise, follow the wall here to the right and don't take your hand off it for a second."

Sam swallowed, and once he was safely back in contact with the wall, we set off. I was holding Gray tucked against my chest with my left arm, with Harold perched behind my head in the hood of my cloak. I held out my right hand to the wall, feeling the rough surface under the tips of my fingers, making sure to keep a connection.

We'd been walking along for less than five minutes when Gray said, "Stop!"

I realized my eyes must have adjusted to the dark, because I could see Sam's faint silhouette as he turned around, and the dim ball of light on the end of his wand bob and dart as he pointed it this way and that. "What is it?" he asked.

"Nothing much, except we're here," Gray answered.

"What, in the Provost's Tower?" I asked.

"Of course not. We're still in Team Itsy-Bitsy's little shop of horrors, but this is where the secret door is supposed to be," Gray answered, turning to stare at the blank wall. "Now, I just need to find the mechanism," he mumbled under his breath. "The guy said it would be the second rock to the right of the crack."

I scanned the area. It didn't look much different than any other part of the dungeon. "How can you possible know this is the spot?" I asked. "The wall looks the same, and in every other direction, there is only darkness and decay."

"Because I know," Gray answered gruffly, while scrutinizing the wall.

"And all these sticky, creepy webs."

"Trust me, this is the thin bit I was talking about," he muttered. "I can feel it, but there are a lot of cracks and rocks here."

"And an enormous pair of eyes, all red and glowing."

Gray was too preoccupied to hear me, because he continued in a brisk voice, "You see, one of the student externs working with the Itsy-Bitsy Spiders found out there was about ten feet of wall between him and an archive of old exams, and so—"

"Spider!" I shouted and pointed up.

"No!" Gray corrected. "He created a secret passage, so he could get in and study them whenever he wanted."

For some reason, rather than panicking as the eyes moved in, ever more quickly, growing larger and larger as they came, I found myself answering quite calmly, "No, I mean there is a giant, monstrous spider that is about to devour us all."

Sam answered with an "eeeep!" while I turned Gray about and pointed up.

"AHHHH!" he screamed, yet another sound demi-liches should not be allowed to make, as it resembles the noise you would make if you put your own hand into a blender and turned it to puree.

"Turn me back around, quickly!" Gray shouted.

While I did that, Sam began to fire off bolts of flame at the eyes. Despite the vast size of the thing, or at least what I assumed was its vast size given the diameter of the eyes and their distance apart from each other, it was quite nimble. It jumped about, dodging and weaving. A web came shooting out of the darkness and struck just above my head.

"We need to hurrrrry!" I urged Gray.

"I knooooow!" he shrieked, mimicking me as well as he could, considering again that his normal voice sounds like a puppy getting a root canal while Pavarotti sings old Iron Maiden songs in a full death growl. "Now let me focus!"

I squinted at the wall, trying see what he was looking for as he began muttering to himself, "Don't worry, it's easy, Gray, second rock to the right of the crack. Bastards! Like trying find a pebble in a quarry."

I left him to it and tried to see if I could help Sam, but he was doing great. While he hadn't been able to score a direct hit, the flaming balls he was firing had begun to ignite the webs. Suddenly a tracery of blazing oranges and reds was mapping the dungeon before us. The chamber was enormous, with a cavernous ceiling arching high above, weird passages with branchings and twistings going this way and that, and a variety of sudden drop-offs, pits, and odd dead ends. And webs—everywhere—webs and more red eyes attached to bulbous bodies. Gray had been right. Had we ventured more than ten feet into that room, we would have been lost in no time.

Luckily, Sam was in full kick-ass mode. Earlier the spiders had been dancing their way toward us, but now they were in full retreat. We could hear their piercing shrieks of terror as they tried to escape the flames.

"Good news!" I said to Gray. "Sam has them on the run."

"Better news, Avery!" he said and his eyes were blazing with excitement. "We're in!"

A ray of devilish light shot from his eyes and hit a pebble that looked like every other pebble in the wall, although it *was* to the right of a crack. The wall gave a shuddering sigh and twisted in on itself. I tensed myself for what might be beyond, but as Gray had said, there was nothing but rows and rows of filing cabinets stretching into the distance as far as my eyes could see.

"Anytime you're done playing with those spiders, Sam!" I cried as I stepped through the door with Gray and Harold.

CHAPTER 18

OUT OF THE FIRE
AND INTO THE FILING ROOM

Sam followed moments later, silhouetted by the burning webs from the chamber beyond, and he looked every bit the badass mage I knew he was. Unfortunately, in typical Sam fashion, he ruined it by tripping over the doorjamb and launching a fireball down one of the corridors of filing cabinets.

We all watched, horrified and powerless, as the glowing ball got smaller and smaller and smaller until . . . Boom! It hit the wall at the far end of the room, which really was an absurd distance away. At first, I thought maybe it wouldn't be that bad, but a second later a blast of heat and light came rushing back at us that smelled of dry paper and ash. In a heartbeat, an inferno was blazing at the other end of the room. It sounded like a tornado or freight train, which sound very similar anyway, so maybe it sounded like both. Anyway, that tornado freight train was advancing at us slowly but surely.

"Tell me we don't have to go that way," I pleaded.

"We have to go that way," Gray said with a hissing sigh.

The door ground to a close behind us, leaving a wall on which was mounted a board full of numbered cards stuffed into a grid of identically numbered slots.

"I guess there's no going back?" I asked Gray.

"What? Into a flaming hellscape of giant spiders? Be my guest," he answered with evil snark. "But if you've not suddenly become suicidal, grab me chit number six-six-six."

I rolled my eyes. "Seriously?"

"Look, we are the undead. Originality isn't exactly our strong suit. Just do it!" he shrieked.

Somewhere halfway down the room, the fire must have hit some old parchment, or paper dipped in kerosene, because there was an explosion and several filing cabinets launched themselves into the air. I stuffed Gray under my arm and ran my finger along the slots until I found a weathered card printed with the number 666. The griminess of it told me a lot of undead had handled it over the years. I reminded myself wipes weren't just for toddlers and picked it up.

I put a hand out to Sam and got him to his feet.

"Sorry about the"—another explosion rocked the room—"the whole fire thing," he said ruefully.

I waved off his apology. "Don't sweat it. Who really needs a millennia of old exam papers anyway?"

"If you two are quite done," Gray barked. "We need to run!"

We did, racing down the endless rows of filing cabinets, while Gray barked out the orders. "Right! Left! Right! Right! Right! Right!"

Yes, I know four rights is a loop, but trust me we did it and found ourselves running along a row of wooden cabinets—and some that I could swear were made of bone—all about twice my height and holding hundreds of drawers so thin that each might have contained one or two sheets of paper at most. The flames had reached us, but only on the left side. I prayed to the gods our next direction would be right again, away from the blaze, but of course they weren't listening.

"Straight!" Gray shouted.

I looked ahead. There was a crossing, but flames would be on both sides. I reached behind me, grabbed Harold, and stuffed him in an inside pocket of the cloak. Then I pulled the hood up over my head. I turned and shouted back at Sam, "Flames ahead! Get ready!"

His eyes went wide, but he put on a little burst of speed so that he was right on my heel when we hit the inferno. Fire raged on both sides of us, creating a tunnel of heat and smoke. It was hard to breathe, and I could feel the flames licking at the cloak. Ahead, I could see the end of the row. There seemed to be no other exits.

"Where to now?" I asked Gray.

"Straight ahead!" he shouted over the roar of the flames. "The cabinet at the end is number 666!"

Of course, given my history with prayers and deities, we were still twenty feet from the cabinet when it burst into flames. I skidded to a stop. Sam crashed into my back.

"What are you doing!" Gray shrieked.

After my spine stopped shuddering, I said, "The cabinet is on fire!"

"It does that all the time!" he shouted as though that were the most obvious thing in the world. "Now, run before you get us all killed, and hold the chit out in front of you."

I hesitated for a moment, glanced back the way we came, only to see three or four cabinets collapsing across the path. We were trapped. I grabbed hold of Sam's arm. "I don't know if this going to work but keep your hand on my cloak." He grabbed hold.

"Run!" Gray howled, and the howl alone was enough to start me running.

With a scream of "I hate Student Records!" I held my hand out in front of me and ran headlong into cabinet 666.

I was still screaming when I realized I was sprawled, head down, across several stairs of a stone staircase that spiraled out of sight below me. The air was blessedly but deathly cold.

"Are you quite done trying to announce our position to every Sealer in Provost's Tower?" Gray snapped.

The hair rose on the back of my neck. I could feel the tower looking for me. I had a sudden urge to reach into my pocket and check on the key, but instead clasped my hands together to keep them from sneaking off. "We're in the Provost's Tower?" I asked.

While I still don't understand how Gray can smile being a skull, I swear that he grinned evilly. "Yes, the very one, and get your knee out of my nose before I incinerate it."

I pulled myself together and then helped Sam pull himself together. We sat side by side on a stair with Gray wedged between us and caught our collective breath. Well, Gray didn't. As we all know, he doesn't breathe. He was humming some hideous tune that sounded like "Sussudio," but I decided even Gray wouldn't sink that low.

"What are you doing?" asked Sam.

"What?" I asked.

"Well, your right hand keeps trying to creep its way into your cloak pocket, and your other hand keeps trying to stop it, but this time it didn't succeed."

He was right, I could feel the key at my fingertips. The metal was cool and smooth as always, and the power crept through me. My heart pounded in my chest, and I wondered, since we were so close, if I should use the key now. Maybe I could pull the tower down around us. Dismantle it stone by stone until I found the provost, and then dismantle him cell by cell. I could then assume my rightful place as head of Mysterium!

It was this last vision that broke the key's spell. I shook my head and pulled my hand slowly from the cloak.

"Sam, if you see that hand creeping again, make sure you let me know." I grasped his shoulder to keep it from doing just that.

"I don't want to stop your game of patty-cake or whatever, but can we get moving?" Gray asked in that gratingly snarky way of his. "I've brought us to a little used area of the Provost's Tower, but this is still the heart of the Administration. Sealers will surround us from here on out."

"Before we go anywhere, exactly where have you brought us?" I asked him. "And what in the name of all the gods was that cabinet we went through?"

Gray tilted to one side, perhaps gathering his thoughts, and then said, "Well, you know how the Administration uses the undead to transport messages? It grew tiresome for us to go all the way from Student Records across all those quads with all those able-*bodied* students throwing their fazediscs and flaunting their limbs. So, we decided to create a short-cut. Thus, the cabinet. And *this* is an old servants' stair that winds a little more than halfway up the height of the tower, and a little more than halfway down the underground bits. We rarely are asked to go even half that in either direction anyway, and if we have to go higher or lower, they assign us a guard escort."

I thought about this and a plan, or at least the first inklings of a plan started to form. "And how often is this passage used?"

Gray shrugged. Again, you'll need to hang around a demi-lich for a while to know what I mean. "We'll probably run into some of my fellow undead here and there, but I can talk us past them. The question, O Magey One, is what we do when we get to the first secure level?"

Something about this stair was speaking to me, I just needed time to listen. So, I sat with my head in my hands and thought. After a time, during which Gray got increasingly antsy, I asked, "How many levels down can you go before you hit the first security checkpoint?"

Gray considered the question before answering. "Not very far. There are three levels of storage and another five or six levels of unclassified archives, but beyond that it's all restricted."

That was about what I'd expected, and I nodded the confirmation of my suspicions. "What about up?"

The demi-lich's eyes narrowed in confusion. "Up?"

"Yes, how far could we go up until we hit a check-point?"

"At least to forty-five or forty-six," he answered. "Below that are the administrative offices that deal directly with students, but—"

"It's perfect!" I said, jumping to my feet. "Don't worry, guys. I have a plan," I assured them. This wasn't exactly true, but it was truer than it had been a few minutes earlier. I picked up Gray. "Right, let's get started."

Sam got to his feet and we both started walking in opposite directions, me going up, him going down. "Where are you going?" I asked.

Sam pointed down the stairs. "Isn't the pattern that way?"

"Yup," I answered.

"But we're going up?" Gray asked.

"Yup."

Sam and Gray looked at each other. "I don't know, kid," Gray said. "He's one of you."

"I can explain later," I said as I began to climb. "For now, just trust me."

From behind, I heard Sam mutter, "Why is it always up?"

We had climbed a dozen floors when Sam, wheez-ing now, finally broke down. "I need to know what this plan is, Avery. Something to give me the motiva-tion to keep climbing."

"The plan is that we find the pattern, I take the key onto it, and melt it to scrap. Afterward, we do our best to escape?" I hadn't really thought much past destroying the key. I figured that, kind of like the big bang, once it happened everything would be different, so planning what to do next seemed pointless.

Sam nodded but then shook his head. "I meant, how are we going to get to the pattern when we seem to be moving away from it?"

"That is a good question," Gray agreed.

I had kind of wanted to keep that part secret, because it was either very clever or very stupid, and I didn't want to know verdict yet. But if talking would keep Sam moving, I would talk. Luckily, I only made it as far as, "You see—" when we heard someone, or I should say smelled someone, coming down the stairs at us. Again, I can't be sure, but from the smell alone it had to be a demi-lich, probably an Administration messenger.

"Quickly, you fool, put me down," Gray hissed. I did and half a moment later, and several hacking coughs on my part, he was levitating in front of us. "Put the wand away, Sam, and hide the imp, Avery," he ordered. "Let me do all the talking and try to look as vacant as possible." As he turned back around, I distinctly heard him mutter, "At least that part should come naturally to you."

Sam and I did as he asked, and I'd just coaxed Harold into my cloak with an outrageous three candies, when around the bend came a demi-lich. This one had formerly been a Cthulhoid, but he was levitating on the same noxious nether cloud as Gray and had the same demonic embers for eyes.

As we approached, the Cthulhoid said, "Evening." Gray responded in kind, and I thought we might go on without comment, but just as Sam and I passed him, he asked, "What are you doing with these two?"

Gray groaned. "Ignore them. They are trainees."

"Don't look very bright," the other demi-lich said. "A shame, you being stuck with them with all the excitement going on."

"Tell me about it," Gray hissed and lowered his voice. "But what can you do? They are relatives of a couple of trustees."

"Typical," the Cthulhoid said with a heavy shake of his bizarre skull. "Still, if you can ditch 'em, come by the break room. One of the banshees was able to tune the nether radio into an on-world pirate station. They're broadcasting wall-to-wall coverage of the strike and protests over the dismissal of that graduate student petition. We're thinking of starting a union. If graduate students are trying to get back pay, maybe we can too. Do you know how rich we would all be?"

Gray's eyes literally lit up. "I'm definitely in, but aren't you worried about the Sealers finding out? There are a lot of good skulls buried around this campus from the last time we tried to organize."

"But that's the great thing about the protests," the Cthulhoid whispered. "Almost all the Sealers not at the front are out on the quads trying to keep the students from torching the campus. I'm kind of surprised you were able to get through."

Gray dropped his voice conspiratorially. "I took 'em through number 666. Minds blown!" They both laughed, and Gray said, "Well, I better get going before one of their daddies gets worried."

"Better you than me," said the Cthulhoid and, with a tip of his forehead, continued on his way.

By silent agreement, we waited until we'd put a couple of levels between us and the Cthulhoid before I said, "Eldrin is doing it! With the Sealers mustered out of the tower, that means our path to the upper levels is going to be a breeze. I should call him."

"Are you crazy?" Gray hissed. "I know Eldrin is very proud of his little coin, but you are in a building dedicated to paranoia! Even if the Administration can't break the encryption, they will still know there is a signal being generated from within the tower and be on us before you and that elf can exchange 'live long and prospers.'"

I hated that he was right, but he was right. "Fine, I suppose we keep climbing."

Sam, who had taken the opportunity to sit down and rest his legs, gave a groan as he stood back up. "Why up again?"

"Because that's where we can catch the express down," I answered. Seeing that both Gray and Sam looked equally confused, I decided it was time to explain my plan. "Okay, if we headed *down* the stairs, we'd have to pass through dozens of checkpoints to get to the pattern level. No matter how fearsome you've become, Sam, and no matter how many Sealers Gray could help us avoid, we'd be bound to get caught. But all those checkpoints are annoying for the upper brass who have to travel around this tower every day. So, there are special elevators on the upper levels that will take you down and skip all those checkpoints. And most important, an express doesn't stop along the way to take on other passengers."

"Genius," Gray hissed with delight.

I was glad he got it, but Sam still looked confused. "But Gray said this stair only went halfway up the tower, and won't there be as many checkpoints to get up to the top as there are to get down to the bottom?" he asked. "I mean, you can't just walk into the provost's office. Can you?"

"No, kid," Gray said. "But the thing is we don't have to get to the top. All we have to do is get to the lowest level that gives us access to an express elevator, which I believe is level fifty."

"Exactly!" I said with a snap of my fingers. "There's only one checkpoint we need to worry about—that's at the elevator itself. If we get past, we are on, and then we get to skip all the checkpoints going down."

"Seems like a pretty big flaw in security," Sam said.

"It is," I agreed. "But it's the way most people think. If you want to guard something, put it as far away from the entrance as possible, which in a tower either means very high up or very low down, because then it's hard to get to. But all that really does is put it closer to the edge of your control."

The examples of this are legion in the annals of Mysterium mages. Take Torak in Eddings's world. He builds enormous armies to stop the chosen one, or whatever he was calling himself, from getting to him, but then leaves a set of stepping stone islands that lead across the ocean to his home turf, and the citadel of his power with no guard whatsoever. Same with Sauron in Tolkien's drama. He literally sets himself behind an impenetrable barrier of mountains and fortresses and swamps filled with dead elves. But at the one place in the world where his most precious thing can be destroyed, he doesn't even bother to post a single orc with an ax. Crazy.

Anyway, these were my thoughts, and frankly my hopes, as we continued up and up. Maybe Moregoth and the provost would be just as blind. Maybe we'd get to the pattern, the source of their power, and no one would be there, because neither could conceive of anyone trying to strike directly at their heart. Of course, since this ran counter to my typical luck, I didn't hold out much hope. But I had to admit, this first stage of the plan was running to perfection.

As we continued our climb, we came across two or three more demi-liches, a couple of humans, an elf, and some kind of crystal skull that kept trying to steal all our loose change. They either hurried by or were put at ease by Gray's banter. But we were growing exhausted. I lost count of the number of times we stopped for Sam to take a break, and even I was beginning to wear. The tunnel we had been traveling through in the Underground had been enchanted with a permanent stasis field for the workers, which meant we hadn't needed food or sleep, but we had done a lot since stepping into that spider deathtrap, and Sam and I were beat. I handed around butterscotches while we waited for him to catch his breath.

"How much further, do you think, Avery?" he asked piteously as he sucked on his candy.

I recounted the levels we'd passed in my head and said, "Ten, I'd say. According to Gray, the stair stops there anyway. However, I think before we hit the top we need to acquire some new clothes."

"What?" Sam asked and first looked and then sniffed at his cloak. The second act made his nose pucker. "Sounds reasonable. We want to look and smell our best for the pattern."

"No, no," I said with loving irritation. "I'm not worried about how you smell. We need some Sealer cloaks and couple of other props if we are going to get onto that elevator." What I didn't say was that since

Gray had started levitating himself again I was pretty sure we all smelled like nether gas anyway.

"How *are* we going to get onto the elevator?" Gray asked. "You've been remarkably vague on that point."

"I have another plan," I said. "Some of it . . . you may not like." His piercing eyes narrowed suspiciously at me, but that was nothing compared to the howls of venomous protest he launched after I explained what I intended to do. I let him go on for a bit, but then said, "You know it makes sense and may be the only way."

"Well, yes," he admitted. "But that doesn't make it any less humiliating."

"I promise, if I could do it, I would," I said earnestly and entirely dishonestly.

He humphed and whined and muttered to himself about skull rights and living-centric worlds for a while, but eventually he agreed. We crept up the next few levels, unsure of where the guard posts would start.

At last, about four levels from the top, Gray stopped suddenly and darted back down to us. "There are two of them up there. On either side of the door. One sitting. One standing."

I nodded. "Okay, just like we planned it, and Gray . . . don't hold back."

Then came that evil grin that is so nice to see on the face of someone fighting on your side. He concentrated for a bit so that the blue cloud of noxious gas billowed around him. I nodded to Sam, who readied his wand. As for me, I reached into that place inside me where I went when I needed magic, but there was still a hole. With all my concentration, I might have been able to conjure a flame or a feeble light, but nothing lethal.

"Um, Avery, you asked me to warn you," said Sam, and he pointed at my hand. The key was in my hand, and it was glowing. I realized that I wasn't sure when I had pulled it out or how I had started it glowing, but it seemed likely to me that I had done both. "Doesn't the key work like a great big beacon?" he asked.

With a silent nod, I shoved it back into my pocket. "Thanks, Sam."

Gray had started to ascend the stairs with Sam and me at his heel, basically hiding in the drifting ends of his cloud. Yes, it was awful; yes, we had prepared by fashioning bandannas from some of Harold's clean diapers (that I suddenly realized he'd outgrown somewhere along the way); and yes, our eyes were watering despite our precautions, but if it worked, we would be that much closer to getting onto the elevator.

Still, there was the problem of me. I was powerless to help them in whatever came next. Desperate for some way to contribute and hopeful to not choke to death before we got to the guards, I held the cloak over my head and looked into the pocket where Harold was comfortably resting. He looked up at me with his big eyes. "I don't know how much you understand me,"

I said. "But if there is a way for you to feed me some power that would be great."

I handed him another candy, and he said happily, "Bang!"

"Exactly! Bang!" I repeated. He giggled and sucked on the end of the candy. I wasn't sure if he understood, but it seemed like we were at least on the same train of thought. Suddenly I heard Gray's voice. I popped my head out of the cloak and saw that, sure enough, we were at the door to level forty-six. There were two guards, literally identical in face and build, both in standard issue crimson Sealer cloaks. One was leaning against the wall next to the door, a rod of lethality loosely held in one hand. The other was just levering himself to his feet with his own rod.

"Gentlemen," Gray said as they both gasped and tried to wave away the cloud of nether gas that was threatening to envelop them. "I have an important message for the assistant associate vice provost for Academic Affairs. I have been charged . . ."

I saw Sam step down a few stairs and aim his wand at the standing guard from underneath the cloud. At that angle, and with the billowing cloud, the guard had no chance to see him. I thought it was clever enough that I copied the move even though I wasn't sure exactly what I was going to do, or if my conversation with Harold had held any meaning for the little imp. I had just decided to tackle the one on the right—and hope Sam took out the one on the left instead of me—when Harold emerged from my pocket and wrapped himself around my right forearm like an imp bracelet. His little paws shot out and he formed my hand into a pretend gun.

"Bang!" he said happily.

Hoping that meant what it sounded like it meant, I dropped to one knee and pointed my finger toward the guards.

The guard on the right, who was clearly having trouble focusing through the smell, cut Gray off. "I need to see your paperwork, and you need to get an emissions test, because you are rank. It smells like a pile of—"

That was as far as he got. A streak of blue lightning connected between Sam's wand and the Sealer who had just risen to his feet on the left side of the door. The man crumpled like a rag doll. Before the guard on the right could react, I pulled the trigger of my fake gun and said, "Bang!" A bolt of pure purple energy sizzled from the tip of my finger and struck him between the eyes. They rolled up in his head and he fell to the ground.

Sam and I moved forward and began stripping the Sealers of their crimson cloaks, while Gray hovered over our shoulders cackling, another sound you can add to the list. "Oh, now who smells! Having a body isn't so much fun when it doesn't work."

Unfortunately, with him that close, the cloud was now surrounding us, making it impossible to see.

Both Sam and I started coughing uncontrollably. Harold, who was used to the infernal (being from the infernal himself), even flew up above Gray to find clear air. "Gray, time to dial it back," I said. "In fact, we are on to stage three, so we need to shut it down altogether."

"Fine," he grumbled, and the cloud was sucked back into his skull as he slowly settled next to us on the stairwell landing.

Now that we could breathe easy, we made quick work of the Sealers. Sam and I each took a cloak, a rod of lethality, and the battle mask they wore while in combat, which I thought would be perfect it we needed to disguise our faces. When we put the gear on, it didn't look quite right. Mine fit fine, but Sam is neither tall nor thin, which meant the cloak both hung off him and hugged him in decidedly non-Sealer ways. Luckily, Sam had a spell for this—something to do with a thimble and a needle—that made the cloak fit much better, although he still looked like the tiniest Sealer I'd ever seen.

I was finishing up my disguise when Sam said, "Hey, these two guys look the same."

I glanced over. "Yeah, what about it?"

"Well, are they twins?"

Despite myself I chuckled, and from the rattling sounds of hell spawn coming from Gray, he was also. "You do know that most Sealers are clones, right?" Gray asked.

Sam nodded and then asked, "What's a clone?"

"A duplicate of someone," I answered. "The Mysterium does it all the time during states of war. There are only a few thousand Mysterium mages here on campus. Maybe ten, if you counted all the students."

"Which you shouldn't, because students are morons!" Gray spat. "'I need some information on the fall of Aslan,'" he mimicked, in his own inimitable style. "Look it up yourself! They're called books. Read one!"

"Anyway," I continued, straightening Sam's Sealer hood on his head and showing him how to hold the rod properly. "The number of actual Sealers is only a few thousand."

"But we've fought armies of tens of thousands of them," Sam protested.

"Right, but the vast majority of those are clones of the true Sealers. They are controlled from here on campus by . . . I guess you'd call them pilots or controllers. Often units like these are set into an autonomous mode with a simple command like 'guard' or 'kill' or 'apprehend.'"

"Are they real people?" he asked.

I knelt beside them, put a finger into each of their right ears, and hit the self-destruct button. In a matter of seconds and with remarkably little mess, they were two piles of dust, which I wiped away with the tip of my boot. "I don't think so, but I also don't think androids dream of electric sheep."

This confused him long enough for me to remind everyone that we needed to keep moving. I got Sam to produce a length of chain from somewhere in his pouch and asked, "Gray, are you ready?"

He nodded, and I carefully fed the chain through one earhole and out the other. He winced slightly but made no other protest. Then I wrapped a piece of cloth around his eyes, and Sam and I lifted him up by the ends of the chain. Gray gave a sort of whimper and Sam asked, "What's wrong?"

"Have you ever had a chain strung through your head?" he asked bitterly.

"Gosh, I don't think so," Sam answered.

"Well, it's damned uncomfortable."

"Does it hurt a lot?" I asked.

Gray, if you can believe it, slumped on the chain. "I wish it did, but it doesn't. However, it does a leave a funny metallic taste in my mouth. Very unpleasant. You know what's also unpleasant though? Dirt. Dirt and worms. Dirt and worms and those burrowing beetles. Very creepy."

With Gray listing off all the most unpleasant things that had ever crawled through him while dead, which was really a lot of unpleasant things, we continued our trek up to the fiftieth floor. Each level above forty-six had its own set of guards, but with our Sealer robes on we were able to march past them without being challenged. Until we got to level fifty.

The stairwell landing looked just like every other stairwell landing, except that the stair went no further. Two guards, again identical and again wearing the standard Sealer gear, stood on either side of a hefty-looking metal door. They snapped to attention as we approached. I introduced myself as Alex, and by previous agreement, so did Sam.

The one danger in our pretending to be Sealer clones was what to do if they demanded that we take off our battle masks, because there was no way we could be mistaken for twins unless we could convince them that we were the DeVito/Schwarzenegger kind of twins. Fortunately, they didn't. Instead, they saluted, a gesture we returned with awkward uncertainty, and gave their names as Bob and Bob. For clarity, I will refer to them as Bob 1 and Bob 2.

"What's the idea bringing a thing like that up here?" Bob 1 asked, pointing at Gray.

"We've been told expressly that the Associate Assistant Vice Provost wants to personally interrogate this subject," I answered.

"Well then, take it down to Interrogation where it belongs," Bob 2 said.

"Look, they told us he needed to be cleared up here before he could be brought down there," I said, and with a nod from me to Sam, we set Gray down on the floor of the landing. I stretched out my arms. "We've carried it up thirty flights just to get it here."

"Well, it's not on my clipboard," Bob 1 said, as though this ended the debate.

"I told you it was no use, Alex," I said with as much bitterness as I could muster. "It's not like on the front. Everything is bureaucracy here at HQ. No one will do you a solid just 'cause you're a veteran."

Sam shrugged and thankfully said nothing, but Bob 1 said, "Wait a minute! You two are vets?"

I looked down at my feet and gave my head a shake. "Two tours. Last one at the . . . Western Bore."

Both Bobs' eyes widened. "You were at the Bore?"

I leaned in toward them and lowered my voice. "Haven't you noticed Alex here is a little short for a Sealer?" They both nodded. "Spell took off half his lower legs. They were able to reattach his feet, but they haven't had time to restretch him yet. You know how the Admin is. They don't have any time for the little guy."

The Bobs shook their heads sadly. "Crying shame," Bob 2 said, and Bob 1 added, "None of us have had it easy since Moregoth lost his corporeal form."

"And then there's all the rumors about the provost," said Bob 2.

Bob 1 clamped a hand over Bob 2's mouth. "Are you crazy? You want us all sent down to Interrogation?"

"He's right," I said. "Let's not speak of such things." I really wanted to encourage these guys to stop all the small talk and let us onto the elevator. We were one Harold sneeze away from blowing everything.

"It's okay, gents," Gray said in his grating voice. "If you can't decide what to do, simply unchain me and I'll find my own way to Interrogation."

"Shut it!" Bob 1 shouted. "If we need to hear from the brainless division, you'll be the first one we ask."

The Bobs both laughed at this, and Sam and I joined in. "Good one," I said. "Have you heard this one? Why was the skeleton so calm?"

Bob 1 and Bob 2 shook their heads, but before I could deliver the punchline, Gray hissed, "Because nothing could get under his skin. Get it? He has no skin? Soooo original. How about this one, why didn't the skeleton eat the cafeteria food?" Gray gave them no time to consider an answer. "Because he didn't have the stomach for it! Another brilliant one about how we have no internal organs. Comedic gold."

"Is this skull always this mouthy?" Bob 2 asked.

I nodded wearily. "The whole bloody way up." I gestured the Bobs closer and dropped my voice. "Look, I don't want to cause problems for you guys. We all know there was a screw-up. But could I ask you a favor? We all know this thing belongs down in Interrogation, but please don't make us drag its sorry excuse for a skull all the way back down the stairs. If you could just put us on the express straight to Interrogation, we all win. And I get to get away from its voice before I tear out all my hair."

"Oh, I have another one," Gray was saying. "Why do skeletons hate winter? . . . You don't know? Because, the cold goes right through them! Right through them!" He laughed at his own joke, and everyone covered their ears until the hideous sound subsided.

Sam gave a little sob, because I think his head really was hurting. I gestured at him. "Please. Have some pity."

Bob 1 and Bob 2 looked each other and nodded. "Come on, we'll get you down there. No one deserves any more of this skull. Especially not vets."

We lifted Gray up on his chains and he gave a horribly theatrical moan. Bob 2 opened the doors and Bob 1 led us through into some kind of war room that had been set up to deal with the student protests. Long folding tables filled with papers and spell cauldrons were set up in rows around a large chamber that probably had a spectacular view, except that all the windows had been papered over with maps and diagrams of troop positions. There was a buzz of conversation, and in the air the smell of bodies that had been awake too long without a shower.

The place was also swarming with mages, some in standard dress and some that were in Sealer robes. And these were not clones, like the Bobs, but originals, and from the insignia on their robes, some were even from Moregoth's own division. A couple looked up at us curiously, but we just kept our eyes forward and followed Bob 1. It was the longest short trip I've ever made. The skin on the back of my neck was prickling from eyes I assumed were staring at us, wondering why we were there. The tension only got worse when we were standing at the elevator waiting for it to arrive. I was so certain someone was going to challenge us that when the elevator chimed its arrival I nearly jumped through the ceiling.

"Settle down," Bob 1 said. "You'll be free of this knucklehead in no time."

"Knucklehead?" Gray asked with a demonic chuckle. "That reminds me of another one. What's a skeleton's favorite musical instrument?"

Trying to ignore Gray, Bob 1 leaned in and swiped his rod over a runic panel. The buttons lit up and he punched the floor for Interrogation. I had very consciously positioned myself next to the panel, so as he hit his button my knee pushed a button much, much further down on the panel: Pattern Control. I swept the corner of my cloak over the lit-up button in hopes he wouldn't notice, but I needn't have bothered. He and Bob 2 were far too eager to escape Gray.

"Can you guess? You don't know?" the demi-lich was saying. The doors were drawing closed. Bob 1 and Bob 2 stepped back as quickly as they could, but it was too late. Just before they shut completely, Gray shouted, "A trombone! Get it! A trom-bone!" Laughter ricocheted around the closed elevator as it began moving back down the tower.

At last, we were on our way to the pattern. Now if we could only survive Gray's stand-up routine.

CHAPTER 19

DOWN DOOBIE DO DOWN DOWN

We were no longer walking. Instead, we were in a very comfortable elevator shooting to our statistically certain deaths, surrounded by the sounds of the most soul-destroyingly bland Muzak the multiverse could produce, 1970s Stimulus Progression, or as I have heard it called, the end credits theme for the death of the universe. If you don't know the work, don't worry; if you were alive during the '70s or the '80s, it was your background music while shopping at J.C. Penney's or Montgomery Ward.

The first order of business was to remove the chain from Gray's head and his blindfold. He stretched his jaw and looked between Sam and me. "Okay, how about this one—what's a skeleton's favorite kind of art? . . . Give up? Skullpture. Get it? Skull-pture."

And to get him to stop telling bad jokes.

He started to laugh again, and I shouted, "Enough! We're all friends here."

"Oh, are we, Avery?" he asked, his eyes blazing. "You're the one who started it."

"I was trying to gain their confidence," I explained, hoping I was not going to be dragged into yet another lecture on demi-lich rights. "Now, can we focus on what we're going to do when the door opens for Interrogation? There won't be just a couple of Bobs down there, I can assure you."

This quieted everyone down, which I was beginning to regret because the Muzak was really grating. It was Gray who broke the silence. "Do we know how long the doors stay open on each floor?"

I put a finger to my chin, trying to recall what I could about elevators. "Depends on whether this is considered a time of high, medium, or low volume. At high volume, elevator doors are programmed to stay open five seconds, and at low volume, up to eleven seconds, but they can be customized within certain limits. Not that Mysterium regulations are at all in line with proper disabilities regulations—as evidence, I will direct your attention to the never-ending staircase at the entrance to the Department of Magical Effects— but the minimum time a door should remain open is three seconds. Of course, that's not the time from no-

tification to closing, which adds another five seconds."
I tapped my chin again. "I'd say you could safely count
on the doors being open for about ten seconds or so."

When I looked at Sam and Gray after this little
lecture, they were both staring back at me, stunned,
but as it turned out, for very different reasons.

"You know a lot about elevators," Gray said.
"Maybe an unhealthy amount."

Sam smiled. "I meant to ask before, what's an elevator?"

"I mean, do you read the manuals for pleasure?"
Gray asked.

"That's what we're in now isn't it?" Sam said, looking about excitedly.

"Because I'm a bit concerned about you," the skull
confided.

"How long do we stand here before something
happens?" Sam asked.

I threw up my hands, and they both mercifully
grew quiet. Putting up my forefinger, I said, "First . . ."
Then thought better of it when I couldn't remember
the exact order of the questions. "Yes, Sam, this is
an elevator, and it's already moving. You can watch
those lit numbers at the top telling you what floor
we're on. No, Gray, I'm not mental. My dad inspects
them, among other things . . . many other things."

Gray mumbled something about that being very
convenient, but it was what Sam said that shook us
both. "Neat! It says we're passing floor zero."

A shot of fear-induced adrenaline raced up my spine, and from Gray's expression, I could see that he was feeling it too. "Damn! This is a fast elevator. Okay, we need to come up with a plan in the next sixty seconds or we're going to get hauled off at Interrogation and tortured to death."

"Oh!" Sam said.

"Indeed!" I agreed. I stared around the little box. It was your standard elevator: six-foot square, door in the middle, panel of buttons on one side of the door, call box on the other, and unlike in all the movies, no convenient escape hatch in the ceiling. I started pacing back and forth, thinking. "We only need eleven seconds . . . eleven bloody seconds. We could hide Gray in my cloak, but then we would be two Sealers standing there, shuffling our feet. They're bound to ask us what we're up to, and there's no way we would survive close inspection by a real Sealer. If only we could be invisible—"

"I could cast a spell," Sam suggested brightly.

I shook my head. "Express elevators are shielded, and invisibility spells on Mysterium are tricky."

This of course was another of my notorious understatements. In most places invisibility is easy: you bend light around an object, and bang, you're invisible. But those sorts of spells are so well-known that Sealers emit a constant screening spell that detects light manipulation and redirects the light toward the caster. As a result, the invisibility spell turns into a spotlight you're shining on yourself. In Mysterium, if you really wanted to be invisible, you have to make every cell in your body transparent. This sort of transformation is incredibly difficult, and getting it wrong can have some hideous results. One mage tried it as a class project but forgot to include the contents of his alimentary canal.

"Maybe we could hide then?" Sam suggested.

"Hide!" Gray shrieked. "We're in a box, you idiot! What are we going to do, pretend to be part of the wall?"

I spun around and pointed at him. "Sam, you are a genius!"

"I am?" he said.

"You can't be serious!" Gray shouted.

"I am serious," I said and, wrapping my cloak tightly around my body, shoved myself into the small corner on one side of the door. It was only about a foot and a half, but if we were careful it could work. I glanced up at the floors. We had about twenty seconds. I pointed at Sam. "Have you ever played hide-and-seek?"

"Of course," he said. "That and kick-the-can were my favorite . . . and Red Rover . . . oh, and—"

I waved away the rest. "Never mind all that. In hide-and-seek, the best place to hide is where?" I asked, but we didn't have time for him to come up with the answer, so I did. "It's out in the open. In a place the seeker would think you couldn't possibly hide. Wrap your cloak and robe around yourself like I have and hide in the corner here." I shoved him against the call box. "I will be in this corner." I shoved myself against the panel of buttons. "When the door opens, no one speak, no one breathe, no one move. All they'll see is an empty elevator. They won't even think for a second that someone might be hiding in here."

"What about me?" Gray asked in my arms.

I opened my cloak and started to stuff him into a pocket. "Sorry, but it's safer this way."

He looked into the pocket with distaste. "Normally I would agree, but did you know that you have baby detritus in here? It's gross."

"I'll clean it out later," I said with a grunt of impatience and shoved him inside.

Harold made a squeak as I put Gray into his pocket, but quieted under the soothing powers of a candy. At this point I was certain I was ruining the imp's teeth and was an awful parent, but comforted myself with the fairly certain knowledge that it was better than getting him killed.

I had only just gotten myself settled when the door chimed for Interrogations. I held a finger to my lips. Sam nodded and took a deep breath. The doors slid open. Outside I could hear a bustle of activity intertwined with distant screams and cries of those being interrogated.

One second, I counted to myself.

"Take Prisoner Number 2358, take him to cell 11B2 for questioning. Next!" a big booming voice shouted.

Two.

"Look, how much longer?" asked a nasty, nasally voice. "We need to get back to Sector B. A mob of students from Reanimation have animated the statues along the Walk of Trustees, and I don't even want to describe what they're making them do to each other. It's not right!"

Three.

"You'll get your turn," the booming voice answered impatiently. Then I heard the words I was dreading. "Is that the express?"

Four.

"Yes, sir!" came a hoarse reply.

Five.

"Well, hold it! I need to send a message back up to the assistant associate vice provost for Discipline."

Six.

The doors had to close soon. I'd already counted to six since they opened, but we must have been in a low-volume mode, which meant there might still be five to go! That's when Harold's little paw shot out of my cloak and started punching the door close button like he was playing *Galaga*. They started to move.

"Hold that elevator!" I heard the hoarse voice shout.

"Sorry" came the nasally reply. "I wouldn't want to lose my place."

The doors closed, and the rest of the conversation was cut off. I still didn't dare breathe until I felt the elevator start to move again. When it did, I exhaled. "Gods, that was close." I took Harold out of his pocket and gave him a high five. "Well done, you." He gave me a thumbs-up and clambered back into the hood, still happily sucking on his candy.

I looked over and saw that Sam was still pressed against his wall. His face was beginning to turn a bit blue. "Sam, you can breathe now," I said. "We are past Interrogation."

"Oh, thank goodness," he gasped. "I wasn't sure who was it."

Slumping to the ground, I laughed. "Hopefully no one from here on out, Sam."

I looked up at the panel. It was quite a way from Interrogation to Pattern Control, which was the last button available. I figured we had several minutes. Enough time to talk through what was coming next and to give Sam and Gray a chance to leave.

I took Gray out, put him on the ground beside me, and gestured for Sam to come sit with us. He did. I looked around this tiny circle. "I can't ask the two of you to come with me any further, because I have no idea what we will be facing down there. An army of Sealers might be waiting. I think that's unlikely, but they could be. Then again, I'm not sure what will happen once I bring the key into contact with the pattern. There might be cataclysm like the one on

Trelari. The backlash might bring the tower down, possibly even the whole world. And last . . ." I looked down at my hands. "This is the end of my plan. Even if there's no army. Even if we get to the pattern. Even if we successfully destroy the key. I have no idea how to get out of Mysterium.

"But." I hopped to my feet, grabbed a piece of fazechalk from one of my pockets, and began sketching a transport circle. "When the doors to the elevator open, the magic shielding will be less effective. Once we reach Pattern Control and the doors open, Sam can activate this circle, and the two of you can jump straight back to Trelari."

Sam shook his head vigorously. "I will activate the circle for Gray, Avery, but I'm coming with you. No matter what. Besides Ariella would kill me if I let anything happen to Harold."

Gray thought about it, his ember eyes glowing dark and mysterious in their sockets. "Yes. I think you should activate the circle, Sam." It was the right choice, but I had to admit to being a little disappointed. I could see Sam felt the same way. Then I saw that evil grin stretch across Gray's skull. "You two will need someone to hold the door open for you. I'm very good at that. I will use my head—get it? Use my head?" This time I didn't even complain about the laughter that followed. After all, he was now our escape plan.

I spent the remaining time finishing the circle

and working with Harold on our "bang" protocols. He added a "boom" and an "uh-oh," which really sounded promising. Sam and I also went over our approach, which was not going to be as subtle this time. A few floors from our destination, he wrapped a piece of parchment around his wand. I pulled my sleeve up over where Harold had attached himself to my arm, and we made ourselves ready at the elevator door, making sure that the travel circle was shielded from view behind us. Gray kindly waited until just before we reached Pattern Control to start levitating. Then we were there.

Gray clicked his teeth. "Right! Let's kick some Sealer ass!"

The doors opened to reveal a small chamber that looked to be a natural cavern; only the floors had been smoothed. Directly across from us was a small doorway carved into the living rock. It was mounted with a heavy gate of iron bars, behind which stood a Sealer's Sealer. His hair was buzzed short and his blue eyes were sharp and penetrating. Certainly no Bob.

We paused only long enough to allow Sam to surreptitiously activate the circle behind us with his wand. Then he and I stepped out of the elevator and marched in unison toward the gate, making sure to keep shoulder-to-shoulder to obscure Gray and the glowing circle behind us. As we got closer, I could see beyond the Sealer a room filled with mages, all hunched over different mystical control panels on which various shapes and runes and patterns spun and moved. I could also see a large sweeping window in the far wall from which came an otherworldly glow. I knew from the quality of the light that it must be Mysterium's pattern.

"Orders?" the man with the piercing blue eyes demanded.

I saluted and said, "Sam, show him the orders." Then I carefully retreated a couple of steps.

Sam stepped forward and pulled out his wand, still rolled in the parchment, and thrust it forward at the Sealer. The man held out his hand and started to take the parchment scroll, but then hesitated and eyed Sam. "Aren't you a little short for a Sealer?"

Sam answered with a blast of pure energy that shot from the end of his wand. The spell lifted the blue-eyed man off the ground and blew him back at least twenty feet. He crashed into one of the panels and the other mages looked up in alarm.

I yelled, "Sam, duck!"

He dropped to the ground, I pointed my palm at the door and said, "Boom!"

My arm recoiled from the shock as a purple burst of energy about the size of a softball launched from my hand and slammed into the thick gate. There was a spray of rock and the entire section of the wall, iron bars and all, went flying back across the room beyond. It caught one of the nearest mages as he was turning toward us and flattened him. Then the battle was on.

The mages outnumbered us significantly, but they were not combat trained. Meanwhile, over the last year, Sam had become a true battle mage, and he was relentless; clouds of black arrows (one of his signature spells), blinding zones of pure darkness, spinning balls of flame, and nets of pure energy rained down upon them. Meanwhile, Harold delivered even more than I could have expected. Between Sam's dizzying array of spells and my bangs, booms and uh-ohs, we had wiped out all the mages and most of their equipment in about two minutes.

When the dust and debris and spinning vortexes of mystic energy finally settled, Sam and I looked about and listened. Apart from occasional bits of stone falling from the ruined doorway we had blasted our way through, the circular control room was quiet. There was no blaring alarm or stamp of feet. The other elevator down to this level showed no sign of activity, and there didn't appear to be any other exits, which did make me wonder briefly how they got down to the pattern. But that was a complication for later. At the moment, it seems that we had succeeded.

"I think we did it," I announced and pulled back my sleeve to make sure Harold was okay. He smiled wearily and held out a paw for another candy. I had never been happier to give him one.

Sam wiped off his wand, gave it a little spin around his fingers, and shoved it back into his belt like a gunslinger in one of the spaghetti westerns. I was about to tell him how Chuck Norris he was, but he spoiled it by saying, "Neato!"

"Indeed," I said with a smile.

"Can I remind the two of you that we are still in the heart of the enemy's territory," Gray called from where he was hovering in the doors of the elevator. Occasionally, they would try to close, bang into him, and reopen. "Oh, and I am still being used as a glorified doorstop!"

"Right! Let's see how to get down to the actual pattern, Sam."

We looked around the room, but the only visible way in or out was through the gate we'd just blasted to pieces. The only other feature of note was a wide window. We rushed over to this. It looked out onto a natural cavern—a vaguely rounded shaft of rough rock that rose a hundred feet or more to a high domed ceiling. Tall statues with vaguely humanoid features were carved at regular intervals around the cave walls. They were so worn with age that it was impossible to tell whether they were meant to represent the Mysterians or some other long-lost race. They stretched from floor to ceiling, their heads meeting at the top of the dome as though bent in study of the floor of cavern that lay about forty feet below us. That was where the pattern was set. I gazed at it in wonder.

My first impression was of a vague circle of glowing light about fifty feet across. But as I studied it further, the blur of white light began to resolve itself into an intricate intertwining of many overlapping lines and patterns each of a subtly different hue that pulsated with a rhythm that seemed to match my own beating heart. It was a weaving of magic that was complex beyond imagining. Nor were the position of the lines static, but with every pulse they would writhe and shift into new patterns. The effect was mesmerizing.

And then the enormity of where I was struck me. This was the true heart of the Mysterium. This was the place where the rules of the multiverse were made, and hopefully where the key could be unmade.

As always, on thinking of it, my hand moved to the key. This time there was not the vague tingle of energy I normally felt when I touched it, but a veritable rush of power. I wondered if the key knew what was coming. That finally I was going to destroy it. I drew it out and it seemed to grow heavier, so much so that it was a struggle even to hold it up. I gripped it in both hands. In the perfect surface of the key, I could see worlds upon worlds reflected. This was the gateway to infinity, something that could take me anywhere. I could barely breathe.

I watched through the window as the pattern began to respond to the key's presence, whirling and sending sparks of possibility and gyres of potential, only to fade or transport themselves to the edges of subworld. It was so beautiful. I wondered if, right now, the pattern was giving birth to new places, different realms of imagination. For some reason, the cost of those new places never entered my mind.

"Avery?" said Sam. "Um . . . Avery?"

I took another pace toward the window, and I pressed the key against it. The heavy glass began to vibrate and ripple. "Not now, Sam. This is the moment."

That's when Moregoth laughed. I spun and saw, across the ruins of the control room, that what I had taken for a blank wall at the back of the room had only been an illusion. As it faded, the true extent of the chamber became evident. The actual room was twice again as big, and standing in this newly revealed space were row upon row of Sealers, rods of lethality already aimed and at the ready.

"You are a fool, Avery Stewart! A grotesque jester that dances on the edge of an abyss of misery," rasped Moregoth as his smoky legs flowed over the ruined consoles and the bodies of the mages we'd battled. Behind him, the ranks of Sealers advanced. "Did you really think you could reach the pattern unnoticed? How exquisitely naïve," he chuckled. "We were aware of your presence from the moment you entered the tower. The only reason we didn't seize you and your pathetic band was our desire to discover your purpose." A flowing black hand brushed back his vaporish bangs from his eyes. "When you boarded that elevator, you sealed your fate. Now hand over the key and end this." His arm seemed to drift out from his body, stretching toward me like a shadow at sunset.

There was no time to think. If I held the key for even a moment longer, Moregoth and the Mysterium would have it. Once they did, they could use it as I had never been able to bring myself to use it. Trelari would be destroyed, all my friends killed. With this truth in mind, I acted.

Holding the key in front of me, I launched myself through the glass window, hoping that my headlong dive would end in the pattern. The key gave one slight vibration as it contacted the window, and the glass exploded into a million shards. Then I was falling with the pattern rushing up toward me. I had enough wherewithal to try to unwrap Harold from around my wrist so he could take flight, but his little body clung to me even tighter. I was ten feet from the ground and bracing myself for the end when I felt something grab hold of my toe. A second later, I was floating gently toward the pattern, Sam latched on to my leg with one hand while in the other he held a little white feather. I recall in the back of my mind thinking, *Oh, so that's what it's for.*

Above us, I could see Moregoth and the Sealers lined up across the window, a wall of crimson and black. He was shouting commands. I could hear the stamp of boots from somewhere and saw that beneath the window were seven openings, a passage from the upper chamber to the pattern room that must have been hidden by Moregoth's illusion. We would soon be surrounded by Sealers. I would only have one chance.

We touched down, landing just inside the boundary of the pattern itself. As soon as my body made contact, its power coursed through me. It rippled up my legs, into my chest, and out again through the top of my head. Bumps and bruises disappeared. Long-lost memories resurfaced. I think it may have even regrown my appendix, which had been removed when I was a child. At last it got to the place in my chest with the little tear. In a great rush of sensation, I was whole, and magic began to flow through me again.

"And now what, Dark Lord?" Moregoth said as he floated down from the window to stand at the edge of the pattern. Out of the doors on either side of him came his army of Sealers. They marched in two columns, one clockwise and one counterclockwise around the pattern. We were surrounded. At a gesture from Moregoth, they all raised their rods of lethality and pointed them at me.

"You know I could destroy all of them," I said, and my voice rang with power.

He laughed, a wheezing, hacking sound. "I have seen what you can do, Dark Lord, and all I will say is, be my guest. Kill me where I stand, if you can. Bring this tower down around us. End the war."

"Your precious provost would die with you," I warned.

"Yes, my provost," Moregoth said with a chuckle. "I don't think he has much to worry about from you." For some reason he found the thought quite amusing and paused for a second, staring off at nothing. As an observation, I think that for the ultimate goth, Moregoth laughs a lot. I don't usually get his jokes, but for a sociopath he seems fairly jolly.

He shook himself out of his reverie, which made for an odd effect, him being entirely gaseous. "Anyway, I encourage you to indulge yourself. Think of the delicious agony you might bring to your enemies. Out in the streets, thousands of future Mysterium mages are protesting. Kill them all before they can be used against you as weapons. Become what you really are. Become the true Dark Lord. But I think you should decide soon, because the pattern does not seem to be agreeing so well with your friend."

I looked down and saw that Sam was on his knees, his hands clasped to the sides of his head, a low moan of agony escaping his lips. I knelt beside him. "Sam, what's wrong?"

"It . . . it hurts" was all he could manage.

"He's Trelarian, Dark Lord," Moregoth answered with a purr. "Whereas for you and me, this pattern is like mother's milk." He reached out and an arc of power rose up from the pattern to greet his touch. He caressed it almost like a lover might. "For him, it might as well be poison. Even as we speak, he is being rewritten."

He was right. Everywhere the pattern touched him, Sam's features seemed to melt and flow, and then some inner power would slowly remold him. But he was exhausted and growing weaker by the second. Harold hopped out of my arms and climbed onto Sam's chest. A shimmering glow of purple encased them both. Sam's face calmed, but how long could Harold hold out against the pattern? This had to end, but looking at the ring of Sealers surrounding us, I didn't know what to do.

Moregoth seemed to sense my uncertainty. "I ask again, what now?"

"What now?" I repeated with a shout. "Now, I destroy the key that you have sought for so long. You may kill us, but I will steal from you and your master the one hope you had of winning this war. Without it, the forces of Trelari will grind you down. I think you will find Mysterium a small and exposed place when all the subworlds and innerworlds that you have ruthlessly suppressed all these years finally rise up against you."

With that, I plunged the key into the pattern, trying as I did to open a direct line between the two. For lack of a better analogy, as Eldrin had said, to short the key out. There was a ringing sound as it struck the stone. I didn't breathe, I just watched, waiting to see the key melt away and its power fade.

Nothing happened.

Where it touched, the pattern there was a sparking and blazing of light. Power pulsed within the key, but otherwise it was fine. I had failed. Again.

Moregoth roared with laughter. "As I said, you are a tragic jester. A buffoon of ignorance and incompetence. If I were not pressed with other concerns, I might even be amused by your suffering." He was gesturing now to the Sealers who also began to laugh, even if it was clear they had no idea why. "You really have no idea what you're doing, but it seems you have served my purpose at least. You have delivered the key to me and now the victory of the Mysterium over your pathetic uprising is complete. I will take great joy in slowly unraveling each one of your—"

Whatever he was about to say was lost in an extreme fit of coughing. Still, a hand formed out of the black fog of Moregoth's body and snaked across the pattern toward me. I stuffed the key, anticlimactically, back into my pocket, and grabbing Sam in my arms, began to back away from Moregoth's grasping reach.

"Where are you going, Dark Lord? Do I need to remind you that you are completely surrounded?" he asked, still very raspy after his coughing fit. My diagnosis was that he badly needed a cough drop.

I didn't actually know what I was doing. I had nowhere to go. I was without hope. But being without hope isn't the same thing as giving up, and giving up was something I wasn't ready to do.

Crawling, I dragged Sam to the center of the pattern. He was not going to make it much longer. His body seemed to be at constant war with itself: flowing at times like water, then rippling like a flame. It was grotesque, and he could no longer speak through the pain. I lay him at my feet and stood. Moregoth had sprouted multiple arms now. He stepped onto the pattern himself and began encircling me with his body, which was as creepy as it sounds. There was no way out. I should have realized that everything had been too easy. I had been blinded by my need to destroy the key. And, well, Moregoth was right. I had been an idiot. Sam had trusted me and now lay dying. Gray had followed me and my only hope was that he'd realized we were done for and jumped through the portal already. If not, he was likely dead . . . or re-dead.

I gave myself a few beats of the pattern, and my heart, to mourn my friends. Then I steeled myself for what was to come, because I had decided that while I had failed them, I would not fail the multiverse. If the only way to keep the key from falling into the hands of Moregoth was to destroy Mysterium, then that is what I would do. I would don the mantle of the Dark Lord once and for all and be the ultimate evil. I took the key from my pocket again, determined to do what Vivian and Rook and so many others had been begging me to do for so long. I would fight. I would use the key, here on this pattern, and I would kill Moregoth and as much of the Administration as I could. And even if I couldn't destroy the Mysterium, I would shake it to its very core.

"Moregoth!" I shouted.

"What, Avery Stewart?" Moregoth snarled, a sick smile creeping back across his face. "Have you come to your senses? Will you now beg me to 'spare the others' and 'take me instead'?"

"Not exactly," I said, rising to my feet, the key clenched in my hands. "Before you asked me to 'be your guest.'" My face twisted into something dark and cruel. "I accept."

There was momentary look of wide-eyed astonishment from Moregoth as I pointed the key at him, and the power of the main pattern of Mysterium began to fill me. Then a very strange thing happened. A yellow circle appeared around Sam and me. The ground seemed to disappear beneath our feet, and we fell straight out of Mysterium.

I'm not sure whether Moregoth or I was more surprised, but he certainly had the bigger reaction. While I gave him a little wave, he screamed, "Nooooo!" as we vanished from sight.

The last thing I heard was him howling, "Stewart! I'll get you and your little imp too!"

Though I'm not sure he heard me, I shouted back, "He's not so little anymore!"

CHAPTER 20

BITTER DREGS

Surprise! We were on Trelari. Again! I was beginning to resent the place. Happily, I was not back in the Citadel of Light. Instead, an unconscious Sam and I appeared in . . . Yeah, I had no idea where we were. It looked like Vivian's tent, but when I opened the flap and poked my head out, I found that the tent was standing in the center of an immense stone chamber. The walls formed a continuous circle around us that spanned at least fifty yards, and they rose to meet a ceiling at least that distance above us. Everything was gray, everything was smooth, but not polished, and there were no obvious exits anywhere.

It was creepy in its cylindrical perfection, but at

least there was no immediate threat. I closed the flap and turned my attention to Sam and Harold, stunned to see that both seemed to have aged. Harold's face had broadened, as had his shoulders. His wings were considerably larger. He was still young-looking and nowhere near as round about the middle as he had been when I first met him. But when he wearily climbed up my arm and settled heavily on my shoulder, it reminded me so much of those early days that I found myself asking him, "Can you explain what happened?"

His response was also classic Harold. He sighed heavily and shrugged, and then a hint of that mischievousness returned. "Butterscotch?" he said, with a twinkle in his eye.

I reached into my pocket and handed one to him with a laugh. "At least that hasn't changed. Now, let's see what happened to Sam."

He was unconscious so I lifted him onto one of the settees, arranged an absurd number of pillows around him, and covered him with a blanket. I studied him carefully. He was mostly the same, but in his face I could see that he had also aged. Before he'd had a baby face, smooth and unmarked. Now, tiny lines traced off of his eyes and across his forehead.

"What the hell have I done to you?" I asked, but of course got no answer.

I'm proud to say it was only after trying to come up with a theory and failing, and then trying to contact

Eldrin to see if he had a theory and failing (the tent or rock chamber must have been shielded somehow) that I wondered if I had also been affected. I went to a mirror hanging on one of the tent supports. My face looked exactly the same. It was monstrously unfair. I should have had a big mark. A scar. Something to let everyone know what I'd done, but I had escaped unscathed. I really was a product of Mysterium.

I stared at myself in the mirror. "You are a monster."

"Oh, Avery," a voice replied. "You're not a monster. It just didn't work, that's all."

As I spun about trying to find a source, a bright light appeared in the tent wall. It began to form the outline of a door. The door swung inward, and Vivian stepped through. She was wearing white robes and looked like an angel.

Of course she already knew it hadn't worked! She must have known that it wouldn't before I even tried. How much more had she predicted? Had she known what would happen to Sam? If she hadn't interfered and sent out all those notes, he would never have been there in the first place. I felt heat rush through my body, and all my frustration and anger came spilling out.

"You knew *everything* that would happen. You let me take Sam and Harold and all the others into that place and knew all along I would fail! You could have stopped it but did *nothing*."

She shook her head sadly. "I didn't know how it

would end, Avery. I rarely do. All I knew was that you would try to sneak away and what I needed to do to give you a chance to succeed. No matter how hard I looked, I couldn't see what would happen when you reached the pattern."

It was her usual excuse, but this time I wasn't buying it. "That would explain a lot, except for the escape hatch," I said, stabbing a finger at her. "The only way you could have known to plan a portal is if you *saw* me on the pattern."

She tried to reach out a hand to touch my shaking arm, but I pulled it away and stalked to the other side of the tent. That close, I was in real danger of losing the force of my righteous anger. She sighed. "That wasn't foresight, Avery. That was me knowing you. I cast that travel pattern on Harold the last time we were together. It was linked to a contingency."

"What contingency?" I hissed angrily.

"Your trying to use the key on the Mysterium pattern," she said and her eyes narrowed a little. "That I couldn't allow."

"What gives you the right?"

"I have every right!" she shouted. "You nearly destroyed yourself here on a pattern you drew yourself. Can you imagine what might have happened to you *and* Harold had you used the key on the pattern of Mysterium?" I had but knew the answer wasn't going to help me seize back the moral high ground. "Do you think you're the only one that's afraid of Moregoth getting the key? Have you thought for one moment how much effort it took me to keep you alive?"

I started to answer but made the mistake of looking into her eyes. She was crying, tears rolling down her cheeks. Harold leapt from my shoulder and fluttered over to her. She hugged him to her chest while one of his paws reached up and stroked her neck.

There was only one thing to say. "I'm sorry. You had every right to fix my screw-up." I sighed. "I just don't understand. I opened the key to the heart of the pattern, but nothing happened."

She was still smiling and cooing to Harold, but something in her eyes shifted. Her brow wrinkled in concern. "Have you thought about what that means, Avery?" she asked, still tickling Harold under the chin playfully.

"I haven't really had time," I admitted and threw myself back onto one of the cushioned couches. Whether the pattern had revived me or not, all I wanted right now was a decent burger and then ten to twelve hours of sleep. I closed my eyes.

A pillow smacked into the side of head. I sat up. Vivian pointed a finger at Harold, but he was one step ahead and already had a thumb cocked nonchalantly in her direction. "What do the two of you want?" I asked.

"I want you to think about the fact that a reality key, that according to everything we know was made by Mysterians on Mysterium, has a stronger reality than Mysterium's own 'pattern.'" She actually made little air quotes around the word *pattern*.

"Okay?"

"God, for a worlds-famous mage, you can be so dense at times," she said, clenching her hands in mild frustration. "We both agree that had the key been actually forged in Mysterium's pattern, it would have unraveled."

I thought about it and nodded. "That's the nature of pattern-forged objects. It's why I assumed the destruction of the key at the pattern was a given."

She started pacing. "Right, that's the difference between objects and beings. I note you're channeling magic again." I nodded stupidly. "That's because your magic comes from Mysterium. You are empowered by its pattern, whereas poor Sam . . ." She stopped next to him and placed a hand on his forehead. A little smile turned up the corners of her mouth. "He'll recover by the way. He just needs some rest."

I rubbed my eyes sleepily. "So do I."

"You're fine," she said with no sympathy. "He, on the other hand, was being systematically unknitted and rewoven by the Mysterium pattern. Luckily, Harold was able to keep him mostly stitched together."

"I know, I know," I said, shaking my head at the reminder. "What a cock-up. The whole thing. The problem is I don't know what to do next."

A wicked grin crossed her face. "Well, since your plan didn't work, we could try mine."

I groaned. "Are we really going to have this fight again?"

"But don't you see? If the key is more powerful than the Mysterium pattern, then it's more powerful than Moregoth and the Sealers," she said excitedly. "We can destroy them with it! We can win this war and conquer Mysterium! Give it to me, and I'll take care of everything." She held out her hand. I noticed she'd trimmed her nails.

I considered giving it to her on the principle that she couldn't do worse with it than I had. Then I remembered the yellow brick road turning gray. Alice popping out of reality with nothing more than an "Oh!" of surprise. The poor faun's beautiful brass knob. The sound Trelari made when I almost cracked it in half.

"Avery? Give me the key," she said, stepping toward me, her hand still held out, grasping. "Once the Mysterium's gone, we can do whatever we like. Imagine the possibilities. We will either find our own happily ever after, or make it."

I wanted to give it to her. But for better or worse, it was my responsibility. I shook my head. "Sorry, Vivian. You know I can't."

A huge smile broke out across her face. "Good."

"What?" I asked, my head spinning by her changing moods. "Was that some kind of test?"

"You can call it that if you want. I needed to see if your heart was still set on destroying the key, because it's going to be really hard for you to go through with it, and I think you know that."

"But what about the whole ultimate weapon thing?" I asked.

"Frankly, I'm also tired of fighting," she said and came to sit next to me on the settee. "The only question now is how to destroy the key, and I think I know who can help us."

"Eldrin?" I asked.

Her mouth tightened in consternation. "No, not Eldrin, and on that point, I think you've been relying on him too much to do your thinking." I yawned and nodded placidly. She smiled despite herself. "Why don't you get some sleep?"

"Sounds good." I laid my head in her lap, tucking my feet behind me. "Where are we, by the way?"

She began to run her fingers through my hair. "This is my undisclosed location," she answered.

"It's . . . it's shielded," I said with another jaw-cracking yawn.

"Mhm," she hummed, and then in the softest of whispers, "Trust me, Avery, no one will find you here. Now sleep, while I invite another guest to the party."

Something about that sounded vaguely ominous, but I was too tired to care. I tried to tell her about how much I missed her, but I'm pretty sure that was just a dream.

I felt like I'd just fallen asleep, when I was woken

in the worst way possible, which is to say, by a dwarf. It was Rook, and he was pissed. "You do realize that you pulled me away in the middle of a bloody battle!" he was shouting. "I do no' give two figs if he's asleep. He needs to wake up an' give me some bloody answers!"

I sat up, blinking and stretching as Rook and Vivian entered the tent. He marched up to me and shook a finger in my face. "I take it yar responsible for me bein' hijacked!"

"I am?" I asked. Behind him, Vivian shrugged.

"Yes!" he said with an emphatic tug of his beard. "Apparently, I'm needed here as a consultant, not back at the bloody citadel, which is under attack—again!"

I rubbed the back of my head, trying to get some thoughts flowing. "I had no idea. Is everyone all right? Do they need help?" I looked around stupidly, as though the battle might be raging in the tent itself. Thankfully it wasn't. The only other person around was Sam, who was still curled up on the settee sleeping.

Rook waved a hand in front of my face to draw my attention back to him. "Nothin' like that, laddie. Valdara and Drake can handle that lot. But Mysterium is gettin' bolder since you and Vivian quit harrassin' them at the borders." He sat with an audible *humph* on one of the other settees and looked around. "You got anythin' ta drink in this . . . whatever this is?"

Vivian brought him a bottle of wine I'm positive

wasn't in the tent a half second ago. He tipped it back and took a huge drink, then wiped his mouth with the back of his hand and let loose a belch. "That's better." Rook looked over at Sam. "What's wrong wi' the kid?"

"Nothing much," I said. "He's just recovering from an attempt to unweave his reality."

Rook nodded, unimpressed, and took another swig. "I've had worse."

He was right. He had. I sat up and looked at his formerly missing leg. "Hey! You can walk!"

The dwarf squinted at me critically. "Of course I can walk, you daft idiot. Ariella and her mother had this on me a few hours after you left." He patted the wrong knee.

"I think it was the other one," I pointed out.

He thought about it for a second and raised his pant leg a bit to reveal a wooden prosthetic, beautifully crafted and carved with the most elaborately interlocking runes I'd ever seen. "So it was," he said with a smile. "So it was. Can't really tell 'em apart now unless I'm in the bath, then the wooden one floats. But enough about me. What's this consultin' you need? Valdara won't notice me gone for a few minutes, but more than that and she'll start lookin', and you do no' want her to find me here. She's still pissed at you for sneakin' off again!"

While I was trying to decide if it was ever going to be safe for me to show my face in the citadel again,

Vivian said, "We need to talk about the location of Mysterium's pattern."

"What? Everyone knows that—bottom level of the Provost's bloody Tower," Rook said and took another draw on the bottle, which I noticed didn't seem to be getting any emptier.

"Not the Mysterium pattern the mages made, Rook," Vivian said and crouched down so her golden eyes were on his level. "Avery and I want to know about the real pattern. The one the original Mysterians made. The one the mages have been using as an energy source all this time."

Suddenly my mind was wide awake. This was what Vivian was trying to get me to realize last night, or morning, or whenever it was. If Mysterium's pattern hadn't been able to unravel the key, then there must be another one. A deeper one. An older one. I sat up and fixed my eyes on the dwarf just as Vivian was doing.

He seemed to pale under our scrutiny, and took another deep drink from the bottle.

"Well?" I asked.

His eyes darted back and forth between the two of us. "How could you possibly know about the other pattern?"

"Because it has to exist," Vivian answered. "As you well know, Avery took it upon himself to sneak away from Trelari and bring the key all the way to Mysterium. There, and at great peril to himself and Sam *and* Harold, he managed to make it to Mysterium's pattern."

"The 'real' pattern," I added, and Rook's head swiveled toward me, his eyes wide. "The one at the bottom of the Provost's Tower."

"Do you know what happened when he opened the key to the pattern?" Vivian asked as Rook turned back toward her. Rook shook his head, his beard wagging like a flag in a breeze. "Nothing!" Vivian shouted, clapping her hands together sharply.

Rook jumped back, his eyes as wide as dinner plates, well, at least saucers. (He is a dwarf, after all.) He seemed genuinely at a loss for words. To drive home the point, I pulled the key out of my pocket and held it out. God, it had grown heavy, and the tingling in my fingers was so enticing. All I wanted to do was taste a little of the magic within it. My hand shook a bit with the effort of resisting, and I slammed it down on a small table next to where I was sitting. It took a lot of will to pull my hand away.

The dwarf was clearly unnerved. He stared at the key like it was a viper and wiped a shaking hand across his beard.

"What is that thing?" Vivian asked, pointing. "And where was it made?"

Rook rocked his body back and forth for a second and buried his head in his hands. "If what you're sayin' is true, then it may be what the Mysterians call the Master Key," he answered, and looked up at us, his eyes wild. "I swear I didna' know, or I never would have let Avery go on that damn fool quest ta destroy it."

"The Master Key? Is it another of these pattern keys the Mysterians made?" I asked.

"Not just another one!" the dwarf shouted and, jumping to his feet, started pacing, taking swigs from his bottle now and then. "It's the key that was used when the Mysterians created the true pattern at the center of everything."

"True pattern? Center of everything?" I asked. "I thought the Mysterium pattern was the center of everything! What is this *true* pattern? We need specifics."

"It's called the Mysterian pattern, and if you want to know more then you're several thousand millennia too late!" he growled. "This is the stuff of legends, stories, even legends of stories."

"What stories?" Vivian asked. "Tell us."

Rook pulled at his beard. "According to the legends, the First Mysterians created a pattern at the center of everythin' to run the universe. Now, these aren't the Mysterians that lost everthin' to the mages, these are the Mysterians who set up the rules of all reality. They are the ones who supposedly brought chaos to the universal order."

"You mean order *to* chaos," Vivian clarified.

"Oh, do I?" Rook asked with peak snark. "You mages think ya know everthin', but like I always say, you know only the unimportant bits. You see, in the beginnin' everything was all ordered."

"What's wrong with that?" I asked.

"Have ya ever experienced perfect order?" he asked. I thought about my aunt's house with all the plastic covers over the furniture, but doubted that counted. After neither I nor Vivian said anything, he said, "No, you haven't. Perfect order means perfect stasis. Nothin' can grow. Nothin' can change. The Mysterians added chaos and random chance to the multiverse, through a great deal of effort, I might add." He shook a scolding finger at us as though we had disputed the point. "It wasna' easy."

The never-ending bottle of wine was beginning to have its intended effect. Rook was beginning to get into his story. Now he stood in the center of the room, holding court. "It is said that long ago at the beginnin' of time itself, or at least before decent calendars and certainly before digital watches, the Mysterians, who are naturally clever and curious, found a portal at the edge of their world. In time, they managed to open it, and they went through it, and what did they find? A land that was connected to every other world in the multiverse. The Mysterians called the land More Doors."

I heard the rattle of something against the table beside me. It sounded like the key had fallen or slipped off, but when I glanced down, it was still right where I'd left it. Dismissing the incident as evidence of my increasing paranoia, I turned my attention back to Rook's story.

"They traveled through some of these portals to other lands, but everywhere they visited was locked in stasis, never changin', never growin'. It was, to put it mildly, a drag." To emphasize the point, Rook took a long drag on the bottle. He was definitely wobbling now, and I hoped he'd get through the story before he became completely incoherent. "Now, seein' as how the Mysterians found delight in change, they decided ta bring their brand of chaos to the rest of the multiverse. How you ask?" He waved an unsteady finger about. "Good question. They did it by creatin' the Mysterian pattern at the center of all these worlds."

"In the Land of More Doors?" I asked. This time I saw the key give a small jump out of the corner of my eye. I turned to stare at it, but it did nothing further and appeared unchanged. Nevertheless, I lay my hand on the table, my fingers cupping but not touching the key.

"Exactly," Rook said, spinning in Vivian's direction. "It only made sense. More Doors was incredibly well connected."

"But how does makin' a pattern spread chaos?" Vivian asked. "Isn't a pattern by definition orderly?"

"They didn't want true chaos," I answered, since Rook was having a bit of trouble focusing his eyes. "True chaos is pure destruction. They wanted to bring organized chaos. Renewal. Rebirth."

"Ayyyyyyyeeeeeee, laddie!" Rook shouted. "And they created keys attuned to the different worlds. Keys that could be used to reshape reality and bring the right amount of disorder to the multiverse. Now, most of those original keys have been lost or destroyed, but there was one key that was supposed to be indestructible. It was a Master Key meant to be able to open doors to any world and guide the pattern itself." Rook paused solemnly, or he had slipped into a standing unconsciousness, one or the other. I cleared my throat and he lurched back into speech. "That is the key that I . . . I mean, Griswald the Guardian, must have passed on to you."

Vivian and I gathered around the table while Rook swayed unsteadily on his feet. "It's like a skeleton key," she said, peering at it. "It can open anything."

"More than that," I said. "It means that this key can rewrite *the* pattern. The Mysterian's *first* pattern. The pattern of the multiverse."

Suddenly Rook slurred, "It was lef' as a safe'y measure in case thin's . . . thin's went wrong . . . But there's one prob . . . prob . . . problem. No one knows where the Lan' of More Doors is. Is lost . . . lost forever." After saying this, he swayed once, twice, and fell back onto the carpeted floor. He was snoring before his head hit the ground.

Vivian and I made sure Rook was comfortable on one of the settees before going back to contemplating the key. "The story answers a lot of questions but raises just as many," I said.

"I agree." She nodded. "If this place Rook mentioned is the most connected place in the multiverse, how did it escape the attention of Eldrin or one of your lot? Surely, someone would have stumbled on it at some point."

"Not necessarily," I said. "The multiverse is infinite, which means it could easily be out there where no one has been. Or maybe someone did stumble on it, or observe it and didn't know what they were looking at. We are also assuming the Mysterians put no protections on the place."

She nodded. "I'm also puzzled about the key. If it was really designed as a safety measure, it isn't working very well. Instead, it has been tearing up worlds, and shredding patterns, and acting like an agent of pure destruction." She curiously tapped at it with one of her nails. I noticed her finger jump when she did. She glanced at me sharply and pulled her hand away.

"It seems to have a mind of its own," I said. The moment the words were out of my mouth, I realized their significance. "That's it! The key has a mind of its own!" I shouted, and jumping to my feet, began my characteristic pacing. All the pieces were there, I just had to fit them together. Luckily, I was with Vivian, and she was amazing at puzzles. I started saying all the random thoughts I was having, hoping some of them would make sense to her.

"This whole time, we've assumed the key has been actively seeking to destroy things, but what if we're wrong? What has the key actually done?" I started counting things off on my fingers. "It took us on that awful journey through the multiverse, during which it revealed to us how Mysterium magic *really* works—the consequences. Without it doing what it did, would I ever have figured out the flaw?"

"Had it not broken your pattern on Trelari, would you have gotten up the nerve to try to destroy it?" Vivian asked.

I shook my head. "No, I kept finding excuses to use it. This battle is too important. That engagement may be the linchpin to defeating Mysterium." I turned and snapped my fingers. "And then, there's the entire journey to Mysterium's pattern. If I had never done that—"

"We never would have known about More Doors," Vivian finished the thought.

As she spoke, the key gave another violent twist, jumping several inches off the table. I turned and pointed at it, my mind finally making the connection between her mention of More Doors and the key's strange movements. "Say it again!"

"What? More Doors?" she asked.

Again, the key twisted and flipped, twining itself briefly into the oddest shape.

She and I both stood over the key and linked hands. In unison we began chanting, "More Doors! More Doors! More Doors!"

The key flipped and twisted and gyrated on the

table, and then suddenly grew quiet. In the tortuous shape of the teeth, we could see runes. I cannot say what language they were in, only that it seemed perfectly intelligible, and read, *The place where shadows die.*

A second later the runes began to melt away, and a second after that the key was as featureless as ever. Vivian and I sat on the settee, hand in hand, staring the key that had been my enemy for so long.

"It's been trying to help us all along, in the only way it knew how," I said in an awed whisper.

"Do you still think we should destroy it?" she asked.

For the first time in a long time I wasn't sure. What I did know was that the key had been trying to show me how broken the multiverse really was and that it needed to be fixed. I couldn't disagree. "I think destroying the key would be the easy way out, but I don't think that's what it wants."

"What *it* wants?" Vivian asked in more than mild confusion.

I stared at the key, nodding. "I think I understand now. It knows the multiverse is out of balance, and it knows the Mysterian pattern is to blame. I think it wants someone to rewrite the pattern. To fix the multiverse. To change everything."

At that moment, Rook rolled over in his sleep and muttered, "How can ya use it without gettin' lost? How?" Vivian put a hand on his brow until his dreams calmed and his breathing steadied.

We were silent for a long time. I hoped her mind wasn't going down the same roads as mine: death, destruction, dread, but I had long since given up trying to divine the thoughts of a diviner. "I suppose at the moment it's a bit of a moot point," she said after a while. "As long as the location of this Land of More Doors is a mystery."

I looked down at her fingers, still interlocked with mine, and wondered if I should tell her I had known where More Doors was from the moment I read the runes on the key. What would it mean for us? Another fight about what to do? More acrimony, this time with the fate of the world in the balance? Maybe I should have said nothing, at least until morning, but I'm not that smart, and I was utterly done with secrets and deceit.

"It's at the Well of Worlds," I said, still looking at her pale thin hands. "The place Rook calls the Waste. That's where we can find a door to it anyway. That's where the scraps and remains of worlds—where the shadows—go to die. The ironic thing is that the key even tried to lead us there . . ."

My voice trailed off, because Vivian's face was filled with a sudden light. As soon as I saw that expression, I knew—maybe the way she knows when she has her visions—everything that was to come. She sprang to her feet and began making plans. We could leave at once, the two of us. At first, we could travel by shifting between worlds, slowly transitioning from one to another, so there would be no gateway residue for anyone to follow. Then to the pattern, where we would fix everything, but mostly Mysterium. It was while she was telling me exactly how the world should be reordered that the Walt Whitman poem I'd read back in my Oxford days came back to me. I recited it to myself:

> I THOUGHT I was not alone, walking here
>   by the shore,
> But the one I thought was with me, as now I
>   walk by the shore,
> As I lean and look through the glimmering
>   light—that one has utterly disappeared,
> And those appear that perplex me.

I stared hard at the key. "Are you good or are you evil?" I whispered.

In my head, there came a voice, an ancient far-off voice that was probably of my own making, some imagining of what I hoped the key would be. It said, "I am what you make of me."

I flopped back on the settee and announced, "Well, we are royally screwed."

CHAPTER 21

A CLOSET FULL OF DARK LORD

Remember how I said earlier that I was at least glad I wasn't back in the Citadel of Light? Well, I was back, although this time by choice. It wasn't my choice, but someone did choose it as our next destination. That it happened not to be either me or Vivian was beside the point. But, since you have no idea what I'm talking about, let me take you back to before we arrived.

We were in Vivian's undisclosed bunker/tent location, which she had bored out of the center of a mountain. There were no entrances, no exits, and it was warded by so many spells that I don't think Eldrin could have found us, even trying his hardest. Air and water and food were conjured into existence as needed. You could live in the bunker forever, at least as long as the magic held. I now knew how it was that Vivian could disappear off the face of the world for months at a time. Needless to say, I was jealous.

We had made all our preparations for the journey. Our extradimensional folded spaces were filled with essentials, which for me mostly meant lots and lots of butterscotch candies and frozen mice. (Quick parenting tip: if you make a pinprick hole in your folded space, the relentless cold of the ether vacuum will turn any pocket into a convenient deep freeze.) Vivian had even written a note for the still-unconscious Rook explaining how to use the tent flap to transport himself back to Valdara. Finally, we carefully woke Harold, which nearly gave up the game but didn't thanks to the aforementioned candies. I was just about to step through the tent when Vivian asked, quite clearly and calmly, "Are you coming or not, Sam?"

Turning, I hissed, "Vivian, what are you doing?"

She laughed; it was light and lovely. "Avery, he's been awake since last night. I doubt he slept for fear we would sneak out on him."

I cast my eye over him. He sure looked like he was deep asleep. "Is this true, Sam?" I asked.

At my question, he sat up. "I did nap here and there. I couldn't help it."

"You've been eavesdropping on me again!"

"I keep telling you, I have nothing to do with dropping eaves," Sam said with great dignity. "All I was doing was listening while pretending to be asleep."

"That's the same thing," I snapped.

"Oh," he replied. "Then I guess I was." He hopped to his feet. He was fully dressed and ready to go. "Don't leave me behind, Avery," he pleaded. "I have to go with you. I want to see the Land of More Doors and learn exactly how shadows die. I want to be there when you destroy the key or the pattern or whatever it is you're trying to do this time."

"Well, that makes one of us," I muttered and chewed on my lip while I thought about him. He had become a remarkably powerful mage, particularly in battle. Without him in the Provost's Tower, I would not have made it. There was also some nice symmetry to having him along. If my suspicions were correct, either Vivian or I wouldn't make it out of the Waste. (I was pulling very hard for it to be me, of course.) Anyway, presuming things worked out the way I wanted, she would need someone to save her from herself. "All right, come along," I said. "But I swear to the gods, if you say—"

"Neat!" he exclaimed and did a little bounce on the tips of his toes. I slapped a hand across my face and opened the flap. My foot was almost through when he said, "But I need to make a quick stop to say goodbye to Valdara and the others first."

I will not bother you with the argument that ensued. Oddly it was two-sided, and I was in the minority. Vivian seemed perfectly at ease with us traveling to the citadel. I know it speaks volumes about the lack of trust in our relationship, but she was so suspiciously accommodating I actually checked my pockets to make sure the key was still there. Outnumbered, I conceded, but said that Vivian and I would only go under a heavy obfuscation spell, and we would stay locked in my rooms while he made his goodbyes. I had no desire for a scene between Vivian and Valdara, or me and Valdara for that matter.

That's how I found myself in my chambers at the top of what the Trelarian locals called Magus Tower. If you find it weird that I would choose to go there because it would be the first place someone would look for me, I would only point out that this is the first time I've mentioned the fact that I even have rooms in the citadel. It is well-known that I avoid them like the plague, and the reason for that?

"You should really get this blood cleaned out of your dread cloak or it will stain," Vivian said. She was standing in front of a large black wood armoire, inspecting my Dark Lord costume. She'd already noted that my skeletal mask was beginning to show signs of wear and been appalled over the state of my platform boots. She popped the mask on and turned about dramatically. "I am the Dark Lord," she announced in as deep a voice as she could muster. "All will kneel before me or die!"

I laughed and threw a pillow at her. "I don't sound anything like that."

"Of course you don't, dear," she reassured me, hanging up the mask and closing the armoire. "I always thought you were going for a kind of Dr. Claw thing."

I sat up in the bed where I been sprawled and pointed at her with a snap. "Exactly! Thank—" Then I remembered that she had been the one that compared me to Master Blaster. "Wait a minute!" I cried. "When we were fighting on the pattern, you told me I sounded like Master Blaster."

I'm not sure I've ever seen Vivian look so abashed, or abashed at all for that matter. She stared down at her feet. "That was mean of me. I only said it because my vision told me that was what you needed to hear to hate me as much as possible. I don't even know who Master Blaster is."

"Why did you want me to hate you?"

"Because I needed you off Trelari before the next attack by Moregoth," she said, as though that explained it all. When she saw I was not satisfied with the answer, she let out a little sigh. "I reasoned that if you hated me, you would go off-world. I admit I was pretty desperate."

I pursed my lips in thought. "It didn't work, you know. I was afraid of you for a while, but hate? Never."

"That's the thing you've never understood about my sight," she said with a shrug. "It gets the big things right, but most of the time it's wrong, particularly about the specifics. For example, I had no idea why you needed Eldrin or Stheno with you, only that you did."

At the mention of Eldrin and Stheno, I jumped to my feet. "By the gods! They have no idea what happened to us."

In an instant, I had pulled out my BIT coin and activated it. Eldrin's image flickered to life. Unusually, he was wearing very formal mage robes; more typically, he was studying a giant stack of papers. "Yes, Avery?" he asked impatiently, still looking through the papers.

"I'm sorry I didn't call earlier, but I am out of Mysterium!" I said, putting as much urgency as I could into my voice. "You can abort your mission and get out of there!"

He looked at me with a bemused expression. "Why would we do that? The student revolt has been a smashing success. We have nearly the entire campus behind us."

"Yes, but you are in terrible danger!"

I heard a snort of disbelief from somewhere to Eldrin's left. He made a gesture and Dawn stepped into view. "Can you explain things to Avery?" he asked. "I have to go over our latest protest schedule."

She nodded and turned to me, hands on her hips. "We are exceedingly busy, but let me just say that the Administration would never move against the students. It would trigger an all-out rebellion from the innerworlds, and they can't afford to lose any more support. Already their resources are stretched tighter than a drum."

Vivian poked her head into view and waved. "Hi, Dawn!"

Dawn waved back and smiled. "Hi, Vivian! It's nice to see the two of you back together . . . and not threatening each other with annihilation." She looked back and forth between Vivian and me, her piercing gaze studying us. "What are the two of you up to anyway?"

I tried to signal to Vivian not to say anything, but she just kissed me on the cheek and said, "Avery doesn't want you to know, but it turns out the key is more powerful than we guessed. We are off to rewrite the pattern at the center of the multiverse."

This merited a blink of surprise from Dawn and a full double take from Eldrin. "You're what?" he asked.

I sighed. "We are going to take the key to a pattern we discovered that appears to be what feeds power to Mysterium. We think we can rewrite it and cut off the flow." I scratched at the back of my head nervously. "I may not be able to talk to you again for . . . for some time."

The papers dropped from his hands. "Avery—" he said, and there was something in the way he said my name that said everything.

"I know," I said, not wanting to meet his gaze, but unable to look away. I considered that this would probably be the last time I would see those star-speckled eyes. "I had hoped—"

I couldn't finish, but he also understood. "Yeah, me too," he said, and then he smiled, one of those perfect, infuriating, Eldrin smiles. "We'll always have McKinley College."

"Yes, we will." I laughed. "Doorknobs that don't work and walls that phase out of existence."

"Good times," he said, and I knew he was saying, *I love you and goodbye.*

"The best," I agreed.

I passed the coin to Vivian so she could say her goodbyes to Dawn, and Eldrin did the same. Vivian turned to me when she was done. Tears were in her eyes and she wiped them dry. "Don't you want to say goodbye to Eldrin?" she asked.

I shook my head. "We've said everything we can."

She broke the connection and began to wander around the room, while I sank into a thoughtful silence. Eventually her meanderings took her to the bookshelf. "Have you read any of these?" she asked.

I shook my head. "The whole thing is a stage prop. I suppose it's what I am also. The only thing here that's mine is this." I picked up a book from my nightstand that I'd been reading back when I had time to do such things and tossed it across the bed toward her.

She read the back. "What kind of wizard is Neil deGrasse Tyson?"

"The kind that changes planets to dwarf planets."

Vivian nodded. "Astromancer then."

I chuckled, and she came and sat next to me on the bed. "Are you laughing at me?"

"Absolutely not," I answered as we leaned against the headboard and I put an arm around her. "It's just so easy to forget that we come from such different places."

"I suppose," she said and plucked at the cuff of my robe.

I swallowed, because I knew I was approaching a sensitive subject. "If you ever did want to talk about where you came from—"

She tensed in my arms. "I can't. Not yet. Not while the end is still so uncertain."

I left it alone until I felt her body relax again. I suppose I would have happily let the silence stretch on, but after a few minutes she said, "You really did make an excellent Dark Lord."

"Thanks . . . I think," I said and thought back to Eldrin and me dreaming up my "look" so many years ago. It had all seemed such a lark. "You know, I actually studied old episodes of *Inspector Gadget* trying to get the voice right. Can you imagine? I can't believe how naïve I was. 'What are you doing for your thesis?' 'Nothing much, I'm just going to save this reality from itself.'"

"We didn't know any better," she said.

"I didn't know any better," I corrected. "You were switched on from the beginning."

"It's only that I had the advantage of disadvantage."

I turned her chin so I could seem those gold-rimmed eyes. "Never minimize what you had to go through, Vivian. You may not like to talk about it, but I know that it cost you a great deal."

"Every morn and every night?" she asked.

"Indeed."

I stared at the flames in the fireplace across the room. I think Sam or Ariella had cast an endless fire spell on it, because the thing never seemed to need more logs. The two of them had tried very hard to make me feel at home. They had decorated the whole place for me, and it had an aura of a wizard's bedroom and study, complete with a perch for Harold, which he was currently using to nap on, inlaid bookcases filled with exotic-looking tomes, a globe of the cosmos that was highly inaccurate, a telescope out on a balcony that the guy who made the globe of the cosmos probably needed more than me. There was even a broken-in leather chair by the fire that had a little table standing next to it on which rested a very beautiful long-stem pipe. I don't smoke, of course, but it sure looked right over there. What I couldn't get over was how much I wanted it all to suit me, but how little it actually did.

For better or worse, I had lived my life in conventional little houses, and dorm rooms, and apartments. Places with microwaves and TVs and, when I was lucky, air-conditioning. In short, I was the least wizardly wizard you've ever met. I found staves annoying and wands intolerable. I preferred blue jeans and sneakers to robes and boots and cloaks. That I was wearing all that now was simply a function of needing as many pockets as possible to carry Harold's stuff. It started me thinking about what would happen after the Waste.

"What do you want to do after?" I asked, taking the opportunity to bury my face in Vivian's hair. Heavenly.

She had been tracing some pattern on the back of my hand with her nail and hadn't heard me. "Hmm?" she asked.

"After we are done in the Waste, what do you want to do?"

"Oh, I don't know," she said dreamily. "I hadn't thought a lot about it. Probably either try to rule the world or go somewhere and have lots of babies. It's a bit hard to decide right now, but I'm sure the two aren't terribly compatible."

A lump of fear rose in my throat, and I'm not sure which future terrified me the most. Fortunately, I never had to take a position one way or the other, because at this point the door to my chambers banged open downstairs.

"Avery!" Valdara called. "Are you hiding up there?"

I heard the heavy tread of feet coming up the tightly wound stairs. Vivian and I jumped out of bed. She began to weave a gateway, but I shook my head. "Ariella is probably with them. She'll detect it for sure. We're going to have to hide you."

I glanced around the room. What to do? The feet were getting very close now.

"Magus Stewart!" Valdara boomed again. "You better not even think of trying to portal out of here, or I'll have Ariella drag you back by your ear!"

"Hey, Avery!" I heard Ariella sing from somewhere below.

We both dropped to our knees and looked under the bed. It was a sea of dust bunnies. "No way!" Vivian said.

"Right!" I pulled her to her feet and looked desperately about. Chair? No. Fireplace? Obviously not. Armoire? "The armoire!" I hissed.

Without waiting for her make up her mind, I opened the door and pushed her inside. She poked her head back out. "They're bound to look in here."

I shoved her head back, slammed the door, and leaned casually against it as Valdara came into view. Drake was behind her, and I could see Ariella and a crestfallen Sam behind him. Valdara and Drake had obviously recently been in battle. Her armor was dented, and his cloak appeared to be singed. She fixed burning eyes on me and advanced, her gauntleted hands clenching and unclenching in anger.

"What the hell were you thinking, running off like that?" she asked.

"I was trying to destroy the key," I mumbled.

"Interesting, I thought that whether and how to destroy the key was still a question for all of us to answer," she spat, and I mean that literally. Still, I didn't dare try to wipe off my cheek.

"You . . . you seemed busy?"

I saw Drake give a shake of his head and knew that had been the wrong thing to say. She punched the door of the armoire next to my head. Inside, I heard Vivian give a squeak of alarm, which I tried to cover by making my own squeak. Valdara didn't seem to notice, because she began stalking back and forth in front of me, raging.

"Yes, we've been extremely busy. The Mysterium has been relentless in its assaults. And just when the pace of war seems to be picking up, what do I find? Three of my top lieutenants gone. If it weren't for Khagad and Burub rallying the Army of Shadow in your and Vivian's absence, there might be catapults and battering rams at the very walls of the citadel itself!"

From inside the armoire, I heard Vivian give a very quiet clap of joy when Vivian mentioned Khagad and Burub. They were two of her top orc lieutenants. She had always urged me to give them more responsibility, something I was loath to do, because each topped nine feet and I was afraid what would happen if we ever had a tactical disagreement. Anyway, I was sure I was never going to hear the end of it, but right now I had to remind Vivian where she was . . . exactly.

As casually as I could, I slapped my hands back on the armoire as though pushing myself off and wandered over to the fire. "I know it was wrong, Your Majesty," I said somberly. "But I felt it was my duty."

Valdara spun on me and roared, "Your duty was here! With your queen! And even if you did think it was *your* duty, why take Sam? Ariella has had to do all the work of four mages while you've been gallivanting about."

"Oh, I don't mind," Ariella said. "I don't sleep, and the extra work gives me something to do while everyone else is unconscious. Otherwise, I just knit, or write poetry, or sculpt . . . something like that."

"And b-b-begging you pardon, Your Majesty," Sam said quietly. "Avery didn't bring me. I kind of followed him."

"Fine! All of you are idiots!" Valdara roared. "At least tell me you were able to destroy this key once and for all."

I swallowed hard before admitting, "No, Your Majesty. We did get to the pattern, but nothing happened to the key. Only through Sam's heroics did we manage to keep it from falling into the hands of Moregoth."

She folded her arms. "I see. Well, if the key can't be destroyed, then is it finally time to use it as a weapon?"

I shook my head. "It is still what it was, Your Majesty. The more we use it, the more of Trelari or some other world it will consume."

Valdara studied me. "So, there's nothing that it can do to help us?"

"We could defeat the Sealers with it, but there's every chance that we would destroy Trelari in the process."

"I will let it go for now," she said reluctantly. "But we are not doing well in this war. With the Sealers' recent victories and the intensity of their latest attacks, we need to strengthen the army and marshal all of our defenses."

"I just told you the key won't help," I objected.

"I wasn't talking about the key. I was talking about one of my greatest archmages—you, Avery. I need the man who was willing to give his life for Trelari. Remember him? I need the most powerful wizard that I know, and I could really use the armies of the Dark Lord too." She stabbed a pointing finger toward the armoire, and my heart lurched. Fortunately, she didn't seem interested in me donning the outfit then and there.

She lowered her voice; it was almost plaintive. "Can you help me with that? Because the you that I've had for the last several weeks has been worse than useless. I can't afford to have a Dark Lord in hiding, a Dark Lord trying to figure his life out, a Dark Lord playing wet nurse to a baby imp. I need you here, now, and helping with every fiber of your being."

I wasn't sure what to say. I certainly wasn't going to make a promise to her I knew I would break as soon as she left. I settled on, "That makes sense."

"Yes, it does," agreed Valdara, clapping a hand to my shoulder. "Now get yourself together and be ready to defend Trelari. We need you."

"Agreed," said Drake.

"I'll . . ." I paused, not sure what I was willing to say. "I'll get myself together."

Valdara nodded. "Report by tomorrow morning. Is there anything you need?"

"Butterscotch?" inquired a suddenly awake Harold.

Drake and Valdara both shook their heads and began to leave when something seemed to occur to her. "One more thing!" She pushed Seamus, who had been screened behind the others this whole time, forward. He was holding a large metal box in his hands. "What exactly is this?" she asked, and at a nod, Seamus opened a heavily padded lid.

The stench of rotten eggs and teriyaki sauce came rolling out, along with a floating skull. "I've heard of rough crowds, but this is ridiculous," he said. "I haven't been in such a tight space since my own funeral. Get it? My own funeral." He giggled at his own joke.

"Be quiet!" Valdara ordered.

"No problem," Gray replied, and then because he couldn't help himself, he added, "I can be as quiet as the grave. Get it? The grave."

Valdara was done. She shoved him back in the box and slammed the lid closed. "I will ask again, what is that?"

"He's a demi-lich," I sighed. "And he's not that bad. What I mean to say is his humor is terrible, but he is actually an ally."

"His name is Gray!" Sam announced proudly.

Valdara glared at him and said, "I will deal with you later. Right now I want to know why this Gray appeared in the Great Hall, unannounced?"

"Ah," I said. "He was on the quest with Sam and I to destroy the key. He was the only one able to transport out using our original escape plan."

She began massaging her temples vigorously. "What do you propose to do with him, because he's not coming out of that box in my presence again unless you tell me he can single-handedly"—the box gave a jolt of protest—"single-headedly," she amended, "take down Moregoth himself."

"You may leave him with me, Your Majesty," I said with a bow. I realized too late it was my first bow since she'd entered. Royal protocol has never been my strong suit.

"Gladly!" She nodded to Seamus, who set the box down on the floor with remarkable alacrity. She began to leave, but just as she reached the top of the stairs, she turned. "I will expect you in the Council Chamber in fifteen minutes, Magus Stewart."

Thankfully she waited for no response before marching down the stairs, because I couldn't think of a reply that wouldn't have been a straight-up lie. Seamus followed at her heels, an enormous smile of relief on his face. I had to admit that dealing with Gray did take a lot of work.

Drake stood at the top of the stairs until Valdara and Seamus were in the room below before turning to me. He leaned on his staff. "Something tells me you won't be making that meeting." I started to protest and he waved my words away with the smallest gesture of his fingers. "It's okay, kid. I know you're meant to be doing other things right now. This war is Trelari's to fight, and as much as Valdara wants every weapon she can get, you're not one of us." He cast his eye on Sam and winked. "As for you, my young wizard, I think I may have a message I need you to run up to Magus Stewart in about five minutes. Understand?"

For once Sam did, completely. He gave a quick nod and scampered down the stairs after the others. With a tip of an imaginary cap to me, Drake started down after him.

"Thank you, Drake," I said and touched my hand to my heart, a gesture that had meant something to him once, before I'd stolen his faith.

He returned the gesture with a sad smile that spoke volumes. "Oh and, Avery, tell that lady of yours that if she's going to make a habit of hiding in people's wardrobes she needs to learn to breathe quieter." I blushed at getting caught and he laughed. "Good luck to us all," he announced and was gone.

At last I was alone. I walked across to the armoire and was halfway there when I realized Ariella was still in the room, standing perfectly still near the fire. My heart leapt to my throat. "Ariella . . . I don't . . . It isn't . . ."

"Be at peace, Avery," she said with a laugh that brought to mind bells tinkling in a spring breeze. "I knew you and Vivian had arrived as soon as you portaled in. I could feel it in the land like the striking of a great gong."

At this, Vivian emerged from the wardrobe. She walked up behind me and put an arm around my waist. "I'm sorry I haven't been around much lately, Ariella," I said. "I know I ruined your chance to study at Mysterium, and I promised to teach you, but something always seemed to get in the way. I'm sorry about that also, because you deserve a good teacher. One who can focus on you."

"You're worried about that?" she asked. "I've thought a lot about what they taught at Mysterium, and I don't think I would have liked it much. In fact, I've decided to start my own school of magic, here on Trelari. It will focus a bit more on time and discipline and consequence . . . and of course it will have loads of electives." She laughed again, a brook babbling through a wooded glade.

Vivian and I embraced her. "Thank you for everything, Ariella," I said. "I saw Rook's leg. It was a stunning piece of craftsmanship. If that is what you will be teaching at your school, then I may be the first to apply."

I had meant it as a joke as much as a compliment, but Ariella's face clouded. "I do not think I would accept you as a student," she said seriously. I drew back, a little hurt. She smiled, but it was touched with sadness. "It is not that I do not think you are worthy of a place. I am sure there is still a great deal more you could teach me about magic than I could teach you. But as much as I love you, Drake was right, you do not belong here. Your comings and goings shake the foundations of the world. If Trelari is to be at peace one day, then it will be without you." She turned to Vivian. "Either of you."

She kissed us both in the fashion of the elves. "Goodbye, and may the sun and stars and the moon grace your path," she said and glided down the stairs.

Vivian and I stood in silence long after the door in the chamber below had closed behind her. At last she said, "I think we've been dismissed."

She was right. I thought about how that made me feel. I'd devoted a large portion of my life to Trelari. First, to try, as I thought at the time, to save it. Then to try to save it from Vivian, who it turns out was trying to save it herself. Then to try to save it from a madman, only to be saved myself by its queen. And now to save it from the entire weight of the Mysterium, only to be told that my services were no longer needed. The only constant this whole time turned out be how wrong I'd been in my assumption that Trelari needed me at all. It turned out what it needed most was to be left alone. And, as was typical, an elf had to explain it to me.

Vivian and I held each other and exchanged stories, both happy and sad, about our time on Trelari. We kept finding ourselves being moved from tears to laughter and back again. We happened to be laughing when Sam made his way back to the room.

"What's so funny?" he asked.

"We've been fired," Vivian announced, wiping the tears from her eyes with the edge of her sleeve.

"Gosh! Sorry!" he said.

"Don't be." I bent and picked up Gray's box, which Vivian and I, by silent agreement, had decided not to open until we were elsewhere. "It was the right choice."

Sam was still confused when Vivian swept an arm around his shoulder and led him toward the armoire where she and I had drawn a travel portal of pretty significant complexity. We all stepped in and closed the doors. The wardrobe deconstructed itself plank by plank, and we were off.

CHAPTER 22

WASTED

The armoire reconstructed itself—and us—at the edge of the Well of Worlds. A gray snow was falling from a leaden sky, and the churning mass of grinding shadows seethed at our feet. Across the frozen landscape, I could hear the wind blowing, seeming to whisper the languages of forgotten souls, which I supposed it probably was. I guess what I'm saying is that the place was as depressing as ever.

It was Sam, with a scratch of his head, that asked the obvious question. "If this is the portal, how do we get in without ending up like Rook?"

"We use this," I said and, pulling the key out of my pocket, held it up dramatically.

"Didn't Rook also have the key?" Sam pointed out.

"Yes, okay, he had the key," I conceded, irritated that my dramatic moment had been ruined by the truth. Also, the key was bloody heavy right now. All it wanted was to get to the Waste, and it kept urging me to dive right in. Fortunately, while I'm an idiot, I'm not that much of an idiot. "The advantage we have over Rook is that we know that this is the Master Key," I explained. "We know that one of its chief functions is to open the way to what lies beyond. All we have to do is let it work."

I started to open my will to the key but stopped. Too many times I had tried to go it alone, and the consequences had been universally bad. Also, the closer we got to the end, the greater the danger that I would lose myself. I gestured the others over. "We do this together."

Vivian and Sam exchanged a glance but grabbed the key. For Sam, it was the first time holding it, and his eyes went wide, his pupils dilating at the feeling of the power. For Vivian, the reaction was more of relief—the shudder of a junkie long denied a fix. I gave them a moment to adjust. When I thought they were ready, I said, "Concentrate on opening the gateway. Together now."

At first I felt nothing but my own will, then Vivian and Sam joined. Our combined consciousness began to build toward a crescendo. It was exhilarating right up to the moment that Gray's box came tumbling out of the armoire and landed at our feet.

"Stop!" I shouted. "Everyone stop. I forgot the bloody demi-lich."

Slowly, I might even say reluctantly, we reduced the flow of power until the key was dormant in our hands. The effort was enormous. While the others recovered, I bent and opened the metal lid of the box. Out flew Gray. His eyes were blazing with the injustice of his imprisonment.

"What is the meaning of this? To be imprisoned without trial. It's an outrage. Do I not have rights? Am I not a man?"

I raised a finger. "Technically, no. You're a soul cage. It doesn't mean you don't have subjectivity, but what recourse you may have to the law is an open question. I think Anthony wrote a lot about the subject in some of his works."

"You must be great at parties," Gray snarked, and it was a fair point. He spun about, taking everything in. "Nice place." And I think he meant that sincerely. "What are we doing?"

"Before you interrupted us, we were going to open a gateway to a pattern at the center of the multiverse," I answered, impatiently slapping the key against my thigh.

"Well, don't let me keep you."

Moments later, Vivian, Sam, and I were directing the power of the Master Key at the portal to the Waste. As we watched, the swirling vortex of dying shadows parted in the middle and a stair of ashen blocks formed from the nothing. It led from the edge where we stood down to a vast horizon of black and purple and gray, like a bruise on creation. It was a spectacle that had likely not been witnessed even in the lifetimes of the elves. Sam summed it up best when he said, "Golly!"

With Gray floating behind us, we descended. I reached the bottom first, and have no words to describe it. That's not to say that I can't describe what it looked like. In fact, that's quite easy. It was flat and featureless. There were no hills, no mountains, no trees, no plants or animals or birds of any kind. It was a waste, the ground covered in black-and-purple grains of sand, with a mix of gray ash—the remains of worlds long since dead. The only striking feature was the sky, which was an inverted whirlpool of dark clouds cut by flashes of ghostly lightning. However, while I can tell you what it looks like, it is impossible to express how it felt. I have traveled to hundreds of worlds. I have seen ocean planets where waves can rise hundreds of meters into the sky. I have climbed mountains that extend to space. I have eaten in restaurants at the end of the universe. But I had never been in a place where I felt so alien. The land was not just dead, because death is a part of the cycle of life.

This was different. It felt like the opposite of life. The opposite of creation.

"This looks like undead paradise," Gray said in an attempt at jest, but his words floated out on the wind and joined the faint chorus of the dead. "Although, it's a bit creepy even for me."

"Creepy," rasped Harold in about the creepiest way possible. I looked back at him. He was clearly not happy to be here. I tried to hand him a butterscotch, but he pushed it away.

Sam came sprinting down the stairs after me. He also looked unnerved by the experience. "I don't like this place, Avery."

"I don't think we're supposed to like it, Sam."

Vivian came last. She looked about with a nod. "No pattern here, do you know which way we should go?"

I shook my head, but the key was tugging at my hand in a most definite direction. "I may not, but the key seems to," I said and pointed across the Waste. There was nothing to see, but something was out there that the key wanted to get to very badly.

Without another word, we set out. I can't say how long we walked. We tried to keep our spirits up by talking or singing songs we all knew, but the voices on the winds would always come and steal the words away. Eventually we stopped talking altogether. We also eventually learned that the land was not absolutely flat. There were great dunes of dust and sand and ash that would rise up unexpectedly in front of us. We would climb for a time, sinking knee deep in the foul stuff, and then descend, sometimes falling and sliding as the ground gave out suddenly under our feet.

We had just come down one of these mountains of ash when Sam broke our communal silence. "I . . . I can't see the stair anymore."

I turned about, and sure enough, it was gone. Its line of gray in the sky had been the one reassuring constant in this featureless and shifting world. Without it, the Waste looked the same in all directions, an expanse of black and gray under a swirling sky. It was demoralizing enough that none of us wanted to go on. Besides, it seemed like the light was failing and the air was growing cold, a grim twilight fading to night. I tried to cast a spell to provide us some warmth, but the magic flickered and died on my fingertips. "No magic," I announced.

Vivian nodded. "Yeah, I tried as soon as we arrived. The whole place is a dead zone."

I expected some kind of crack from Gray, but he seemed exhausted. As soon as we made the decision to stop, he dropped to the ground, the embers of his eyes glowing dimly, like coals on a dying fire.

"Are you okay, Gray?" I asked.

He shifted slightly, nodding. "Just . . . tired."

Vivian and I looked at each other with concern. This confirmed that the Waste was having an effect on all enchantments, even the one that kept him animated. It was possible that if we stayed here too long, he might simply fade away.

Harold climbed off my shoulder and went to lie in Vivian's lap. He had grown a lot lately, but in this place he seemed more and more like the old, old Harold, the one that started this journey with me what seemed like ages ago. Vivian handed him a butterscotch to try to raise his spirits, but he fell asleep, the candy still unwrapped in his hand. It reminded me that imps are also creatures of magic. Could the Waste be draining him, too?

I closed my eyes and felt at the line of magic that connected us. He was most definitely weaker. I could almost feel the drain on him, like air running out of a pierced balloon. I gathered what little of my own power I could find and fed it to him through the connection. I was relieved to see that it seemed to have an effect. His body relaxed and his breathing steadied.

"You won't be able to do that forever," Vivian said, putting a hand on my shoulder.

"I don't have to do it forever," I replied, "just long enough."

While Vivian and I contemplated Harold, Sam was unloading his pack. He pulled out several blankets and began laying them over the purple-gray sand. The colors seemed to fade from the cloth as soon as they touched the ground. Then he began pulling a few sticks from out of his pack.

"What are you doing?" I asked.

"Building a fire," he answered, looking at me as if that were the most obvious thing in the world.

"Won't that be seen for a hundred miles?" I asked.

"I don't think so," said Sam. "I chose this place because it's in a hollow in the dunes. Besides, there doesn't seem to be anyone else about. Should I not?"

The moaning wind picked that time to swirl around us. I shivered. It was definitely getting colder. "Go ahead," I said.

"How are you going to light it?" Vivian asked. "This place seems to devour magic."

"Don't worry!" Sam said excitedly. "We have the power!"

"What power?" I asked, sitting up.

"The power of Gray, the skull!" He pointed at the demi-lich.

Gray's eyes flared to life for a moment. "Sorry, Sam, not tonight."

"But I've seen you shooting eldritch fire from your eye sockets."

"Sam, have you not noticed the magical drain?" I asked.

He nodded. "But Gray isn't a mage."

"But he is magical," Vivian pointed out.

"Oh, right," Sam mumbled. "Sorry."

A little of Gray's old fire seemed to return. His eyes flared to life and he said, "I am magical though.

If you cut me, do I not bleed?" No one said anything. "Okay, bad example, but you know what I mean."

"Yes, we do," I said. "Now, I happen to have a way to light the fire, and it doesn't require magic or other impossibilities, like me striking stones against each other or rubbing sticks together." I reached deep into my folded space and pulled out my lighter. "I give you, the BIC."

"I thought you didn't smoke," Vivian said accusingly.

"I don't. This is for exactly one circumstance." I held the lighter up, lit it, and shouted, "Free Bird!"

The voices took up this chorus, which quickly dampened my enthusiasm. I handed the lighter to Sam, who studied it suspiciously. After explaining how to work it, and what a free bird was, he bent to his task. Fortunately, he turned out to be a wizard (no pun intended) with fire. Soon the logs were burning brightly, and we crowded together. The warmth was nice, but even better, the light from the fire made it impossible to see the surrounding desolation.

I'm sure we should have been worried about whatever terrors might be lurking out there, or setting watches, or any of the things that come with camping while on an adventure, but no one mentioned them, and I certainly wasn't going to be the killjoy. I was perfectly content to lie down next to Vivian and watch the shadows of the flames dance across the dunes. Gods, I was tired.

I drifted off to sleep and soon found myself dreaming of Moregoth. I saw him searching for me, floating between worlds, seeking, seeking, his vaporish arms coming closer and closer. "Avery! Avery Stewart. I will find you." The words came out in a whispered rasp.

I sat upright, startled awake by the dream. Harold was huddled against my chest. He felt cold. The fire had gone out at some point. I wrapped my cloak around him and was settling back when I realized that Vivian wasn't beside me. I started to rise, looking for her, when Sam grabbed me and bent close to my ear.

"Quiet!" he ordered with a hiss. "Something is out there."

I waited, unmoving and silent, straining to see and hear in the quiet darkness. It took a few minutes, but then I began to sense what Sam had: that something was moving out there. I heard it more than saw it, and felt its presence even more keenly as a kind of chill deeper than the night. Eventually I saw the faint outlines of a dark, floating silhouette against the dunes.

My first thought on seeing it move was that it was Moregoth. However, it had an unsettling emptiness about it that I had never felt before. I'd like to make a Moregoth's-brain joke here, but I really wasn't in a joking mood. My throat tightened and I broke out in a cold sweat. When I thought things couldn't get worse, it shrieked out a single word: "Key!"

That was all the warning I needed. My hand was in my pocket in a flash. I didn't know what would happen if I used the key in this world, but I wasn't about to let this abomination roam free while Vivian was out there alone!

I was just rising to my feet when a putrid blue fog covered me. Gray had levitated himself between us and the faceless cloak. I nearly gagged from the odor, and my eyes started watering. "Hiya!" he said, addressing the creature. "I'm Gray, though if you want a formal name, at least one of my friends calls me Gray Skull."

There was no response for a breath, but then it answered with another shriek of "Key!"

"Nice to meet you, Key. I'm a demi-lich who has lost his way while traveling across existence. What's your story?" The cloak only drifted a little closer. "I'm a comedian. Do you want to hear a good joke about a banshee, a werewolf, and a vampire who go to a revival meeting?"

While Gray distracted the creature, I rose slowly to my feet. Now that I had some perspective, I could see that the creature was enormous, or at least that the edges of its body blended so perfectly with the darkness that it was impossible to tell where it ended and the night began. It seemed to tower over Gray. "Key!" the creature screamed again.

With the key in hand, I took aim at the creature. At the same time, Gray's eyes blazed with infernal light. We were both a heartbeat away from attacking when a purple light appeared behind it. The cloak wheeled about with a cry, and then darted across the sand and over the dune like a shadow running from the light.

Gray and I tensed, waiting to see what was behind this new threat, but it turned out to be Vivian. She stepped forward, hands raised. "Stand down, boys. It's just me."

The demi-lich let out a rattling sigh and dropped out of the air like a stone. He hit the ground and rolled down a little slope in the dune, coming to rest on his side. I dropped to the ground next to him and set him upright. "Gray? Gray?" I called, but he said nothing. The only sign I could see that he was still animated were two very faint pinpricks burning deep within his skull.

"What the hell was that?" I asked Vivian. "And where did you come from?"

"I was just out . . . looking," she said and knelt to the ground so she could cradle Gray against her chest. "As for that thing. It was a Hollow."

"A Hollow?" I asked.

"Yes," she said. "I've run into them before in subworld. They are the empty remains of a being whose world has been destroyed, and roam through the multiverse seeking essence from the living. Usually, they don't bother with the undead."

"He was trying to defend us," I explained.

She nodded, and her hand stroked the side of Gray's skull. To my great surprise, I saw a small blue spark arc from her fingertips into him. His eyes seemed to brighten, and Vivian let out a sigh. I almost asked her what she was doing. She had no connection to Gray that I knew of, and I also knew how much that little jolt must have cost her.

While I was contemplating the riddle of Vivian, Sam asked quietly, "Do Hollows kill people?"

"Only the deathly ones," Vivian replied, still lost in her own thoughts. She gave her head a little shake and jumped to her feet. "I think the light is beginning to return. Let's move on." She carefully set Gray into one of the pockets of her robe and went to rouse Harold.

"Fine by me," Sam said. "I want to be miles from here, and the sooner the better."

While he bustled about packing the blankets back into his bags, I studied Vivian. I had known her long enough to know when she was hiding something. She hadn't simply been wandering about in the night. Somehow, she had known something was coming. Could she still be playing the angles, even now?

I was still lost in these thoughts as we began our second day in the Waste. The dawn, or what passed for one, made us feel better. Well, "better" considering that we were still in a desolate landscape with a cease-less wind that sounded like the cries of the damned. But after hours of walking, and with no sign or landmark to show us that we were making progress, our steps began to slow. My thoughts turned more and more frequently to the key. Despite its continual pull, I wondered if I was missing something. The gate to the Land of More Doors had to be here! The waste couldn't just be nothing for no reason.

"Sealers," hissed Sam, tugging at the sleeve of my robe and pulling me to the ground.

Vivian dropped down beside us. "Where?"

His hand shot out to our left. It wasn't easy to make them out, but now that I knew where to look I could see them. They were still pretty far off, small dots of red in a world of gray. Harold definitely knew they were there. He was agitated and kept hissing, "Sealers!"

I hoped that they hadn't spotted us also, but there seemed little doubt that they were tracking us. Some-how, Moregoth had found me—again. I suspected it was the key, or perhaps opening the gate had drawn him to this world. It had taken an enormous amount of energy to break the seal to the Waste.

"Okay, I have a new plan for where we go," I declared. "Anywhere they're not."

Vivian shook her head in disagreement. "The Sealers don't matter. We need to follow the key. We won't survive long in this abyss if we let Moregoth dictate where we go."

Putting together his longest and most disturbing set of words to date, Harold said in apparent agreement, "Nasty evil Sealers!" I didn't disagree, but I was also hoping he was just in a phase.

I decided to see if we could follow both my plan and Vivian's at the same time. Focusing on the key, I followed the arrow it was drawing in my mind. At least it wasn't the worst case scenario. Although Moregoth was heading the same direction we were, he wasn't directly between us and where the key wanted us to be. I really didn't want to have a showdown with Moregoth and an army of Sealers, but Vivian was right—we wouldn't survive long in this hellscape. Gray was almost gone. Harold would be next. The rest of us might be able survive on whatever we'd tucked away in our cloaks and pockets for a time, but this place was worse than death, worse than decay, it was unlife.

"Right!" I said, making a decision. "We go as fast and as hard as we can toward whatever it is the key is leading us to. But we are going to have to be careful. If the Sealers see us, they'll be on us in no time, and the only magic we have now is the key."

Everyone nodded agreement, and we slithered back down the dune. We made our way as directly as we could toward what I hoped was the gate. We kept as close as possible to the valleys and depressions between the dunes, but there was precious little cover. Often, we had to make mad scrambles over ridges or across vast stretches of slate-flat ground. Although we couldn't see them anymore, we all felt Moregoth's eyes on us, and we all knew we were being hunted.

We were taking a break in another little valley between dunes when they found us. The sky was beginning to darken when Sam cried out, "Sealers!" He stabbed his finger to the ridge of the dune on our right, and there they were. A line of crimson with a spot of black in the center.

They must have seen us at the same time, because there was dark laughter on the air, and the line of crimson came flowing down the side of the dune toward us like a wave, with the black spot at its crest.

"Up!" I shouted. "Run for the ridge!"

Sam reached for his pack, but I shoved him forward, pulling Vivian up beside me. Up, up, we drove our weary legs. Behind us I could hear the shouts of the Sealers, but I dared not turn around. I had no idea what we were going to do when we got to the top, but I thought there was a chance that if we could just reach the rise of the next dune that there might be some salvation beyond.

Sam made it to the top first. He threw himself down on the crest of the ridge, and then seemed to slither backward with a cry of horror. He pointed down the other side of the dune and gasped, "Hollows!"

I peered down the slope and sure enough, only ten paces below the ridgeline, there stood an army of Hollows. They were arranged in staggered rows—a sea of empty cloaks exuding dismay. I looked back down the way we'd just climbed. The Sealers were at the bottom coming up now. We were trapped.

I clutched Vivian and Sam to me. "I'm so sorry. I was a fool to bring you here. I had no idea. I'm so sorry."

"Avery—" Vivian started to say.

"It's okay, Vivian. Stay behind me. Both the Hollows and Sealers are only after the key. You two make a break along the ridge back toward the staircase. I'll stay here and take out as many as I can."

"But, Avery—" she pleaded.

"It's the only way," I said and kissed her hands. "I love you, Vivian."

Sam rose to his feet beside me. "I'm not leaving you, Avery." I nodded and clasped his arm in a traditional Trelarian handshake.

He pulled out his wand, stared at it, and put it away again. Then he drew a small knife from his belt. We stood back-to-back so we could face both of our foes. While the Hollows hadn't advanced any further, the Sealers were halfway up. I took the key from my pocket and began to pull in energy. Immediately, the ash and dust began to swirl around us.

"Avery, Sam—" Vivian barked.

"It's okay, Vivian," Sam said. "We'll hold them back long enough for you and Harold to get away. The stair was back that away." He pointed to the right. "I've been keeping its location in my mind."

"Shut up, both of you!" she shouted. Sam and I stopped what we were doing and stared at her. "Good. Now, if you two will stop trying to martyr yourselves and follow my lead, I think we can all get out of this."

She stood at the top of the ridge, hands on her hips, her robes billowing out behind her. With a couple of gestures, she positioned us so that I was on her right and Sam was on her left.

"What are we doing?" I asked.

"Watch," she answered and turned back to the advancing Sealers. By now they were no more than thirty yards away. Moregoth's vaporous body was flowing up the dune side like a cloud blown by the wind. He looked different in the Waste, grayer, thinner. I could almost see through him.

"Moregoth!" Vivian's voice rang out strong and loud so that the voices on the wind took up a chorus of his name. "One more step, and it will be your last."

At first, I thought he would ignore her, but I had forgotten Moregoth's penchant for drama. He held up his hand, and the advancing Sealers stopped with only twenty paces to go. For a moment the only noise came from the incessant wind and the fluttering of robes. Moregoth's eyes met mine. He seemed tired, as if even the dark powers that kept him alive were being tested by this desolate land.

"I am not here to bargain or parlay, Dark Queen," said Moregoth. "We may have no magic in us, but we outnumber you ten to one. If need be, I will gladly beat the life from you and take the key from your battered corpses. Or you can hand me the key now, and I will let you all go. I wish to be gone from this place." He reached out a dark-gloved hand that managed to stay tangible in the wind, but only just.

I was about to tell him where he could stick that hand, but Vivian spoke for me. "I am not here to parlay either, Moregoth, but to give you a chance to save yourself from utter destruction."

Moregoth seemed to droop. He coughed before rasping. "I am a candle, flickering in the void. I have no time for word games. If you aren't going to give me the key, then you will die." He paused, but only long enough to read the resolve in Vivian's eyes. Without preamble, he barked, "Sealers! Advance! No quarter!"

Wearily, the Sealers came on. Each pulled two wickedly curved daggers from their belts. I felt like this was going about the way I thought it would. "Vivian?" I called, pulling the key out again.

"Don't you dare, Avery Stewart," she hissed. "Not this time."

With that, she raised an arm. Suddenly from behind us, the Hollows sprang to life, rising up the dune and flowing over it. I nearly lashed out then, but something about Vivian's preternatural calm stayed my hand. To my amazement, the creatures passed right by me, even with the key in plain sight. The Sealers saw them, and they stopped.

The ranks of Hollows all shrieked a word, but this time it was, "Sealer!"

The midnight-black cloaks met the line of crimson. It was not so much a battle as a slaughter. Wherever a Hollow reached a Sealer, they would loom over their red-cloaked victim, surround them, and drain their essence. A few of the Sealers tried to stab at them with their knives only to find their hand passing straight through. In the work of a moment, each of the men in Moregoth's army was reduced to motes of sparks, which danced away and faded on the blowing wind.

Moregoth did what any sane being would do. He ran for his life.

I watched a hangman's grin curve across Vivian's face. Her eyes blazed purple for a second, and she said a single word: "Moregoth."

Instantly the Hollows took up the chase. The last I saw of Moregoth was a mist of gray struggling against the wind on a distant dune, a line of pitch-black shadows in pursuit. Long after they passed from view, I fancied I could still hear their shrieks of "Moregoth" drifting back on the voice of the wind.

"Vivian?" I said, taking her hand.

She shrugged and gave me her most cunning smile. "What? A girl can't have her own private army? What do you think I've been doing all this time wandering through shadow? Knitting?" She gave me a playful slap, turned, and walked down the dune toward whatever lay ahead.

Sam, who had trudged all the way back down to retrieve his pack, came huffing back up. "Begging your pardon, but you have one scary girlfriend, Avery."

"Amen to that," I murmured, and for once I meant it entirely sincerely.

CHAPTER 23

THE LAND OF MORE DOORS

I let Sam catch up with Vivian before following. There were so many questions I needed to think through, and they only seemed to multiply when I was around her. Here is a small sampling of questions I was seeking answers for: Vivian said that she had gathered the Hollows while roaming subworlds. How had she convinced them to follow her? What had she promised? Why had she not revealed them before? Were there still more secrets to come? Would there ever be an end to them? Would she ever feel enough at ease with me to be truly and completely honest?

It was ironic—secrets were the one constant in our relationship. I had even grown to expect them. I suppose there was a sort of comfort in knowing that somewhere there was always another shoe ready to drop, but the same way I had grown tired of lying, I had grown tired of being lied to. It was not so much that I believed Vivian had evil intentions. She had saved me so many times, probably more than I knew, that I had no doubt she had chosen not to reveal the Hollows because she believed to do so would have endangered me or Sam or Harold. But in some sense that was the problem. Trust went two ways, and while she had earned mine, I had clearly not earned hers. It hurt.

I walked down the dune after them. The wind was picking up, throwing the ash and sand into choking clouds, and bringing with it the whispers of more forgotten voices. It was creepy as always, but it also made it difficult to see anything more than a few dozen paces away. The last thing we could afford right now was me getting separated from the others because I was sulking, so I jogged a little until I was right on Sam's heels. True to form, Sam was doing what I hadn't the courage to try: he was interrogating Vivian.

As I finally got close enough to hear, he said, "Well, they seem scary to me."

"And so they should," Vivian replied, her voice drifting back on the wind, quiet and calm. "They yearn for what they've lost, and in the depths of their want, they can do great harm to the living."

"Gosh!" Sam said with typical understatement. "Then how did you know they would work with you?"

"I didn't," she said. "In fact, they had every reason not to help."

"Why?" he asked.

Her voice quavered a bit as she answered. "I have what they call the stain. It's an . . . It's difficult to translate, but I suppose you would call it an aura. It hovers over people who have destroyed shadows. The Hollows hate people with the stain."

"Why didn't they hate you?" I found myself asking.

Vivian stopped and turned. "They did. Maybe they still do."

She was cradling Harold in her arms, and he was clearly suffering. His body was curved in on itself and his breathing was shallow and wheezy. We stared at each other over Sam's head. He looked back and forth between us before stepping to one side.

I stroked Harold's head. He gave a little whimper and turned in his sleep. "Will he be all right?" I asked. She nodded, but her eyes glittered with unshed tears. Something told me her emotion was less about Harold than about her memories of that first meeting with the Hollows.

"Why didn't they kill you, Vivian?" I asked in a low whisper. She started to turn away and I grabbed her arm. "They had no problem slaughtering the Sealers at a word from you, and I suspect the one that came to our camp would have destroyed me without hesitation had you not intervened. Why are you different?"

She looked back in the direction we'd come from. "I suppose in part because I said I was sorry, in part because I told them I wanted to make sure that the things I had done would never happen again, and in part because I offered them my soul if I failed."

"You what?" I said, just before Sam murmured, "No, Ms. Vivian. No!"

She smiled at both of us. "You needn't worry. We won't fail. I've checked innumerable possibilities, at least fourteen million six hundred and five or so."

"That does seem like a lot," Sam said with a whistle. "And so specific."

"Too specific," I said behind narrow eyes. "You made that number up to make your prediction seem more plausible. Computers and Vulcans do the same thing all the time. I mean really, seven thousand eight hundred and twenty-four point seven to one? Ridiculous!"

Vivian repositioned Harold against her body with one hand. "I might be exaggerating slightly, but I've seen a lot of outcomes. The visions told me that we would ultimately find our way here." She held up one finger. "They told me that the Hollows were the only beings in the multiverse that could thrive in the Waste." She held up a second finger. "They told me where to find them and what to promise them—"

She started to raise a third finger and I shouted, "Yeah, your soul!" I immediately regretted the outburst, as the voices picked up the call of *your soul* with unseemly and frightening glee.

"Yes, my soul," she said with a sigh. "But is it so much, Avery? If we fail, and the world continues as it is, then let them have it. I am tired of being evil. Aren't you?"

She didn't wait for my answer but turned and started walking again. The light was failing fast now, and with the wind kicking up the ash and sand, she was soon just a vague smudge. Sam looked after her, bouncing from one foot to the next, clearly anxious to follow. When I still showed no inclination to move, he said, "I don't think you're evil."

"Thanks, Sam," I said as he continued to fidget about. "Now, go after her before we lose ourselves."

He gave a little bob of his head and started running, calling out, "Wait for me, Ms. Vivian! Wait for me!"

I waited as long as I dared and then walked slowly after them, following the sounds of Sam's calls on the wind. Maybe it was just guilt triggered by Vivian's question, but the key was suddenly weighing on me and it made every step a struggle. As I trudged along, I thought about the nature of evil. It was true that I had done many classically evil things over the years. I had been responsible for the deaths of thousands in wars of my own making, and many more than that, whether wittingly or unwittingly, as the result of my use of Mysterium magic. In most cases I could point to some higher purpose, but not always. There were things I had done for my own convenience, or to protect myself or those I loved at the expense of others. Still, despite the undeniable truth that I had done evil, I found it difficult to hear myself called evil.

I wondered if that was true of all evil people. Did Sauron really consider himself to be a vile abomination or abhorrent, which was the literal meaning of his name? How about Torak? Did he think of himself as evil, or merely as the servant of the true prophecy? What about the Wicked Witch? Did she justify herself because Dorothy killed her sister? And what about Darth Vader? I bet if you asked him, he would tell you that the Empire must endure or all hope of stability and order in the galaxy would fall. Then he would Force choke you to death.

On the other hand, there were a few villains that clearly embraced the label proudly. There was the bad guy from *Time Bandits*. He was up-front that he wanted to rule the world and digital watches, which was pretty evil. There was also the fact that his name literally was Evil. Master Blaster made no bones about the fact that he wanted the pop group, Kidd Video, to be his personal musical slaves, and that's about as evil as you can get, but then he was a music executive. Cruella de Vil hunted puppies to make a fur coat. I'm pretty sure there's no defense for that either.

That was all the truly evil people I could think of before I caught up with Vivian and Sam. By then what passed for night in the Waste had truly fallen, either that or the ash storm had blotted out what little light there was to begin with. Whichever it was, we were basically walking blind over featureless lands. It was absurd. Besides, the key now felt like a lead weight in my pocket. I needed to stop and rest, and we needed to figure out what we were doing and where we were going.

I called out, "Jaws wasn't evil! He was just a bit peckish and had a craving for human."

This bizarre statement, apropos of absolutely nothing, had its intended effect. Sam and Vivian stopped and turned to stare at me. She had fashioned a sling out of her cloak to keep Harold protected from the blowing sand and ash. Vivian put her head to one side and considered me for a second. "We aren't mindless eating machines, Avery, and you're lucky I had a boyfriend from Earth who was into horror movies or that reference would have been lost on me."

"Perhaps not mindless," I conceded. "But we were as ignorant of the truth of reality as that shark was to the idea that killing a human is *malum in se*. And you never told me you had a boyfriend on Earth."

She thought about this for a moment, biting her lip. "We can't let ourselves off that easily. Jaws didn't kill out of malice but because that was his nature. The shark didn't have the capacity to *question* why it was doing what it was doing, or whether it was right or wrong. We did." After a pause, she added, "How did you think I knew about Dr. Claw or Master Blaster? And do you really want me to tell you about *all* my old boyfriends?"

"No, of course not," I said irritably, although I really did. "And your *boyfriend* obviously never showed you *Jaws: The Revenge*." Then I mumbled, "Poser."

I think she heard me, because her mouth tightened and her eyes narrowed. "*He* did not, but *I* did read the original proposal you wrote for your Trelari experiment. In one of the appendices you wrote, 'This proposal does raise a larger question as to whether the Mysterium has a right to step into and perhaps permanently alter the development of a subworld, and once a decision to do so has been made, how long our duty as guardian of the subworld would extend.' You knew. You knew even then that what you were doing might not be right, and that the people of Trelari should have a say in their own destiny."

"*That* wasn't the point of that appendix, and you *know* it," I said with more venom than I intended. It wasn't that I was mad at her, but hearing how I'd thought about things then frankly made me ill. As did the idea of her having a boyfriend from Earth who was into horror films. I decided it would be better to drop the subject of the boyfriend altogether. "The irony is that I was actually making an anti-Donaldsonian argument about Mysterium mages having a *duty* to intervene in subworlds where we could. The question of whether it was right or wrong was a throwaway. I ended that section by saying the issue was—"

"A philosophical one," she said and put her hand in mine. "I know, but how many Mysterium mages would have even bothered to write it? I knew when I read it that you were the one."

I met her eyes again. The wind, which had continued to pick up, was swirling her hair about in flashes of gold. "Then our meeting really was chance," I said, reaching out to tuck a loose strand behind her ear. "No one reads appendices."

"Avery! I'm surprised at you," she said with a tsk. "You know as well as I do that if you haven't read Part V of Appendix A of Tolkien's writings on Middle Earth, you've missed the best part."

Around us the night was black as pitch, but Vivian's face and eyes were luminous, like molten gold on the rising moon. I had never loved her more. We kissed and might have continued to do so had Sam not cleared his throat. I broke away from Vivian's embrace and asked impatiently, "What is it, Sam?"

"Who is Jaws?" he asked.

Vivian and I laughed. "One of us will tell you the story later," she said. "Right now we have other things to do."

"What are we going to do?" Sam asked, looking about. "Is this where we are going to camp?" He began to shrug off his backpack.

Vivian shook her head. "No, Sam, this is where we are going to open the door out of the Waste."

"Here?" Sam asked in disbelief, but it was me who answered, "Right, here, Sam."

I had known the truth of it as soon as Vivian spoke. The key had been trying to tell me how close we were getting for a while now, dragging more and more as we moved closer. In this place it was like an anchor. I realized that moving, even a pace to the right or the left, would be an effort. As unlikely as it seemed, this was the place.

Sam spun around, confused. "I can't see anything different about this particular piece of the Waste."

Neither could I until Vivian pointed up. Our eyes followed her gesture and saw that what we had taken for night wasn't the setting of the sun, but the falling of the sky. While we had been walking, the whirlpool of clouds that had been swirling far above since we'd arrived to the Waste had descended around us. We were currently in the relative calm of its eye.

"Gosh! What do we do now?" Sam asked with a gulping sound.

"Eventually, we will use the key to open the way to the Land of More Doors, but for now we sit and we talk," she said calmly and, folding her legs beneath her, sank to the ground. I joined her, and she leaned over to me and whispered, "And decide which of us dies."

Of all the things she'd ever said to me, this may

have been the most expected. I had known for some time that this moment was coming. I didn't know it would be here, on an alien plane of existence, in the eye of a tornado of dead worlds, but I knew this would be the topic of our last conversation. The good news was that I already knew who it was going to be: me!

While Harold yawned himself awake in her lap, Vivian pulled Gray from a pocket in her cloak and set the skull beside her. His eyes flickered weakly around the circle at us. "Please don't tell me you brought me all this way for a game of spin the bottle. I swear to all I hold unholy, I will incinerate the first one of you that tries to tongue me!"

Sam shook his head. "No, we don't have a bottle. We are going to open the door!"

Gray let out a soul-rattling sigh. "Well, that's a relief." He paused for a half beat, waiting, and then asked, "Well, what are we waiting for? I'm not getting any less undead."

"Before we go through the door, we need to decide what we are going to do when we get to the pattern," Vivian answered.

"Aren't we going to destroy the key?" Gray asked and swiveled his eyes back and forth between Vivian and me. When no one answered, he said, "Don't tell me now that we are here it just doesn't seem right to destroy it. You've convinced yourselves that it would be better to use it to do something or other."

"It's not like that—" I started to say, but Gray shook himself sadly and shrieked in that way only demi-liches can.

"Of course, it's different this time. You two are the chosen ones, or some such nonsense. Have any of you actually read any of the stories from Mysterium, because this is what happens in every one of them."

"If you will let us explain," I interjected.

"Explain! Explain!" he howled. "No need to explain. It's always the same. The good guys can't quite bring themselves to utterly defeat evil and so evil has a chance to creep back and the whole story gets repeated again. I always thought it was the mages setting themselves up for future grants, but now I think it must be some kind of pathology with your kind. And that's coming from an undead! We are the literal source for the 'back from the dead' trope."

"If you must know, and apparently you must," Vivian snapped, "we are not planning on destroying the key, because that won't actually solve the real problem with the multiverse. Instead, we are planning on using the key to rewrite the original Mysterian pattern, although likely this will result in the destruction of the key. What I meant about discussing what we do when we get through the door is that we need to decide whether I redraw the pattern and die, or Avery does."

"Oh," Gray said. "Well, in that case maybe we could just flip a coin and be done with it."

"Gods, why be so dramatic, just play a couple of rounds of roshambo," Harold said with an irritated grunt. Vivian and I both looked sharply at the imp. He was no longer a baby or even a toddler, and apparently in our time in the Waste he had skipped right through the childhood years to land squarely on grumpy teenager.

Sam took no notice but said angrily, "Well, I for one don't like either of those choices."

"Whatever," Harold said and pulled Vivian's cloak back over his head.

"It could be best three out of five to give them both more chances," Gray proposed.

"That's not what I mean," the young mage said, his voice quivering with emotion. "No one ever said anything about someone needing to die. There must be another way."

I shook my head. "If we are going to end Mysterium's dominance over the multiverse once and for all, as Gray urges quite rightly that we do, then the pattern that has been feeding it all this time must either be destroyed utterly or redrawn. It is the only way."

"But why does someone have to die?" he asked, running the back of his hand over his suddenly wet eyes. "We didn't die when we were on the Mysterium pattern?"

"You almost did," I pointed out. "And the only reason I was unaffected is that my entire magical existence was formed by the Mysterium pattern. For me, it was like coming home. But this pattern will be alien to all of us, and even if it weren't, drawing or trying to alter a pattern of such power exacts a price."

"But . . . but . . . I . . . we need you," Sam sputtered.

"Yes," Vivian agreed emphatically. "You do need Avery. He is the multiverse's leading expert on what has been happening lately. It is his voice, through his books, that will inform the world on what is to come. That is why I intend to redraw the pattern."

"Very persuasive," I said with a laugh that didn't quite disguise the steel in my voice. "But I have the key, and ownership is still nine-tenths of the law, so I will be redrawing the pattern." To emphasize the point, I put a hand very deliberately on the pocket that held the key.

"Yes, I suppose you could do that, but I have a trump card," she said.

Her eyes flashed purple, and Hollows began to step out of the black swirling clouds around us. They did not immediately move against me, but I could feel their eyes, not that they had any, fixated on me. Vivian smiled like a chess player who has just announced checkmate.

I suppose I should have been scared. Sam certainly was, if the shade of white his face had taken on was any indication. The funny thing is, I wasn't. I was tired. I was bone weary of playing this game of poker with her. So I decided to end it and go all in. Call her bluff. (For those of you who are not card players, these are all terms I learned while watching a week of professional poker during what I call my TV sabbatical. I assure you, the analogy is perfect.)

"I thought we were past this, Vivian," I said with a shoulder-drooping sigh. "If you want to take the key from me by force, then order the Hollows to destroy me, because that is what it's going to take. I won't raise a hand against them or you, but I also won't give up the key willingly."

"Oh, Avery, you are so melodramatic," she said with a dismissive chuckle.

"Melodramatic! Me?" I spluttered. "You're the one threatening people with killer cloaks."

She laughed again, but it was filled with regret. "Avery, I am not threatening you. In fact, the Hollows aren't here for you at all. They're here for me."

"For you?"

In reply she did this thing she does when I'm being dense where she rubs her temples. "Yes, Avery, they're here for me," she explained with forced patience. "If you go through the door, then I will have failed my pledge to the Hollows, and they will take their price."

It took me a second to understand what she was saying, but when I did I rose to my feet and tried to put my body between the Hollows and Vivian. "Sam, to your feet!" I urged. "Don't let them get too near!"

In a flash Sam was up, his dagger already in hand. Even Harold emerged from Vivian's cloak and began flapping about. I noticed that at some point while hidden in the cloak he had managed to spike his hair and get a nose ring. I made a mental note to have a serious talk with him the next time we weren't in mortal peril.

Together we circled Vivian, trying to keep an eye on all the Hollows. In response, the creatures began to sway and moan something that sounded like, "Stain!"

Vivian stood and put a hand out to both Sam and me. "There's nothing you can do, Avery. You have no magic to counter them, and they will not stop until they have their payment. I understood the consequences when I made the bargain."

"They are not taking your soul!" I said and pulled the key from my pocket.

"Don't, Avery!" she cried. "The key can't harm them. They are the remnants left after the key has drained everything else. You will accomplish nothing and provide a beacon the Mysterium can follow straight to where you are."

Even as she said this, the wall of Hollows began to advance forward. Now their cries of "Stain!" were clear and the word began to echo about us. I was wondering if she was right about the Hollows being immune to the magic of the key, when something she'd said earlier about them being shadows of the living struck me. Could it be that simple?

"Vivian, you said that they were shadows of beings. Were you being poetic or literal?" I asked in a rush of words.

"I don't . . . Why does that . . . ?"

I spun about and held both her hands in mine. "I know I'm often vague and that I can be infuriatingly tangential in my thoughts, but this time I just need a yes or no. When you called the Hollows shadows, did you mean that in a precise and uncomplicated way, or were you trying to convey a meaning beyond the ordinary? In other words, is the definition of shadow here a denotation or a connotation?"

Her mouth curved into the smile I knew so well. "You know, it's pretty hard to give a quick answer when your questions are so damn long, but yes, I meant that they are literally the shadows of dead realities."

I kissed her. "That's what I was hoping you'd say."

I spun back around to find that the Hollows were no more than arm's length away. They had begun to rise up and engulf us with their bodies, all the while their moans of "Stain!" growing louder and louder.

"Gather round!" I cried to the Hollows. "It's time we all went to the land where the shadows die." I dropped to my knee and plunged the key into the ground.

There was a roar of sound as the clouds closed around us. Beneath our feet, the sand and ash began to shift and swirl, drawing us down. Sensing their danger, the Hollows abandoned their attack and tried to retreat, reaching out their shadow arms to claw at the ground, but we were all caught in the land's pull. Then, with a sudden jolt, reality slipped out from under us, and like sand through an hourglass, we were drawn out of the Waste and through a pinhole of consciousness into the Land of More Doors. The last I heard of the Hollows were their shrieks of "More Doors!" rebounding about us in a never-ending choral canon of terror. That this was accompanied by Harold humming something that sounded an awful lot like "Killing in the Name" by Rage Against the Machine only made the effect all the more disquieting. Definitely long past time for a talk.

CHAPTER 24

THE DARKEST LORD

In one of those disorienting reorientations that happens sometimes when traveling between worlds, we did not so much fall into the Land of More Doors in a great rush of sand and ash as tumble through a door. We found ourselves lying, all jumbled together, on a floor of smooth, gray stone. There was no Waste and there were no Hollows. I had the key in one hand and a suspiciously familiar doorknob in the other. I turned back and looked. Sure enough, the door we'd come through looked just like the one from my old dorm room. Or rather, it momentarily looked like the one from my old dorm room, before remolding itself into a kind of conceptual door: featureless, gray, and rectangular.

We slowly got to our feet and looked about. Apart from the dozens, hundreds, thousands of identical featureless gray doors, the land was utterly empty. It was also eerily quiet. I was acutely aware of how accustomed I had become to the incessant howl of the wind in the Waste. It was a feeling similar to when an air conditioner cuts off after it's been blowing for a couple of hours. You hear the absence of noise, and you notice other sounds like footfalls on pavement or the beating of your heart. It was creeping me out.

To distract myself, I turned my attention to a study of the doors. I could see no particular order or arrangement to them. They simply stood, scattered, here and there, alone or in groups, for as far as the eye could see. There were a million questions one might ask when confronted with such an alien world. I asked the one that was weighing on me. "Why was the portal from the Waste the door to my old dorm room?"

Vivian and Sam looked at each other and shrugged. "I was going to ask you the same thing," she said.

Harold, who definitely had a nose ring and what looked like an AC/DC tattoo on his forearm, sighed impatiently. "I can see why it takes mages so long to graduate."

"If you're just going to insult us—" I started to say.

"Save the lecture, pops," he muttered. "The reason the portal manifested as the door to your dorm room is because when you called forth the door, you didn't specify a form, so it went digging through your subconscious and that door is the one you most commonly think of as a door when you hear the word." He picked at his teeth with one of his long, sharpened nails that he had somehow had time to paint a ghastly shade of purple. "Now had you properly bounded the spell—"

"I understand!" I snapped and, shaking a finger at him, asked, "But, if you're so smart, then answer this—where is the pattern? If the Waste is what feeds the pattern energy, then why did its gateway not bring us straight to it?"

He sighed and rolled his eyes. "The Waste isn't a real world, it's just a byproduct of the pattern. It doesn't have a door of its own. It has to steal one from another world. Probably a world it's about to consume."

On cue, there was a flash of brilliant blue light around the door, the gray rectangle morphed into a beautiful stone archway in a Romanesque style, and then there was that familiar moaning wind and the archway dissolved into ash and rubble. As the doorway disintegrated, a bolt of pure energy shot out from the circle and raced along the ground out of sight. The doorknob I'd been holding melted away in my hand.

Harold smirked in a way I can only describe as Eldrinesque. I shook another finger at him. "Well, who gave you permission to get piercings? And a tattoo? Those are permanent! Ask any midforties ex-hipster, they'll tell you, it's not so much fun getting them taken off!"

"'Ask any midforties ex-hipster,'" he mocked, and then added with a sneer, "Shows how much you know, nothing is permanent on an imp." He slapped a paw over the tattoo and it changed into a hand giving a very rude gesture.

"Wipe that off at once!" I shouted.

"That's not very polite, Harold," Vivian said calmly. "If we can't tattoo anything nice on our bodies, then we shouldn't tattoo anything at all."

She tried to stroke his head, but he pulled away and flapped over to perch on top of a nearby door with a muttered, "Whatever."

I was about to lay into him about his attitude, but then noticed he had changed the tattoo again, this time into something that looked a bit like a complex magical circle. I decided arguing with him was not going to get us any closer to finding and redrawing the pattern.

"Okay, if the Waste dropped us at random in More Doors, how do we find the pattern?" I asked.

"I don't know for certain," Sam said. "But if the energy that came out of this door was going to the pattern like Harold said, then I suspect we could follow this little line."

He pointed at the ground. Around each of the doors was etched a mystic circle, but from the circle around our door extended a thin line, actually more like a hairline crack in the gray stone of the ground. I started tracing the ragged track and saw that it was continuous and ran in a definite direction. We scouted about for other vacant circles that the Waste had consumed, and we soon saw that from each issued a similar crack, and that each crack went in that same direction.

I clapped Sam on the shoulder. "Excellent eyes! These must lead to the pattern!"

"What an incisive mind," Harold said with heavy sarcasm.

"That's enough of that," I said, and then did a double take because in the last few minutes he had somehow found a black leather jacket with a giant red anarchy symbol painted on its back. "And would you stop messing about with your clothes . . . it's . . . it's distracting."

He ignored me with elaborate indifference, and I could feel myself working up to a real top-notch harangue when Vivian laid a hand on my arm. "Leave it, Avery. As you said, we need to find the pattern."

"Quite," I said and turned to follow Sam with a grunt of disgust that would have made my father proud.

Not that I would admit it to Harold, but she was right. All my fussing about with the imp was merely a way for me to avoid thinking about what was to come. As we began following the flow of the cracks, weaving our way around and about the doors, I turned my attention to the problem of the pattern itself. Now that I was aware of the significance of the disintegrating doors, their presence was pervasive. Empty circles filled with piles of ash and rubble could be seen scattered all about, and every so often there would be another flash of light, and another door would crystallize for a second—a heavy wooden door bound in iron, a circular portal of brass, a stone triangle—and then, in a moan of wind, it would disintegrate with a flash of lightning. The pattern was even now consuming worlds. If I had still needed convincing, this would have settled the question of whether the pattern needed to be redrawn once and for all. But there still remained the issue of who would do it.

Vivian was walking ahead of me. Her face was troubled, and I wondered if she was thinking the same thing. How could I convince her to let me do what needed to be done? I had given up trying to outmaneuver her. Every time I thought I had managed—at the pattern in Mysterium or in the Waste—I found out that she was one step ahead. Frankly, I was losing faith in my ability to win this particular contest. I walked up beside her, and in one of those lovely synchronicities that you experience when you've been with someone for a while, we reached for each other's hand at the same time.

"I've been thinking about divination lately," I said. This appeared to pique her interest and she raised an eyebrow quizzically. "Don't get too excited. I still think it's terribly squishy, but I do admit that the art has been taxing me lately. I think I can live with the idea that I will never be able to throw you a surprise party or give you a gift that you didn't anticipate, but what no one tells you about diviners is how damned aggravating it is to try to outsmart them. I really want to be the one that takes the key out onto the pattern, but I confess I don't know how. I fully anticipate that we will get there and you will have built a wall around it that only you can enter, or have an army of creatures standing by that are genetically engineered to steal keys from guys named Avery—"

"'The One That Survives,'" Gray screeched out of nowhere.

I actually jumped when he spoke, because he had been so weak in the Waste that I had grown accustomed to him not being so . . . himself. Now I saw that the glow from the balefire pinpricks of his eyes were ablaze again. He was also floating again—right behind our heads. This explained why Sam had been so eager to go to the front, and why I had been growing increasingly nauseated. It also could mean only one thing.

I reached out with my will and found lines of magic flowing all around us. It seemed to be concentrated in the cracks that ran from the doors, but it was so strong that it permeated everything to some extent. The power available was essentially limitless.

"Well?" asked Gray.

"Well, what?" I asked.

"That idea about genetically engineered creatures," he said impatiently. "Come on, admit it, you got it from the *Star Trek*, season three, episode seventeen. You know, 'I am for you, Kirk.'"

It took me a moment to understand what he was saying. When I did, I stopped in my tracks and looked at him. "How does a demi-lich from Mysterium know anything about *Star Trek*?"

"Oh, after you ditched us back when we were all trying to escape Student Records—"

"You mean transported you to safety?" I corrected.

"You say skeletons, I say skelatons," he retorted. "Anyway, Eldrin, Trevor, and Tanner all got to talking about their favorite *Star Trek* episodes. We ended up having a bit of a Trekathon. Did you know that in *Catspaw* the witches were supposed to be floating heads?" He shook himself in disgust. "The director was a fool. You can clearly see they're wearing turtlenecks. If he had used demi-liches, he wouldn't have had any problems."

I wasn't sure what to say. The entire scene his story painted seemed so unlikely and absurd that my mind refused to contemplate it. Plus, I had this nagging feeling that I had been in the middle of something important. Thankfully, Vivian was there.

"Go away, Gray. We were in the middle of something important," she said, but took the sting away by giving him a kiss on the top of his skull. He didn't blush so much as turn a less bone-pale shade of white. But he did float away to join Sam and Harold as they scouted ahead. Vivian squeezed my hand. "You were saying?"

I sighed deeply. "I was saying that since you already know what's going to happen at the pattern, can't you just tell me how things turn out? For once, I want there to be no secrets between us."

Vivian stopped and so did I. She stared down at the cracked ground. "Is that what you think of me? Do you think that all this time I have held the secret to all that is to come and kept it from you?" When I didn't respond, she let out a shuddering breath. There were tears in her eyes. "That's not the way it works. It never has been. If I saw a vision of us on that hill in Trelari, surrounded by Sealers, or you back in New York, unmoving, while dark forces drew near, or you on the Mysterium pattern facing a vast evil alone, Sam dying at your feet, or us in a terrible Waste surrounded by shadows, what should I tell you? My visions see moments, but they give me no insight as to what I should do about them. It took all my skill to trace *my* possible actions, hundreds, thousands of choices I could make or not make to get you beyond each moment of crisis, and even then most didn't turn out the way I intended."

She laughed ruefully and began pacing back and forth across the remains of a shattered door. "I threatened you on that hill in Trelari because I had a vision that you would die in the next battle we fought with Moregoth. The only course I could see to keep you from the fight was to drive you away from me. Then you go and decide to destroy the key on Mysterium's pattern! I've been going crazy this whole time trying to keep you from leaving me or dying, and even then it was my plotting that nearly got us killed in the Waste. So, no dear heart, I'm not omniscient."

I grabbed both of her hands. "But have you seen what happens next?"

"There it is!" Sam shouted.

We both turned. The others had gotten quite far ahead, but in the direction of Sam's cry, I could see a vague iridescence. My question forgotten, we walked forward, still holding hands. As we advanced, the cracks grew wider and more jagged, and the doors crowded in thicker and thicker until I felt that we were stumbling through a forest of gray rectangles with tangled roots of broken stone.

The pulsating glow grew brighter, and then we edged between two doors set nearly shoulder-to-shoulder and found ourselves in a broad circle of gray stone. In its center was the pattern surrounded by a dense spiderweb of fissures. Despite my purpose and my knowledge of what it stood for, I found myself struck breathless by the pattern's beauty. Unlike the

Mysterium pattern, which had been flat, this was a sphere, some of which rose above the ground and some of which, almost mirrorlike, rested within. It was formed of the most brilliant light that I had ever seen and contained a swirl of every color and of every hue of every color. While it was bright, bright beyond reasoning, it didn't hurt my eyes. Rather, it held me in its grip—fascinated.

Entranced, I moved forward and the inner structure of the sphere was revealed. Although technically it's not possible to describe what I saw to the types of three-dimensional beings who are likely to read this, the best I can do is to say that it contained a tangle of geometric patterns—euclidean and non-euclidean—that were constantly shifting and unfolding to show different forms—a kaleidoscope of infinite dimension.

I might have stepped straight onto it without any thought had Harold not landed on my shoulder. "Not without me, old man," he said with a disgruntled hiss.

Vivian came over and touched my arm. "Avery?"

"Yes," I said, unable to tear my vision away from it.

I found that I was standing at the edge of the pattern, the key in my hand. In this place it seemed alive, pulsing and twisting in tune with the light as it reflected this central flame of the universe in its form. The movements seemed random, but in my mind I could hear the voice of the key echoing over and over again: *It is time. It is time.*

"I have to go," I said, my body poised on a knife's edge.

"I know," she said with a sad smile. "And so do I."

I wanted to say no, but I couldn't speak, I could hardly think beyond the need to take the key onto the pattern. But I knew if I went, Vivian would go, and she would die. It was this thought alone that gave me the strength to remain motionless on the boundary between this world and the one that lay beyond. I was still frozen when there was a flash of brilliant light from behind us. I knew without turning that it was Moregoth. I could feel the touch of his evil like a chill in the air.

"Moregoth," I said with an animal growl.

In reply there came a voice that was not at all like Moregoth's. In fact, it was not at like any living being that has ever existed. It was vast as the multiverse and as deep as time itself. "Avery Stewart," it said, every syllable of my name dripping with hate. "We meet again!"

The power of the voice broke the key's spell. Freed from its implacable will, I spun and saw something that both looked like and nothing like Moregoth stepping from a door. What I mean is that the thing had all the familiar hallmarks of Moregoth's body—his pale skin, the black sweep of hair falling across his face, the cadaverous, black-cloaked body—and yet it had been rendered devoid of all humanity. The face was a mask with two swirling voids for eyes. The hair and body, shadows that had form but no texture or life.

The door this creature had emerged from had taken the form of the massive front gates of the Provost's Tower, and I knew at once that it must be the portal to Mysterium. It sat at the apex of an oblong circle of doors that surrounded the pattern clearing, and a massive fracture connected it to the pattern. Even now, I could see power flowing from the pattern through the door and back into the shadowy mass. As the being stepped from the circle, the world shook and the flowing shadows swelled until they blotted out everything but the pattern itself, and even its light seemed to dim and its colors to fade with the creature's approach. Everyone sensed its menace, and we all drew together in a tight circle with our backs to the pattern.

I drew courage and strength from the key and found myself gripping it so tightly that my arm hurt. "What are you?" I asked in a broken voice.

My question was greeted by laughter, or at least the semblance of laughter, for it was not only devoid of all humor and emotion, but it lacked even a reference to such things. The effect was horrible. "Everyone calls me the provost, but you should know better than that, Avery Stewart. We are very close, you and I. You might even call me your benefactor, for without me you would be nothing."

"You lie!" Sam shouted. "Avery has been fighting you for years. You are everything he despises."

The being turned its eyes, two pools of deeper glowing darkness, on Sam. "What do you know, little shadow? Your ignorance is so profound that I must assume the others brought you along as a pack mule, because you could serve no other useful purpose. However, if *Avery* will but say that I lie, then I will concede the point." The shadow bowed its head in my direction, inviting me to speak.

The problem was I could say nothing, because every word was true. I could feel my body resonating in its presence with such familiarity that the only comparison I could make is the connection that must exist between an infant and mother. I also knew where I had felt that touch before: on the pattern of Mysterium. As impossible as it seemed, the provost, this thing, was the Mysterium pattern embodied.

"No witty response?" it asked with another terrible laugh. "I'm disappointed. I've been following your adventures with rapt attention and had understood that you always have some clever retort at the ready." It paused, but even if I'd had some comeback, I couldn't speak. It was like a hand was gripping my throat. "Tell them. Tell them that I am written in every fiber of your being. Tell them that without me you would not be Avery Stewart, mage and Dark Lord, but Avery Stewart, a friendless, failed student of sociology and overall disappointment."

"Avery?" Sam asked, taking a step back.

Still I could say nothing. The voice roared, "Tell them!"

The hand that had gripped my throat released suddenly. "It's telling the truth," I gasped. "This is the pattern of Mysterium. The source of my power. It has been running the university all this time."

"No!" Sam cried. "I don't believe it."

"You are a little fool, and you have picked your companions poorly," the provost said derisively. "Let me show you." The figure raised a hand and pointed it at Gray. "Demi-lich, your services are no longer needed."

A dagger of darkness shot from its hand and struck Gray in the temple. The infernal glow in his eyes flickered and vanished, and he crashed to the ground with a sharp, hollow rap.

"Gray!" Sam screamed and then, turning to Vivian and me, shouted, "Do something!"

I wanted to cry out myself, to raise my hand, to use the key to lash out, but my body would not answer, and from the rigid way Vivian was holding herself I suspected she was also under its control. While she was originally from a subworld somewhere, she had tied herself to Mysterium and its magic as much as I had in her time at the university. We were caught, and I could think of no way to break free.

"They can't help you," the provost said with mirthless glee. "I am Mysterium, and they are mine—every particle and atom. Let me give you another demonstration." He raised his hand again and pointed at Vivian. "Kneel!"

At my side, Vivian's knees buckled and she pitched forward, falling to the ground. Knowing I could not move, I tried to open my will to the key. I could feel its power surging just out of reach. But even that part of me was inscribed—and in fact, rebuilt in the last few days—by the Mysterium pattern. My body and my will were at its command. I ground my teeth in impotent fury.

"And now I bring to an end to my long search for the one instrument that might have stood against me. How fitting that the agent that has finally brought it into my grasp is the mage everyone thought would be the great savior of the multiverse." That awful laugh rang out again as it pointed its finger at me. "Bring me the key!"

I was moving. Despite having more power at my fingertips than I had ever thought possible, despite every cell in my body screaming to stop, I was moving. It was at this point that something happened that none of us, not Vivian with her visions or even the soul of Mysterium with all its power, could have foreseen or predicted.

Sam stepped in front of me and pointed at the provost. "Your search will not end today, creature." Then he turned to Vivian and me. "I'm sorry, but it's the only way." He extended his hands, there was a flare of power, and Vivian and Harold and I were lifted into the air and thrown back into the pattern. A rush of energy, like fire, ran through my body. I felt the provost's constraining bonds lift. I was free.

A terrible, bestial roar of frustration and anger issued from the provost to echo through the Land of More Doors, but it was so far away and so faint that it seemed more like a dream.

"I think someone is having a really big feeling," Harold said, using words I'd so often repeated to him in his brief infancy.

CHAPTER 25

WHAT THIS MULTIVERSE NEEDS
IS AN EDITOR

I was in *the* pattern, the *first* pattern, and every molecule of my body danced. It was a place of color and light and endless energy, but also of smell and sound and texture. I could feel through every mote of my being power flaring around me and rushing through me in exhilarating waves. At my feet I could see strange ribbons of undulating color that turned and twisted and interwove together like a labyrinth of pathways in space. It was sort of like being in a Country Joe & The Fish album, or anything from Pink Floyd pre–Syd Barrett going off his nut.

As soon as my mind stopped racing long enough to focus, I looked for Vivian. She was sitting nearby holding her head, a look of rapture on her face. I called to her, and after a long delay, she waved back at me languidly and slowly rose to her feet. As she did, I noticed that the pattern seemed to clutch at her body, and scattered in the wake of her movements were little motes of her being that drifted off and disappeared. I looked at my feet and lifted one. Sure enough the boundary of my foot stretched as the ribbon clung to it, and as it pulled reluctantly away, a shower of particles was left in its wake. We were being consumed by the pattern.

It wasn't that I hadn't been expecting something like this, but it was still a little sobering. It also meant that we didn't have much time.

I did not so much go to Vivian as I did think of going to her, and then we were standing next to each other on the ribbon path. I was getting less sensitized to the pattern's mesmerizing effect and could see that Sam's spell hadn't thrown us far beyond its boundary. We were, in fact, very near to the edge. Through the shimmering haze, I could see Sam standing before the looming form of the provost. He looked so small, but in his hands he held a fierce light that the shadow could not touch.

I pointed at him, ignoring the little particles of my finger that came off from the violence of my movement. "We have to help!" I shouted and raised the key.

It was Harold who shouted for me to stop as I unleashed a torrent of energy at the shadowy form beyond. Power rushed from the key. I felt every bit of it like fire running through my blood. I dropped to my knees with a scream as a bolt of pure magic shot out and then swirled and bent and faded as it got caught and carried away by the eddies and currents of the pattern.

"Stop! Stop!" Harold moaned with pain. "You aren't attuned to this pattern. Trying to channel through the key will get us both killed."

"But we have to use the key to rewrite the pattern," Vivian said.

The imp put out a hand and stroked her cheek. I noticed faint lines around his eyes and along his forehead. His hair had begun to thin. "Exactly," he said. "We can do one, but not both."

I understood. If we saved Sam, then we would not have enough reality left to redraw the pattern. Vivian came up beside me and put a hand around my waist. "Then we need to go."

I nodded but didn't move. It seemed impossible that we would abandon Sam to his death, but that was exactly what we were going to do. Even now I could see the shadow of the provost flowing toward him and could hear its inhuman laughter.

"All you have done is delay the inevitable," it said. "I am quite attuned to the Mysterian pattern. I shall deal with you and then destroy them, if they are not consumed by it first."

A hundred seeking tentacles stretched out from the creature and began to surround the young mage. Oddly, Sam seemed unconcerned. He stood, quite at his ease, the glowing balls of light in his hands still shining. He had woven a circle around himself, but there was no way a simple protection ward would hold against all the power of the Mysterium. I found myself pressed against the shimmering boundary, shouting for him to run, but either he didn't hear or he ignored me.

Sam answered the Mysterium's threat with a laugh of his own. "Moregoth, or whatever you call yourself, I've studied enough Mysterium history to know that you're expecting to fight some kind of final climactic battle with the Dark Lord and the Dark Queen, but it isn't going to happen. This isn't that kind of story. It's an Avery Stewart story, which means I am going to say something witty and rude and then do the thing you least expect and that you will have no answer for." He examined the back of his nails for a second with studied indifference and then looked back up at the looming figure. "Shall we begin?"

If nothing else, Sam had struck the provost momentarily speechless, and I didn't blame it. Somewhere along the way Sam had become a force, and despite our own peril and the urgency of our task, Vivian and I found ourselves frozen, unwilling to turn away and miss whatever was about to happen. Harold did mutter something about Sam buying us time and perhaps now being a good time to go, but even he didn't sound convinced.

In response, there was a choking, cackling, rasping noise that I can only assume was laughter. Either that or the creature had swallowed a great big Electro Who-Cardio Shluxe. "You actually believe you're going to stand before me? You were not even able to handle your first day as a novice. You are less than nothing, and worse for a mage, you know less than nothing."

"You are right, of course," said Sam. "I'm not the best wizard. In some areas of magic, I'm a very poor wizard indeed, but there is one field that I have studied intensely. One area of magic where I have studied under the multiverse's greatest master. Do you know what that is?"

The creature was a wall of shadow rising up and over Sam, its swirling eyes staring down at the mage from far above. "Please enlighten me. Your unaccountable arrogance will only make your destruction all the sweeter."

"You know what they say about being careful what you wish for?" Sam said with a shout. "You're about to get a visceral lesson in karma. At least, I think you are. You will if I'm using the word right. Avery's definition was a little confusing."

The circle Sam had drawn around himself flashed with an intensity that was blinding even behind the barrier of the pattern, and he vanished. The creature drew back momentarily, and then when nothing happened, it laughed again. I know I have used words like *terrible* and *awful* and *horrible* to describe the sound of the provost's laughter, but I really don't think they communicate the true effect. Imagine listening to Grunthos the Flatulent recite his poem, "Ode to a Small Lump of Green Putty I Found in My Armpit One Midsummer Morning," but set to the tune of a song like "La Macarena." It's more or less that without that charming little dance to make it fun. Anyway, the provost had reason to laugh, which he made plain a second later.

"Well, I'll admit, he got me. That was the last thing I expected." It flowed closer to the pattern as Vivian and I began to retreat. "The little fool is smarter than I gave him credit for. More's the pity for you."

I had begun thinking the same thing. Sam was gone, which was great for him and I didn't begrudge him his escape even for a fraction of a second, but the consequence was not so great for us. We found ourselves standing more or less face-to-face against the full power of the Mysterium.

Tendrils of the shadow's body were just beginning to edge through the boundary when Sam's voice rang out again, this time from somewhere to our left.

I located him standing beside the portal to the Mysterium. "I never got a chance to enlighten you," he shouted. "The answer is portals! I have studied under Avery Stewart, the world's greatest expert in portal manipulation, and we happen to be standing in a world filled with portals!"

There was another flash, this time from the door to Mysterium. It swung shut with a thunderous boom, severing the shadowy umbilical that had been feeding the being. The provost had only enough time to turn and appreciate its sudden mortality when another, larger, surge of magic issued from the Mysterian pattern and shot out along the multitude of fissures that ran from the pattern's edge. Columns of light burst forth across the horizon as countless doors began to open about us, and from the doors issued every kind of creature and beast and hero that the multiverse had to offer. It was a spectacular sight, probably only rivaled by the opening credits of *Super Friends*. Not the regular old *Super Friends*, but the 1978 *Challenge of the Super Friends*, where you had Superman, Wonder Woman, Hawkman, Batman *and* Robin, Aquaman, Green Lantern, and the Flash all racing out of the Hall of Justice as one to fight the Legion of Doom. Sam even had a great line.

"Say hello to my friends!" he crowed, and I'm pretty sure that wasn't a reference, because there is *no way* he'd ever seen *Scarface*.

"It's amazing how many worlds the Mysterium has managed to piss off over the years," Harold observed dryly.

And so it was. Sam had filtered his spell to open only those doors at the end of fissures; that is, doors to worlds from which the Mysterium had been draining reality. He had managed, with simple elegance, to summon together those worlds, all those little shadows, that the Mysterium had for so long abused. Still, despite the sheer numbers arrayed against the provost, with the power of the Mysterian pattern at its command, I wasn't sure which side would ultimately win out. However, I did know how we could help.

"It's time to go," I announced.

Vivian nodded and slipped her hand in mine so that we both had hold of the key. "Do you think we will ever see him again?"

I looked down at the blurred edges of our hands wrapped around the still very real key, and the increasing transparency of our bodies. "Certainly. He seems to have everything well in hand."

We turned our backs on the battle and began walking deeper into the pattern. The last I saw of Sam, he was popping from door to door like a jack-in-the-box, firing bolts of energy into the shadowy body of the creature and shouting abuse as an army as diverse as the multiverse swarmed it.

By comparison, our own journey was quite placid.

Though the pattern was a chaotic maze of intersecting paths and seemingly impossible geometries, with the key as our guide, it was impossible to get lost.

"Have you thought about how you are going to redraw the pattern?" Vivian asked.

"I have not," I answered and gave her hand a squeeze, a wave of sadness washing over me as it gave unnaturally beneath my grip. "Because, I don't intend to redraw it at all. I had decided to let you do it."

"Really? After all that arguing, why give in now?" she asked.

I drew the back of her hand to my lips and gave it a kiss. She followed my movement with her eyes and nodded. "I understand." And she kissed my hand in return.

What she understood, what she had seen in the contrast between the solid reality of the key and our own bodies, is that we were fading more and more rapidly now. In painting terms, we had entered the pattern as examples of realism, had slowly turned painterly, and now were rapidly becoming impressionist.

Harold sighed from my shoulder. "Well, if you ask me, and I know no one is, but I always thought you two were better off together. I'm not sure why you'd want to change that now."

We both looked at him. For reasons that had everything to do with what it is to be an imp, a subject I was still profoundly ignorant about, the pattern was not fading him. Instead, he was aging. In the last few minutes of walking, he had had taken on more and more of his former appearance. The lines, which had been hints or rumors before, now ran clearly across his forehead and sprouted from the corners of his eyes and mouth. His hair was gray, and he had begun to develop a stoop and a familiar rasp in his breathing. I wondered if he was spending himself to keep us from disintegrating even quicker, but the answer seemed unimportant. Like Vivian and me, his choice to be here had been made long ago. Still, I handed him a butterscotch, and he took it with the same twinkle in his eye he always had when a candy was on offer.

"What do you think?" I asked Vivian. "Together?"

She put her head to one side. "Yes. That feels right. But it doesn't answer the question of what we actually want to do." Gesturing at the swirling colors, she asked, "What would you change?"

I looked around at this beautiful place and could see the Mysterians' original intent. It really was a near-perfect expression of freedom and imagination. Or it would have been if not for the original sin at its heart: the Mysterians' perverse need to be at the center of their own creation. It could be heard as a dissonant counterpoint in a song of otherwise perfect harmony, or smelled as a rot in an exquisite bouquet, or seen as an occasional stain coursing through the breathtaking swirl of colors around us.

"A bit like a jelly donut, isn't it?" Harold wheezed.

And strange as it sounds, that was the answer. "It is exactly like a jelly donut!" I said with a laugh.

"A what?" Vivian asked. Her hair no longer had enough substance to spill over her shoulders and was flying out behind her like she was standing in a strong wind.

"The answer is to treat the pattern like a jelly donut," I replied with another laugh, but the reference had given Vivian a miss. "Don't you see? Donuts, as even the most cynical will admit, are inherently delicious. They are, in fact, an almost perfect vehicle for the delivery of two of the four basic food groups, fat and sugar, salt and caffeine being the others, of course. The problem with jelly donuts is the presence of the jelly. You take a delicious, fried, sugary cake and inject it with cold, sickly sweet goo. If you could remove the jelly, they would go right back to being perfect. The answer here is to remove the jelly and none of the donut."

"I think I understand. You don't want to rewrite the entire pattern."

I shook my head. "Only the cold, sickly sweet, gooey bits."

"So, the plan is to do as little as possible?"

"Exactly."

She rubbed at her chin with a hand that was becoming more of an abstraction by the moment. "Not really my strong suit," she admitted.

"I'd let Avery take the lead on that," Harold grunted. "He's been doing practically nothing for years."

Even Harold's insults made me happy, and I handed him a blur of butterscotch that melted away to nothing in his hand. It was not that I had forgotten that we were dying. Indeed, it was becoming harder and harder to ignore the fact. Our bodies were entirely translucent, and now when I looked into Vivian's eyes, they were little more than smudges of white in a blush-pale frame, although the gold rings still shown as bright and crisp as ever.

She leaned her head against my shoulder. "I am going to miss this."

"Me too," I replied and pulled her closer until the smudges of our bodies merged.

Some time, a minute or an hour later, we came to a very dense tangle of ribbons that took us looping and spinning and twisting through impossible folds in space. Moving through it was so dizzying that it took me a moment to realize that we had arrived at the heart of the pattern. Sitting in a small clearing, in this mass of chaos and creative destruction, was a perfect disk of what looked like iridescent metal inscribed with layer upon layer of Mysterian runes. It was exquisite in the artistry of its execution. It was also the sole point of order. As for the runes, they were quite definite as to their purpose: no creator or creation would ever surpass Mysterium. All realities would be subject to Mysterium's rule. Despite the shimmering beauty of the object, it repulsed me.

Our notional hands were still clasped around the painfully real key. I looked at Vivian. She was a ghostly outline, a translucent envelope in which atoms of her being spun and fluttered like motes of dust in a ray of sunshine, but I could still see the gold rings of her eyes. We both knew that once we destroyed this single anchor of reality, we would be swept away—extinguished.

I took Harold from my shoulder. All traces of his youth had been erased. His hair had fallen out, the lines in his face were deep crevices, and a hazy film covered his eyes. "I think it is time you were off," I said, my voice itself only a vague notion.

"Almost," he agreed with a wheeze.

"Do you know where you'll go?" Vivian asked and reached out a lazy brushstroke that might have been a hand to his head.

He shrugged. "There are a couple of mages I've had my eye on. That elven friend of yours."

"Eldrin?" I asked.

Harold bobbed his head. "That's the one. He seems pretty clever and better educated than most. Then again, maybe I'll pack it all in. I'm getting too old to train a new mage."

"Nonsense!" I said with a grin that was likely lost on my abstract countenance. "You don't look a day over four thousand."

"You are too kind," he said with a sarcastic bow. "Now, you two better get on with it before you float away for good."

I nodded, or thought I did. "You will be okay, won't you?"

"I'm an imp. We always survive," he said with a sad smile. "That's our curse."

Being unable to put into words what my time with him had meant, I simply said, "Thanks for . . . for everything."

He hugged Vivian around the neck and then put out a paw and rested it one last time atop my head. "You are a *good* mage, Avery Stewart."

With a wheezing sigh, he flew from my arm to settle on a nearby ribbon of pattern. Vivian and I turned back to each other. "I suppose this is it," she said, and a few fragments of blue dropped from the golden rings of her eyes.

"I suppose it is," I agree, and reached out a ghostly blur of color to wipe away her sorrow. "Look on the bright side. We made it all the way to the end and never became what we feared the most. You are simply Vivian, not the Dark Queen."

"And you are my Avery, not the Dark Lord."

"So, does that mean your vision was wrong?"

I saw that little tilt of her head I knew so well. "I only said that we wouldn't live happily ever after."

"Ah, but that only depends on your definition of 'ever after,'" I pointed out. "I'm certainly happy now!"

She wrapped her arms around me and buried her face in my chest. I found my being melding with hers. As one, we turned toward the perfect disk and raised the key. "I wonder what will happen to the others," I said. "To Eldrin and Dawn, Valdara and Drake, Sam and Ariella? Will the university survive? Will magic still exist?"

Vivian laughed, and if that was the last sound I ever heard, I decided I could happily die. "Only you, Avery Stewart, would spend your last moments of existence worrying about whether magic will be around after you're gone."

I shrugged. "What can I say, I would hate for there to be a multiverse where people think Criss Angel is the real thing. Besides, I'll miss it. I'll miss all of it. That feeling that anything is possible. Opening a plain red door in Oxford and finding yourself in another world. Won't you miss it?"

She shook her head, and I could feel her thoughts before she spoke. "Not even a little, but I will miss you. Oh, and strawberries and cream."

Then, because it was me, and I couldn't help myself, I asked, "Do you think it would be wrong if we left the multiverse a few parting gifts on our way out?"

I didn't have to tell her what I was thinking of doing, because by now our minds had also merged. She laughed at the notion, and with her laughter still echoing through my body, we unleashed the full power of the key. It was like nothing I'd ever felt before—the ultimate spell. The key began to melt under the strain, and our bodies were consumed until the magic of us was all that remained. I had a momentary thrill of fear that, after everything, we might fail. Then there was a terrible crack.

The disk split in half, and then in half again, and again.

"I love you," we thought.

I felt a pull somewhere just to the right of my heart, and—

EPILOGUE

My name is Sam Noble, and I am not Avery Stewart, nor am I any kind of Dark Lord. I'd also like to apologize a bit in advance for not being Avery, but I felt that this part was important to share. So, enough about what I'm not. What I am is one of the very few to witness the birth of the new multiverse.

I was standing on the edge of the Mysterian pattern, and before me raged the monstrous provost. Cornered against the closed portal to Mysterium, it lashed out with shadowy tendrils at the host of elves and dwarfs and men and orcs and undead and things I have no name for that had answered my summons. Every attack left corpses in its wake. But the army of the worlds fought on, roaring its defiance in a thousand voices and a thousand tongues.

Though the provost was outnumbered, the outcome of the fight was far from certain. It had sealed off the doors to the other worlds so only this first wave of allies had made it through. We could expect no reinforcements. And while I had cut the provost's access to the Mysterium pattern, the growing pile of bodies littering the broken ground was a testament to the power it still possessed.

I had made my mind up to do something dramatic and foolish, like Avery would have done. When the pattern behind me began to vibrate, I turned and saw ripples running along its boundary. The ripples combined and combined until the whole surface of the pattern sphere was undulating violently. The hum become a buzz and then a whining screech that was so painful I covered my ears. But there was no escape. It seemed to be coming from within my own head. Around me the sounds of fighting waned and then stopped altogether. Across the field of battle, weapons dropped from hands and knees buckled in pain. Even the provost's shadowy form shrank in on itself.

When I thought I would go mad, the sphere gave one last violent tremor and contracted before bursting outward in a noiseless flash of impossibly bright light. A force lifted me off my feet and threw me back so that I flew across the open space in front of the pattern and hit hard against one of the doors that ringed it.

I sat, dazed, as dazzling lights in rainbow hues

raced out from the pattern along the lines of cracked rock, relieved that the sound had stopped. Wherever the lights went, the stone of the ground reknitted itself, leaving behind a smooth, unbroken surface. Most of the lights soon passed out of sight, but the largest of them traced its way from the pattern to the portal of Mysterium. The circle around the portal blazed to life, and the provost cringed and cowered as the light surrounded him.

The circle grew brighter and brighter. A cry, terrible and inhuman, issued from the provost as his shadow body withered under the glare until it was little more than a deep black hole in the air. With a last flare of blinding brilliance and an otherworldly shriek of terror, even this splintered to pieces, and those pieces to fragments, and those fragments to motes too small to be seen. The portal to Mysterium opened and the remains of the provost were sucked through. The portal closed again with a slam of finality, and the light of the circle flickered, then died. The provost was gone.

I think I may have said, "Gosh!"

Those of us that remained, and there weren't many, had started to pick ourselves up when brilliant lights surrounded us. The nearest one was coming from one of the ruined doors. I watched in wonder as the door reassembled itself stone by stone and timber by timber. And this was happening all around, in every corner of More Doors. A cheer erupted from the host of creatures as the doors to countless worlds reemerged from the rubble.

I felt a sudden pressure in an area of my chest to the right of my heart. A moment later, there was a weight on my shoulder accompanied by a wheezing sigh. I smiled, but the moment was bittersweet. If Harold was with me, it meant that Avery was truly gone. I reached into my robe for a butterscotch and handed it to him. He took it and rasped, "You about ready to blow this place?"

"Almost." I walked over to Gray's skull, picked him up, and stroked the yellowed bone. That's when the tears started falling. I didn't notice the ray of light attach itself to me until it was too late. It grabbed me and ripped me backward and through a portal to Trelari. Fortunately, I held on to Gray's skull and Harold held on to me.

I would like to say that everything changed after that, but this is not that kind of story. This story ends as it began, with a flawed narrator and a lot of regret. That isn't to say that Avery and Vivian sacrificed themselves for nothing. Far from it.

Legend has it that half of Mysterium's Etherspace Astronomy Department quit when the sky lit up with thousands upon thousands of reborn worlds. In many of those worlds there is still a high holiday devoted to "Avian," which Eldrin explained to me once is how the multiverse decided to combine Avery's and Vivian's names à la Brangelina, Bennifer, or TomKat (whatever he meant by that). Regardless, Avery and Vivian saved the lives of countless billions, and in a larger sense that makes this a happy story. The pain, as always, is in the details.

But I am a good-news-first person, so I will start there. On my return to Trelari, I took Gray straight to our resident semi-lich. After I apologized several times for stealing his coffin, Aldric reanimated Gray. It was great to have Gray back, but an odd thing happened when he started to levitate. Out came a blue cloud of nether gas, but it was no longer noxious; rather it smelled like roses and sunshine. Nor was this change to demi-lich biology isolated to Gray. Undead across the multiverse suddenly smelled fantastic. By the way, if you haven't smelled sunshine yet, find a demi-lich because you're missing out.

Of course, those of us who knew him detected Avery's sense of humor and a contest developed to see what other Easter eggs we could find. (For the record, I'm not sure why they are called that. It has something to do with an Earth bunny cult. Sounds terrifying to me.) Most of the rumors turned out to be false. According to Dawn, Criss Angel (which sounds like a made-up name to me) did not die in an illusion gone wrong, and David Hasselhoff (again, I did not make this name up) was not appointed the German chancellor. On the other hand, Eldrin swears that now when he watches *Danger Mouse* reruns, whatever those are, Dr. Claw, whoever that is, sounds exactly like Avery's Dark Lord voice.

It was Eldrin who first discovered that Avery and Vivian had left little presents behind for creation. A few hours after the pattern was reset, he found an "unpunched" (though why anyone would bother punching a game is beyond me) copy of *The Campaign for North Africa* sitting on his desk. He still hasn't had the heart to open it, although Dawn says that's only because he knows it will lose half its value the moment he takes it out of some kind of containment spell she called "shrink-wrap."

If there is a moral to Avery's story, perhaps that is it: some things can't be undone, even if you completely rewrite the rules of existence. For my own part, I got back to Trelari to find that peace had not miraculously broken out. Far from it. The war continued for eighteen more terrible months before the last handful of Mysterium's innerworld allies finally broke and threw their support behind Eldrin and Dawn's student-led revolution. Without the support of the innerworlds, the Administration became entirely reliant on the Sealers, and that's when Valdara's war of attrition began to take its toll. The goal with any engagement became to kill as many Sealers as possible. It was during this time that I learned to hate war. It was also when Drake left the citadel.

He had grown increasingly repulsed by the things Valdara, as queen, did in the name of victory, and she felt duty bound as Trelari's queen and commander in chief not to change her strategy to appease his morality. In the end, their love could no longer hold them together. I've heard many rumors about where Drake went after he left: that he fell to drink, that he rededicated his life to the gods of his youth, even that he joined Luke on his island of contemplation. The truth is more prosaic. He became a healer in Valdara's army, traveling wherever the fighting was the worst, and spent the years after the war helping the poor souls whose minds could not escape what they'd seen or done.

Ariella also left the citadel around this time. She had grown bored with a war she saw as pointless. Her plan, as I understand it, was to spend some little time in Mysterium studying magic under Eldrin's tutelage and then travel the innerworlds and subworlds learning all she could about different mystic disciplines before coming back to start her own magical school in Trelari. How long that journey will take I do not know, but four years after the end of the war, she is still in Mysterium and, with the list of subjects she wants to study, will probably still be there when I die.

Of all Valdara's advisors, Rook and Seamus stayed the longest. Their strategy of grinding the Administration down eventually succeeded. An isolated and resource-strapped Mysterium could no longer replace Sealers as quickly as they were lost. First, the Administration was driven out of Trelari, then the subworlds, followed by the innerworlds. Their reach was ultimately reduced to the Provost's Tower.

Although I was not there, I've been told that when Eldrin's forces broke down the doors of the Provost's Tower, he found the place filled with the most unspeakable horrors. What few mages remained were mad beyond redemption, and many had taken to sacrificing their fellow inmates in dark rituals attempting, in vain, to resurrect the provost. It became clear that, while the pattern of Mysterium had been cleansed by Avery and Vivian, the remnants of the provost's spirit lingered in the tower. After many failed attempts to exorcise the place, the structure was dismantled brick by brick and a vault built around the pattern room. On top of this, a library stocked entirely with student dissertations was erected. Eldrin said it would discourage anyone from visiting the place and that Avery would have found the idea amusing.

As for me, I eventually returned to Trelari to take up my post as royal archmage and help oversee the birth of that long-promised new golden age for our world, one in which prosperity reigns and men and elves and dwarfs live in peace. I regret that, despite her service during the war, we have still not fulfilled Vivian's vision and found a way to integrate the orcs and other creatures of the Army of Shadow into society. Some hatreds are simply too old and run too deep to heal quickly.

It was the peace that drove Rook out of Trelari. He found everything was becoming far too "touchy-feely." He particularly hated that we officially referred to the age as the Golden Era of Peace, which he said was something "Hallmark" would print on a "greeting card." (I'm not sure who Hallmark is, but I think he sounds lovely.) Rook and Seamus moved to Mysterium where Rook was installed as a professor in the Department of Epochally Ancient History, and Seamus was given a position as his teaching assistant. Although, to be honest, the two of them spend most of their time running the Mysterium Chess Club, and arguing over who owes whom money.

Rook's return to Mysterium was a signal to the other Mysterians that it was safe to come home. Many of them took the invitation, but what they found was not the Mysterium they remembered. No longer is it the center of the multiverse. Indeed, there is no center. Eldrin told me it would be so, but I had to see for myself, so I journeyed back to the Land of More Doors after the end of the war.

The positions of the doors had changed. The pattern is still there, but it constantly shifts about. There are no innerworlds, no subworlds, just worlds. Mysterium can no longer subjugate other realities, nor do its mages have the power to do anything they wish. Manipulating the stuff of existence is difficult. It takes real study. And to their astonishment, and my amusement, sometimes it requires a focus: a pebble or even a white feather.

But Mysterium's waning status in the multiverse is nothing compared to the scars left from the provost's rule. Shortly after the Mysterian pattern was recast, Eldrin and Dawn were appointed co-chancellors of Mysterium University by a new and student-elected board of trustees—the title of provost, for obvious reasons, has been retired. They, along with their lieutenants, Susan and Stheno, have spent the years since the war trying to heal what they can and purging what they can't. They disbanded the Sealers and imprisoned loyalists, but agents of the Administration and provost-acolytes continued to terrorize, staging guerrilla attacks and spreading mayhem across the innerworlds and within the university. For a time, I helped hunt the renegades. My tally was fifty-two. Somewhere around thirty-six, I learned to hate killing.

For all its limitations and flaws, there is still something magical about Mysterium, and there will always be those drawn to it. Students, like Avery, that open a door and find themselves in another world—home at last.

As for Avery and Vivian? Officially, they are dead. Eldrin believes they are, but I think that's because his divination magic can't find them, and he has infinite faith in the infallibility of his spells. I know that's probably not the most satisfying answer, but it is the official line. I didn't believe it and, more important, didn't want to believe it. Finding out the truth of what happened to them became my obsession.

The multiverse was reborn, Trelari was at peace, Eldrin and Dawn had Mysterium as in hand as anyone ever could, but I was restless and moody. I wanted to believe that somehow, Avery and Vivian had survived. It also seemed to me that everyone else was all too happy to forget about the two people who had sacrificed everything for the rest of us.

I spent days going to all the places on and off Trelari that Avery and Vivian had frequented, looking for clues they might have left behind about what they were planning to do in the pattern, and for some sign that they might have arranged a mystical escape hatch for themselves. What if Avery had devised a complex portal that could work within More Doors itself, or Vivian had cast a prescient charm like she did when we were on the pattern of Mysterium? I even took to interrogating Harold on the subject.

He had been with them at the very end, and I had long suspected he knew more about what had happened than he was willing to tell me. But anytime I questioned him about whether they were alive or where they were, he would shrug and give me some enigmatic answer or say something like, "Your questions are just like Avery's, simple to ask and impossible to answer."

It was with this question of their ultimate fate weighing on my mind that I took a sabbatical from my duties as royal archmage to search for them. In the spirit of full disclosure, something Avery always demanded in these books, I did not leave my post voluntarily. Valdara got fed up with me mooning about the citadel and dashing off to this place and that without warning, and dismissed me. I didn't blame her, and in her own way I think she was giving me permission to leave. I suspect that she knew I wasn't going to be happy until I learned what had happened to Avery.

I wish she would have come with me. She had sacrificed so much to ensure Trelari's survival during the war and she deserved a rest. Only those of us in her inner circle knew that she had considered giving up the crown after the war. I think she wanted to find Drake and see if they could start again. But who would rule in her absence? Who could we trust to protect the peace the people of Trelari had fought so hard to win? Who was selfless and noble enough to put the people's good above their own? Her tragedy is that there has only ever been one answer: Queen Valdara.

I was being entirely selfish, abandoning her to go hunt for someone who was, likely as not, dead. I could accept this, but what I couldn't do was figure out how to begin. Despite all my searching and prying, I found nothing. I decided to change tactics and went to places Avery and Vivian had actively avoided. That was how I found myself in Avery's rooms in the citadel, aimlessly going through the books and clothes and odds and ends that Ariella and I had planted for him in our attempt to make him feel at home. I picked up an unread copy of *The Dark Lord* and flipped through it, laughing again at my naivete. To think I didn't know why I needed sand and a knife!

I was about to put the book back when I happened to flip to the inside of the back cover. In bold, it had the author's name: Jack Heckel.

Early on, I had thought of tracking down this Mr. Heckel to see if he had any information, but I hadn't been able to find him. I even consulted Eldrin, but he was emphatic that it was a fool's quest. He told me that when the first book came out, he had used every tracing, tracking, and finding spell he knew— and trust me, that's a lot—and had found nothing. He attributed this to the fact that, whether Avery knew it or not, Jack had always been a pseudonym of Avery's, and that I was overthinking things, which was ironic coming from him.

However, that day in Avery's room, I actually read about Jack Heckel. And there in black and white were explicit directions on how to find the mysterious author: *Jack aspires to be either a witty, urbane world traveler who lives on his vintage yacht,* The Clever Double Entendre, *or a geographically illiterate professor of literature who spends his nonwriting time restoring an eighteenth-century lighthouse off a remote part of the Vermont coastline.*

Harold pointed out that Vermont has no coastline and therefore would have no lighthouses, and that the whole thing was probably meant as a joke. Of course, I was not going to let a little thing like facts get in the way of my mania. I made a portal and we traveled to Burlington in Vermont, which I thought was a good starting point since a university was located there.

It is my understanding that this part of Earth has trees with leaves that people like to peep at, which sounds extremely naughty. We must have missed the season, because it was early spring and the trees were still bare, which also sounds extremely naughty now that I think about it. The point being, we made it to Burlington and found that it sat on a large lake that has not one lighthouse but twelve!

I obtained (stole) a sailboat, much to Harold's displeasure (not that we stole it, but that I was intending for him to go on it), and we set off across the lake. I will not bore you with the travails of trying to sail a boat when you have no knowledge of sailing, but I will say that being a mage and having the ability to summon wind on command has a wonderful smoothing effect on life's little bumps. It was on the evening of the third day of our survey that we reached the lighthouse at Windmill Point—the ninth we'd looked at so far. The others had either been empty or lived in by the type of older people who can afford to spend all their time taking care of a lighthouse. I had to admit that I was losing hope.

When we were close enough to shore that a simple far-see spell would give me a good view but far enough away not look suspicious, I dropped the sail and let the boat drift to a stop. The lighthouse was charming: two stories with a stone tower standing at one side. A bright green lawn sloped down to the water's edge. Sitting on a blanket, hand in hand, were a man and woman. Her head, a blaze of yellow in the setting sun, was resting against his shoulder. With the glare of the sunlight on them it was impossible to make out their faces, but they seemed like the right age, and her hair—

Suddenly, there was a peal of high-pitched laughter and a little girl, no more than four, came running out of the house and down the lawn. For a moment she turned her head so that the light fell on her face from the side. My breath caught, because I saw in her eyes a glint of gold. It was only a flash, and then she spun away again and, with a squeal of delight, flew into her parents' arms. They pulled the child between them and closed her in their embrace.

I turned away with a smile, dropped the spell, and began to raise the sail again.

"Well?" Harold grunted impatiently. "Was it them? Can we drop this bloody *Rhyme of the Ancient Mariner* kick?"

"Yes, Harold, we are going," I answered and called up a wind that would take us back to Burlington.

The imp was staring toward the lighthouse now, shading his eyes with his paws. "So, is it them?"

"It's enough," I answered, and in a whisper just to myself, "Time to go home."

ACKNOWLEDGMENTS

We would like to acknowledge everyone that helped get us to this point, but since listing everyone is impossible, we offer the following. For everyone who isn't listed, we want you to know that you made a difference and we appreciate it.

As always, we would like to thank our families: Heather, Taba, Isaac and Carleigh. In the words of the poet, you are our North, our South, our East and West.

We would like to thank our new editor, Nate. We've enjoyed the ride and appreciated your insights. Let's do it again (hint, hint). Also, Chris, who fact-checked us and did copyedits. Anytime you want to edit one of our books, we'd love to have you back. To rest of the team at Harper, this is book number five.

What a wonderful journey! Thank you for continuing to believe in us and laugh with us.

To our fellow Harper authors, thank you for your continued support. We would like to give a special thanks to Bishop O'Connell for always sharing great stories and being infinitely supportive, as well as having a strong t-shirt game. Rook is probably a reference to you. Probably.

Finally, to Evan, thank you for being our biggest Charming fan. Please stay with us and let's discover what the future holds.

Harry would also like to thank:

The Hanover Writers Club. I appreciate my monthly dose of encouragement more than you know.

Everyone at Ravencon! What a spectacularly fun event!

All the independent booksellers out there. You connect us with our readers.

My amazing Unboxed team—Connor, Drew, Kim, Mark, and Terry, thank you.

Kayla and Cathy for being wonderful friends and fantastic cat-sitters.

Quasar and Nebula for being fantastic human-sitters, including sitting on authors while they are trying to write, not to mention keyboards.

Bishop, Meriah, Bud, and Dennis for the critiques of my future novels.

Dad, thanks for always supporting my writing. Mollie and Ben, thank you for all the roleplaying and lots of good stories.

Heather, none of this happens without all you do, and Carleigh, everything I write is for you. I love you both.

John would also like to thank:

Isaac and Taba, who always have the most wonderful suggestions for how to make my stories better. Avery and Harold and all the rest appreciate all you've done for them.

Thanks also to the Chiweenies, Sam and Frodo. There isn't much you can't learn about life by watching two dogs joyfully fighting over a plastic bone.

Bim and Oliver, Joy and David, and everyone else in Long Beach that continues to agree to play games with me. Whimsy is a precious thing and you all help me keep it close at hand.

To my niece, Ariana, and my nephews, Nathan and Daniel, resilience is a remarkable quality. I marvel and celebrate in each of your successes. Always keep striving and know that you are loved.

Finally, to Harry. What can I say? I will never be able to tell you how glad I am that you picked up the phone all those years ago to tell me that we were going to write a book together. These have been happy days.

ABOUT THE AUTHOR

JACK HECKEL's life is an open book. Actually, it's the book you are in all hope holding right now (and if you are not holding it, he would like to tell you it can be purchased from any of your finest purveyors of the written word). Beyond that, Jack aspires to be either a witty, urbane world traveler who lives on his vintage yacht, *The Clever Double Entendre*, or a geographically illiterate professor of literature who spends his nonwriting time restoring an eighteenth-century lighthouse off a remote part of the Vermont coastline. Whatever you want to believe of him, he is without doubt the author of the Mysterium trilogy and the Charming Tales series. More than anything, Jack lives for his readers.

Despite whatever Jack may claim, in reality Jack Heckel is the pen name for John Peck and Harry Heckel.